THE WORSHIPPER AND THE KING

The Inside Story of Solomon's Love Song

Judy Pendell

Speak Fire Publishing

TABLE OF CONTENTS

DEDICATION

I dedicate this book to my Heavenly Father, my Bridegroom Christ, and Holy Spirit, the source of my inspiration.

As a daughter of the Most High, whom I desire to please, I bring my book as a gift from the giver of all gifts. All things come from you and without you, we can do nothing. I bring this work, Heavenly Father, as a young child brings a picture they made in school, or their first attempt of writing a poem.

I say, "Daddy look what I made for You."

You know the heart of Your children, and our desire to make You happy with what we create. I know, as a loving parent, You will say, "This is wonderful my daughter. I love this gift."

You are the greatest of musicians, artists, writers, and poets. No one can compare to You. But we are growing to become like You because you put it in our hearts. Someday, we will see you as you are. For now, the next natural step is to imitate You completely. It is my attempt to be like You with this creation, for it is my worship and love-gift to You. Your love, redemption, blessing, and promises give us a future and a hope. I cannot help but respond with gifts of love and creation.

I love you forever and bow before You as I now present my gift. Thank you for accepting it.

INTRODUCTION

A friend of mine asked me about my book and taking on such an overwhelming project.

"What were you thinking?" she said to me that day.

Thinking?

Was she talking about the tremendous amount of work, travel, and time it would take to do the research? Did she mean the writing skills and insights it would take to write such a story? *Thinking?*

No, I was not thinking, if you mean using clear, logical, and organized thoughts. If I think, I think like a poet. I performed with a Jewish dance group for a short time and the leader was always talking about the Bride of Christ. One day I realized, in Song of Solomon, this Bride of Christ was the Shulamit. I read it through and through and could hardly understand it. But I loved the poetry.

Shortly after that, I read *Captivated*. My takeaway from that book was discovering the main theme of the Bible. In the old covenant, God *married* the Israelites. He was in covenant with them and, when they sinned, constantly wooing them to return to Him. It expanded into the new covenant with the bridegroom Jesus pursuing his bride, the church. Our Heavenly Father is, even now, pursuing his bride in love. So, the main theme of the Bible is not good versus evil, light versus darkness, hate versus love, but God pursuing a loving relationship with his bride.

My other takeaway from *Captivated* was that the story of Cinderella was inspired by the Song of Solomon. As one of my friend's said, "No one gets through life unscathed." We all long for a savior to show up and rescue us from our pains in life just as Cinderella did. Even the most loving parents can't always protect their children from what life throws at them. Many times, just to survive, we find ourselves working or being forced to do things outside of our genuine identity. But we know in our hearts we are made for more.

Around this time, I had a dream which was actually a visitation from Jesus. He proposed to me as I was looking down at myself. I was standing on a bridge next to a lady with long, flowing black hair that hung to her knees.

Soon after this, the idea of writing about the Shulamit was conceived in my heart.

In my story, Shulamit was a dreamer, just like Joseph had been a dreamer. God puts dreams into our hearts. But those dreams require an *intervention* from God. When you dream dreams that are out of reach of your possibility, that is where God shows up. Without supernatural help they will not come to pass. In this story, Solomon shows up as a figure of our Divine Bridegroom. He is continuously supportive and helpful as his humble country bride grows her destiny from a worshipper to a queen. He even provoked the warrior queen as necessity brought her forth.

Before I started writing, I spent many nights after work reading all the interpretations of Song of Solomon I could access. With the Song of Solomon, people step into the story and give their own personal interpretations of the Shulamit's story. The main voice in Song of Solomon's dramatic poem is the Shulamit. There are more interpretations of Song of Solomon than any book in the Bible, including Daniel and Revelation.

As I continued to read commentary after commentary, I had more questions. Who is this Shulamit woman? What was she really like? What would it have been like to live in the historical times where she grew up? Israel was a thriving country at that time. While the temple was being built, worship was possible before the Ark in the tabernacle of David, in the actual presence of God. What was the Shulamit's experience? She worshipped at the dedication of the temple when the glory of God came down, and she was able to meet the Queen of Sheba. What was that like for her?

I found inspiration from the commentary of J. Vernon McGee, who wrote of Shulamit falling in love with a shepherd who sang and danced. Later she found out the shepherd was a king. I think that is so like real love. Often, we fall for the heart of a person and later learn of any status there may be. Anyone could fall in love with a great king (but our God tests our hearts).

Most people today do not really understand marriage through the lens of Biblical times. In that culture, marriage involved a Ketubah agreement and a large betrothal before the actual marriage celebration. The bride-to-be had a long time to prepare for her marriage. As in the Old Testament, we (the Bride of Christ) have time to prepare for our time to reign in the Kingdom of Heaven.

We are growing into reigning as priests, kings, and queens. As each day passes, we are learning to worship, and how to turn that very worship into deep intercession to overcome the hard battles of our times. Our perseverance will lead to heavenly rewards as prophesied in the book of revelation.

They that overcome shall:
- Eat from the *Tree of Life*
- Receive a crown of life
- Be given hidden manna to eat
- Obtain power over the nations
- Be clothed in white garments
- Our names will not be blotted out of the book of life but instead confessed by our father and the angels

- Be a pillar in the temple of our God
- Sit with our bridegroom Jesus on His throne as He sits with His Father on His throne.

Several friends who read my early chapters told me I was writing a musical. I thought about that but decided on a book where I could detail more of how the protagonist took steps toward her destiny. I also wanted to talk about how key figures in her life helped her within the context of the Hebrew culture. I was raised a Christian and research showed me how Jews and Christians became disconnected just before the dark ages. So much real understanding of the history of God's love for mankind was lost. I wanted to engage that.

From the very beginning, I kept getting poetic lyrics that could be songs. I was surprised at how I would wake up in the middle of the night and write out a poem. I learned that, in Hebrew, the word for poem is the same word for song. I believe that if a musician, poet, or dancer can read Song of Solomon and not write a song, dance, or poem, then they are missing the Spirit of the Song. It remains the standard of great love songs and stories. Even Shakespeare drew from the well of Solomon's dramatic poem.

Nothing would make me happier than to see a musical come out of my book. But I am not a musician, so I wrote a story with poetry.

I also believe that there is a touch of prophecy in all great songs and writings. Many verses in Song of Solomon relate to the Book of Revelation (Daniel and Revelation are also books of prophecy just opening in our time). Shulamit's dreams must therefore be prophetic. So, I see my story as prophetic, historical, and romantic. Solomon's greatest love song is not an allegory, but there is poetic symbolism, metaphors, parallels, and figurative speech throughout. It is full of the language of heaven—too beautiful to describe in earthly terms. God put Solomon and the Shulamit together, and from their love story Solomon was able to write his greatest song. Theirs was a marriage made in heaven.

One final word about the Shulamit. Song of Solomon commentators disagree on many things, but they all apparently agree upon one point.

Whoever this Shulamit woman was, *she was a good wife.*

1 GOING UP TO JERUSALEM

"Look!" Shulamit shouted, "Jerusalem!"

"Yes, the *City on a Hill!*" Papa proclaimed.

"The *City of David, the City God has chosen!*" Gran-papa announced.

"The *City of Zion and our Great King!*" a voice in the crowd yelled out.

"Now we rejoice and sing," Gran-papa commanded.

The sight of Jerusalem was the sign to sing the songs of ascension. The multitudes sang these songs as they approached the chosen city every time they journeyed to Jerusalem for the feasts.

Voices rose in unity, "*I will lift up mine eyes unto the hills, from whence comes my help. My help comes from the Lord who made heaven and earth. He will not suffer my foot to be moved, he that keeps me will not slumber. He who keeps Israel shall not slumber nor sleep…*"

The happy family moved amongst the great multitude of pilgrims ascending the hills toward Jerusalem. Shulamit, a young girl of seven years, was going to Jerusalem with her family for the first time. She was full of excitement. They had been singing on and off most of the way, except when listening to Gran-papa. He told stories of going to war with King David. While stories abounded in Israel of King David and his battles, Gran-papa's version always made her heart step into the wonder of worship.

"There we were, on a hill surrounded by our enemies," Gran-papa recounted, "We were prepared for war. Our slings in our hands and our pockets full of well-chosen rocks. Our bows were easy to grab from our shoulders, and our arrows were sharpened. Our swords were in their sheaths at our sides. Yes, we were ready."

"Suddenly, King David gave an order to lay aside our weapons and worship. He said he had to inquire of the Lord. There he stood, lyre in hand, surrounded by a group of musicians and the high priest who had joined us. Those of us who knew how to play an instrument were instructed to join. With enemies surrounding us, we began to worship and give praise to God. I thought to myself, *this is crazy, our enemies outnumber us and are ready to attack us, and here we are worshipping with King David, who is dancing around and playing his lyre.*

"However, the whole camp was soon dancing and singing to the music. I wondered what made me join up for the war. But somewhere amid the questions in my heart, a spirit of worship came over me. I, like King David, was overcome. I looked around me and saw we were all overcome. Heaven had come down and joined us.

"Shortly afterwards the shofar was blown. The king's inquiry from the Lord was answered. A strategy from the Lord had been given, and the shofar was our call to battle. The sound of the loud ram's horn had always caused a fire to burn within our spirits. That burning continues even today when the shofar is blown before the Holy days and special occasions.

"We grabbed our weapons and marched forward to meet the enemy. We were in a haze. Every move we made hit its intended target. Our enemies fell before us with the slightest swing of the sword, as if angels fought with us. It seemed we had walls of fire protecting each one of us, and the enemy couldn't even see us. We had sight, and they were blinded. The battle was soon over, and the enemy that hadn't fled like cowards lay on the field before us. Only a few of us had skin wounds."

Shulamit loved Gran-papa's stories.

But what she loved the most was the songs he had learned worshipping with the king. He said, "King David wrote them, often spontaneously as they went. The songs were alive with inspiration and the living, breathing presence of God coming from the anointing on the king's life." Shulamit longed for this living, breathing presence of God. She was excited about going to Jerusalem to worship in the Tabernacle on Mt Zion. Her greatest desire was to worship in the presence of God.

While she had that thought, a song came into her heart. She began to sing a simple melody, tapping a beat on her tambourine:

> *Get you up into the high mountain,*
> *Get you up into the high mountain,*
> *Get you up into the high mountain,*
> *He shall feed His flock like a shepherd,*
> *He shall feed His flock like a shepherd.*

Papa chimed in after the first line and sang, "Get you up into the high mountain," in his own deep voice, and Mama and her two brothers added their varied voices, and a beautiful harmony came forth in song.

"My daughter, you have written your first song," Mama said. "It is a simple melody with a profound thought. Great things happen on mountains in Israel. We ascend, and we receive revelation from encountering the Lord in the high places."

King David had surely been a great shepherd over Israel. He led his people well and was loved by all. But now he was old, co-reigning with his son Solomon. It seemed the end of an era. No one knew where Solomon would take the kingdom, so Papa was bringing his whole family to the tabernacle to worship. No one knew how long the worship with the Ark, holding the presence of God, would be open to the public. He wanted his family, especially his children, to experience the anointed music and divine presence while it was still open to the common people.

As they continued walking up the steep hill, they could see the walls and gates of Jerusalem. Crowds of people entered the city. Shulamit asked, "Are we going to sacrifice our little lamb at the tabernacle of David?"

Papa responded, "No, I will go with your brothers and sacrifice the lamb at the temple in Gibeon."

"No sacrifices here, Papa?"

"Here in Jerusalem, we offer the sacrifices of praise at the Tabernacle of David."

"Oh, Papa, I can be a sacrifice with my praise?"

Papa laughed. "Yes, my little lamb, you can be a sacrifice of praise. You are my little worshipper with a heart full of praise. When you hear the music of the tabernacle, and stand in the presence of God before the Ark, your heart will rise, and you will dance and sing like King David did before the Ark. The King taught us how to worship. When the Lord looks down upon our worship he is delighted, and He pours down his blessings upon us. Worship brings favor."

"Wow, Papa," Shulamit responded, hugging him in joy.

***

As the family entered into the gates of Jerusalem, they ascended the steps of the city in the direction of Mount Zion. From there, the palace could be seen in the distance. They followed the crowds until they could see a large tent behind the palace on Mt Zion. As they approached, they could hear music in the air. Shulamit began to jump up and down joyously.

"Papa, I hear the music, I hear the music," she cried.

"Yes, my little lamb, the music in King David's tabernacle is played evening to morning without ceasing, every day of the week throughout the year. The worship never stops. There is continuous giving thanks and praise, and psalm-singing as the Levites ministered before the Ark of the Lord. The priests minister in great courses of singers and musicians. They sing with instruments of music, psalteries and harps and cymbals, and lift up their voices with joy. There are even women singers and dancers with tambourines."

"Dancers," Shulamit said with surprise.

"Yes, Shulamit, there is dancing and clapping of hands, and sometimes shouting to the Lord and lifting up of hands. We have done this at the festivals in our village."

"Are there trumpets?"

"Yes, there are trumpets on special occasions. There is also the worship of bowing, stooping very low, and prostrating ourselves on the ground to show deep adoration and devotions, and prayer for our petitions. We want to seek God's face by worshipping with our whole heart."

"I want to seek God's face and worship with my whole heart."

"I know you do. You have been worshipping, clapping your hands, and dancing to music since before you could even say your first words."

The joyful sound of worship was now ringing in their ears as they came near to the entrance of the great tent. Already, Shulamit could feel her foot tapping to the music and her body wanting to dance. Her father whispered into her ear, "You are entering into a Holy Place, and you must observe and be in awe of the presence of God. Do not talk loud or interrupt. Listen and pay attention to your mother."

As they came to the door of the tent, the two doorkeepers greeted them. Shulamit and her mother were ushered over to the woman's side. Shulamit could see the Ark of God with the Golden Cherubim on a Platform in the center of the tent. Just below the platform to the right was a full orchestra of musicians in greater number than she could count. Harps, large and small and of different shapes, flutes, and pipes of various sorts, even a type of organ where pipes of various lengths were tied together. There were drums of all sorts, large and small, and a priest was seen holding a cymbal. Papa had told her, when King David wanted a new sound, he created a new instrument to make that sound.

Shulamit was overcome. Her spirit was lifted to the heavens in the presence of God. The joy in the tent began to overflow within her. Never had she experienced anything like this. Even the air was heavy. It was greater than her father and grandfather had described. She grabbed her mama's hand and tried to get her to move as close to the Ark as possible, but the crowd was large, and it seemed everyone desired to be close to the Ark. To her amazement, like the parting of the Red Sea, the way opened for her and Mama to move up closer to the Ark.

A song of halal, a Hebrew praise song, began from the instruments, and soon the crowd sang, "Praise the Lord! Praise, O servants of the Lord! Praise the name of the Lord! Blessed be the name of the Lord from this time forth and forevermore! From the rising of the sun to it's going down, the Lord's name is to be praised!"

There was a men's choir and a women's choir, sometimes the men would sing, and the women would respond in their high voices. Shulamit began to sing the response with the woman's choir. She raised her hands into the air to show her praise, and her feet began to jump under her. It was as if she had no control over her own body. She moved with a flow that came from the very Presence of God. Shulamit's mother, Miriam, was singing and raising her hands also. That song ended with the sound of cymbals followed by much clapping and shouts of joy.

Harps began to play a new song, and a priest stood up before the Ark. He began to sing with a powerful, loud voice that carried throughout the tent. It seemed to almost split the air as the entire crowd throughout the Tabernacle heard him. The people stood silently as he sang, "Oh give thanks unto the Lord, for He is good."

His hands motioned for the chorus and crowd to respond with, "For His mercy endures forever."

The priest then sang, "Let Israel now say."

The chorus and crowd answered back, antiphonally, "His mercy endures forever."

Back and forth, as the priest initiated, the chorus and people responded. Everyone was participating in this joyous event.

Shulamit pondered how her Gran-papa taught them that King David had an intimate relationship with the Lord when he wrote the psalms. King David put his psalms to music to sing in the tabernacle. He desired to give the people of Israel an understanding of how to have a relationship with the Lord through worship. King David poured out his heart to God and to his people. By his example, the people learned "the Lord inhabits the praises of his people." When the people of Israel would worship, the Lord drew near. He drew them together into unity with Him.

Another psalm was sung with a joyous melody, and Shulamit became lost in worship.

She began to sing and dance as she twirled around and around and moved and spreading out her arms in the full freedom of her joy. Her feet tapped out steps, as she moved her arms down and then up in showing her honor to God. Shulamit was unaware of herself, and what was happening, for she was drawn somewhere before a heavenly throne into God's presence. She was no longer dancing alone. The Lord inhabited her worship. Angels were dancing with her. Soon the women around her were drawn into her dance and joined a company of dancers with her. She knew King David saw a revelation of another Zion. That vision inspired him to bring that Zion to earth on this Mt Zion, where the music played continually just like before the throne in heaven.

As the song ended, Shulamit felt her body descending back to the tabernacle. Soon, she was once again aware of her surroundings. Her mother was signaling her to sit down as the High Priest was now about to speak.

The High Priest was dressed in glory with his robes, and breastplate of twelve brilliant stones of different colors representing the tribes of Israel. He lifted his arms out wide as he chanted, "*Smah Yisrael Adonai Elohenu, Adonai Echad*; Hear oh Israel, the Lord our God is one God."

The High Priest spoke of God's glorious blessings over Israel, and the bounty of the harvest. He spoke about how Israel was the most blessed nation on the earth, and about how Israel was called and chosen to bring blessings to the whole earth.

While the high priest exhorted, Shulamit's mind wandered into what a blessed life she had, and how blessed she was to be born into a family who joyfully worshipped the one true God. She had never been exposed to the world of the heathen, but she had heard about it. If she should ever encounter a foreigner in her land who did not know her Lord, *Adonai*, she would share her joy with them and help them to know *Adonai*. She would follow King David's example in the tabernacle.

While she pondered that joyful thought, the High Priest spread out his arms toward the congregation again and began to speak the Aaronic blessing. She refocused to hear his words.

"The Lord bless and keep you, the Lord make his face to shine upon you, and be gracious to you, the Lord lift up His countenance upon you and give you peace. So shall they put My name on the children of Israel, and I will bless them."

Shulamit looked around the tent to see sparkling eyes and faces shining on the people. The congregation had been caught up in the glory of God, and their countenances were shining. Peace and joy permeated the atmosphere.

Shulamit would have stayed all night and day in the tabernacle, but Mama took her hand and told her they had to go. As they were departing, a priest walked up to them and began to prophesy over Shulamit.

"Young maiden, you have a heart and gift for worship," the priest said. "And there is an anointing upon your worship." The priest then laid his hands upon her head. "I speak over you this day, that you will be a blessing in Israel with your worship. Hold to this gift. Hide it in your heart and memory, and do not settle for less than God's call upon your life."

Mama heard the prophecy spoken over Shulamit and knew she too carried a part in protecting this prophecy in her daughter.

Inspired by the anointing of her experience, Shulamit turned to her mother and also prophesied.

"Mama," she said, smiling, "you are going to have another baby, and it is going to be a girl."

"I know," Mama confirmed, "I heard the Lord tell me that while we were worshipping. Surely, the Lord has blessed us this day before the Ark of God's glory."

A seed was planted in Shulamit's heart that day in the Tabernacle of David. That seed set her on a journey that would change her life forever.

2 THE BATTLE CRY

Shulamit's family were winemakers. Today they celebrated a glorious harvest and the Sabbath out in the countryside, with a picnic outside, near a clear water stream on a beautiful, bright and sunny day.

"We make the best wine in all Israel," Papa boasted, as he held up his goblet of wine, "the vineyards on our mountain produce the best grapes anywhere." The vineyards of their small village were high on a mountain called Baal Hamon. Papa exclaimed, "The Ruach wind of heaven blows upon our mountain. That is our secret. Yes, the four winds blow across Baal Hamon, each in their season on the mountain. The cold winds come from the North, dry and hot winds from the East and South, and fresh breezes from the sea. Together these winds bring the rain and the sunshine that creates the sweetest of grapes."

Papa was not the first person to say that their mountain, Baal Hamon, produced the best wine. It was King David who had first made that proclamation. Shulamit's family had given wine and food to King David when he fled from Saul, and some of their family members had joined with him. When David finally became king, he insisted on buying a small vineyard in her family's village and had asked her family to be the vineyard's keepers. They valued their connection with the king, and his friendship, and enjoyed being of service to the king. They rejoiced to know their wine would be served in the palace.

On rare occasions during the harvest season, the king came by and visited their family, sharing a communal meal, and drinking wine, as no celebration in Israel was without wine. The king sang with them and brought gifts as well as news from abroad. But nowadays, one of his agricultural overseers would come by and inquire about the harvest, bring gifts, and occasionally share a meal with them in passing.

These high mountain warriors of Shulamit's family didn't need the king's protection. But they honored the great warriors of their history. They told and retold the stories of David and Goliath and David's mighty men, as they desired to inspire courage into the next generation. Every child in Israel knew the story of David and Goliath. As mountain people, they prided themselves on being strong people who had conquered their mountain. They were loyal to the king, who had helped them conquer all the rest of the territory Jehovah had promised to them.

Shulamit's family loved to celebrate. The love of celebration was part of the culture of their day. It was a happy time in Israel's history. The country was united; it was a time of peace. Blessings abounded. It was a time when people could dream. Papa was a dreamer, and he inspired in his children the gift of dreaming. "Your life is as great as your dreams," was what he had always spoken into the lives of his family and everyone he encountered.

In the heat of the sun, Shulamit's brothers were playing David and Goliath with wooden swords they had made themselves, and their slingshots. All mountain people knew how to use slingshots very well. Protecting sheep on high mountains was sometimes perilous. Shulamit, too, knew how to use a slingshot very well. Watching as her brothers played aroused her desire to be a warrior like David to take down the giant Goliath.

"I want to be David. I want to be David!" Shulamit shouted.

"You can't be David, you're a girl!" Joshua shouted back.

"I don't care if I am a girl. I want to be David!" This time Shulamit yelled it so loud enough that it could be heard by Papa and Mama sitting a distance away. She turned to her father, shouting, "Papa, they never let me play. I want to be David."

Papa, tired of their bickering, intervened, "Joshua let your sister be David, you are just playing, and even a girl needs to know how to proclaim a battle cry. Girls have to grow up to be strong women. It takes strong women to bear babies and be mothers.

Joshua conceded to his father's request with an impish grin. He picked up his wooden sword and proceeded to speak out the lines Goliath boasted before all the warriors of the Philistines and Israel with his added variation.

"Am I a dog that you send a girl to fight with me? Come to me, and I will give your flesh to the birds of the air and the beasts of the field."

Shulamit started to show her hurt feelings, but she quickly summoned her resolve to fight back. "You come to me with sword and with spear and with a javelin, but I come to you in the Name of the Lord of Hosts. We women of Israel are fighters too. This day the Lord will deliver you into my hand, and I will strike you and take your head from you. And this day I will give the carcasses of the camp of the Philistines to the birds of the air and the wild beasts of the earth. Then all this assembly shall know that the Lord does not save with sword and with spear: not with boys only, but also with girls; for the battle is the Lord's and He will give you into our hands!"

Shulamit picked a rock out of her pouch and put it in her sling and slung it at the nearest tree, hitting the trunk. Then she took another rock and slung it at the trunk and hit the edge. Joshua was so angered he threw down his wooden sword and walked off.

He huffed, "I'm not playing anymore."

Shulamit's mother, Miriam, who was sitting beside Papa with their new baby girl in her lap, glanced at her husband, Joseph, and questioned,

"Joseph, how are you going to solve this problem?"

His wise brother, Jehiel, jumped in, "You taught her to love and honor King David. You have always told her what a great king he was. Is it any surprise she wants to be like the king whom she so greatly admires? But what is King David most admired for? Is he not most admired for his praise and worship that brought the *presence of God* to the battles? You know that your daughter loves to sing and dance, and she plays well the lyre and tambourine. Perhaps you should suggest that the best way for her to be like King David is to become a "worshipper" rather than a "warrior." She can be a "worship warrior" and fight the battles of the spirit.

Miriam agreed. "Jehiel is right, remember the prophecy the Priest at the Tabernacle gave to Shulamit about her gift of worship?"

Joseph called his sons and daughter. They obeyed their father and came and sat near him. "Children," he said with calm authority, "we are all called to be fighters, and all of you are shepherds protecting your sheep. But Shulamit," he said, turning to look into her face, "as time goes on, Joshua and Caleb will grow to be tall men with strong muscles and deep voices. You will develop into a beautiful young woman with a sweet, woman's voice." The boys were appeased, and Shulamit listened eagerly as Papa continued to speak.

"Shulamit, there are better ways for you to win battles. A beautiful woman only has to smile. Look at your beautiful mother. When she smiles at me, I will do anything for her. When she sings for me with her beautiful voice, my heart melts. Mama rules my heart, not because she is physically stronger. The secret of the woman is to be beautiful from within and without. Deborah went as a spiritual leader to battle with Barak. It was her favor with God that brought the blessing of God upon them. Worship is the secret of winning the battles of the Lord. When you worship you touch heaven to fight for you."

Papa began singing a spontaneous song.

When you worship
Heaven smiles
Upon you

Our Father delights
Your countenance lights
And you shine

When you dance
Heaven dances with you
Our Father's heart is touched

The Worshipper and the King

He says
"You're mine!"

When you Worship
The angels
Surround you
The Father dances with you
As the angels take
Your hand

You are carried
Before the throne of Heaven
Ten thousand angels standing
At attention
For command

And the Father says
"Ask of me
My favor is upon you
As you worship
An army of banners
Fight your battles
As you stand

When you dance
Two camps come together
You bring Heaven to Earth
Hearts come together
In new birth

When you worship
My winds blow upon you
The North winds,
The South winds
The East and the West

When you worship
Heaven smiles upon you
You are blessed

Heaven Smiles
Heaven Smiles
Heaven Smiles

Judy Pendell

When you Dance

They were a worshipping family.

Papa played the lyre. Joshua played the trumpet. Caleb played the flute. Shulamit danced with her tambourine. Mama sometimes danced with her tambourine or played the flute. But today she sang, her melodious voice in harmony to Papa's deep voice.

While they were singing, Shulamit went to her brother Joshua in tears and asked him to forgive her. He did the same with her, and they hugged each other. After a short time of worship, they thanked the Lord for the bread and dipped it into the common bowl of lentils and legumes.

Shulamit's family was a happy family.

The afternoon was hot, and later Papa shouted, "Let's go up to the lake and swim!" Shulamit and her brothers took off running up to the lake. Shulamit could run fast. Her feet were light, as though they had wings, and she gracefully danced as she ran. Her brothers were the only ones in the village who could outrun her.

When they reached the lake, they jumped in with no fear. Papa taught them all to swim. He told a story about how, once, a lamb wandered off, falling in the water. He had to jump in and rescue it. It made Papa decide that they all needed to know how to swim, just in case they ever had to rescue sheep.

Papa had a gift for making everything we needed to learn into some kind of game and fun. To Shulamit, there was no one like Papa. She adored Papa.

3 A COUNTRY GIRL DREAMS

Shulamit and her best friend, Rebecca, were practicing their leaps while watching their sheep in the family fields. Leaping was Shulamit's new creative dance move.

The idea came from watching nature. When she saw the gazelle and deer leaping, she interpreted the joyful jumping as their own way of dancing. Now her goal was to include leaping in her worship dance. "Run as fast as you can, Rebecca. Then jump. Point your right leg out in front of you and glide until you land on the ground on both feet. They took a few tumbles in the learning process. But it was also a fun way to pass the day and the baby sheep were frolicking around them, making things even more fun.

They had a beautiful view from the hill and could see down into the valley where the King's Highway, one of the great trade routes of their civilization, wound between two high mountain ranges. Caravans came from Lebanon to Damascus, traveling the silk roads of the East to Jerusalem and Egypt. They also came from Egypt, in the South, up through Jerusalem on their way to Damascus, Lebanon, or toward the Exotic East. Shulamit and Rebecca could see a few of the watchtowers along the highway, protecting the people and the travelers.

Fresh water flowed down their mountain in streams where visiting people would refill their water vessels. Occasionally, a caravan would stop in the town nearby. The common people were able to see merchandise and exotic clothing worn by the people passing through. No matter where the processions came from, or where they were going, all their roads took them through Jerusalem because Jerusalem was the center of the universe.

Rebecca noticed a new group coming and shouted, "Look Shulamit! A caravan is headed towards Jerusalem."

"Yes, I see the flag with the gold lion on the blue," Shulamit observed. Throughout her childhood, Shulamit's family taught her to recognize the various flags of the tribes and other countries that passed through. "It is the flag of the tribe of Judah. It might be the king's caravan returning to Jerusalem."

"Look at the white horses, they are so majestic!" Rebecca said, rejoicing at their beauty.

"Look at the soldiers riding on the horses, with their swords on their thigh. There must be fifty or sixty of them."

"I wonder if the one wearing the long purple robe is the king."

"Look at the beautiful golden carriages. Do you think they are carrying women to the palace?" Rebecca asked.

"I wonder what it would be like to live in a palace," remarked Shulamit.

"Me too."

"You know Rebecca, this may seem strange, but something inside tells me someday I may visit a palace," Shulamit mused. "Years ago, this priest told me that I would be a blessing in Israel with my worship. I wonder if I'm a blessing in my worship as the Rabbi said."

"I remember you telling me that."

"My dream is to marry a Levite and be able to worship in the tabernacle, sing with the choir. Maybe dance."

"How would that happen?" Rebecca asked

"I don't know. Maybe, someday, a Levite will come and see our worship. Or maybe Papa will take me back to the tabernacle again to worship when I am older."

"You are a dreamer. You have to take me to the palace with you if you go."

"OK, deal. We will be best friends for life. Now, we need to go back to practicing our leaps, so we can put them into our dance for the Harvest Festival. You know what my mama always says, 'A person's gifts make room for them.'"

"I love your mama. She knows how to inspire everyone around her to learn new things by saying things like that. I remember when our fathers came back from Jerusalem with new looms, and your mother was teaching us all how to use them. We didn't feel like learning. But she talked about excellence, beauty, selling our goods at the marketplace, and bringing honor to our community. She made us interested. Remember how proud we were of the pretty cloth we wove."

"Yes," Shulamit laughed, "It was work though. But it became fun when we produced something of beauty." Rebecca joined her in laughter.

"Let's practice our leaping some more, so we can have a really beautiful dance for the festival. I want to leap higher, over that big bush."

Rebecca warned. "Don't you think it's a little too high?"

"If I start running from further back, I can get a good jump and I'll leap right over it." Shulamit walked back and ran very quickly. With her final moment, she took a big leap, but she did not make it over the bush. Her foot caught on the bush's edge. She fell headfirst down the hill, rolling over several other small bushes and rocks before she came to her final stop. Scratches and bruises adorned her arms, legs and both sides of her face. Her dress was torn, and her hair was matted with weeds and parts of bushes.

At first, she couldn't get up and had to make sure no bones were broken. Rebecca ran down to help her stand up. Thankfully, she was okay, but she looked a sight.

"We better gather our sheep and go back home," Rebecca advised. We can stop by the stream where you can wash off,"

Shulamit limped down the hill, and her body ached. The last people she wanted to run into were her brothers. They saw her coming and started laughing. "What happened to you?" one of them asked.

Neither Rebecca nor Shulamit said anything, because they knew how her brothers liked to tease her.

Then Shulamit's Mama saw her and began to take care of her injured child. She directed Shulamit to her private bed chamber where she applied healing balm to her wounds and combed the brambles out of her hair. It was almost time for dinner, and she wanted Shulamit as presentable as possible before Papa came home for their Sabbath dinner.

Shulamit usually helped mama put the dinner on the table, but not tonight. The best she could do was hold her baby sister. But that was just fine.

Shulamit loved Miriam. "This is my little sister," she always said. She loved so much being a little mama to her sister. When Miriam was learning to talk; Shulamit was the translator telling everyone what little Miriam said and wanted. Shulamit was very protective. No one or anything would hurt her little sister. But now Miriam was looking at her with sympathetic eyes. Her childish intuition told her to be good and sit still because her big sister hurt. Such was the bonding between them.

Soon dinner was ready.

Mama lit the candles and blessed the Sabbath. As they began the meal, Papa looked over at Shulamit and saw all the wounds. He gave her an inquisitive look but said nothing. Her brother, Josh, snickered, "I bet she was doing her leaping again. She thinks she is a gazelle or something."

"I don't think I am a gazelle," Shulamit answered angrily, "But as I watched them one day, I saw that their leaping is a dance. Their worship. They are graceful and elegant. Dance should include leaping. It shows joy. At certain high points in the music I can feel the leap. It is like when a bird takes off in flight, they speed up into flight and then they spread their wings and glide. After the leap, I can spread out my arms and turn in circles like I am gliding, and it makes the dance more beautiful."

Papa listened with an amused smile on his face. Then he said, "Sometimes we have to know our limitations. You have to learn how high you can safely leap, and if you leap too high before you are ready, you can take an awful tumble. We all have to learn to go slower, and take smaller steps, when mastering new skills. You also have to make sure your feet land on solid ground and not on a slope. We all want to make things happen in our lives. We want our dreams and desires to happen right away, but often, we just have to practice. When we are really ready, our leaps of faith happen. Don't give up on creating a dancing style, though. You are creating art."

Papa grabbed his lyre and said, "I have a new song to teach you. Grab your flute Mama. Joshua, play the other lyre. This is one of the last songs King David wrote before he died. The last words of a person's life are the most powerful. As a shepherd who has lived a blessed life, I almost consider it my song too." He sang:

> *The Lord is my shepherd, I shall not want.*
> *He makes me to lie down in green pastures;*
> *He leads me beside the still waters. He restores my soul;*
> *He leads me in the paths of righteousness for His name's sake.*
> *Yea, though I walk through the valley of the shadow of death, I will fear no evil; for*
> *You are with me; Your rod and your staff, they comfort me.*
> *You prepare a table before me in the presence of my enemies;*
> *You anoint my head with oil; My cup runs over.*
> *Surely goodness and mercy shall follow me all the days of my life;*
> *And I will dwell in the house of the Lord forever.*

The song struck a heart string in all of them. Shulamit could hardly sing because her ribs were so sore. Yet the song, coming through the voices of her heroes, King David and Papa, spoke deeply to her of the goodness of God. She pictured in her mind the still waters of the pond where she bathed and swam. The pond was surrounded by cool cedar trees that provided rest and refreshing from the heat of the day. That picture would stick in her mind for the rest of her life whenever she sang that song.

As calm came over the family, Papa sighed, lifting his wine glass in praise of God. "Thank you, *YHWH*, for a blessed life and happy family. We must always be thankful for our blessings and each other. Shabbat Shalom!"

***

Seasons had come and gone in the small mountain village where Shulamit lived. Her small village consisted of houses joined together with their front doors facing outward and back doors facing into the village. As a community, they had protection from any attack, even though they were now living in a time of peace and could focus on the blessings of their produce. In the back of homes were large walled in gardens where they cultivated green produce: Cumin, peas, lentils, lettuce, endives, leeks, garlic, onion, cucumber and cabbage. Fruit trees and some flowers could also grow in their gardens to beautify them, but that was more of a luxury. Since the front of the house faced outwards, shepherds and harvesters went out of the village through the front doors. Sometimes they walked long distances to harvest and take their flocks. Sukkots were often built during harvest season to stay near the harvest and keep watch from invaders or thieves. Sukkots, temporary shelters, were small huts. The walls were made of roughly hewn wood and topped with vine or palm branches. They were comfortable enough, but nothing like a family home in the village.

Shortly after the fall harvest came the early rain, which began the time of plowing and sowing of seed for the spring harvest. The first harvest in early spring was the barley harvest, which occurred at the time of the Feast of Passover. The wheat was harvested at the time of the Feast of Pentecost fifty days later. Wheat was not grown on their mountain, but they were always ready to help families who lived in the valley at a time of need. The whole mountain functioned as a one big community. First as a family home, and then as a village of extended families, and finally as a part of their tribe in Israel. They had to stick together to survive, especially during the wheat harvest where a sudden rain could destroy the crop. At such times, folks would pitch in to gather the crop in quickly. Everyone had to be prepared to help. The biggest harvest of the year was when the Feast of Tabernacles was celebrated in early autumn. That season was when the fruits were harvested: grapes, figs, pomegranates, olives, and dates from which they made honey.

Papa always called the Feast of Tabernacles the "Happy Harvest." In Israel, wine was the symbol of joy. It was considered a sin not to be happy at this harvest time.

As Shulamit and her brothers grew older, Papa taught them how to know the taste of good wine. "Swirl it around in the glass, sniff it, and then sip. The more flavors you smell and taste the better the wine is. If it is deep and complex the taste will stay in your mouth longer." The wine at Baal Haman was very sweet. Papa was always mixing wine with fruit and herbs, experimenting with different kind of grapes to create new flavors. To Papa, wine, like life, was a big experiment.

There was one more great harvest in their village. This was what Papa called the "crowning glory" of all their produce. That happened when the beautiful young women came of age to marry. When they wanted to express themselves ready for marriage, they would dress in white and dance with the other maidens at the festival.

Shulamit had grown into a prized beauty. She was taller than her mother, her friend Rebecca, and most of the other women in the village. She was as tall as her brothers. Mama said, "Don't worry, your brothers are still growing, and men reach their full height later than women."

Shulamit grinned, "You know mama, I don't mind being as tall as them, even if it is for a short time." Shulamit enjoyed being a pretty young woman. But she would never accept that, because she was a woman, she was any less mentally and emotionally developed than her brothers. Though she could run as fast as they could, when she tried to shear sheep, she discovered it took a lot of strength, and it was not a job she cared to do.

Papa said, "Be proud you are tall. God has made you tall for a reason. When people have to look up to you it is easier for you to lead. And you appear as a queen among women. You are tall and graceful like a palm tree blowing gently in the wind."

Shulamit's beautiful black tresses rolled past her waist in ringlets down her back. Her nose was long, and her mouth produced a wide smile with evenly matched white teeth. Her eyes were large with long, thick lashes, and her eyes sparkled, bouncing to show her quick wit and dreaminess at the same time. Her cheeks were pronounced, and her neck was long. Her figure was slim and yet full in all the right places. Her long, slim legs were designed to move quickly, yet delicately. Papa affirmed to her that she was a prize, and he was not going to give her away to, just anyone.

Papa told Mama, "I don't want to lose my pretty daughter, and she has this idea of marrying a Levite. I've promised her I will not make her marry someone she does not want, and that I will try to find her someone she wants. But does she really know what she wants?"

"Joseph," Mama said, "We all know the song you sang about Heaven smiling when Shulamit worships. That song did not get there by itself. Her dream is important. There was also the priest who gave her a prophecy about being a worshipper who would bless all of Israel. I doubt she will change her mind too easily. You know how I am from the valley, and my parents thought I was marrying too far away from home to move up to the mountains. They could not change my mind."

Papa sighed, "Shulamit never forgets anything. What are we to do? She has made me promise to take her to the tabernacle in Jerusalem again when that feast comes up. I cannot break my promise. But I question my own wisdom sometimes."

"This is where prayer and trusting comes in. Joseph don't forget you taught us all to dream, and it has made our lives more fulfilling. I remember when you dreamed of making the best wine in Israel. And out of the king's mouth, your dream came true."

"My wise wife, what would I do without you?" Papa relented.

***

But Papa never took her took to the Tabernacle in Jerusalem again, and Shulamit did not dance at the festival in the coming season.

Papa was getting old and tired, and one day he didn't wake up.

Shulamit's life as she knew it shattered when her father passed. Her whole family was in shock. Shulamit, in her pain, withdrew. For the first time in her life, she was oblivious to the pain of others around her. She hid from others as much as she could. She grew silent. Whenever she could, she grabbed her lyre, and took the sheep up to the pond, or ran there to be alone on Sabbath afternoons. She called this her secret place, but of course her family knew where she was, so it was not really a secret.

There she wailed.

She had been taught not to ask God why, and so, while she was alone, she sang the psalms that expressed her feelings best. She sang the Psalm, *The Lord is my Shepherd*, because she identified it with her secret place, and it comforted her the most. She would sing, stop and cry, and then sing it some more.

One day, as she sang, "Thy rod and thy staff they comfort me," she became aware of arms like those of an angel, embracing her. Something shifted in her spirit in that moment. She sensed *Abba*'s love in a very real, very precious way. She felt the presence of God, like she remembered it in the tabernacle as a child, but this presence was close and personal.

There were no soft words spoken into her spirit. It was all in her sense of feeling. Her heavenly father was speaking to her in a different way through this special embrace. It reminded her of the times she sat on her Papa's lap, and he just held her until she fell asleep before carrying her to her bed. She felt deep compassion. She knew in her spirit that the prayer within her heart was heard. Her life was not over. God was still with her, and He cared about her and her situation. She still had a future. The depression and grief begin to lift from her spirit. She felt strengthened in the Lord, and she knew she could go on.

When she returned and tried to put her experience into words to tell her mother, Mama said, "I know, Shulamit, I know. *YHWH* loves us all so much. He gives us the strength to go on. And go on we shall." Then she hugged Shulamit.

Two shifts happened that day: Her relationship with her Lord deepened. And Mama took on a new role of guidance in her life that had always been overshadowed by Papa and sometimes Gran-papa.

4 THE MAIDEN'S PRAYER

Suitors started asking about Shulamit, but she found no interest in any of them. Despite not being married yet, her brother Joshua took the responsibility of his father's place in the family. He was the oldest. Everywhere he went, he found himself pressed by the same question.

"Is your sister betrothed yet?"

One day, a few months later, Shulamit faced what she, at first, thought was the betrayal of her best friend, Rebecca. They often took their sheep up the hill together to let them graze, and of course, shared their hearts. They talked about the festival coming up and what they were making to sell there. Shulamit was embroidering vests for women. "Mama said, 'we might not be rich, but the embroidery on our clothing can make us dress as beautifully as women of wealth.'"

Rebecca told her about the tapestry she and her mother were making. But that was not what Rebecca really wanted to talk about. After exhausting the subject of all the raisin cakes and special deserts they would sell at the festival, she broke into what she really wanted to say.

"You know Shulamit, I feel like kissing Joshua." Shulamit looked at Rebecca, unable to speak. "I like him, and I am considering marrying him."

"You like Joshua?" Shulamit asked, lost in disgust. After a moment she cried, "Yuck!"

Rebecca said nothing, waiting for Shulamit to speak again. She knew she would.

"Yuck!" she repeated. "Joshua? Didn't he always pick on us, and say we were silly girls?"

"I know," Rebecca said, smiling. "But haven't you noticed how handsome he is becoming?"

"He's my brother."

"But haven't you noticed that your brothers are the best-looking men around? And they are hard workers, and more practical than most men."

"They are my brothers. I don't think about that. Papa and Mama taught us all to be practical. Papa taught us all about running a vineyard, and making wine, and caring for the animals. Papa taught the boys to build furniture and houses. Mama taught me how to cook, spin wool and weave, and sew. She taught me how to create beautiful clothing and tapestry, run a home, and care for children. Just a few days ago, I helped her deliver a baby. That is just how we were raised."

"Also, your family sings and laughs and tells good stories and entertains the community. I have always loved your family. Why shouldn't I love your brother?"

"I don't get it. My best friend wants to kiss my brother. I just don't get it." Shulamit sat in silence, almost in unbelief of what she just heard from her best friend. The silence between them was deafening.

Shulamit got up to walk around and be able to think. She couldn't. Her best friend was betraying her for her own brother. She looked back at Rebecca, who was almost in tears, and then she knew.

Rebecca would never betray her.

Rebecca had just seen something in her brother that, as a sister, Shulamit could never see. And she herself had never seen, had never met, a man she 'desired to kiss.' After pondering the idea for a while, a positive thought came into her mind.

She ran up to Rebecca and gave her a big hug. "We would be sisters. We would be best friends for the rest of our lives. We would be family!" Rebecca gave Shulamit a big smile through tears of joy.

"Does Josh, like you? Have you talked to him?"

"He has been smiling at me, and he gave me a flower one day."

"If he gave you a flower, that means something. I have never seen him do that to anyone." Shulamit looked at Rebecca again. "You really want to kiss him?"

Her blush was confirmation. "Please, Shulamit. Help me find out if he likes me."

"How am I supposed to do that? I can't just go to him and ask him."

"Oh no! Don't do that!" Rebecca thought a moment. "I don't know, maybe say something like, 'I think Rebecca likes you.' Then see what he says."

"Okay. I will talk to him." Shulamit looked at her friend again. "You really feel like kissing him?"

Rebecca's face opened into a smile that reflected pure sunlight.

At the end of the day, Rebecca and Shulamit returned the sheep to the fold and went their separate ways, a plan basically in place. As she walked home, all that was on Shulamit's mind was that Rebecca wanted to kiss her brother. "She wants to kiss him. She actually wants to kiss him," was all she could say to herself.

Returning home, Shulamit was faced with another issue.

As she walked in, Mama's eyes gave her a knowing look. Shulamit sighed. Her mother had invited someone to join them for dinner, so Shulamit had to greet a suitor at the dinner table.

This was the third friend of the family to come by in a short period. Someone doing business had asked Josh if she was betrothed, then unexpectedly showed up for dinner. In Israel, when people were passing by, it was considered hospitable to invite them to dinner. That often included fellow citizens passing through. Hospitality was considered a high virtue in their culture, and visitors rarely came without some kind of gift to add to the meal; be it wine, fruit, or nuts. This suitor brought a large basket of figs and pomegranates, and a vase of white and purple irises.

Shulamit was polite as always, but did not eagerly engage in the conversation. She still hadn't finished processing Rebecca wanting to kiss her brother. Anyone who knew Shulamit knew she enjoyed talking and laughing with people and even singing. They knew her quietness was not a good sign. Fortunately, the young man could sense she was not interested and didn't approach any question of marriage with her brother.

After he left, Joshua angrily asked, "What was wrong with *this* man? The last man you said couldn't sing, and the one before you said was uninteresting to talk with. So, tell me," he demanded.

Shulamit tried to evade the question, but Caleb got involved with the conversation. He agreed with his brother and also demanded, "Tell us, Shulamit, what is wrong with this one?"

In distress, Shulamit snapped back, "I have no desire to kiss him!"

Tempers began to flare in their home. "You have no desire to kiss him?! You have topped it all!" Joshua said. "I can't take it anymore! Papa put too many dreams into your head. You have no sense of reality."

"Oh, yeah, then why does Rebecca want to kiss you?"

"What?" Joshua's face turned red.

"Yes, she told me. My best friend wants to kiss my brother. She said she wants to marry you, and that you are handsome. Have I topped it all?"

"Stop!" Mama said. She could no longer hold her peace. "This is getting out of control. We are a loving family. We do not say things to hurt each other. Joshua, I know you are carrying a lot of responsibility at a young age. It is not easy. You do need to let Rebecca know if you are interested in her, and if you choose her, you have my blessing. She is from a good family."

"I like Rebecca, and I am considering marrying her," he paused, then continued on the issue with his sister. "But Shulamit needs to bear some of this responsibility. Maybe she needs to be in charge of the grape harvest this year. Then she will see what responsibility is."

"I'll do it!" Shulamit shouted, "Papa taught me how to manage the harvest the same as you. I may be a girl, but I can handle responsibility as well as you."

"Good, maybe you will be more humble, and not have such haughty ideas about who is good enough for you," Josh replied.

Mama went outside to pray, "Heavenly Father, help our family. Help my daughter not to despair. Surely you have someone that she will find attractive and worthy to be happy with. Give her brothers patience."

Shulamit ran out of the house, crying to her Mama. "I'm so confused, Mama. I know you and Papa loved each other. I know how excited you were when Papa came home from the field or a trip. I want what *you* had."

"Yes," Mama sighed. "Your Papa lives in my heart as a happy memory of the joy of my youth, and it can't be taken from me. I've had as a great love as ever there can be. Every maiden should have such joy with the man they consent to marry. If, after the harvest festival, you have not found a suitor you care for, I will take you to visit my family in the valley. But Shulamit, there is no perfect man. I was attracted to Papa before we married. And he sang wonderfully. He was funny and was a great storyteller. He knew how to tell stories that brought the characters to life and made you understand how God worked in the men's hearts of Israel's great history. But I knew when I married him, I would have to help him manage things. I knew I was practical and I was willing to do it."

"I know Mama. You were always the rock behind Papa."

"Good wives are, Shulamit. That is why I know Rebecca is good for your brother. I also know that you can manage as well as your brothers. You got that from me. But, you also got the dreamy side of your father. Let me say this, you have to have a list in your head of ten things you want for your husband to have. Habits, talents, whatever you want. If you find a man you are attracted to, and he meets seven out of ten requirements on that list in your head, then he might be a good person to accept. I know you don't want to be bought and marry out of duty, but it is true that you can learn to love. You have to trust God. I know He loves you. I know He has a plan for you."

Shulamit kissed her mama and went outside to sing a prayer.

YHWH, please help me
My spirit faints within me
I yearn to be thankful
I just want someone
Who lights a fire within me

Abba, a marriage
Must be more than bride price
And dowry
More than rules and
Regulations
Ketubah's and duty
I just want somebody
Who lights a fire within me

Is there someone who sees me

As more than just property
I'm just a simple maiden
But I know within
You've made me for something more
Someone who finds me worthy
Who lights a fire within me

Abba, I'm fainting
Please come and help me
I know You gave me beauty
For a special somebody
I will reserve myself
For your chosen man
Who lights a fire within me

Then she had a thought: *And someone I desire to kiss, though I don't understand those feelings.*

5 THE HARVEST

"This calls for celebration!" King Solomon proclaimed as he held up his golden goblet to his inner circle of friends and counselors in his private chamber. "The Foundation of the courtyard for the temple is almost finished. Mt Moriah is beginning to take shape."

"Indeed, we are seeing progress," announced Solomon's overseer of the labor force and builders. "The stones cut from the quarry are now being overlaid with silver for the temple. And there is more cedar from Lebanon being transported and cut into columns for building."

"This is good news indeed."

King Solomon, his chief council, and various overseers reclined on layers of luxurious carpet around an elaborately designed cedar wood table. It was low to the floor and inlaid with precious stones. Fresh wine poured into their goblets before Solomon raised his hand for the toast blessing. The others followed, joining him with the refrain, "*L'chaim tovin ul'shalom* (For good life and for peace)."

The king looked at the burgundy wine with interest. He gave it a swirl to let it breathe as he inhaled the sweet fragrance. He took a sniff and then a sip of the wine, allowing it to roll over his tongue. Finally, he savored the first burst of different fruit components as he held it in his mouth and swallowed. The sweet wine lingered in his mouth for some time changing into new flavors and leaving a pleasant aftertaste. "This is good wine. Where did it come from," he asked.

"This is the wine from the vineyard your father purchased in Baal Hamon, in Ephraim," Zadok, the High Priest, answered. "After they give their first fruits to the priests, they always send a portion of wine from the harvest to the palace and sell the rest for their own profit."

"Baal Hamon. Hm. I guess my father knew how to pick the best wine and the best vineyards to produce it." Solomon pondered for a moment then asked, "But why would a family sell a vineyard, even though they keep most of the profits?"

"They made an arrangement," Benaiah, commander of the army, one of David's mighty men finally spoke up. He had been very important in helping Solomon become king, and a soldier who had always been a loyal friend of the royal family. "This family has been friends with David since before he was king. They wanted him to come, visit, and sing his new songs in worship with them. Your father would go in the month of Elul, when it was custom for the king to be in the field. He always said the time of the harvest was the time to go out and enjoy visiting the common people. It was the happiest season of the year. I went with him as his bodyguard until his majesty was too sick to travel."

"So, you know the family," Solomon inquired. "Tell me more about them?"

"They are a family that loves to worship. King David always said that if Joseph had been a Levite, he would have made him charge over the tabernacle music. He was that good, but mostly it was his heart toward God. King David knew how to pick out the true worshippers. His majesty always said it was more about inspiration coming from the heart than true technical skill. This man Joseph was a rare man with both heart and talent."

"And what of the family?"

"Joseph's father fought with His majesty. He wanted to be a mighty man.

"Seems every warrior who followed my father desired to be a mighty warrior at that time."

"Perhaps. But his majesty convinced Joseph that his skill as a worshipper and providing provisions for his majesty's small army was more valuable. His majesty gave him some money from the spoils of war to pay his debts, and Joseph promised to keep a vineyard for the king."

"Interesting," Solomon said. "Can you tell us more about this family?"

"Joseph married a woman named Miriam from the tribe of Issachar. It is not often people from one tribe marry into another tribe, but they met in the crowd going to Jerusalem shortly after the Ark was placed in the tabernacle. Miriam is a graceful dancer named after Moses's sister, known in history for leading worship after the Israelites miraculously crossed the Red Sea. But she also carries the gift to know the times and the seasons. It is a gift of the Tribe of Issachar. They were the first tribe to recognize that David would be king after Saul."

Benaiah added, "I always enjoyed going with David to visit them."

"It is time for me to see how the fruit flourishes in the vineyards. My brothers can take care of business while I go out to the harvest fields. I want to visit my vineyard," Solomon laughed.

Benaiah laughed with him. "Perhaps I need to share just a little more about visiting them. Your father always visited them dressed as an ordinary shepherd. His majesty did not wish to draw attention to himself. He wished his visit to be private. You also have to take a gift when you visit there; and you have to have a song. That is the family tradition. If I may be of further service, perhaps I should go with you and introduce you. At least Miriam will remember me. I heard that Joseph died some years ago, but the older sons may remember David's visits."

"Yes, I would appreciate that. Going with someone who knows the family makes getting to know them easier." Then Solomon pondered, "The Family tradition, hmm. I have been designing a small winepress made from the cedars of Lebanon. You put the grapes in, lower the presser onto the grapes, then you turn the handle, and that makes the center screw press the grapes tightly so fresh juice comes out.

Zadok, the High Priest, laughed, "Your wisdom and creativity never cease to amaze me."

Solomon, still focused on his thoughts, sighed. "A song too? Hmm. I guess I will have to go to that mountain to view the beauty and see what song comes forth."

He turned to his servant and said, "Load up mules with some of those pistachio nuts from Persia and spices from the far East. Oh, and perfume for the women of the house; please include building tools for the men and whatever else you deem appropriate. He turned to Benaiah, saying, "You are going to go as the king's overseer of the harvest." Pointing to another man in the room, he continued, "Zabud and I are going to dress as shepherds and go with you as fellow travelers. I want to get to know this family as just an ordinary Israelite. Make sure you use the name Jedediah for me, in case any stranger asks questions. It is the name Zabud's father gave me at birth. I want to be one of them. I want to have some fun!"

"It sounds like an adventure," Solomon's counselor and friend, Zabud, answered. "We haven't had one in a while. As your friend, I am honored."

"Their harvest festival is about to begin," Benaiah added, "and the mountain is beautiful with streams flowing down, fresh water to drink, and small ponds and lakes that are great for swimming. It is the perfect time to."

***

"There it is. Behold the beautiful mountain, with vineyards all around. See there, apple, pomegranate, and various fruit trees are scattered about. It is a sight to behold," Benaiah declared.

"I have been too long at the palace. This is a breath of fresh air," Solomon acknowledged.

"You spend too much time admiring beautiful women at the palace," added Zabud. "It is time for you to admire the beauty of nature."

As they rode up closer to the vineyard, they heard the sound of harvesters singing. Particularly the lovely sound of a young woman's voice. It couldn't help but stand out. They drew closer to see where the voice was coming from.

Sing a song for the harvest

Sing a song for the vine
Sing, sing, sing a song
Sing for the joyful wine

Sing to the Lord of the Harvest
Who sends the rain in His time
Sing, sing, sing a song
Sing for the joyful wine

Sing a song for the harvest
For the blessed abundance
Sing, sing, sing a song
This is the season to dance…

Suddenly they saw a tall young woman dancing. Her long black curls swirled around her, bouncing down her back while she balanced a large basket of grapes on her shoulder.

Solomon jumped off his horse and pulled it behind some trees. "Change of plans," he said. "I need Benaiah to go and inquire of the woman. Find out whom she is and if she is betrothed. If she is not betrothed, I wish to meet her as an ordinary shepherd. Zabud," he said, motioning to him, "you stay with me."

"I am looking at her, and her way of singing and dancing," said Benaiah. "She could be Joseph's daughter. So, what shall I do if she is betrothed?"

"Then you can come back and get us. But, if she is not, be discreet. Come back and get the donkey. Give her the presents, and perhaps this gold necklace," which he took from his neck. "Give it to her as a sign to wait for the right person. You have always been wise in encountering women. Use your wisdom and charm now. Sing with them if you must."

Benaiah rode up on his horse to where she could see him. He called out, "How goes the harvest?"

Shulamit was startled. Women in their culture did not talk to strange men. But the older man was riding a horse with the seal of the king. She perceived he must be an overseer sent by the king, so she responded, "The harvest is great this year! We are truly blessed. The Cypress grapes we planted some years back have finally come to bloom. This crop has produced the sweetest grapes ever." She reached for a bunch of grapes handing it up to him. "Here, taste these." Shulamit looked around her to see her cousin was nearby; and, of course, all the harvesters were curious.

Benaiah tasted a few grapes and confirmed, "Sweetest grapes I have ever tasted."

Shulamit smiled, showing the joy of someone proud to have the acknowledgement of hard labor appreciated, especially from one of the king's overseers. It had been several years since anyone from the palace had come to visit the vineyard. After King David's death the visits became scarcer.

Shulamit inquired, "You must be the king's overseer?"

"Yes, I am. And who are you? "

"I am the overseer of our vineyard this year. This vineyard on our family's land we keep for the king, but you are the first person from the palace to come this way in many years."

"My apologies, fair maiden. I always enjoyed coming with King David to visit your family before he became too sick to travel. I enjoyed the music then, just as I enjoyed your singing just now."

"Thank you. My papa always said that you can add a song and dance to anything and make it better. Harvest is a happy time as we reap the fruits of our labors."

"Your song is lovely."

"Oh, I just make it up as I go. It's worship, thanking God for all his greatness and blessings to us."

"That is quite a gift you have."

"My mother said, 'King David imparted the gift of worship to our family. My Saba (grandpa) said that King David had a song for everything—for war, for victory, and for thanking God for blessings. So, we make a song for everything and turn it into worship.'" Shulamit began another short work song to make her point.

Work is work
Mama taught me
To value a work well done
Papa always told me
To make sure work is fun!

"Amazing! Your worship makes work fun." Benaiah laughed before he said, "So you *are* Joseph's daughter. That sounds like the Joseph that I knew. But a woman is overseeing the harvest? Where are your brothers?"

"My brothers are mad at me. They wanted to teach me a lesson by making me oversee this year's harvest. But I find it an opportunity to show them and others that I can manage a harvest as well as any man. Look how happy my workers are. We sing as we work. We have fun in our labor."

Benaiah tried to hide an amused smile. "Indeed, I see that. But why are your brothers angry with you? You should be proud of being a beautiful young woman who knows well how to manage a responsible assignment."

"They are mad because I have not agreed to marry any of my suitors."

"So, you are not betrothed?" Benaiah had to admit, he was impressed by this woman's intellect. "It is wise for a young beautiful woman to wait for the right man. If I were not an old man and already married, I would love to marry you myself."

Benaiah noticed the Shulamit blushed at the very personal comment and he wisely changed the subject. "The king sent me here to see how the harvest on his vineyard is going. But he also sent me with a message that your wine is the best wine he has tasted in years. He wished to send your family some gifts. Give me a moment to fetch my mule."

Benaiah went to gather the mule and whispered a quick message to Solomon. "She is not betrothed."

Solomon whispered back, "Give her the gifts and leave as quickly as you can before more questions are asked."

While he was gone, Shulamit called her cousin over to join her. Her cousin was a big mountain of a man, already making his way toward her when she began speaking. Shulamit knew someone had already sent for her brothers, though she did not think it necessary. She felt quite safe.

Benaiah was not surprised when he returned to see she was no longer alone. He climbed down, reaching out his hand and showing the first gift. "Here we have a small winepress of King Solomon's own design. You put the grapes in and turn the handle. Wine comes out this spout."

While Shulamit was standing amazed at the hand winepress, Benaiah showed her other presents for building, spices for cooking, and handed her a small, sealed flacon of perfume. "Oil and perfume bring joy to the heart," he mused.

Shulamit was overjoyed and did not know how to thank him. "I cannot wait to share these gifts with my family. My brothers love to experiment with new ways of doing things. My family would be delighted to have you dine with us."

"I have to meet the king at the horse stalls in Megiddo. I have no time. But wait, before I go, I would like to give you a special gift from the king." Benaiah opened another pouch on the donkey and pulled out a long thin golden necklace. The design was very delicate. Shulamit thought it was breathtaking.

"This is for you," he said. "As overseer of the harvest, I believe the king would like you to have this. Put it on your neck and tuck it under your robe. A woman wearing gold says she is valuable, and not going to settle for any common suitor."

Shulamit, holding back tears, took the necklace and held it in her hands. It was something so special she did not feel she could accept it. But something in her spirit said, *this as a sign of the favor of God and you must receive the blessing and have faith.*

Finally, she said, "I am so honored. Surely you will pass our way again and bless our family with your presence? The harvest festival is about to begin."

"I will try," Benaiah responded as he jumped back on his horse and prepared to ride away. "Let your cousin take the mule to your family with the gifts. I will retrieve it on my return. If not, consider it a gift too."

"Please bring the king when you return."

Shulamit's face flushed as she watched the overseer turn and ride away. She could not imagine what made her say such a presumptuous thing. As wise as she was, at times she was known for opening her mouth to hear things come out she had not thought out. As she wondered where those words came from, all she could think was, *they have been said and I cannot take them back. God knows.*

6 THE SHEPHERD AND SHULAMIT MEET

"She's not at the harvest festival?" Solomon queried. "Have you inquired as to her whereabouts?"

"I heard say that she is at her secret place," Zabud, responded.

"And where is this secret place?"

Zabud pointed to a group of trees up the hill from where they were sitting. The water flowing down the ravine was cool.

"I see happy hills," Solomon said, "and I feel a song coming on. I'm taking my lyre and will wait outside her secret place until she comes out of her hiding."

Solomon trekked up the hill. Thoughts swam in his head about the beautiful harvest time and the rejoicing of meeting beauty in the hills. He began to compose as he walked:

And the little hills rejoice on every side, lai lai lai lai lai lai
They shout for joy they also sing
They shout for joy they also sing
They shout for joy they also sing

Thou crownest the years with thy goodness
And thy paths, they drop fatness
They drop upon the pastures of the wilderness
And the little hills rejoice, on every side

And the little hills rejoice on every side, lai lai lai lai lai lai
They shout for joy they also sing
They shout for joy they also sing
They shout for joy they also sing

They shout for joy they also sing, lai lai lai
They shout for joy they also sing, lai lai lai
They shout for joy they also sing, lai lai lai
Lai lai lai, lai lai lai lai
Lai lai lai lai
Lai lai lai lai lai lai lai
Lai lai lai lai

And the mountains shall bring peace
To the people
And the little hills, by righteousness lai lai lai

And the little hills rejoice on every side, lai lai lai lai lai lai
They shout for joy they also sing
They shout for joy they also sing
They shout for joy they also sing

Solomon continued singing, adding verses to his song about the glorious time and place in nature as he sat behind the shade of a tree. He liked his inspiring vantage point, sitting outside of paradise and seeing a touch of blue between the trees.

A voice from within the trees began to sing along to his music. The beautifully-toned voice carried in echoes across the mountain ranges, harmonizing with his voice. Their voices blended together majestically. As the singer emerged from the trees, Solomon almost stopped singing, full of awe.

Before him stood the most beautiful woman.

She sprang forth dancing, her eyes closed as she twirled and twirled to the feeling in the music. Her powerful, joyous dance moves reflected what she felt. Her arms stretched out wide as she turned, and her hair flowed around her in the wind as she spun. The expression on her face was pure joy, lost in the music as if she were in another dimension.

Holding his lyre in his hands as he played the song, Solomon could not resist the impulse to get up and dance around her. She was so lost in the song, she did not even notice that he had come nearer. When she suddenly opened her eyes, surprise came upon her face as she saw Solomon dancing with her.

Yet she continued to dance.

She did not wish the dance to stop, and it was clear, Solomon did not either. They continued dancing around each other until, exhausted, they collapsed to the ground laughing. Gasping for breath, they kept laughing and laughing and laughing. They stopped for a moment, gazed at each other, and started laughing again.

As she looked into the man's eyes, Shulamit had a feeling of wonder. That wonder shone through her. She blinked, as if to question whether or not she was dreaming. *Was this incredibly handsome man sitting across from her on the grass? Sitting there, with his curly black hair down to his shoulders, was he real?*

Solomon knew she was real. He could not take his eyes off of her. *Beautiful.*

Perhaps out of joy or sudden, nervous shyness, they began to laugh again. The laughter increased like before, and they stopped trying to figure out why. If it was heaven that kept them laughing, they didn't know. Solomon and Shulamit only knew something amazing had just happened, and it was a gift for them both.

When they finally managed to stop laughing, Solomon remarked, "I have never laughed so much in my entire life."

Shulamit, as though awakening from a dream by his voice, suddenly became aware of her behavior. She scooted back on the grass to put distance between them. She didn't know if she should run away. Solomon noticed her expression and rising anxiety, so he said, "Do not worry. A beautiful maiden like yourself is one a man would desire to marry so much he would only show you the utmost respect. Your honor is safe."

Marry? Shulamit pondered that thought, and her face flushed. She tried to remember the list—the one her mother told her to hold in her mind—to see if this man met the qualifications. But with the handsomest man Shulamit had ever seen sitting in front of her, her mind would not work properly. Before she could stop herself, a big smile came across her face.

Solomon, as a king, had always carefully weighed his words. But at this moment, he found himself surprised at the words from his heart. They came to the surface so easily. He had the welcome, though uncomfortable, feeling of being vulnerable and out of control. For a man in his position, those feelings were not something he was used to.

But her smile set him beside himself.

Shulamit's mind and feelings were all over the place, but she tried to hold her composure. She could feel butterflies within her chest and stomach, fighting to explode out of her. After a pause, she admitted, "I don't think I have ever laughed so much either. You sing and play music the way I imagine King David would have."

Now Solomon tried to hide his uneasiness. Did she know who he was? How could she?

Shulamit sensed she had said something wrong. "I don't mean that in a bad way," she interjected when she saw his expression. "My brothers sing very well, and so did my father. But I have never met anyone who sang as well as them."

"Oh, I see," Solomon responded breathing an internal sigh of relief. "Your voice is as lovely as these very hills. I feel as though I have been singing with an angel."

Shulamit lowered her gaze, humbled by the compliment. She'd heard it so many times before, but never from the handsomest man she'd ever seen. "Do you think," she said, "that angels might sing through people sometimes?"

"What do you mean?"

"I once felt as though an angel was singing through me. My father said that heaven likes to worship with us. "

"I am sure that heaven would want to dance and sing with you." Solomon smiled, not taking his eyes from her. "How come you are not down making merry at the harvest festival?"

Shulamit would have liked to have averted the question, but for some unusual reason, she felt there was something in this man she could trust.

"I'm hiding," she said.

"Hiding? Why would someone as beautiful as you ever hide?"

"I know of a few suitors who are coming because they have been talking to my brothers about becoming betrothed to me."

"Oh," Solomon said, considering. "And you don't want to be betrothed to any of them? May I ask what it is that desire in a man you want to marry?"

Shulamit's face turned to fire. "Where are your sheep? I don't even know your name. Where are you from? Where is your family, and why are you in our village?"

Solomon knew she was right to ask about him before she answered any questions and shared her heart. "My name is Jedidiah," he said. He'd practiced this story. "I come from the tribe of Judah. If you follow the trail of the sheep down the hill, you will find my sheepfold. I am passing through with sheep I bought from the mountains in the North. I wish to breed them with my sheep to create sheep with thicker wool. I also wish to visit the harvest festival as I pass through here. I have heard the wine from up in this hill country is some of the best in Israel."

"*The* best," Shulamit corrected.

Shulamit's mind had cleared a bit. She remembered her list of ten things she wanted in a husband. She decided to put him to the test, right then and there, and see how he responded. "My name is Shulamit. My mother said I was an easy birth and a peaceful baby, and I was born in a time of peace. I want a man who can give me my own home, not a home built onto his family home, but my own home. I want my own home and my own vineyard."

"I can do that," Solomon said, urging her on.

His response gave Shulamit boldness. She looked him in the eyes and said, "I want a man who is quick of wit and curious about life. Someone who wants to learn as much as he can. I want a man who is a hard worker and likes to be creative in his work with new ideas and ways to do things, like business."

"I am a creative businessman," he said, smiling.

"I want a man of strong faith who likes to worship and sing and dance. I want a man that I would desire to kiss."

"Would you like to kiss me?"

Solomon could not help himself. He had been staring into her sparkling brown eyes, watching her beautiful mouth move as she spoke.

Shulamit blushed deeply within her milk chocolate skin. She realized she had spoken without one bit of discretion to this man. She started to back away again, this time standing to her feet. She snatched up her slingshot in case Solomon made a move to kiss her.

"Do you know how to use that?" Solomon said, smiling.

"A shepherdess in the hills, of course, I do."

Solomon held his hands up in surrender. "Don't worry. I won't kiss you. Not until after I have married you."

Shulamit stood there, stunned into silence. For the first time in her life, it suddenly dawned upon her, she might have met someone she could desire to kiss.

Yes. She desired to kiss him. Very much.

Solomon watched her. He knew by the expression upon her face that he had his answer. This beautiful woman was attracted to him, and not just because he was a king. She was attracted to him as a man. He wanted to know this woman more.

"You will have to meet my brothers and mother," Shulamit said as if she weren't already captivated. "If they like you, and if I like you as I get to know you, then I will consider marriage."

Solomon let out a big sigh of relief. "When can I meet your family?"

"Tomorrow at the harvest festival," Shulamit answered. "I will dance with the single maidens, and you must be the first to come up to take my hand when the dance is over."

"I will be," Solomon said.

7 LOVE AT THE HARVEST FESTIVAL

Shulamit awoke the next morning with a song in her heart and an expectant mood.

She knew it would be a great day. Her dream was coming true she could hardly wait to see Jedidiah and introduce him to her family.

As she dressed and groomed for the day, she danced with excitement. She washed and combed her long black curls, humming to herself. The flowing white dress she and Rebecca made from flax would be perfect for the day. They had belabored many hours at the loom for this garment, worn only on special occasions. She would wear her red scarf with the long fringe around her waist. The way it moved against the air made it lovely for dance.

Not only that, it was also a present from her father bought from the markets in Jerusalem. In a way, having on that sash made her feel like her father was with her, blessing this day.

For the final touch, she opened the perfume given to her from the king's friend. When she was done and felt ready, she went to find her mother. When she saw her, Shulamit lifted her chin and said, "I am going to dance tonight with the maidens at the festival."

Shulamit's mother, Miriam, busy kneading the leaven into the bread dough, was surprised but did not give it a lot of thought. There was just too much to do to prepare for the day. She had her prepared dough, almond and fig cakes, and lots of fruit to load onto the wagon to take to the festival. Shulamit's little sister, Miriam, enjoyed helping her mother decorate their booth, decoratively arranging the food. Before they left, Miriam decided to run out to the fields to pick flowers and herbs to adorn the platters of food. She enjoyed making small arrangements of flowers. When she returned, Miriam tied her picked flowers, small herbs, and branches together with straw bows, making little bunches. She liked giving them as presents to people. It was her special gift.

Shulamit's widowed aunt came into the room and saw Shulamit dancing around. She said, "You are looking very joyful today, Shulamit. There is a glow about you that I have never seen." She smiled and said, "Are you in love?"

Shulamit smiled back. "The festival will be special today. I expect many surprises. I am going to dance."

"Whenever you dance, it is special indeed," her aunt remarked.

***

Solomon also awoke early in his tent. His small campsite was pitched down by the stream, where a newly accumulated flock of sheep were feeding on the green pasture land. He began planning his day with Zabud and his trusted bodyguards disguised as shepherds. He turned to Benaiah and smiled, saying, "Thank you Benaiah, for what you have done during our travels thus far. You did a good job getting the information I needed about my bride to be; but I feel no more need to hold you from your military duties. You may go on to Megiddo and check on the horse stables. See how the army is learning how to train horses and riders."

Benaiah was happy he pleased his king. Bowing deeply, he left the tent, preparing his mind for the trip to Megiddo. Solomon's greatest horse stables were not far from Ephraim in the Valley of Jezreel in Issachar, and they were due an inspection.

"Zabud," Solomon said, "you are in charge of making sure all the men are spaced around the maiden's dance this evening to run interference against anyone blocking my goal of reaching my chosen maiden. In the meantime, have a small unit stay by the flock. Make sure they do not draw attention to themselves and keep guard over the palace mules. Keep them well covered from anyone guessing what may be loaded on them. Zabud, you will come with me as my friend. While I am speaking with the people of the village, take note of the situation around us. I will need you to direct the men when the time comes to grab my maiden's hand."

Solomon placed gold chains and silver coins with a few other jewelry pieces in the pouch attached to the belt around his waist. He slung his lyre on a strap over his shoulder and walked to the nearby creek to fill his flagon with the mountain water. As he sat on the hillside, watching the sunrise, he began to compose a ballad about "The Harvest Maiden."

He envisioned how this beautiful harvest maiden would look with gold around her neck, dressed in beautiful garments accented by her tall, lovely frame. He imagined a crown upon her head. As he thought about her, he sensed majesty in this country maiden. Solomon's gift of wisdom, which he was continually discovering, included being able to visualize the end from the beginning. And as he sang about the harvest maiden, he was given revelation about her being transformed from lowly maiden into a majestic queen.

She was one chosen by the Lord. And He had been preparing her to become his bride and queen.

In his blossoming song, he was opening this gift from God. He sang out,

"I've watched you from a distance,
I take pleasure in you
When the time is right, I'll reveal myself
And make a queen out of you."

As he heard his words, he understood he would have to save that song until later. That had to be a song he would sing when the Ketubah was officially signed, and she knew who he was. Until then, he had to keep his identity secret. That would be somewhat difficult. His servants were instructed in their duties to act as the shepherd's peers and keep their eyes open. And most importantly, they were to make sure no one got in the way of his being the first to take Shulamit's hand at the dance.

Zabud joined him near the water. He observed, "My king, I believe you are in love. Joy is bouncing off of you. Who will be able to resist?" His tone softened as he added, "But tone it down as you arrive at the festival, you do not want to alert Shulamit's mother too quickly. Kings can be fooled, wise men deceived, but mothers," he paused, "mothers see the intentions in the heart of anyone near, especially when it comes to their offspring. Pray God gives you grace with her mother."

Solomon gave a slightly anxious laugh. "Come," he said. "Let us take the mules with their gifts. If the brothers are hard to negotiate with, the gifts and money will answer all things. I will give whatever it takes to have this beautiful woman for my wife."

Zabud chuckled. "Remember sire, you are a king, and who can say, "No" to a king?"

"I will never use my position as a king to force love upon anyone. And I will not make a woman chose against her family's wishes." Closing his eyes, he prayed, "*Elohim*, God, give me wisdom." Then to Zabud, he said, "Pray they want her happiness as well. Pray this is a happy occasion."

Over the hills and into the village, Solomon and his companions came, pulling their laden mules. The market bubbled with jubilant activity. Sukkots were set up all around the open center. Fruit hung on the booths, enticing passersby and shading sellers with roofs thinly covered with branches. They were made this way to leave room for the sun, stars, and moon to shine through the roof. Low tables inside the Sukkots displayed flowers in vases and baskets of many items like pomegranates, figs, grapes, and apples. The spices mixed with olives, and honey, making the air pungent and inviting. Colorful mats on the ground displayed lentils, seeds, and vegetables in colorful pottery.

Displays of raisin and almond cakes adorned many sukkots. And dumas (rolled grape leaves filled with rice, meat, and vegetables) were arranged on large pottery platters. Nearby, an open-pit-roasted lamb. Branches from the grapevines burned as fuel, flavoring the meat with their smoky fibers. Small clay stoves were set up to bake the fresh bread as large vessels of water and juice from the grapes were set up for drinks. Everyone was displaying their gifts and talents.

There were, of course, many tables of crafts, clothing, and homespun cloth at the harvest festival, including Shulamit's. She was proud of her embroidery skills in the vests, jackets, and tablecloths she had made. Her brothers and their friends displayed their woodworking skills. Caleb, who liked carpentry, presented his tables, stools, and cabinets.

Animals, looking their finest, were in the stables. Acknowledgments were given on the best sheep, goats, and other domestic animals. And sheep shearing became a contest of who could shear the fastest. Travelers came to the village during this time, exchanging their goods for wine, grapes, and fresh products. The bartering could go on for a long time while people ate and laughed. But the focus of the festival was giving thanks for the bountiful harvest of wine and fruit. And give thanks they did, with all that made gathering together in celebration joyful. Music played, and children were dancing and running around making merry.

Into this joyful festival, Solomon, the handsome stranger, and his friend Zabud tried to walk unnoticed. But a stranger in a village where everyone knew each other was hard to miss. The young maidens turned their heads as he and his fellow shepherds tied the mules to the trees. But he was not deterred.

Solomon's spies told him who Shulamit's family was, and he wanted to ingratiate himself with them. Solomon made a quick glance and took note of where all Shulamit's family was located. Walking with a nonchalant gait, he proceeded over to where Joshua had a table set up covered with vases of the family wine and baskets of grapes. Joshua showed off the winepress the king had given his family, offering samples of his fresh grape juice and wine.

"You are welcome to try a cup of juice from our fresh harvest grapes," Joshua said as he handed a cup to Solomon. Joshua loaded the press with grapes and turned the handle while Solomon held the cup up to the spout. Once the cup was full, Solomon took a drink. He was delighted.

"Excellent. Your harvest is blessed. That press you have works very well. Did you design that?"

"It is actually a design of King Solomon himself, given as a gift to our family for the wine we send to the palace."

"Let me taste a cup of your wine," Solomon asked. Joshua happily acquiesced. "It is excellent. I must fill some of my ampullas with your wine when I leave. What can I give you in exchange? How about a gold ring?" He patted his pouch. "Are you betrothed? I have rings for a future wife. I also have chains and earrings. I even have silver cups to serve your wine in?

And I can trade you my sheep too."

"Tonight, I will take the hand of my future wife, and afterward, I will look at your rings and jewelry. Let me fill your flagon now with fresh juice for you to drink as you look at all the other products and enjoy the festivities."

Solomon looked over to where Shulamit was giving fresh bread with legumes and cheese to people coming to their table. Rebecca saw him looking at Shulamit and said, "That handsome shepherd over there keeps looking over here at you? Have you noticed?"

Shulamit giggled, "Do you know something, Rebecca? He is handsome enough to want to kiss. His kiss would be better than our wine, I believe. And today," Shulamit announced, "I will dance with you and the other maidens, Rebecca."

Rebecca gave her a curious look and then said, "I think he is coming our way."

Solomon came over and looked at the raisin cakes Shulamit's Mama was giving out. She handed him one and said, "Please taste."

Solomon took a bite and said, "I would like to know your family secret. I assume you are passing this secret on to your daughters?" He asked as he looked at Shulamit and then at Rebecca, to pretend he did not know she wasn't her daughter.

Miriam introduced herself, and then lifted her palm in Shulamit's direction. "This is my oldest daughter Shulamit, her best friend, Rebecca, and my youngest daughter Miriam."

Little Miriam looked up at him with a big smile and handed him a flower. "And what is your name?" she asked.

"Oh, yes," he spoke as he looked down at little Miriam. "My name is Jedidiah." Looking back to the elder Miriam, he said, "You are blessed to have such lovely daughters and friends. What else do you have here?"

Being the mother she was, Miriam gave him samples of all her loaves of bread. She placed legumes on flatbread right out of the oven, which he ate with obvious delight. He went on to look at the clothing they had made and made remarks about the embroidery designs Shulamit had made.

"When I create a design," Shulamit explained, "I think of the meaning of the flower or fruit that I put into the design so that every design speaks something to the person who would trade for it.

Solomon saw a design of red pomegranates with the seeds in them and asked, "What does this mean?"

"Seeds are about fruit. It means there will be the blessing of much fruit: children, or harvest blessings, or whatever you want the seeds to represent in your life."

"I like the rose," Solomon voiced. "A rose to me symbolizes beauty." I will take this cloth with the rose design and place it on my table at home to remind me of all the beautiful roses in this countryside."

Shulamit blushed as he was looking at her when he said it. Miriam noticed and hid her small smile. Rebecca pretended not to notice. Little Miriam smiled widely.

"I would also like some of your raisin, almond, and fig cakes to take with me for my trip home. And I have a gift for each of you ladies."

Solomon reached into his bag, removing four scented pouches with colorful braided string to hang around their necks. He held one out for each of them to put on, placing one around little Miriam's neck as she giggled. She held it up to her nose, taking a big whiff before tucking it into her dress. The spices in the pouch contained the smell of cinnamon, myrrh, frankincense, cedarwood, and other rare spices. It was a gift often given by men to their beloveds to say; now you have my scent with you all the time.

Shulamit's mother, filled with hospitality, decided to invite him to dine with them after the main festivities were over.

"I would be delighted," He replied as he turned to the neighboring sukkot. "I will find you at the end of the festival ceremony."

"We look forward to it," Miriam said.

Solomon continued to walk around the festival marketplace, admiring the local products. He sauntered over to where Caleb displayed his woodworking skills. Bending down, he looked at the trunk Caleb had built. Opening and closing it, he complimented, "You are a skilled carpenter."

Caleb was pleased. "I wish I had more time to build, but as you can see, we are country folk who spend most of our time sowing, planting, harvesting our grapes, and caring for our sheep."

"I know what you mean," Solomon agreed, "As a shepherd, I too would like to spend more time building which is my favorite thing to do. Just keep doing what you love, who knows where the future will take you. I need to go and see your animals. I like trading in sheep and other animals."

Solomon continued wandering around the festival grounds looking at the animals and the flower arrangements in pots, laughing with the children, and talking with the people. He was having a lot of fun.

As the sun went down, a trumpet was blown. The ceremonies were about to begin. People left their booths and gathered around the open center of the festival where men and women played their instruments. Caleb played a long flute, and Joshua the lyre. The women kept the beat with tambourines. Then the music stopped as a priest stepped forward, holding a silver goblet of wine. Lifting it, he blessed the Lord for the bountiful harvest and declared, "As long as the earth remains, seedtime and harvest, cold and heat, summer and winter, and day and night shall not cease."

This signaled the makeshift band to begin playing and singing a traditional song called, Seedtime and Harvest.

As long as the earth remains
Seedtime and harvest
Seedtime and harvest
Seedtime and harvest
Shall not cease...

Spontaneous verses, "The summer heat and winter rain, seedtime and harvest will remain," were added as the children danced in a large circle. The laughter bloomed as magnificent as the harvest while the songs were sung. A village man saw Solomon's lyre and invited him to join the musicians.

The women began to gather in a circle to dance with their tambourines to a lively tune.

Sing, sing, sing a song,
Lift your voice in rejoicing,
Drink a cup of the harvest wine,
Join in the happy dancing.

While the women danced in a circle with their tambourines, the men dancing alone began to jump and leap around, circling spontaneously. Solomon got up and danced with the men. Shulamit noted how limber he was. He jumped about like a gazelle leaping about on the hills.

Joshua, watching Solomon dance, began to jump about also, laughing with him. The village people cheered them on. Shulamit kept pace with the women dancing with tambourines, but her eyes were on Solomon. Thankfully, she knew these harvest songs inside and out. She flowed so naturally with music, it didn't take much effort to do both.

Caleb began to notice the glances and stares between his sister Shulamit and this stranger. He pulled Joshua to him, speaking in his ear. "Keep an eye on this man. He keeps looking at our sister."

Solomon's friends also took note that Joshua and Caleb were talking together while watching Solomon. The tension was beginning to build as they watched Solomon, Shulamit, Joshua and Caleb. Zabud appointed them positions, but they still were concerned about how were they going to keep the way clear for Solomon to reach the young maiden's hand? And when He grabbed her hand, what would the repercussions be? Those strong brothers of hers did not look like men you wanted to anger.

With a break in the music, Shulamit's uncle, Jehiel, who now replaced her papa as master of ceremonies, stood. He welcomed all visitors to their village, even looking at Solomon while he spoke. He then went on to acknowledge the outstanding wines in their village, the prize animals, and the skilled crafts. Her uncle was very wise and made sure every family was represented in some award. He was very detailed in acknowledging local talent, especially in the youth, the future leaders of their village. Finishing the awards, he called forth the priest to offer the final cup of wine as the ceremonies were ready to end in their grand finale.

The Priest held up his cup of wine and again gave thanks for all the blessings *Elohim*, the God of creation, had poured upon their village and the great seedtime and harvest they had this year. Then he said, "But the real symbols of crowning glory, are the beautiful young maidens of our village who have come to full harvest in this season of their lives. They are beautiful flowers, prepared by the hand of God for the men who shall be blessed to betroth them. They have prepared a dance to share the glory bestowed upon them."

Into the circle of maidens came Shulamit, Rebecca, and five other maidens. They were all dressed in flowing white dresses and scarves of various colors with long fringes hanging from their waists.

As the musicians played their prepared music, they begin to dance slowly. They started in a circle, facing inward, opening their arms widely above their heads, like flowers opening to the sun. Then they lowered their arms, grabbed hands and turned a full circle to the left, coming to a slight pause before turning another full circle to the right. Still facing inward, they took hands and raised their arms up as they danced into the center, bringing them down again. They all turned outward and raised their arms as they had done in the beginning–flowers opening in worship. Turning inward, they repeated those same steps two more times. The third time, instead of turning outward, they each began twirling around in circles, arms spread out at their sides.

The music sped up and each maiden turned sideways, facing the back of the maiden in front of her. Like wheat in the wind, they began waving arms from side to side, leaping in their dance. The beat of the music sped up, and they ran and bound higher landing gracefully upon their feet every time. They repeated the leaping and bounding until the music slowed down. Then they turned, facing the circle inward, and grabbed hands again, repeating the steps at the beginning of the dance. Finally, coming to a stop, the entire village clapped.

This was the time for Solomon to run forward and grab Shulamit's hand. Solomon's men took their places to block anyone who would try to stop him from being first. Joshua was walking to take Rebecca's hand, as Caleb saw what Solomon was about to do and ran in front of Shulamit. An unknown suitor tried to come to Shulamit from another direction and was blocked by one of Solomon's men.

Shulamit showed her speed at running and dashed to the other side of Solomon, who stretched forth his hand as she grabbed his.

Caleb's countenance showed grave concern at what just happened. He called to his brother Joshua, who had to let go of Rebecca's hand and run over to where Shulamit and Solomon were. They held hands so tightly it would take an army to pull them apart.

Joshua began yelling, "Who do you think you are? A stranger who comes to our town offering gifts thinking you can buy our sister? Our sister is a dreamer and vulnerable, and you would take advantage of her innocence? She probably thinks she loves you because you can sing and dance. But that is not cause enough to marry. Who do you think you are? We would not allow our sister to be betrothed to anyone we do not know."

Joshua wanted to punch Solomon but stayed his hand out of concern about his sister's feelings.

Solomon caught off guard, not by the brothers being angry, but at the question, "*Who do you think you are?*" Solomon did not know how to deal with an identity other than being a king. He felt at a loss, and suddenly his own vulnerability came to the surface, "I guess I am just an ordinary man, who finds your sister the most beautiful woman I have ever met, both inside and out. I love her. She is a prize above all women. I would willingly give you whatever you want to gain her hand in marriage and far more. I promise you I would dedicate my life to make her happy, and I wouldn't expect you to give her away without knowing my family. Whatever you wish, I will do."

Joshua softened, as he knew he would do the same for Rebecca.

Shulamit, standing there, began to cry. Joshua immediately felt terrible about making his sister cry. But he knew his responsibility to protect her.

"You really love me, Joshua," she said through her tears. "I thought you didn't really care about my happiness."

"Of course I love you," he said, soothing her with a softer tone. "You are my sister. I know you are an honorable sister, but you are still a woman who though very intelligent, has a heart that can cloud your judgment. We men have to protect our women," he said, turning to Solomon. "We would wall you in if we had to in order to protect you."

Shulamit didn't like being spoken of as a woman considered inferior to any man, and quickly replied, "I am a wall."

Solomon could not help but laugh.

Joshua, trying to keep a straight face, said to him, "She is really impossible, wait until she tells you all her dreams, desires and everything she wants, then you might decide you want to run from her."

Solomon stopped laughing, though he was still very amused. "I would run after her, but never from her," he said. "A person is only as great as their dreams. I love dreamers. They challenge me to be better than I am."

Caleb wanted to roll his eyes at that response, but then a thought came to him. This man might actually be a match for her.

Mama came up to them and said, "The food is ready, I have invited Jedidiah to dine with us. Nothing has to be decided tonight." To her son, she said in a soft but firm tone, "Joshua, your beautiful Rebecca is standing over there waiting for you. Best you go to her before she cries too. This is your night to celebrate your betrothal, and we want all happiness." To Solomon, she said, "You were right Jedidiah. Rebecca is soon to be my daughter."

8 UNDER THE HARVEST MOON

The Harvest moon shined bright in the night sky as the stars came closer to the earth to share in the special occasion. Love was in the air. Two long, low tables sat parallel to each other, connected at each end by a shorter table where Joshua and Rebecca sat. They were the center of activity.

A *Shiddukhim* was taking place, where families made arrangements prior to a legal betrothal. Rebecca's family sat at the left table, her table. The male members on one side, and the females on the other. Joshua had Caleb at his right hand, along with the local Rabbi and Uncle Jehiel. His mother Miriam sat at the head of the table on the other side with Shulamit, her Aunt, little Miriam, and other female relatives. Solomon, still disguised as Jedidiah, was seated as an honored guest on the corner of Joshua's table, enjoying his view of everyone.

Servants and friends placed large bowls in a beautiful array at the center of the table. There were vegetables and roasted lamb, along with large platters of mixed fruit, smaller platters of fresh bread and cheese, and vases of wine and water.

The local Priest stood up and sanctified the food. "Lord, we praise you for this food we are about to receive. We are grateful for your bountiful supply, and offer our thanks to all the hands that prepared it. May we have sweet fellowship as we fully enjoy all the many gifts you have given to us tonight. Amen."

Once the food was blessed, a hushed, "amen" was heard throughout the area. Joshua, being the head of Shulamit's family, took a piece of bread and, after choosing the largest piece of meat, handed both to Jedidiah. As he accepted the bread, Jedidiah said, "I am honored."

After this showing of hospitality, typical to the region and the people, the servants filled everyone's goblets with fresh wine. Guests began taking bread and dipping into the common bowl.

Rebecca's father raised a glass of wine and indicated for others to do the same. He was about to proclaim a blessing over his new son and family.

"It has been many decades that my family knew Joshua's family," he began, "yet this is the first time our families have actually come together in marriage. May this be the beginning of a new day for both our families!" Cheers and laughter went up, celebrating the blessing as everyone took a drink.

Solomon looked at Shulamit, smiling as if to say he wished her to be a part of his family legacy. He knew this was not their day to officially celebrate. This was Rebecca's day, and Shulamit knew how to step aside and allow another person to shine. Her best friend, with whom she wished all the happiness in the world was the first person she wanted to tell. But Shulamit bowed her head, smiling sweetly in reply.

One by one, guests and family members began telling the history of the two families. Each friend or kinsman came forward jovially, with stories about building the wall around their village and their homes, or how their two families protected the animals in the sheepfold—bringing the livestock into the village during times of threat from enemies. There were stories that went back as far as conquering the promised land and taking their mountain. Israelites had no better pastime than communing, drinking wine, and telling stories together. In their oral tradition, being a good storyteller was an honored talent. As the stories of their family connections died down, it was time to move into the most important moment of the evening.

Joshua stood up with another glass of wine, from which he took a drink. Others followed in good cheer. It was his time to be the honored storyteller and share his story of knowing Rebecca and growing to love her over the years. He proudly shared his tale.

"Rebecca was always just my sister Shulamit's best friend to me. She went along with all my sister's crazy ideas," he said as people laughed, "like jumping off the high rock into the lake below when she was scared out of her wits, or learning how to make high leaps over rocks and bushes for dance." They interpreted clouds together and designed beautiful embroidery for the market. He looked at his bride-to-be and said, "My sister was always dreaming and talking, and Rebecca was always listening. She was always quiet, but always cheerful and strong. I never saw such a loyal friend in my life. Then one day she grew pretty," he said. Everyone cheered and laughed, and he continued. "I looked at all the pretty girls, and Rebecca stood out. A wife should be a best friend, and Rebecca will now become my best friend and partner in life." Rebecca smiled deeply.

Shulamit jumped up to speak, taking over. "At first I felt Rebecca was betraying me for my brother, of all people, my own brother; but then I realized, now she would be my sister forever." At that statement all the family laughed. Joshua laughed deepest, from pride, or love, or joy. Perhaps all three.

Solomon listened with delight to these happy families in their happy village. For a moment, a touch of envy tried to take root in his mind. He had grown up in a palace full of privilege, but also full of strife and division. His mother was so protective of him she prevented him from joining his half-brothers sheering sheep. She feared they might be jealous of him and kill him.

Here there was no jealousy.

The beautiful woman he loved sat at her best friend's Shiddukhim, ignoring her own desires to be recognized for a newfound love. She looked after the joy of her best friend with meekness and honor. Being willing to take a low seat and let others shine was, to Solomon, a sign of great love, and even greater humility. That trait was rarely seen in a world where everyone sought their own desire for recognition. But he knew that Shulamit would have her day.

As king, he would see to it.

Solomon's thoughts went deeper. He realized that though he had known other wives and concubines, he had never really been in love. And then Shulamit would glance over at him periodically with her sparkling eyes. They showed her love for him, and yet she hardly knew him. Shulamit had a sensitivity to see in him what no other woman had seen and had indeed taken a big leap of faith in accepting the hand of a stranger. She had taken a risk that could have made her look like a fool in front of her whole village. He appreciated her faith.

Yes, he appreciated her faith.

Other women had seen his wisdom, and his talents in leadership which were obvious. But Shulamit was the first to sense in him that he, too, had a gift to worship like his father. Solomon had never felt he could ever come anywhere near his father's gift of worship and song. He didn't think he could compare to his father's deep intimacy with their God, *Elohim*. But around this woman, he felt he could touch heaven in song and prayer and worship.

She pulled it out of him.

She pulled it out because she had it. It was her gift. Shulamit's gift of worship pulled out the spirit of worship in everyone around her. *What an amazing gift,* he thought, continuing to look her way. *I can see her worshipping with me on Sabbath evening in the palace. I can see her worshipping in the Tabernacle. I can see her standing beside me as a great queen as I dedicate the temple.*

I need her, he realized. It wasn't a sense of owner's need. He was not hungry to consume her. It was more akin to recognizing she was worth whatever price or covenant required. Shulamit was a pearl, many times more valuable than ever imagined.

I thought I just loved her. But I need her like Joshua needs Rebecca. She is the kind of queen I have always longed for. I see her as my queen who will bring out my joy to praise and dance. Her joy will bless my court, palace, and me as king. She will bless me with her song and dance. She draws in the presence of God, which every king needs to rule well.

As the excitement began to die down, Solomon asked Joshua if he might offer a gift to the future bride and bridegroom. He had his servant bring over a bag, full of gold rings. Reaching in, he offered a large gold ring to Joshua and a smaller gold ring with a bright sapphire stone in it for Rebecca. Then he started to speak, humbled. "I have been blessed to be here in this village and experience all of your wonderful hospitality. Your love for each other is something I have never experienced anywhere else." As he spoke, tears came to his eyes. "I know now why King David loved to come here and visit your family. If I were king, I would come here every chance I got."

Joshua almost hesitated, not wanting to accept such lavish gifts. But so he would not offend his esteemed guest, Joshua accepted graciously.

Honoring one another with gifts, especially on special occasions such as this one, was their lifestyle. Joshua took the ring with the brilliant blue stone and placed it on Rebecca's finger. She sat and looked at it with great admiration. "This is so beautiful," she said, thankful. "I am so glad you came to our village, and I hope you will become part of our family," making Shulamit look down, even as she smiled. Rebecca continued. "My best friend, now sister, is a dreamer, and we all feel protective of her. Her dreams have always been fun and challenged me to a more interesting life, and so I listen to her. I also believe God really speaks to her."

"Friends like you are worth all the gold in the world," Solomon acknowledged. He turned to Joshua again and declared, "Joshua, I wish a long and happy marriage, with many children. I hope that when you meet my family and know more about me, I may also be accepted into such a wonderful family."

Shulamit's Uncle leaned over to Caleb and whispered, "I know I have seen this man before, but I can't remember where. He must be from a family of influence."

The evening carried on with more stories about their large extended family and individual love stories. Caleb saw his mother with a faraway look on her face, thinking of days gone by, and he knew she was thinking of their father.

Not wanting to leave her out of all the family love stories he called out, "Mom, you haven't told your love story tonight, about how you met our Papa, Joseph. Tell us again Mama. We love your story."

Miriam hesitated, but her family insisted. Her faraway look changed to a sparkle in her eye as she recounted meeting Joseph. "It started with a dream." The family laughed. Everything about Joseph started with a dream. "Your father, Joseph had a dream. Just like our famous ancestor Joseph, the forefather of the tribe of Ephraim, he had prophetic dreams. In his dream, he saw my face, and what I looked like, and that I would be worshipping with my family on the road to Jerusalem.

"The Ark of the Covenant had just been moved into the Tabernacle. As it happened, I was with my family singing and dancing as we journeyed to Jerusalem for the Holy Days. We were full of joy and anticipation, on our way to worship before this unveiled Ark. It had never been so, in our history. We knew the Ark of the Covenant would remain unveiled for only a short time. Once the temple was completed, it would go back into the Holy of Holies. So, my family saw it as a small window of opportunity to step into the presence of God.

"I was singing and dancing with my sisters and other friends as we played our tambourines. Suddenly this young man ran into the midst of us and began dancing. He told us to pick up the beat so the dance could have more life. As he danced, he showed us faster jumping steps while he twirled in circles with his hands held out to his sides. We followed him. He was fun." Everyone laughed, remembering his dancing days. "As evening came upon us and our tribes began to make our separate camps. We told him we were from the tribe of Issachar. He said he was from Ephraim. He asked my name and what city I was from so he might find me again. It was easy to get separated in the crowd. Then he told me he had seen me in a dream, and I was the one he was supposed to marry. He wanted to know more about me.

"I was taken aback. I thought, *this man saw me in a dream?* It was hard not to laugh," Miriam said. "But he was completely serious. I told my mom about him, and she said, 'Invite him to dinner and your dad and I will see what he has to say.'

"As we sat around the campfire, Joseph properly introduced himself to my family. He said he was from Ephraim and spoke of his family as successful winemakers and shepherds. Then he asked my dad for my hand in marriage. My dad, sympathetic to the young man's request, asked, 'You hardly know her, how can you be sure of this marriage?'

"'When I asked the Lord for a wife,' Joseph earnestly expressed, 'I saw her face in a dream, the clothing she was wearing, and her worshipping group playing tambourines.'"

Miriam continued, "My whole family could hardly hold back from laughing. But something happened to me at that moment. I liked this man Joseph, he was funny. He made me laugh. When he had told my sisters and me to add more rhythm to our tambourine beat, it did make our dance more alive. He was handsome. I watched what my dad would say. To my surprise, my father actually took a liking to Joseph.

"'With a name like Joseph, what can one expect? My daughter is in a new season in her life. Your timing is good. I will let you get to know her on this trip, under my watchful eye, of course,' he said. My heart skipped a beat. I hardly expected my dad to give his approval to a stranger. I guess that is why I invited Jedidiah to dine with us. Something in my own memory came to life."

Solomon looked at Shulamit again. He knew they were in a somewhat similar situation. She glanced back at him, the same knowing look in her eyes. They couldn't help smiling at each other. They knew somehow it would work out.

Eventually, the party began to break up. Shulamit stood with her mother and the other women to help clear away the food. She said to her mother, "Thank you for telling your story. If Papa was here, I know he would approve of Jedidiah. Isn't he wonderful? God has answered all my prayers for me and my new sister. I am so happy."

"I surely hope you are right about this man," her mother said. "I like his sensitivity and nice manners. He has a gentle nature that would treat a woman well. He also appears to be successful and intelligent. But we must make sure. Men can be very charming in the presence of a beautiful woman, and when they want something. So, we must be wise Shulamit," she said before lowering her voice. "But I do like him," she admitted.

Rebecca excused herself from what she perceived was a need for a private conversation between Joshua, Caleb, and Jedidiah. Shulamit watched the looks upon her brother's faces from a distance. There were intense looks of concern as they conversed with Jedidiah. And what he was telling them no one in the village would know.

Shulamit watched and prayed, her thoughts a whirl. "Father, God, give Jedidiah wisdom. I mean, give my brother's wisdom. I mean, please keep this man for me. I love him. I believe he is the right man in my heart and spirit. But I have to trust you Lord. You know what is best for me."

The three men talked for a long time. Some parts of their conversation were serious business, but there was some joking around as they started to get to know each other. Uncle Jehiel, as the patriarch of their extended family, had come to join the conversation. But it was Joshua who anticipated further issues and brought them up. He said, "We Ephraimites have the gift of prophetic dreams. But don't let that make you think that is all we are. We are dreamers who *do*. We put feet to our dreams. Just because our sister is a dreamer does not mean she is not a hard worker and manager in her own way. She can lead and is a quick learner. She proved that this year by managing the harvest. She knows how to sell too. Take her to market and there will be nothing left on your sales table."

Solomon nodded in agreement. *This Joshua is a real salesman himself,* he thought. He knows how to sell his sister for the best price. I should have him on my business council. "I believe everything you are saying," Solomon replied. "I will be happy to have her as my partner in life."

Caleb, who had consumed several glasses of wine, couldn't help interjecting, "Our sister didn't say she dreamed about you, did she?"

They all laughed and it lightened the discussion.

51

Solomon, enjoying this moment of fun, said, "She didn't say she dreamed of me, but she did say she dreamed of someone to worship with. Now, I am a businessman, but I am a businessman who considers worship essential for making important life decisions. A person who worships seeks the heart of God and brings the presence of God into the situation which helps any leader make better decisions."

Jehiel heard the word worship. He thought of his niece, and one time they were eating outside on the grass on the Sabbath. He counseled Joseph to declare that Shulamit could touch heaven with her worship. He knew back then she would never settle for a man who would not worship with her. Jehiel began to consider this man Jedidiah. He looked into his eyes and studied his face, suddenly realizing where he had seen that face before. He had seen that face in another man.

King David.

When he said the word worship, it rang a bell. This must be his *son*.

Solomon knew that Jehial had now recognized him. The realization settled on him like a coat. But he also saw that Jehial was an honorable man. One who kept important secrets. He would not reveal his king's secrets.

Caleb broke the momentary pause and added, "But she did mention the word dream." This elicited another laugh from them all.

"She has sought God for her life choices." Solomon surprised them all with his insightful response. "I appreciate that. She has a gift of prophetic dreaming. And I see from your history, it is a gift that runs in families and throughout tribes. Ephraim dreams and Issachar knows the times and seasons. We are a chosen people. In your sister's dreaming, I perceive purity in her. She is without guile. I would never take advantage of that nature in a woman but would guard and keep it."

Shulamit's heart began beating hard in her chest—so hard she almost wanted to rest a bit. Rebecca walked over to her, and Shulamit said, "I wonder what they are talking about. Are they talking about me? I now know for sure my brothers are looking out for my best interest. I know my uncle has been more in my life since my father died. But why aren't they calling Mama into the conversation?" They sat together. "Do you suppose, since Mama invited Jedidiah to dine with us, she had already spoken her approval? But I guess if they are talking about the Ketubah; then you are talking about the marriage bargaining. That is men's business. Do you think that was what they were talking about."

"It will be alright," Rebecca consoled Shulamit. "One thing we both know about Joshua is he has never undersold anything in business. He is probably just trying to find out how sincere this man is. Crazy in our culture that a wife's value is measured in how much gold a man is willing to pay, but at least he doesn't seem poor, Shulamit."

"I don't care if he is poor, because I can manage a vineyard and business for both of us."

"You are thinking with your heart and not your head," Rebecca said, sighing. "Thank God for your brothers."

"Let this dream be real," Shulamit sighed. Shulamit's sister joined them. Rebecca, Shulamit, and little Miriam watched, trying to guess what was going on. It seemed that no one was going to sleep this evening—not until the results of that conversation were over. But soon enough, little Miriam closed her eyes in slumber. Shulamit could not sleep. And Rebecca, her faithful friend, sat with her, looking at the blue sapphire stone on her one hand and holding Shulamit's with the other.

"How did he know my favorite color is blue?" she mused.

Shulamit looked over toward her brothers and saw Caleb pour a glass of wine. He passed it around while each took a sip. Then they grasped each other, as was their custom, and stood up. Joshua walked over to Shulamit and Rebecca and said, "We have agreed to allow you to get to know each other more. You may talk under the open moon by the fire, in plain sight of us all." Shulamit clapped her hands and jumped for joy. Joshua turned towards the fire. "Rebecca and I will be sitting on the other side of the open fire on this lovely night." He looked at his bride to be. "Rebecca, I apologize for so much interruption on this night meant for you. But we will have many more."

Rebecca stood, taking Joshua's hand.

She did not know all that happened, but she knew that, somehow, Jedidiah had won her brother's hearts. They were now giving Shulamit a chance to get to know this handsome stranger and decide on her own if he was what she really wanted. Something shifted. Shulamit could feel it. Her brothers were showing her the respect of a woman about to be elevated to the status of marriage.

Solomon and Shulamit came together and began walking. Shulamit was skipping her way beside Solomon on the way over to the fire. Solomon's heart was skipping as well. They begin to laugh again. "My brothers like you. I can tell. I am so happy," Shulamit giggled as she sat down on the grass.

"Your brothers love you, I can tell," Solomon laughed. "You are quite the family. You can fight and forgive, disagree, and still accept one another for your differences. And yet there is a unity between you that must agree before you let any outsider in. I like that."

"Yes, I guess. How many brothers and sisters do you have?"

"I have three other brothers. I am the oldest and responsible for the wellbeing of everyone. But we work together very well. When I go on a trip, they take over my responsibilities."

"Do you have a lot of responsibilities?"

"Since my father died, yes. I took on quite a bit."

"Your father died too? Oh, I am sorry," Shulamit said as she sat. "I will help you. I know how hard it is to lose a father. My mother always reminds me to not give my brother Josh too hard of a time. I don't try to."

Solomon laughed as he sat down. "I'm sure you don't try to. But I can assure you your brother is a strong man, stronger than he knows. He is a tough man to bargain with."

"You bargained? Whoooo." Shulamit had a quizzical look upon her face.

"Don't you worry about anything. Your brother was just looking to see if I loved you. And I assured him I do. You are so beautiful; I can't stop looking at you. Your eyes are like doves."

Shulamit blushed. She could feel the heat of her face increase, despite the evening coolness.

"Your voice touched my heartstrings first, and your dancing on the hill mesmerized me. But when you opened those doves' eyes and looked at me, I was captivated. I danced, but I was not aware of dancing. I sang but I was not aware of singing. I was not aware of anything but you when I looked into your eyes. Now, I am not aware of anything but you. You transport me to another world."

Shulamit bowed her head under the weight of such compliments. "When you looked at me," she said in reply, "I begin to feel something I'd never felt before. You too have dove's eyes. And when our eyes connected that first time, I felt heaven connect to the earth. Do you believe that heaven can bring two people together and connect our eyes so that we choose each other for life, like doves do?" Shulamit wondered aloud.

"We are here, aren't we?" They both smiled. "We are sitting under a full moon with the stars of heaven all around us," Solomon said as he looked up, "We have a bed of green earth under us, and our spirits full of love within us. Yes, I believe."

"We are not in the tabernacle in front of the Ark, but I feel the presence of God," Shulamit said.

"Wherever there is love, there is God." Solomon paused and looked around. "I wonder how many people are watching us."

"Probably my Mama," Shulamit said. "Josh for sure, and who knows? Maybe half the village, resting on the ground in their sukkots enjoying the night sky. Perhaps they are glancing over here from time to time," she laughed. "Rebecca is still sitting by Joshua. I don't think anyone is getting any sleep tonight."

"How could I think of sleep? I could sit here and stare at you forever. I am memorizing every feature on your beautiful face. When I close my eyes, I still see you. This is how I want to remember you. I want to remember this night forever," he said, leaning on his arm in the grass. "Tell me more of your dreams. I want to hear what ticks inside of this pretty woman's head."

"Well, let me see. You already know my first desire is to sing and dance and worship in the tabernacle and on Sabbath Evening with my family. After that, I want many children. I want to learn all the songs in the Tabernacle and teach all of them to my children."

"Hmm."

"I would like to have my own copy of all the Psalms, and I would like to be able to read them. I can read letters of the alphabet, and some words."

"Hmm."

"You just say, hmm, but do you not think women should be able to read?"

"I think it is amazing. I'm just thinking of how to make all of your dreams happen."

"Oh," Shulamit said, smiling widely again. "Well, actually, I dream of having my own copy of the Torah, so I can read some of it every day. And I would like to learn to write it myself too."

Solomon was having a hard time keeping a straight face. Never had he heard a woman speak like this. As king, he had his own copy of the Torah, which he kept by the throne. He read from it every day for keeping the Word of God always in his heart. It helped him to be a wise judge. "You certainly are a dreamer. But I would have to help you lift the large scroll or divide it into smaller scrolls," he jested." Without saying, Solomon recognized Shulamit's sincere desire to learn more of the scripture. He realized that the desire to know God better was a characteristic of a noble person.

"And I want to be able to write the song you wrote," Shulamit played along with him, "Can you sing that song again?"

Solomon grabbed his lyre and began to play and sing.

The little hills rejoice on every side,
Love is in the air and everywhere,
Like a flock of goats, running down the hills,
Are the waves of my loves, black flowing hair,
And like a helpless man, I sit and stare,
I shout for joy, I also sing,
Yes, I shout for joy I also sing,
I shout for joy I also sing.
Lai, Lai Lai Lai Lai Lai Lai, Lai Lai, Lai Lai
Lai, Lai Lai Lai Lai Lai Lai, Lai Lai, Lai Lai

Joshua and Rebecca glanced their way but did not come over as they were engrossed in their own conversation.

"That is not exactly the same song," Shulamit laughed.

"Yes, but that is before I saw you. As your rabbi declared, the best of these mountains are the beautiful maidens. The flowers sing and blow in the wind," He began humming another melody. "I now have another song. I have a song in my heart. You inspire me. I look at you and want to sing."

"I hear you sing and want to dance."

"I watch you dance, and I want to dance with you, and never stop dancing. I watch you dance, and I see an army of banners. Nothing that can stand in your path. You could conquer heaven and earth when you dance. You could conquer kings, and you have conquered me."

"My Papa said I made heaven smile when I worship."

"Your Papa was right. You do carry a touch of heaven. It is something I have never experienced before. The wind of heaven blows through you. Together we could create beautiful music. We have not even begun."

"That is what I want to do!" Shulamit rejoiced.

"Your brothers are right about your dreams," Solomon stated. "I'm fascinated. I don't know where you get all your dreams, but I believe it must be the hand of God. It reminds me of Joseph's dreams."

Solomon was beginning to see Shulamit not just as a worshipper, but a woman born to rule.

As the hours passed, Shulamit talked at length of her dreams. It was as though she was discovering a part of herself in a man who listened and really cared. Papa and Mama had cared and listened some, but it was her friend Rebecca who had listened the most. Perhaps, as they sat out watching sheep, they had time to dream up things to talk about. Her brothers had always teased her for her dreams and thought it was their duty to keep her in touch with reality. Perhaps, without Rebecca, her dreams would have died. Now they were coming to life again.

"The only person who has listened to me as much as you was my friend Rebecca. You make me feel...valued. I think you really believe such dreams can come true. You have faith. But I have been selfish. I haven't asked you about your dreams."

"Right now, you are my dream. I am thoroughly enjoying you. I enjoy the excitement and expression upon your face as you talk about your dreams. My dream is to kiss you, but I will not awaken love until it is ready. And I couldn't anyway with the whole town watching," he said. They both laughed. "As I look at you and listen, I see you are like a flower opening up. I am getting to know the person inside your beautiful appearance."

"Yes, but tell me more about you and what you like," Shulamit pleaded.

"You made me realize how deeply I like to sing and dance and enjoy worship. I get busy with responsibility, but you remind me of that side of me I love. You have awakened that love in me. I feel many songs rising in me right now, but I don't want to wake up everyone," he said, smiling.

"What do you like to do?"

"I like to build, create and design. I like to observe animals and their natures. I like to design beautiful gardens, plant trees and flowers in ways that make a little paradise outside of the house."

Shulamit listened intently, discovering this man to be fascinating; He was more than she expected.

The night went on with them discussing their favorite flowers, trees, and colors, and many other subjects. As they spoke, they each fell more in love, not taking their eyes off of each other.

Soon the morning star appeared in the sky.

Joshua walked Rebecca to her family's sukkot, then walked back over to where Shulamit and Solomon were sitting.

"We have been up all night, and it looks as though you two have enjoyed each other's company," Joshua teased.

Solomon stated, "Your sister is a very rare woman, indeed. I love her dreams and shall do my very best to see all of them fulfilled. Now, if I may, I would like to give gifts to your family as only a small example of what more I have to offer until we confirm the betrothal."

He called the servants over with the packed mules. Solomon grabbed two large packages and set them on the low table. As he unwrapped the leather skins protecting them, Shulamit's family could see they had colorful clothing inside. "These fine linens here are for the women." He picked up a blue garment with gold trim on the top of the pile and handed it to Rebecca. "This is for special occasions, or you may save for your wedding day." Rebecca's face lit up. She had never seen such luxury in all of her life. She could hardly hold tears from her eyes as she thanked Solomon for his kindness.

Now to the mother of the family, he said as he held out a white dress with gold trim. Shulamit had never seen her mama delighted over any present. The material of linen was so much softer than the sometimes scratchy wool clothing they made for themselves in the country. He handed her a matching soft cotton robe to wear over the dress. Miriam was overjoyed as she accepted the wedding clothing so beautifully made. "You make me feel like a queen."

"You are the queen of your family. Clothing can help us discover things within ourselves that we already are." Miriam felt, for a moment, that she should bow, but she thanked him humbly instead.

"Little Miriam had been standing there anxiously waiting for her turn. She was too cute for Solomon to ignore any longer. He pulled out green material of soft linen as he said, "Mama will help make this fit for you." As she stared wide-eyed with excitement, Solomon announced, "I have something else for you. He pulled out a handful of small gold bangle bracelets and put them on her arm. Little Miriam shook her arms with delight and began jumping up and down. "These are real gold! And I will treasure them forever." She boldly threw her arms around Solomon, and cried out, "Thank you, thank you, thank you."

Solomon turned to another package, opening it. He picked up the elegant tunics and robes inside, handing them to Shulamit's brothers saying, "Robes for the wedding." He put a gold chain around each of their necks. "My new family must be honored," he added. They nodded in gratitude.

Solomon pointed to another package which his servants handed to him. He handed tools to Caleb for sawing, chiseling, and hammering. There were also knives of various sizes in the gift. "A carpenter must have his tools," he said. Caleb was ecstatic. He picked up the tools and held them in his hand as he visualized how he would use each one.

Opening a small package, Solomon gave Joshua a golden serving pitcher and six golden goblets to match. Solomon appraised his gift by saying, "He who makes the best wine in Israel must drink it in the appropriate style." Joshua held up the empty goblet, smiling. He couldn't help thinking, *I wonder the value of these*, but he said, "We shall celebrate with glory. I am honored."

At last, when all of the family had been given gifts, Solomon turned his attention to his bride to be.

He picked up a purple gown. It was intricately decorated with gold design throughout it and trimmed in gold borders. He held it up to her, beaming.

"I look forward to seeing you wearing this, I visualize how beautiful you will look dressed for glory."

Shulamit blushed. She was beyond words. Solomon then asked Miriam to help him place a delicate gold chain around Shulamit's neck. He then handed her golden bracelets for her arm. While Shulamit held her arm extended to admire the bracelets, Solomon bowed before her, took her ring finger and placed a gold ring with a ruby stone on her.

"This ring is my promise to love and honor you forever," he said. While Shulamit admired the ring on her finger, her family clapped and rejoiced over the joyful occasion.

Having offered his gifts, Solomon and Joshua gave each other a customary embrace. Solomon looked endearingly at Shulamit, "I will be back as soon as I can, before the winter rains."

9 Bathsheba's Advice

I brought you out of the harvest fields
Where you worked hard for me
I saw your heart in the harvest field
You gave your all for me

And when you discovered my love
You labored as unto me
I saw your heart in the harvest field
You labored in love for me

You knew my words from a distance
You sang my words to me
You put your heart into worship
As you danced before me

I love your soul in worship
I'm coming closer to you
I've been watching your outflow
And I like what you do

Now I am coming to visit you
And draw you closer to me
I'll visit you in your dreams and your song
I want you to dance with me

I've watched you from a distance
And I take pleasure in you
When the time is right, I'll reveal myself
And make a queen of you

I'm pouring my grace upon you
I am grooming you
My beautiful maiden who works in the field
I'm already in love with you."

Solomon's heart was full of joy. He was almost exploding with song as he rode back to Jerusalem.

Zabud rode beside him on his own horse, singing along. "You are very much in love, my king," he said. "I am the prophetic one, but you have taken her out of the harvest fields in your song to become a queen. I'd say this woman has stirred a gift in you.

"I see people's gifts in them and what they can be," Solomon said. "Is that a prophetic gift?"

"God has given you great wisdom and seeing the end from the beginning is part of wisdom and prophecy. Calling forth gifts is also prophetic. You are not a prophet, but you have some gifts of prophecy."

"As a prophet, Zabud, how do you see this Shulamit?" Solomon asked.

"Solomon, I see through the eyes of a prophet, and you see through the eyes of a king carrying wisdom and understanding to rule. You see gifts from the perspective of leadership and service to the country. I see gifts as a spiritual anointing of worship, prophecy, and intimacy with God. I see gifts in another realm than you do. I see this woman as prophetic. I also see her completely surrendered to worshipping God. She will worship Him and do all He asks of her. As a wife, she will be dedicated to serving you as she serves God. She will do for you all you need to reign as a king.

"Her heart is not to rule. Her heart is to worship her first Love. The Heavenly Kingdom, Mt. Zion, where Yahweh dwells and King David sang about is her first Love. She sees you as a shepherd to guide her in a calling of God, but she loves you too. She is attracted to you. She is a young virgin, Solomon. She is following her heart, but she has not thought through where her heart will take her. Her heart is good Solomon. That is what I discern as a prophet."

Solomon took a moment to digest the words. "I trust your judgment, Zabud," he finally replied. "I honor you as the son of Nathan the prophet, who reminded my father, before his death, of his promise to my mother to make me king. Something I never expected. It is amazing that we have been friends since childhood. How often I have depended upon your spiritual leadership to guide me. I see I have fallen in love with a very unusual woman, but I also see her as becoming a great queen. Your words have proven this beyond all doubt." Spurring his horse on, he began humming and singing to himself again.

Solomon continued singing as he traveled, processing the words of Zabud in his heart. Soon enough, his royal responsibilities crept in, stealing his focus and his songs. His thoughts turned to the reality of the chores ahead and how he would prepare the chamber for his bride to be. He visualized her beauty in all the elegant clothing he would have made especially for her. He thought of all the gifts he wanted to give his bride. He was also planning the return with his family to Baal Hamon. He longed to see the surprise on Shulamit's face when she realized the man she had fallen in love with was really a king.

A thought occurred to him. He began to wonder if his being a king might be too much of a surprise. He needed to talk his mother. She might not be the best advisor on affairs of state, but she was an excellent Queen Mother and understood managing the household of women and children. When he wanted a woman's opinion on love, she was the person to talk to. Besides, Shulamit's family had asked to meet his family, and he would certainly oblige.

He would not return without his mother.

Solomon had always honored his mother from the day he took full authority as king. He even placed her on a throne to his right. No one would ever dare speak ill of his mother as long as he lived. Any slander regarding the Queen Mother was considered an assault against the crown, and not to be taken lightly. Bathsheba had always been the favored queen of his father, and because of that, there was always a certain amount of jealousy. Only Abigail had treated her with kindness when she came to live in the palace. The other queens, jealous and spiteful, had treated her with disdain. They went so far as to excluded her from friendship circles, always accusing her of causing David to sin.

Solomon knew God had shown great mercy to his mother. He made sure she was treated with absolute respect. She and David had repented together of their sin and cried out for forgiveness.

Ever since Solomon could remember, his mother told him he was a special child. She named him Jedidiah which meant beloved. He represented God's mercy and love in her life, and every time she looked at her baby boy, she knew God was good. God was so good, in fact, that she was favored with three more sons: Shimea, Shobab and Nathan. Bathsheba had always protected Solomon and his younger brothers from the wrath of his stepbrothers from other queens.

Solomon grew up fully aware of the deep love his father had for his mother. He knew they both understood a deep love of God and worshipped together in that unity. They sought the Lord together in prayer and worship. Bathsheba had always been the wife David came to when he wanted to share his deepest moments of spiritual intimacy. Solomon's mother had obtained the promise from David that he would become king after Absalom's rebellion and death. She had held to that promise and called for Nathan the prophet to come and help her present this promise to the king as he was dying. Now she was honored as Queen Mother for her loyalty and love to the king.

Solomon did not have to announce himself as he neared his mother's chamber. The servants could hear him singing as he danced down the corridors.

Bathsheba greeted him at the door, "Solomon, what a surprise," she said, smiling as she hugged him. "You appear very happy. We all heard you singing as you arrived. What brings you here? I know you never come to see me in my private chambers unless you have something important on your heart. Is it about your trip? How was it?" She motioned for servants to prepare a table. "Come and join me for tea."

Solomon sat down to a low table on the plush carpet. As the servant poured his tea, he told about his whole adventure to Baal Hamon.

"Mother," he continued, "I realize I have never really been in love before. It is the first time I have ever been just an ordinary man in love with a beautiful woman for no other reason than the simple joy from being in her presence. She is tall and stately, with long flowing black wavy hair, like yours. She has large, dark brown sparkling doves' eyes, encased in long lashes, a long nose, and a wide smile with perfectly matching teeth. Her features are perfect."

"I can see you are enthralled," Bathsheba interjected.

"Her expressions come from a deep joy inside of her, and it enlightens her very presence. There is a touch of heaven upon this woman that makes her beauty stand out from all the other women I have ever beheld. The first time I encountered her we laughed so hard, I thought I wouldn't be able to stop. I felt totally out of control. We sang and danced. I have never had so much fun. I almost got into a fight with her brothers."

"What?"

"They were just doing their duty as brothers to protect her. I like them. I love the whole family. They love to drink and eat and laugh and worship. They loved David and kept a vineyard for him, just so he would visit them and they could worship with him."

"Baal Hamon, I think I heard of that family. They helped your father when he was fleeing from Saul. They always believed he would be king. Your father told me he always remembers the people who loved him and believed in him before he became king, for they had their eyes on the true King of the Universe."

"Yes!" Solomon smiled.

"So that is where you got your song. Your father used to return from visiting them with a song. Every time. They always joked about the good wine there, but they always knew it was more than the wine; it was a bond of friendship." Solomon looked at his tea when he could see his mother becoming wistful. "You know that a king has to know who his true friends are. True friends are rare and deserve honor. As is true love, and true worship." Changing her tone, she asked. "How well did you get to know her? What is her name?"

"Her name matches my name. Her mother named her Shulamit. It comes from Shalom and means peace, just like my name Solomon." We spent the whole night talking. She can talk. She's funny. She has more dreams than I imagined any person can have," he said, laughing. "Wait till you get to meet her. She has a sharp and curious mind. She challenges me. She makes me desire to create more just to see the excitement on her face. She wants to learn to read. She wants to learn all the songs in the Tabernacle. She writes songs. She inspires me to write songs. We bounce inspiration off each other.

Could we be more matched? She carries a lovely gentle peace, but she is strong, she can run like the wind, and she knows how to use a sling shot and defend her sheep. Do you think mother you can meet a person and after a short time feel like you have known them forever? I look into her eyes and I see a reflection of all my own dreams. Dreams that I never thought I had. When she told me hers, she awakened dreams in me. Is that possible?"

Caught up in her son's wonder, Bathsheba responded enthusiastically, "when a person awakens your dreams, it is like heaven coming and opening a door that says you have been brought together to do great things."

"Yes! When she told me her dreams, I could hardly keep a straight face. This woman makes me laugh. She said she always wanted to marry a Levite so she could worship in the Tabernacle and be a part of the worshippers. Then she said when she met me, that perhaps just going to the Tabernacle to worship with me was OK, and that we could have a great Sabbath night worshipping together in our home and village. She wants to be my worship partner forever."

Bathsheba chuckled, "Your father and I were worship partners."

"I remember. Some of my happiest memories were when we worshipped together as a family. I remember when we fled Absalom and we were hiding out. People were feeling down, and my father insisted we worship. I will never forget how he set us down around him to be calmed by his song."

"That is why your father was a great king. David's strength came from his worship and faith in his Great God."

"When she sings, there is strength that comes from her voice. She is deep. She is full of substance and faith. She draws heaven out of me. She said her father wrote a song about her worship bringing a smile from heaven. She makes me smile. She inspires me. While she was talking to me, songs were coming to me."

"I can see that smile on your face, Solomon. Your happiness is radiating, and I feel it. She sounds good for you. You should marry the person who helps you write your best song. The person who inspires your best song has to be from God."

"She carries a lightness that makes me forget all my earthly responsibilities. When I told her I had responsibilities as the oldest brother, she expressed her desire to help me." Solomon was only too happy to talk about Shulamit all night. "She just makes me laugh. And above all, she loves me. She loves me as a shepherd. She doesn't know I am king. She risked being made a fool in her village to love me, a stranger. She ran past her own brother to grab my hand after the dance of the maiden's coming out. She told me I sing like King David. She knows nothing of me, yet her intuition amazes me."

"Solomon, my son, you can sing and worship every bit as well as your father. I suppose he had more time in his youth, sitting on a hill with sheep to develop that talent. But you have it. You cannot compare yourself to your father. He was a warrior and a worshipper; but he never had your wisdom, and the creativity to build and design as you do. You are a man of peace who knows how to create unity. You have your own identity. There is no one like you Solomon. I like what I hear of this woman, she brings out another side of you."

"I hope I am worthy of her."

"I can't believe what I am hearing Solomon. Now I really know you are in love. Love has a way of bringing out a vulnerability in us that throws out all rational thought and wisdom. As wise as you are, this love takes away all your wisdom. Of course, you are worthy. She must be really beautiful to affect you this way. Beautiful women can intimidate the greatest of men." Bathsheba sighs, "I know. I once was beautiful."

"You are still beautiful mother."

"Thank you, my son."

"I hope she will love me as a king."

"Loving you as a shepherd is much more important," she said. "That is where the heart is tested. She loves the person of the heart, and not just the glory. Everyone wants to enjoy the glory and the power, but it is the hidden things of the heart that matter the most. It seems she has passed that test. Did you know I was in love with your father long before he became king? I was a young girl, and as I sat around the campfire with my grandfather and heard your father sing, I wanted to be able to be with your father and sing with him forever. I am sure this woman, Shulamit, will love you as a king."

"Do you think it will be hard for her as a country girl to enjoy a life in a palace?"

"It's all about love, Solomon. You are the one with the love to carry her through and draw out of her what she already has in her, to become what she is meant to be. You know I was not born a queen. I became a queen being in the presence of your father, and the anointing upon his life. His love and anointing were imparted into me as his wife and queen, and the raising of his future king. Everything that I am is because I loved a king.

Bathsheba begins to sing.

In the presence of the King
My heart begins to sing
In the presence of the King
A bride becomes a queen

There is peace
There is pleasure
There is joy without measure
In His presence that I treasure
I delight to be His queen

In the presence of the King
He becomes my everything
As I rest in His presence
I grow in the essence
Of a queen

Wisdom in the heart
Of the King
Unveils the beauty that's unseen
From the fountain of my soul
Love begins to flow
In the grooming of a queen

There is peace
There is pleasure
There is joy without measure
In His presence that I treasure
I delight to be His queen

There is awe
In the presence of the King
Whose Glory transforms everything
He can choose a favored bride
And make of her a queen

There is peace
There is pleasure
There is joy without measure
In His presence that I treasure

I delight to be His queen

"Wow! Mother, that was beautiful! You could not explain it better than in that song. And now I have one last request. I am preparing to go back to the village for my wife. I will have a betrothal ceremony there with her family before I bring her back to the palace, and I need you to come with me as the most important member of my family, along with my brothers."

"You want me to come and meet her family? You have never done this before. Kings come here with their daughters, and you set me on the throne to honor me, and never have I had to interact on such a level. What if they think badly about me having heard of David's sin?"

"Mother, this family loves King David; they don't care about such things. They are not that kind of people. They don't care about problems in the palace and the correctness of society. They care only about the 'Presence of the King of the Universe, and the king who carries that anointing.' They are different. You will love them. Perhaps they will bring deeper healing to your life. They have a joy that is contagious."

"Solomon, you already know as your mother, I have always honored your requests. I will give her one of my own best servants to help her. Choose for her amongst the best servants in the palace to help her learn palace protocol when she arrives. Do you need help preparing her chamber?"

"I knew I could depend upon you." Solomon's face lit up, as he gave his mother a big hug.

10 THE KING RETURNS

Solomon's heart overflowed with joy as he mounted his elegant white horse with long flowing white mane and high tail. He too was dressed in white, covered by a robe and girded with a sword. He sat upon a blue saddle decorated with gold tassels. Behind him, his brothers dressed in royal garments. They too wore their swords. They were followed by sixty horseback riders wearing the different colors of the tribes of Israel. They had swords girded. Everyone prepared for any danger to the king or his bride to be. Behind the riders, a majestic gold carriage raised banners of the royal tribe of Judah—a gold lion on a sky-blue flag, was waving in the wind. The carriage was cedar wood of Lebanon and inlaid of gold in intricate patterns. The seats inside were covered with purple cushions embroidered with flowers of gold, red and blue. Queen Bathsheba rode in the carriage wearing her crown and a magnificent, multicolored robe that seemed to outmatch the splendor of the royal interior. Behind her was a carriage of court maidens, followed by other coaches and camels bearing burdens.

It was a glorious display of grandeur.

As the villagers ran out to see the procession go by, they were surprised to see it stop at their village. A messenger was sent to the house of Joshua and Caleb, asking permission to dismount on the green hills where shepherds often herded their sheep. This location was directly below the hill where Solomon had first met the Shulamit coming out of her secret place.

Joshua and Caleb came to salute the king, only to find it was the shepherd they had met at the harvest. As they bowed before the king, Solomon dismounted, reaching out with joy. He embraced them as he would embrace a lifelong friend. "With your permission, I would like to set up my royal tent on this hill and tents for my servants, for this special occasion." The brothers affirmed him, and Solomon made another request, "Go and put on the nice clothing I gave you at the festival. Have your sisters and mothers do the same. Then come up to the tent when it has been set up."

"What if she asks questions?"

"Tell her it is the king's command. She has to obey the king's commands, and not dishonor the throne of Israel. I want this to be a total surprise."

Joshua and Caleb acknowledged the king as they left almost shaking their heads about how to not give away any clues that might ruin the surprise.

Shulamit and her mother had just returned home from helping deliver a baby in the village and had missed the excitement of hearing that the king had arrived, but they could feel the excitement in the air. They were preparing to bathe and clean up when Joshua came into the house and told them, "The king is here, and he wants to see you, Shulamit. He asked the family to come to his tent. Put on one of those pretty dresses the shepherd gave you. You too, Mama and Miriam."

"What does he want with me?" Shulamit asked with a look of shock on her face.

Joshua saw her shock, but ignored it, demanding she just hurry up and get ready, "And do not keep the king waiting," he said.

Shulamit confessed to Joshua, "When the king's servant came by the field looking at the grape harvest, I invited the king to the harvest festival. I hope when I invited him, I wasn't being presumptuous."

"It is too late to worry about that now. Get ready." He hoped by pressuring her to get ready quickly, she would not have time to think too much.

Shulamit's heart beat hard as she went to prepare. She started to fear in her heart that she would never see her beloved shepherd Jedidiah again. *What have I done?* She asked herself repeatedly. She was tempted to run and hide, but she knew that would not solve her problem. She might get her family in trouble, and besides, she could not hide forever.

Little Miriam had put on her pretty dress and was jumping up and down when Shulamit entered. "I get to meet the king! I get to meet the king!" she sang as she moved.

Mama was busy getting ready, trying to comb little Miriam's hair as she wiggled around. She also worked on her own, making sure they looked good. As she watched her smallest daughter bouncing around, she realized she needed to show them how to curtsy. "When you go before a king, you must show proper honor. This is how you curtsy. Take hold of the sides of your dress; put one leg behind the other, then bend your knees, and lower your body." Shulamit understood and complied graciously, as she curtsied, in a dazed absent-minded manner. Miriam curtsied once, almost fell, and then tried again. The second time she wobbled, but the third time she did it perfectly.

"Can I go out to the garden now Mamma," little Miriam asked, "and pick some flowers for the king?"

Shulamit was very confused and could not bring her thoughts together. She kept combing her hair as she tried to understand what was going on. She was thankful that her brother Josh took charge so well, and her mother's ability to organize everything. She had just helped her mother deliver a baby, she was there, alert and present, and right now she could hardly keep herself together. Too much too fast, she thought, and behind the anxiety was a fear of losing her beloved shepherd.

Mama said, "No one should go before a king empty-handed. I must ask your brothers to bring some jugs of our best wine."

Finally, when the whole family gathered together, they looked at each other and laughed. They had never dressed this nicely before, even for a local wedding. The women were even wearing perfume. Shulamit and little Miriam were so used to going barefoot that they felt awkward wearing sandals. Shulamit planned to take the sandals off as soon as possible. But they were proud of how nicely they dressed for their special meeting. As they walked towards the king's tents, they brought the attention of the locals with their finery. For simple mountain people meeting a king in his formal array, they did the best they could.

It was a beautiful day to walk towards the hills where they could see the king's quarters—a large blue tent with gold tassels, set at the base of the hill. Smaller, less elegant tents surrounded it. Servants built a large pit outside the tent, and the scent of roasting lamb danced in the air with the smoke. The majestic, trained horses wandered on the hill and ate, while the carriages that were unable to go up the hill waited on more level ground. It was an amazing site to see.

Solomon stood by the tent with his brothers, admiring the beautiful sunset and countryside while watching the family begin their climb up the hill. He said, "As she comes closer, I must turn around, so she only sees me from behind. You signal when she is close enough for me to turn around."

As Shulamit's family came close enough to greet the king and his brothers, Shulamit saw the king in purple robe with black curly hair, and crown on. His brothers were adorned in opulent arrays of color, gold chains and finely made sandals. She was feeling overwhelmed already, when suddenly the king turned around to face her.

She instantly bowed her head and curtsied. Suddenly, it dawned on her that the king was her shepherd. In shock she almost fainted. The king reached forth to take her hand and keep her from falling. She looked into his eyes. Tears and a smile came forth at the same time as Shulamit stood, shocked and speechless. She did not know what to say. Her mind flew all over the place and then she stopped thinking altogether. A sudden shyness came over her. She felt embarrassed and didn't know what to do.

King Solomon broke the silence as he said, "My love, I hope you do not feel I was dishonest with you. I had to know that you would love me as a shepherd. I have not stopped thinking of you since we were apart. I have come back as soon as I could. Can you love me as shepherd, a husband, and a king?"

Shulamit blurted out in a quivering voice, "I love you every way that you are."

There was not a dry eye in the group as they clapped in joy. Except little Miriam, who put her hand over her mouth and giggled.

Giving Shulamit a few minutes to regain her composure, Solomon took the lead to introduce his family. "At your request, I have brought my family. This is my brother, Shammua." Shammua gave a polite smile of acknowledgement. Pointing to another he said, "This is Shobab."

"All the way here," Shobab commented, "My brother has been talking about you. We are so pleased to finally meet you."

Solomon introduced his next brother, "And this is my youngest brother Nathan." Nathan appeared just a few years younger than Shulamit, but he was still growing and stood near her height. He greeted her with a gentle bow of his head.

At that moment, Bathsheba made her appearance, and Solomon announced, "And now I want you to meet my mother, Bathsheba."

With a crown on her head and multicolored robes, Bathsheba carried an amazing presence of beauty. Shulamit, her Mama and little sister curtsied deeply to show their respect. Bathsheba opened her arms and greeted each of them with a warm embrace. Then she spoke to Shulamit, "My son has not stopped singing since he met you. It is good to meet the woman who inspires his song. We joyfully welcome you into our family."

Little Miriam held out her flowers to Bathsheba. "I brought these beautiful flowers for you, and the king. It's hard to bow and cross my heart as I hold them."

Bathsheba laughed quietly as she took the flowers. "You are a darling young girl," she said.

Solomon turned his eyes back to Shulamit, "I thank you for waiting for me. I am honored that a woman would hold me in such a way and wait. You have had great faith in believing for the man of your dreams. I thank you for taking the leap of faith to grab hold of me at the Harvest Festival." He took her hand and squeezed it gently. "That took a great courage since you knew very little about me. You went with your heart. God has given you a gift. That level of discernment belongs to a woman destined to be a great queen. As king, I have need of such a woman. As a man, I have need of your joy and laughter. I want to sing and dance with you through life. You are a special delight to me, such as I have only dared to dream myself." Shulamit laughed as he turned her in a circle. Solomon laughed too. "God gives dreams. And He honors those who believe and wait. God called you to me before the beginning of the world. He created you especially for me. This is a day of great gladness in my heart."

Solomon released Shulamit and turned to Miriam to bless her, "Mama, I honor you with appreciation from deep within my heart for raising such a lovely daughter. She comes from your heart, and I thank you for all you have done to love, protect, and raise her to be who she is. She is a priceless gem."

Mama stood with tears in her eyes, glancing toward Bathsheba, who stood with moist eyes also. A moment of bonding happened in that glance. It was a bonding that only mothers that have spent a lifetime pouring their hearts into their children can understand. Unspoken words passed from one mother trusting her daughter to the care of another, saying, "Love her as I have loved her." She knew her plea would be honored.

Solomon then addressed Shulamit's brothers, "I thank you for keeping her protected all these years. I know it has been hard stepping into a father's role at such a young age Joshua, but you have done well."

Little Miriam did not want to be left out and was bouncing around trying to get his attention. "Little sister," said Solomon, "your laughter and giggles come from the heart of a happy family. Thank you for the flowers you brought. You are a bud beginning to bloom. You will have your day too. Be patient and wait like your sister, as I know blessings await you too. Come let us go into the tent and dine."

The dining table was low to the ground on carpets that had been laid down with pillows behind them to lean against. Solomon seated Shulamit to his right in the position of honor. Solomon's scribe sat to his left. His brothers sat next to the scribe. Shulamit's brothers around the left side of table, with the women on the right. Servants came and set down appetizers of eggplant and tahini, roasted garlic with goat cheese, chickpea patties, lentils with spinach and lemon, vegetable salad, a flatbread to pick the food up with. They poured tea into small gold cups with handles as harp music played in the background.

After everyone had taken sips of tea, Solomon had his scribe pull out a scroll. The scroll was a Ketubah, a wedding agreement of all that he had promised Shulamit's brothers as a dowry for his wife. The scribes began to read from the top of the scroll.

First, the king was giving back the vineyard that his father had purchased from their family with an agreement that the wine would be sold to the palace for a good price. Next was the promise that his wife would have her own palace attached to the main palace he would build after the temple was finished—including her own private vineyard, and garden. The family was promised a weighed amount of gold, sheep, mules, goats, and servants to help with labor. The king would build for the family a large wine cellar with vats made of wood from Lebanon. The king also promised marble and large beams from Lebanon to help Joshua and Caleb build a larger house. Harps and musical instruments would be given to Shulamit and her family. Shulamit would be given five servants to meet all her personal needs. Gold jewelry and clothing was agreed upon with no limitations on the amount. Shulamit would have her own special tutors to teach her to read and write the Hebrew language. She would also, as a queen, have access to the Torah. She would be given permission to sit in on all the classes Solomon taught to the heads of state. The family had visitation rights to visit Shulamit with full accommodations when they came to Jerusalem. And her final and greatest desire—to worship in the Tabernacle—was granted, along with permission to worship with the Priest on Sabbath Evening, on religious holidays at the palace. She would have Levites to teach her the songs of the Tabernacle as well.

The scribe finished reading all that was written and asked if there were any questions or additions needed to be added before signing.

Shulamit's family sat stunned at the list of gifts. Only little Miriam asked a question, "Will my sister be able to come home and visit us?"

"Of course, little Miriam," Solomon said. "But guards will have to come with her to make sure she is safe. Shulamit will now have guards to protect her wherever she goes because she will be a queen. A queen must be protected."

Shulamit was still in shock over the reality of her beloved shepherd being a king; she gave a startled expression that she could never just run free in the fields without guards around. But when she turned and looked into his eyes, she forgot everything. She trusted her brothers to know everything was fair and they were happy. All she wanted was her beloved.

Joshua was about to sign when he asked if he might have a private word with the king. Stepping away from the tables to where they could not be heard Joshua made a solemn request. "I know you are a king and have other wives. But I must have an agreement that if my sister is not happy in her life at the palace that she shall be able to return to her home."

Solomon was rather shocked at the request. Covenants in their culture were all binding. Breaking them with foreign kings often meant war and was not something taken lightly.

While he was still thinking on it; Joshua still trying to exert what small bit of authority he had in the whole situation. He stated, "Your tribe of Judah has the throne as promised by our forefather Jacob. The tribes of Israel submit to your authority out of honor to the prophets, King David, and unity of country and our Holy City Jerusalem. But remember that Ephraim was also given a promise of a crown. My sister carries our promises within her, and we expect she will be treated with respect and dignity, or the covenant will be forfeited.

"I understand your request," Solomon responded with calm. He was trained to control his inner feelings when unsure exactly how to respond. But he understood national pride, pride of tribes and families. He understood honor. Forgetting his pride as a king, he showed respect to the head of a family losing a much-loved member. "I don't expect that to ever happen," he admitted, "I promise to do my very best to keep her happy. But should it ever come to pass, we will find a way for her to return home without any dishonor to country or tribe. I am most happy to have the tribe of Ephraim in service to the kingdom."

They called the scribe aside and added a line of writing on the Ketubah. Then they returned to the table without more ado, and nothing said about their private agreement, finalizing the covenant between two powerful tribes.

Joshua pressed the seal of his ring on the marriage agreement. Solomon signaled for wine to be poured into his goblet. He said, "I will drink this cup with you now, and the next cup of wine we drink together will be at our wedding." King Solomon took a drink, then the cup was passed around the family for each to take a sip. Solomon said, "Now let us eat, drink and be merry."

Music continued in the background as they all dipped their bread into the food served on golden platters. All the utensils on the king's table were gold, with intricate designs of lions and flowers, and cups studded with jewels. The tablecloth was blue with gold designs woven into it.

Bathsheba turned to Shulamit's mother and said, "I will make sure that your daughter is well cared for," she said. "I am giving her one of my personal servants who speaks perfect Hebrew and is well trained in how to serve and advise a queen in every area—clothing choice, hair, nails, shoes, food, and protocol in the court. She shall remain by Shulamit's side at all times to assist her in any question she may have. It is a transition to move into the palace. But I see that Shulamit is a bright young woman who will learn more quickly than any other princess who has come to live in the palace. I see she has a quick wit and a mind to learn. She shall be a blessing to us all."

"Thank you so much your majesty. I appreciate your coming all this way to honor our family."

"You can call me Bathsheba. I am honored that I have been invited. I like your family. You are real people who show your heart without pretentiousness, and I love that. As a queen in a court, I have seen so much correct behavior without heart. People who are in touch with their heart are a breath of fresh air."

Shulamit's mother gave her a warm hug. "We shall be friends? Shall we? If you ever need to get away from the palace and hide out with your people in the countryside, you are always welcome. Come for Sabbath evening and sing with us. We have missed the king coming to visit his vineyard. We have missed his coming to dine with us and singing his new songs. We had always hoped his queen would come with him sometime, but he said he stopped by while out doing a lot of business in the kingdom and it was hard to bring his queen who was needed to care for his sons. King David did say once that his queen Bathsheba loved to worship with him."

"Did he say anything else about me?"

"He said you were beautiful, had a tender heart open to the Spirit of God, and you were a very protective mother to your princes."

Bathsheba gave a sigh and wiped an eye. "You have no idea how much you just said, means to me." I do not know how history will remember me, but I love to remember how much the king loved me."

"We have a great God, with a big heart. You were meant to be a queen, and a Queen Mother. A woman with a tender heart is needed to keep a king tender. A woman, who worships with her king, keeps the whole family and kingdom moving in the right direction."

"That is what I see in your daughter. Even when Solomon came to me singing, before I even knew he had chosen Shulamit, I knew she was special because I never heard him sing like that. The Holy Spirit even gave me a song to sing about the "Presence of the King." The King makes a queen into a Queen, but she also makes him a better king. Marriage is a beautiful gift from God. A good marriage is a blessing to the whole kingdom. Yes, we shall be friends. We are family. The hand you extend to me to be welcome in your home is also extended to you whenever you visit Jerusalem."

The conversation at the table flowed. Shobab was all about talking business with Joshua. However, Nathan liked hearing the brother's talk about how they remembered their father, King David, on his visits to the countryside when Nathan and his brothers were children. "Fun, fun, lots of worship and fun," Caleb laughed. "Fun is what we remember. And we remember all the songs he taught us."

Young Nathan listened with joy about his father, between glancing over from little Miriam to her older sister Shulamit and wondering. He whispered into his mother's ear, "Do you think that Shulamit's little sister will be as beautiful when she is older?"

Bathsheba responded with an inquisitive smile, as if to say, *What are you thinking my son?*

King Solomon was engrossed in conversation with Shulamit. She seemed to be concerned about their friendship since he was a king. "We will still be friends," she asked, "Like we were talking the evening of the festival? Where we shared our hearts so intimately?"

Solomon smiled, "I assure you we will become better friends, and even more intimate."

There was an authority in Solomon's voice that gave an assurance of every anxiety that would enter her mind. His strength covered her weakness. She loved it. She accepted it. She received it as a peace within her soul.

As the meal was coming to an end, Solomon asked for his lyre. "I have a song to sing to my bride."

All eyes turned to the king and his bride as he began to sing his song about the Keeper of His Vineyard.

The keeper of my vineyard
Sang a song for me
Of the joy of harvest
And so, I went to see

The fruit was ripe for harvest
She harvested for me
All the while she danced and sang
Working cheerfully

Who is this beautiful maiden?
Keeping my vineyard for me?
I sent my friend to inquire
And she invited me

A king loves his festivals
He loves to be invited
She opened her heart to me
The king was delighted

This maiden is a beauty
My friend said to me
She had many suitors
But she has waited for her dream

She waited and didn't know it
As she served me in my vineyard
And now the king of the vineyard
Shall be her great reward

She is my blessed reward
My bride who sits by my side
I love you, I love you my queen
You are my chosen bride

My vineyard is yours
And all I have too
My heart, my soul and my vineyard
I am entrusting to you

My vineyard keeper
You are my bride

Judy Pendell

In my presence you abide
Reigning with me at my side
My queen, my queen
My beautiful bride

Laughter and clapping came from them all. Shobab lifted a goblet of wine in cheer, "When the king is happy the whole kingdom shouts for joy."

King Solomon signaled for the musical gifts and gave them to Shulamit's family. Two large gold harps, a silver trumpet, several kinds of flutes, tambourines, drums, and even a cymbal for the family. They moved out of the tent to the fire pit on the hill and Solomon sang of the beauty of his bride.

Shulamit, Mama, and Little Miriam got up to dance with tambourines, and even Queen Bathsheba joined them in the dance. Spontaneous words flowed from all their hearts as they celebrated this evening.

Shulamit's extended family came together for the betrothal celebration, knew that the next day the king would take his bride to live in the palace. They knew that her new life would begin. The village people came out and cheered Shulamit into her new life.

Love and joy brought them together.

11 THE ROAD TO JERUSALEM

Shulamit said goodbye to her friends and beloved family. And each one had a kind word with which to send her off.

Her uncle held her for a long moment as he reminded her to keep the heart of King David. "I believe all future kings will be measured by King David's standard of worship and warfare," he said. "They are the peak of our time. Who knows of the time to come?"

Mama reminded Shulamit of the prophecy given by the priest long ago, saying, "Your beauty and your faithfulness to persevere under pressure have brought you to this place. You now have an open door to be a blessing to our country through your worship as a queen. Keep the fear of God, and you will be blessed."

Caleb reminded Shulamit of the lesson Papa had taught on the importance of Selah when he spoke. Selah moments were times to stop and consider the significance of the words spoken before you move in another direction.

"Always listen to the king and his words," he said. "And take time to hide the Word in your heart to reflect upon. You are in a moment of Selah right now in your life as you transition to your next phase. Papa and Mama have taught us all well, and you have a strong foundation."

Joshua stood back, waiting for his turn to speak. He always considered it his duty to keep her humble and in her place. When his moment came, he reminded her, "Do not allow yourself to be worshipped for your gift of worship, or your beauty, lest the glory may depart from you. Remember what God said to Saul: 'When you were little in your own eyes, God made you great.' Keep God and His Word ever before you."

Last to speak, because she was so sad, little Miriam wiped tears from her eyes and muttered, "Don't forget to come back and visit us."

Shulamit gave her a big hug even as she wiped the tears in her own eyes.

Rebecca waited as Shulamit exited the home she knew all her life. With a long, tearful embrace, Rebecca's was the first to wish her all the happiness in the world as she joined Solomon and began the walk to join her new family. Shulamit's extended relatives and village friends also blessed her with all joy in her married, royal life. While waving excited hands, they called out prayers of long life and miracles as she took Solomon's extended hand.

He helped her step into the ornate golden carriage that waited just near the entrance. It was canopied on each side with heavy blue cloth, gold fringes, and the flags of Judah. The interior carriage was scented by frankincense and myrrh. Shulamit sat down on soft cushions and leaned against large pillows of matching purple embroidered with gold threads. The white stallions pulling the carriage were adorned with decorated gold bridles and were brushed and combed until their crested manes and coats shone over gleaming black hooves. They stepped grandly as their groomed tails flowed out, proudly arched.

Solomon and his brothers mounted their own majestically groomed stallions. Sitting stately on his horse while wearing his golden crown, the king also waved goodbye to the people of the village before he gave the signal to his soldiers before him to march forward.

Shulamit sat quietly beside the Queen Mother, reflecting on things her family told her before she left. Indeed, she sat pondering all that had happened in her short life. Part of her was so excited she hadn't slept much the night before. With only a few hours of sleep, she felt hyper-alert as the whole entourage began the descent down the hill to the King's Highway.

She thought back to how she watched these kingly processions as a child. She and Rebecca used to look down at all of the royal processions and caravans with such awe and wonder.

Now she was in one.

Back then, she and Rebecca had only imagined what it was like to be a princess or a queen in a palace. She never considered it would ever really happen to her. This was a more magnificent dream than she had ever thought of, and the Lord had blessed her with great imagination. Shulamit concluded, after much thought, God's dreams for his people are better than anyone could think up. Despite spending this time thinking of other things, her deepest thoughts were on the king riding before her on his stallion.

It wasn't the palace, the servants, the clothes and robes Shulamit wore, or the golden sandals that hurt her feet. Only her king truly thrilled her at that moment. But it was still quite a shock.

Her love, the humble, funny, musical shepherd, was a king. She pondered the idea that a king was really a shepherd, in a way, but on a much grander scale.

Suddenly the impressive weight of responsibility came over her.

The Queen Mother, Bathsheba, seemed to catch the anxiety young Shulamit showed on her face, though she tried to hide it:

"If you considered the responsibility and it didn't humble you," the queen said quietly, "then you would not be worthy of the calling to your position. It is good to have a fear of God and awe of the power and respect for the mighty King of Kings."

Shulamit tried to smile, bowing her head and saying nothing. "Solomon is writing a book of proverbs," the queen continued. "In them, he says, 'The fear of God is the beginning of wisdom.' Solomon was overwhelmed to be a King at such a young age. He didn't feel qualified to lead such a great people, much like you feel now." She patted Shulamit's knee tenderly. "The Lord, in His great wisdom, then came to him in a dream and offered him whatever he wanted." Shulamit's eyes widened in renewed shock, but Bathsheba smiled, raising her hand as if to ask for Shulamit's patience. "Solomon searched his heart for how he could best serve the country and asked the Lord for wisdom and understanding to lead and discern between good and evil. The Lord was pleased with his selflessness. Because Solomon asked not for his own blessings, the Lord told Solomon he would be given honor and wealth, in addition to wisdom." Bathsheba was silent for a moment, "As a queen, your most important responsibility is to love and honor the king. All of your blessings will flow from that love."

"Oh, I love him. I just pray that I can love the king the way he needs to be loved. I'm just a country girl, and I don't know the ways of a palace," Shulamit said, running her hand over the embroidered pillow beside her. "I've only been to Jerusalem once, as a young girl, and I can't remember that much. I only really remember the Tabernacle of David and the powerful presence of God. All I have truly dreamed was to experience that worship again, as a wife, with my family."

"You shall, sweet Shulamit. Now you shall have someone very special to experience worship with," she paused briefly, "like I did with my husband, King David."

Shulamit smiled. "When Jedidiah, I mean Solomon and I, first sang on the hill," she confided, "I knew we were meant for each other because we had something special together singing and dancing. I think that is why we laughed so much. You desire a dream and cry out to God, hoping against hope—and when it comes, it is a tree of life. A fountain inside comes to life that just keeps bubbling over." Shulamit sighed. "But, a King! A King! I should have known! But how could I know? Deep inside, perhaps I did know, but I should have known."

Solomon turned his head around to look at his beloved. She gave him a big smile. Watching him sit straight and tall upon his horse only seemed to grow her love and attraction for him all the more. "I think I must be the happiest woman in the whole world!"

"You are in love," Bathsheba said, smiling. "Love does those things. You make me remember my own youth."

While they were speaking, the caravan slowly descended the mountain road. The procession came to a wide-open road known to all as the King's Highway. This dirt road was level and smooth on the horizon before them. Bathsheba changed the conversation to explain, "Solomon has engineered a lot of work on the road to remove the large rocks and bounders. This made the route smooth for travelers and traders to carry their merchandise over it. Now, it serves as one of the main trade routes from the East, West, and South toward Jerusalem. All roads lead to Jerusalem.

Upon entering the main road, Solomon ordered a halt and rode back to the carriage. "We are going to speed up, and dust will be flying, so it is time to put the canopy down." As the servants worked, he smiled at Shulamit. "You will want to hold on to your armrest, as we are about to gallop into full speed."

Once the canopy was down, Shulamit heard Solomon call out his command to go forward. The chariot jolted into motion, and Shulamit was almost thrown from her seat. She braced herself on the side of the carriage with one hand while she grabbed onto the mother queen with the other.

"Aah, aah, wow, wow, wow!" Shulamit screamed out in joy and laughter. "This is fun! I've never ridden anything so fast. My mule cannot move like this. Wow! Wow! Wow!"

Bathsheba laughed along with Shulamit jostling as she spoke. "I remember the first thrill of my ride in a chariot, but I think I was more afraid than joyful. Getting used to the speed of horses takes some adjustment. I see that you are of an adventurous nature. We can only ride fast on the open road."

Shulamit peaked out through a crack in the side of the canopy as the road curved toward the right. "I love looking at the riders on horses in front of us," she said as she appreciated the speed. "I have never been this close to horses. They move with such power and gracefulness compared to my family mule."

"They are created for war. It takes a lot of training for them to be able to pull chariots or let men ride them. They can be dangerous. But our chariot driver is part of the king's special squadron of horsemen."

Shulamit closed the canopy. "Why do we need so many horses if we are not at war?"

"Solomon teaches that a strong man armed keeps his house. We have enemies all around us. King David was a man of war. Through war, David gained all the land promised to Moses and Joshua. Our forefathers had not been able to conquer them. Do not ever think that the people of these lands accept that this land was promised to us by God. They will gladly fight to get their land back if we show any signs of weakness. As royal leaders of a strong nation, no matter how we feel internally, our public face must always be one of strength."

Shulamit understood what Bathsheba said as she reflected on her own battles with her brothers. She remembered how they often teased her and how she refused to show her hurt feelings. She learned at a young age how to put on a strong face.

Taking a deep breath, Shulamit changed the subject, sharing her excitement about going to Jerusalem. "My grandpapa told us stories of King David and how he conquered Jerusalem. After 400 years of living in the Promised Land, we finally conquered the greatest mountain. 'The greatest mountains are the hardest to conquer,' he said. But Saba said that the king knew it was to be the City of Zion and the habitation of the Lord. Here I am going to the most magnificent city in the world, perhaps of all history."

"You are well informed for a country girl, and very intuitive. When you step into Jerusalem, you step into the center of history. But the season of war is over now. It is a new season—one of peace. This season of peace allows Solomon, a man of peace, the opportunity to build the great temple. From there, the Authority of our God will be so strong, and our worship so great, our enemies will be confounded. Peacetime allows a country to prosper. We can have a bountiful harvest that no one can steal. It allows us to trade, build, and use our skills to build up a strong kingdom. Keeping the people of the kingdom safe, healthy, and happy is the first duty of a king." Bathsheba stopped speaking abruptly as the carriage hit a bump that bounced them into the air. "We had best rest for a while. I will tell you about Solomon's book of wisdom he is writing later."

The carriage slowed down for a length of uneven road, and Shulamit peaked out through the side of the canopy again. She gazed in joyous curiosity at the pale golden fields of harvested hay. Yellow-green mustard flowers covered other nearby areas. The farmers were busy plowing to prepare for the autumn planting. Wadis were down to a trickle of water, but the winter rains would begin at any time, and they would be full again. Shulamit watched the landscape as they passed. Terraced hillsides of harvested grapevines dotted the hills while olive, pomegranate, and fig trees, mostly bare from harvest, were scattered in groves. Pale blue mountains could be seen in the distance, and occasionally they would pass a village. Women could be seen carrying pitchers of water back to the nearby villages on their heads and shoulders.

Bathsheba had dozed off, but Shulamit could not. There was too much to see and too much to think about. Her mind was going over every moment of the time she met Solomon until now.

So much had happened.

She tried to recall her journey to Jerusalem when she was young. She remembered walking past the palace and seeing the tabernacle. Now Shulamit would live right near the tabernacle she dreamed about ever since she'd been there with her father. She began wondering about what life would be like inside the palace. But then the carriage picked up speed again, her exhaustion set in, and Shulamit leaned against a pillow, closing her eyes.

When she awoke, it was sunset, and the walls of Jerusalem appeared golden in the distance. The royal procession had stopped on a hill, and the bridles were taken off the horses. They ran toward the smell of fresh, cool water in the high pasture. One black mare ran ahead and the stallions ran after her.

Solomon came and took her hand to help her out of the carriage, pointing out the beautiful creature. "You are like that mare from Egypt," he said, smiling. "All the male horses run after you, but I am the fortunate one who caught you."

Shulamit laughed. "Race you up the hill!" she said as she released his hand and ran toward the pond. Solomon ran after her, laughing while trying to match her surprising speed. He could hardly keep pace with her. The soldiers, who were supposed to be protecting them, could not keep up either.

Reaching a side of the pond, Shulamit sat under a cedar tree, took her sandals off, and dangled her feet in the water.

"I can't run well in these sandals," she said as Solomon reached her.

"You can run faster?" Solomon was catching his breath as he sat down beside her.

"When my brothers said I was a silly girl, I had to prove that I could chase down the stray sheep as fast as they could."

"I don't think you are a silly girl."

Shulamit smiled shyly. Realizing she had admitted the vulnerability of feeling she had to prove herself to her brothers, she realized it was not necessary with Solomon. He seemed to see only good in her. It made her feel so confident. "I've been restless to run after sitting in the carriage for so long. But I dozed while you galloped your horse so majestically."

Solomon looked out at the purple and white autumn crocuses in the field. "Compared to you, all the other roses are thorns." He reached over and picked a wildflower growing beside the pond. He handed it to her. "You look so beautiful in the gown and robe you are wearing. And you will get used to wearing sandals."

Shulamit felt a bit awkward at being told she was beautiful. But she could feel deep within her that she was beginning to enjoy being a woman.

"It is pretty here," she said. "But not as lovely as my secret place at home."

"It is not so secret here. But you are right, your secret place is one of the most beautiful places I have ever seen."

"You saw it? You walked through the trees up to the lake, and saw it?"

"Yes, of course. I knew you would not take me where you would create unsafe temptation. But after you left, I ventured in to see your secret place and swam. Someday when we are married, we will go back there and swim in secret."

Shulamit tried to hide the pink flush that came over her cheeks at the thought of swimming with her beloved.

"I have designed you a secret place at the palace where you can go and be alone. Even in the palace, we have to have places to hide from the constant activity. I will also take you to my secret place after we know each other better. I go there to do my thinking and praying. I believe God's spirit comes upon me there because I get many creative ideas. I even see in my mind the blueprints and plans for how to carry out my many ideas."

"I feel the presence of God with us right now."

Solomon gave a surprising look of acknowledgment and said, "I do too."

"Do you believe God brought us together?"

"You are a gift from God only He can bring."

Shulamit's face grew hot and flushed again.

"Do not worry, my love. I will not hurry love. I will give you all the time you need for your love to awaken to me. We will know when you are ready. I realize, so far, I encouraged you to talk so that I could get to know you. But now, as you come into my world, I know it is a transition for you and will take time for you to get to know me in this place. As for me, I am ready for you right now. But I enjoy watching you bloom." Solomon looked towards Jerusalem. "Come," he said, "you must be hungry. Let's join the rest of the family and eat." Shulamit, in her excitement, hadn't thought about food all day. She was starved.

The family sat on mats for a small but luxurious meal before traveling again. Fruit platters, cheese, nuts, and bread were set out with bowls of wine on large, colorful cloths that were spread out on the grass a little way down the hill.

Soon after they finished, Solomon's brother, Shummua, noted a small cloud forming in the sky. He said, "We had best bridle up the horses and make our way to Jerusalem. It appears as if the winter rains are about to begin."

Quickly, Solomon walked Shulamit and Bathsheba back to the carriage. He mounted his horse, joining his brothers and the soldiers as they began their descent into the valley around Jerusalem before going up into the city. They had just arrived inside the walls of Jerusalem when the heavens opened into a torrent. Making their way quickly to the palace, they were greeted by Solomon's personal palace staff. "It looks like you brought the rain with you!" said the chief manservant. "Rain is always a blessing!"

12 LIFE IN THE PALACE

As Shulamit took her first steps on the polished marble floors of the palace, she knew she had entered another world, and did her best not to stare open-mouthed at the grandeur of her new home.

Solomon noticed her and said, "You must be tired." He saw that her excitement was as evident as her exhaustion. Smiling, he told her, "Come. I will show you to your living quarters. Tomorrow you can rest all day and let your servants care for all your needs. I will see you in the evening."

He and Bathsheba escorted her down a long hallway lit by golden candlesticks on the walls. She arrived at her chambers. Shulamit's new head attendant stood at the entrance to greet her with four other handmaidens who bowed graciously. Shulamit did not know how to respond and managed an awkward nod of her head.

"Meliba has been part of our household for many years," Bathsheba said as an introduction. "And now I am giving her to you for as long as you need her. She will personally assist you with all you need to learn about living in the palace."

Solomon, with a gentle touch to her back, led her into her quarters, "I hope you will be pleased."

Shulamit could hardly believe her eyes. 'Pleased' was not the word she would have used. She had never seen such luxury in her life.

She stepped onto several layers of plush carpet with colorful flower designs and walls with bright, rich tapestries of expertly embroidered gardens hanging on them. The ceilings were high and built with large cedar beams from Lebanon and curtains, which pulled back to show off the latticework on the walls. Pillows with threads of gold embroidery lay piled beside painted vases filled with aromatic flowers. Large, golden lampstands stood on the floor, as well as wall sconces with candles burning around the room. The censors released a sweet smell of frankincense and cinnamon that mingled with the scent of flowers.

Shulamit breathed in.

Overwhelmed by the opulence, she could not help but give a broad smile. A girlish laugh escaped her, even though she tried to maintain her composure and not act overly excited.

"It is absolutely beautiful," she said through her smile.

Solomon glowed with pride from her response. "Rest now," he said. "Tomorrow evening, I will introduce you to more of my friends and family." He took her hand and kissed it. "I bid you a pleasant night's sleep, my bride-to-be."

When Solomon left, Shulamit lifted the hand where Solomon had kissed it and placed it against her lips. She held it there, basking in the joy of a simple touch of his lips.

Bowing again, Meliba stepped forward, pulling Shulamit from her reverie.

"I want you to meet Sheriti and Kiya. They are from Egypt." The two women bowed to Shulamit. "This is Shanifa; she is from Phoenicia, and finally Aesha from Syria. I am also from Syria." Shulamit nodded to them and repeated their names out loud so she could remember them.

They led her into a bathing room lined with white alabaster tiles from ceiling to floor. She stood, a little confused, beside the large round basin as the servants gently removed her clothes. Shulamit was used to caring for herself, but too tired to resist. They assisted her into the bath while they poured the decadently warm, scented water over her. "I have never felt such smooth texture against my skin," Shulamit said as they washed and dried her body with cloth made of soft white materials.

"This is made from cotton in Egypt," Meliba replied.

"Egypt," Shulamit reflected. "The land Moses delivered our people from."

The attendants dressed Shulamit in a white silk sheath and combed out her hair. Shulamit was too tired to ask where this cloth came from, but she ran her hands all over the sleek, smooth material. She would save questions about where things came from for another day. Life was certainly beginning to change.

She noted a low table set with wine, fruit, bread, and cheese, and her maidens offered her warm goat's milk and pieces of bread stuffed with spiced cheese. Shulamit wanted a little something, but she had to admit, she was just too tired so, they escorted her to her bedchamber.

It was another site of beauty her eyes could not fully take in due to her tired state.

The bed was the center of beauty, made of dark wood with legs designed like to look like lions. The claws almost seemed to dig into the ground. The bedspread was a gold cloth with red flower designs. Gold fringes hung around the edges, and the bed was covered in pillows of various sizes and shapes. The servants removed the pillows and pulled back the spread to reveal soft, thick white lamb's wool. Everything was perfumed.

Shulamit lay herself down and, within moments, fell into a deep sleep.

When Shulamit awoke, the high noon sun was pouring through the clouds. She had never remembered sleeping that long in her life. It took her a few minutes to even remember where she was. Meliba, sitting on a soft pallet placed just outside of Shulamit's bed chamber, rose to her movement. She had already given directions to the other maidens for when their mistress awoke and the sweet sounds of melodious harp strings drifted to Shulamit from the entry. The music sounded to Shulamit's ears like flowers dancing in the wind.

Meliba addressed Shulamit, "Today we will transform you into a bride in full raiment, ready to greet a king. She offered Shulamit a drink of warm mint tea, as she led her into the bathing room. Shulamit's Egyptian maidens Sheriti and Kiya, bathed her in oils of frankincense, myrrh, and rose, and they scrubbed and rubbed the oils deep into her pores. They also washed and smoothed Shulamit's hair with a sandalwood comb that gently tickled her scalp. They took great care with her hands, clipping, filing, and polishing her nails to a shine. Kiya massaged more scented oil into her skin, and soon enough, she felt relaxed and supple as a gazelle.

When they finished, Shulamit looked at her changed body in the polished brass mirror that hung on the wall in her bath chamber. She said, "I kept the other vineyards, but my own vineyard I have not kept." to no one in particular.

Meliba smiled. "Your vineyard will be well kept from now on, now that you are in the care of the king."

Meliba explained about the oils and scents Shulamit had been bathed in. "Come," she said as she led Shulamit into her bed chamber and pointed out the many vials from a large chest in her bed chamber. She handed Shulamit the various vials to breathe, while she asked which scents she preferred. She assisted her mistress Shulamit as she learned to recognize the smell of perfumes which were spicy, flowery, woody, or resin scented.

"This is a lot for you to appreciate," Meliba said, "and we will learn more about perfumes later." Shulamit's mind attempted to relate this new information to her life experience, wandering back to memories of her father. She loved new experiences and always had a hungry mind to learn new things. She remembered her father adding cinnamon to his pomegranate wine, and how her family had experimented with spices in their winemaking. She would now regard learning about all the perfumes as an experiment.

Sheriti slipped the white undergarment over her head. "This is so soft," Shulamit acknowledged. "Softer than the rare linen cloth I have had in my life, and not scratchy like wool. I would love to dance in this material. I can see it flowing out gently as I turn around. What is this material made of? Where does it come from?"

Meliba explained, "The material is silk. It comes from the Far East by way of the Silk Road that goes through Damascus. Jerusalem is the world's biggest market. We live in the center of world trade. I can't tell you exactly how silk is made. You may have to ask King Solomon. But silk is made from cultivating silkworms on mulberry leaves. When the worms spin cocoons and start developing into moths they are taken out and boiled. Threads are spun from them and woven on looms like other material."

Shulamit made a curious face. "I have watched butterflies come out of cocoons."

"Similar, I guess," Meliba said.

"I saw caravans coming from Damascus as a child. Realizing I now live at their destination is a daunting experience," Shulamit said. She was becoming more and more aware of how much her life was changing. She was no longer the simple girl doing physical labor in the fields. Shulamit thought, *Perhaps this work will be harder.*

But she was never one to turn away hard work.

The day was half spent, and she was already tired from taking in so much new information. The new luxuries were a thrill, but ultimately a lot to master.

Shulamit's other Egyptian servant, Kiya, opened trunks filled with silk dresses of various colors, designs, and trims.

"I have only ever had one special dress to wear for festivals," Shulamit said, "and now there are so many to choose from. Which one do you think Solomon will like? I want to please my beloved."

Kiya suggested a light blue dress with a gold sash, with a dark blue robe to go over it. She showed Shulamit some gold earrings embedded with blue lapis lazuli, and a matching necklace with blue lapis hanging in rows down the center. Shulamit pondered over the Solomon's thoughtfulness, choosing these gifts for her.

Kiya read her thoughts and said, "The king likes to give good gifts to his bride. Wear his gifts as a beautiful bride who will make the king proud, and you will give him much glory."

"That is what I want to do above everything, bring glory to my king and his kingdom."

"And you shall, my mistress. You have been chosen to a high calling, and that transition involves a change in clothing. Your glory must match your call. No one would go to a wedding without a proper garment, nor would you go before a king without the proper attire."

Sheriti brought several pairs of gilded gold sandals. When Sheriti saw Shulamit's look of being overwhelmed with so many choices, she said, "If I may, mistress." She held up a pair, "I think this pair with the blue lapis stones will be perfect with your robes and adornment."

Relieved, Shulamit agreed.

Sheriti added, "These gold circlet bracelets will look beautiful on your wrists." Again, Shulamit thanked her handmaidens for their assistance. Though they knew far more than she did about how to groom and dress;

they were careful not to make her feel inadequate. They seemed to enjoy their work of easing in a new queen.

It was soon evening, and Shulamit had spent the better part of the day preparing to meet her beloved. Solomon sent Ahishar, the palace overseer, to escort her to dinner with him. Shulamit was anxious as she walked into Solomon's private chamber. But when she saw her beloved's face light up, her self-consciousness turned into delight. All the hard work of preparation for her king was worth it. It dawned on her that it could be fun learning how to adorn herself and take delight in Solomon's response.

Solomon sat with his family and close friends on cushions at a round table. The king stood up to greet his bride, and his family followed suit.

"This, my friends, is my beautiful new bride, Shulamit." Shulamit bowed her head as all of the guests glowed with approval. Solomon introduced her to the High Priest, Zadok; his son, Azariah; Asaph, a tabernacle worship leader; and his friend and counselor, Zabud, and the military commander Benaiah. Shulamit bowed her head with each introduction. Bathsheba, Shammau and Shobab, who were in attendance with their wives, along with Nathan who was younger and not married, greeted her.

Solomon led her to sit at his right side, between him and Bathsheba, then signaled his servant to pour wine into her goblet.

Shulamit took a sip of the wine. "This is good wine," she said, "like the wine from my family's vineyard."

Laughter arose in the room, and Shulamit could not understand what was so funny.

Shobab spoke up, "It is because this wine *is* from your family's vineyard."

"She knows her wine," Solomon laughed. "This is the way the story began and how I came to meet Shulamit. Most of you were here when I tasted this excellent wine and asked where it came from. Someone said it came from my own vineyard. One my father bought, which was being cared for by his friends. I said I must go there and see for myself. I also wanted to meet my father's old friends. I came upon the vineyard with Benaiah. I brought him with me because of his time with King David when he visited the family. I knew he would know them. We heard a beautiful voice and sought it out. From a distance, I saw the frame of a beautiful woman and sent Benaiah to inquire who she was and if she was spoken for."

Shulamit suddenly realized where she had seen Benaiah. "So, you knew who I was when I met you singing on the mountain?"

Solomon smiled knowingly. "A king must know everything. I have many eyes and ears, as I must stay aware of what is going on within my kingdom. Benaiah came back with a glowing report of your beauty and wit. He said that you were definitely the daughter of Joseph, the man my father loved to worship with. He also told me that you had invited me, the king, to the festival. Hence, I came at the fair maiden's request."

Shulamit's face blushed, but she covered her embarrassment with a laugh. "I feared I had been presumptuous to invite the king, but perhaps an angel must have whispered in my ear. I didn't expect you to come. When you did come, I feared I had lost my shepherd and regretted my presumptuousness."

"I love this woman full of spirit," Solomon acknowledged to his friends and family, "She speaks from her heart and not her head. She wasn't groomed in a palace. Her country style is a breath of fresh air. Is it not?" Many nodded in agreement.

"Now, tell us, Solomon," The High Priest asked, "how did you actually meet?"

"My mother suggested I dress as a shepherd and take my lyre. She told me to discover the woman who inspires my best song and sing. And so, I did." The guests laughed at Bathsheba's good sense and savvy. "I went to find the woman at the festival, but I was told she was not there. My clever friend Zabud was able to talk to the local people and find someone who would tell where she was. He came and told me where she was hiding."

"Hiding?" Several of Solomon's friends inquired through their enjoyment.

"Yes! She was hiding in her 'secret place.' Of course, everyone knew where it was." When he said that, everyone laughed. "Zabud sent me up the hill to a beautiful lake, hidden in the tall cedar trees. I went and waited. I did not know what she was doing and did not wish to invade her privacy. As I waited, a song came to me about the beautiful hills," Solomon remarked.

"And it was a beautiful song," Shulamit added, "I heard it when I was resting after my swim. I came to see where it was coming from. At first, I thought I was hearing the voice of King David in my head and went to see if it was real. I closed my eyes and danced my way toward the voice. When I opened them, there he was. The handsome man matched the loveliness of his song. I thought it was a dream. But he was a real person. Joy overtook me, and I couldn't help but laugh."

"We both laughed. I never laughed so much in my life." Solomon laughed again, just thinking about it. Some of the party joined in the laughter.

"Sing us that song Solomon," Bathsheba requested.

"I can't deny my mother," he said as he waved for a servant to bring his harp.

You crown the years with your goodness,
And your paths they drop fatness,
They drop upon the pastures of the wilderness,

And the little hills rejoice on every side,
They shout for joy they also sing lai lai lai…

Shulamit began to sing with him. Nathan handed her a tambourine. Solomon signaled for a lyre and stood up to dance with his music. Shulamit began to dance around the room, beating the tambourine in time to the music.

Zadok commented, "They are in love! The king is really in love this time! I have never seen him like this."

The room, almost at once, began clapping and singing as they joined in the chorus, *"They shout for joy they also sing, they shout for joy they also sing!"* Soon enough, the room was full of joy, and music, and dancing. When they finally stopped singing and laughing, Asaph, the tabernacle worship leader, announced, "Those are inspired lyrics! I would like to arrange them in a new song for the tabernacle worship. It is a song of thanks and worship of the beauty and blessings from God."

Solomon said, "I have another song I wrote about my maiden who worked in the field. It is a song of my observations and feelings toward her. It was those very thoughts that moved my heart to make her my bride." Solomon signaled the servants to bring appetizers. "As a king, sometimes, I feel the heart of God toward people in my kingdom that God wants to reward. That was the feeling I had when I met Shulamit, my beautiful maiden, working in my own grape harvest. Here, I will sing it, for I am inspired. You all may sit and enjoy your meal," he said as he lifted up his lyre again.

Out of the Harvest Fields

I brought you out of the harvest fields
Where you worked hard for me
I saw your heart in the harvest field
You gave your all for me

And when you discovered my love
You labored as unto me
I saw your heart in the harvest field
You labored in love for me

You knew my words from a distance
You sang my words to me
You put your heart into worship
As you danced before me

91

I love your soul in worship
I'm coming closer to you
I've been watching your outflow
And I like what you do

Now I am coming to visit you
And draw you closer to me
I'll visit you in your dreams and your song
I want you to dance with me

I've watched you from a distance
And I take pleasure in you
When the time is right, I'll reveal myself
And make a queen out of you

I'm pouring my grace upon you
I am grooming you
My beautiful maiden who works in the field
I'm already in love with you.

The room was silent after the song. It was a true Selah moment—one King David had taught the musicians in the tabernacle.

The king's military commander Benaiah broke the silence, "When the king sent me to inquire of the woman in the vineyard, I thought I was to meet just another pretty face. But when she spoke, I saw that she cherished the honor of managing a vineyard in earnest—work her brothers meant as punishment. I saw a heart yearning for more, but faithful in the work given her. And she did it joyfully. I knew I could sway the king's heart either way, yet I saw something in this woman meant for more. She thinks she was presumptuous. But Shulamit was fighting for the call to more in her life and against those who would keep her from her destiny. I gave her gifts from the king—perfume, to let her know that she was valued. And I gave her gifts to give her family. Then I returned to the king and gave him a glowing report and ignited his curiosity."

"Thank you, Benaiah, for being such a trusted man. Thank you for your discernment. You swayed my heart. But the moment my eyes met hers, I was already in love," Solomon said, and sounds of approval drifted throughout the room. "Perhaps I did not know I was in love, for I have never been in love before like this." Solomon turned to face Shulamit, "When I saw you dance at the festival, I would have run through a barricade to grab you, but thankfully you made a quick movement to run past your own barricades and reach me." To the room, he said, "We fought for each other, though she knew nothing of me. She is a strong woman and my favored queen. You are the queen I have always wanted."

The High Priest raised another cup of wine and decreed, "As beautiful a love story as I have ever heard. May your love for each other grow deeper with time! I sense this is a love that belongs to our history and should be written about for others to learn from. God bless King Solomon and Shulamit, our new queen-in-waiting. May their joys multiply and bless our kingdom forever!"

Shulamit felt that the High Priest proclaimed a prophecy, and she took it to heart. She wondered if he had been the one who had given her the prophecy about being a blessing to Israel as a worshipper when she was younger. Now that he was older, the voice seemed to resonate as the same, but she could not tell. It was so long ago.

The servants removed the appetizers from the table and replaced them with main dishes. Shulamit was overwhelmed the elegant platters of food displayed before her that she had never seen or eaten before. She watched as others ate and followed their example as she took a small taste of each dish.

She liked the spices that came from the Far East; they were new to the market of Israel, and a luxury on her tongue. But she was too nervous to really think of eating. Instead, Shulamit watched her husband-to-be as he talked to the people around him.

Solomon had a fantastic way of putting everyone at ease. During the small banquet in honor of her, he kept the conversation light and happy. *Of course*, she thought, *when love is in the air, it is always light.* They were all happy to know the weather was cooling down. Asaph spoke of new songs of the Lord that had been written spontaneously in their worship services. He was arranging the music for the tabernacle.

Solomon said, "Our Shulamit has been looking forward to worshipping in the tabernacle."

"Yes. I can see she is a worshipper," he said. Asaph addressed Shulamit, "You are welcome to worship whenever you wish. There is a special place for the women of the royal family. It is always reserved up close to the musicians and the ark."

Shulamit's face lit up, full of excitement. "It has been my dream to return to the tabernacle to worship ever since the time I was a young girl. I love singing and dancing in the presence of God. I love learning new songs. My family used to worship with King David before I was born when he came to visit. My father loved to worship, and he put that love into my heart from as far back as I can remember."

The High Priest suddenly remembered the young girl years ago worshipping in the temple with her whole heart. *Could this be her? Hmm?* He wondered.

Asaph was amazed at Shulamit's desire to worship. "Music is a gift from birth, but the desire to worship is developed through a love of singing God's Word and rejoicing to bless and thank God for all He has done for us. It comes from the heart. Touching the heart of God and bringing Heaven to Earth, that is the heart of worship."

Noting Asaph's mention of love for singing God's Word, Solomon injected into the conversation, "My bride also desires to learn to read."

The High Priest's son, Azariah, who had been silent until now, spoke up. "I will teach her Sire, if you like," he said. Perhaps Asaph's daughter, Shira, who has a gift for writing songs, may join us. She has expressed a desire and learned to read so she could write her songs. Might I bring her with me to help?"

Asaph gave his consent. "Even the girls in my family write songs."

"Delightful," Solomon said, as he turned to Shulamit. "You see my love; God cares about your desires and has already been making a way for your dreams to come to pass."

Shulamit, beaming with joy, answered, "I can't wait to go to the tabernacle and thank my God, Yahweh, for all my blessings."

"We all have many things to be thankful for," Solomon replied. He gazed into Shulamit's eyes. They looked like two doves in love—never to be separated. The observers could not remember a time when the king was so happy.

13 THE TABERNACLE OF DAVID

Awakened to the sound of rain outside her window, Shulamit went out to see her lovely courtyard garden and to greet the gentle shower. Breathing in the fresh, sweet scent of the garden air, she began to sing, jumping barefoot from stone to stone as she thanked God for the rain.

Thank you, Father, for your showers of blessings
That makes these lovely flowers grow
Thank you, Father for your clouds releasing
The rain and wind you gently blow

Thank you, Father, for the raindrops on my face
The refreshing moisture on my lips
Thank you Father I can touch and embrace
Your loving gift upon my fingertips...

While Shulamit was admiring the beauty as she danced around in her garden, Ahishan, the palace steward, came to her chambers with a message from Solomon. When Meliba answered the door, he announced, "I have a message for your mistress from the king."

"She is singing in the garden. Do you wish to give it to her directly?"

"Singing in the garden," Ahishan said. "In the rain? I should like to see that."

"Come and see then. Then you can deliver your message to her," Meliba replied with a gesture.

When Ahishan saw the joy of Shulamit's song and dance, he was so taken in by the beauty of the scene he did not dare to interrupt. He turned to Meliba, saying, "Don't interrupt her, I am running to the king to see if he would like to come and see this."

Ahishan hastened down the hallway, bursting into the king's private business chamber. Solomon looked up and acknowledged him, curious about the reason for his hasty entry.

"Sire," Ahishan blurted, "I went to deliver your message, but your young bride was dancing and singing in the rain. She has a lovely voice and her dance was delightful. I thought you might want to come and see for yourself."

"I would," Solomon said. Rising, he instructed a nearby servant, "Grab my robe."

The servants had a tough time keeping up to put on his garment as he rushed down the hallway. He was greeted by Meliba at an open side door to Shulamit's chamber, and she directed him toward the garden where he could hear Shulamit's lovely voice drifting through the open air.

Shulamit was still caught up in her worship and praise.

> *Thank you, Father for the rain*
> *Thank you, Father for this early rain*
> *Thank you, Father for the rain*
> *And the blessing of the season*
> *Thank you, Father for this early rain*
> *Everything you do is pleasing*

She picked a flower and raised it to her nose, inhaled a deep breath of the sweet smell as she continued singing. Solomon crept in behind her to join in her song.

"Thank you, Father for the rain," Solomon echoed after her.

She turned, surprised to see Solomon and responded with a bright smile. Without skipping a beat, they continued singing, together.

"Thank you, Father for the early rain," Shulamit sang, and Solomon echoed. "Thank you, Father for the rain," they sang together.

Solomon joined her in leaping across the steppingstones. They held out raised their arms toward the sky to the source of the rain as it fell upon their faces. They were both soaked, but they did not care. As they had done when they first met in the hills, they began laughing, deep belly laughs. Ahishan and Meliba watched from a distance, captivated by their joy.

Ahishan quoted a proverb, "When the king is happy the whole kingdom is in peace." Then he and Meliba, too, began laughing to themselves.

Solomon took lead of their dance, and Shulamit followed him to a small pavilion enclosed by vines and climbing red roses. She had never been here before. As they walked through the entrance, they were sheltered from the rain by a colorful blue tent. Chairs that sat off the ground were placed around the edges of this pavilion, along with small tables near potted plants. Shulamit's eyes lit up, and Solomon smiled at her surprise as he said, "I made you a secret place."

"I love it, Solomon! I love this beautiful garden. It is wonderful!"

"So, you are pleased with your new home?"

"I feel I am living in a dream. I am very pleased!" She looked at him, her eyes sparkling through long dark lashes. "I have never been happier."

She was a vision of beauty to Solomon, even with rain dripping off of her hair. As she wiped it from her face, Solomon chuckled. He guided her to the chairs and they both sat.

"I haven't sung in the rain since I was a child," Solomon disclosed.

Shulamit smiled again. "When you live in the country," she started, "you always celebrate the early rains. It is the blessing from heaven upon our livelihood. Papa used to run into the house when the rain came and shout, 'The rain is here time to dance!' And out we ran, dancing and singing, making up songs about the first rains as we went. After the long hot summer, it was always a joyful occasion."

"I wish I could have met your Papa."

"I wish I could have met your father too." They looked at each other for a moment, but then Shulamit sighed and dropped her gaze. "We both were blessed with great fathers. But now we have each other."

They sat in silence for a moment, considering the depth of their loss and gain.

"It's profound when one realizes the heart's emptiness has at last been healed by a new love to fill the void. Ah, sweet Shulamit, you are the gift of love I have been waiting for all of my life." Feeling a sudden urge to kiss her, Solomon stood up. "We are both soaking wet, and perhaps we should dry off and have some warm tea. If we stay here, I am going to kiss you, and it is not time yet."

On the way back to her chamber he said, "I will teach you about all the plants in your garden and their names at another time. I have so much I want to share with you."

Meliba rushed to them with large towels, offering them seats near a fire in the large guest chamber. As they drank the warm tea, Solomon relayed the message he had sent Ahishan to deliver earlier.

"Are you ready to go to the Tabernacle of David and worship? Tonight, while Asaph is leading the worship, I invite you to come and worship with me and my family." Shulamit couldn't hide her excitement and began nodding, sending rainwater from her hair into her lap. Solomon chuckled. "I have designed a special dress for you to wear for this significant occasion as you enter the presence of the King of Kings." He stood up. "I must dismiss myself now, to get back to my business. This has been a refreshing time. We shall have many more, my love. I will see you this evening."

***

Shulamit couldn't pull the smile from her face. There were so many wonderful things happening. She was surprised when a sudden pang of anxiety came over her mind. She walked into her bed chamber and sat on the edge of her bed. *I shall be going into the presence of God. Is my heart perfect before God? Do I have any secret sins?* Praying within her heart she mouthed, "*Abba*, father, help me to come before you with purity. *Abba*, help me to honor you as you deserve to be honored. Solomon is a king, and my husband on earth. But You are my King of Kings, and Israel is in covenant with You. Help me, *Abba*, to carry my part of this marriage covenant as a Godly wife."

Sherita, her maiden from Lebanon, came into the bed chamber discreetly, and Shulamit smiled when she noticed her. Sherita reminded Shulamit that she had not eaten all day, then asked if she wished for some fresh bread and curd.

"Oh, I will drink some warm milk, but I cannot eat. My stomach is in knots, and I must fast and pray before I enter the tabernacle with the presence of the Ark of God."

"Then let us prepare a bath for you and help make you ready," Sherita said. "Which of these oils would you like?"

As they had done before, her maidens presented Shulamit with several different scented oils. She started to feel overwhelmed, but the small bottle with scents of frankincense and myrrh with roses and sandalwood caught her attention. It was a relaxing scent that made her doze off and remember the song her father once wrote for her as a child. The scent was added to the bath and she slipped in, feeling her body unfurl to enjoy the warmth.

Her maidens scrubbed her feet and massaged more oil into her calloused heels, caused by a lifetime of running through the countryside barefoot. She smiled at the memory of her beloved father, waiting for her to run into his arms on occasion. Shulamit had not thought of that song for so many years, and now it came to her as a comforting balm to her spirit, so she began to sing.

When you worship
Heaven Ssmiles
upon you

Our Father delights
Your countenance lights
and you shine

When you dance
Heaven dances with you
Our Father's heart is touched
He says
You're mine…

"What a lovely song," Kiya said. "Was that written about you?"

"Yes. My father wrote it for me when I was a young girl. I wanted to fight battles like a boy and be like King David. But my father told me I had a different gift. He said I could move the heart of heaven to fight our battles. But I would do it in the spirit through my worship."

"I'm sure *Adonai* was touched by your song of thanks this morning," replied Kiya. "I know the king and the rest of us were blessed. You have a gift."

"Thank you Kiya," Shulamit said, smiling. "I guess I needed to be reminded."

After the bath her maidens dressed her. Just as they finished, a knock came to the door. Meliba answered, and a servant bearing a wrapped bundle said, "A present from the king to his bride." He handed the package to Meliba and bowed before he turned and left. Meliba brought it to Shulamit, who opened it with a delightful squeal. "Aah!" she cried with delight. "This is perfect!" She slipped it on.

It was a gold vest with fringes hanging down the length of the dress. Shulamit began to twirl around and around as the skirt flared out in waves around her. While she turned, the gold fringes spun out with the dress, adding resplendency to the movement. Solomon included a pair of soft golden leather slippers and Kiya tied them to fit her feet. Shulamit was grateful for the comfortable movement.

"I told his highness you wanted a dress that could flare out when you moved, and he designed it," Meliba said. "He had the daughters of Zion make it especially for you."

Shulamit gave her a hug. "So thoughtful. That is so thoughtful of you and Solomon. I have never been given so much care in my life. I don't know what to say but thank you. So, thank you, Meliba. Thank Solomon. Thank everyone."

"You are a bride and a queen, and the king spares nothing for those he loves. You, too, are a bringer of joy. Delight yourself in worship and the king, and in the King of Kings. That way, the whole kingdom will be blessed. Come, let's finish up your preparation."

Shulamit spent the rest of the afternoon praying and repenting. She remembered from her youth the holy awe, majesty, and power of *Adonai*. She wanted to enter His presence with a perfect heart. As the day passed, she continued to thank her heavenly Father for all her blessings. Her mother and father had instilled in her the importance of thankfulness and honoring her God for all her blessings.

In the early evening, Solomon sent his servant to escort her to his quarters. Before she walked out, Meliba tied a gold scarf around Shulamit's head. It covered part of her hair, as was the tradition of modesty before entering the tabernacle. Shulamit bowed her head in thanks.

Shulamit met a group at Solomon's chamber entrance. Solomon, Bathsheba, the High Priest Zadok, Zabud, and Solomon's brothers greeted her warmly and complimented her appearance. Once pleasantries were completed, Solomon lead them all toward the temple. They followed a royal escort outside of his chambers to a flight of steps directly behind the palace. Solomon's party headed up the steps to the special entrance of the tabernacle.

The doorkeepers welcomed the group with ceremonial quiet, yet their visages were happy. Solomon and his people were led to their seating areas in the front, facing the podium where the musicians played. Solomon sat with the men, while Shulamit sat with Bathsheba and other women of the court she did not know.

The Ark sat, resplendent, in the middle on a higher platform.

The gold wings of the cherubim on the ark shone brightly, reflecting the candlelight in the tabernacle. A palpable glory seemed to come from the Ark. It floated in the room like a thickness to the air. Shulamit could feel it. She hadn't gotten this close to the Ark as a young child. And although she had felt the presence of God before, tonight, it was overpowering.

A remnant of the musicians from the previous hour continued playing while Asaph's musicians entered and set themselves up to take over the worship duties. She watched as the musicians arranged themselves. The large ensemble of instruments was divided into the harps and stringed instruments, woodwind pipes and flutes, various sizes of drums, cymbals and tambourines of various sizes. There were also many new instruments she did not recognize. She would inquire later.

Bong, Bong, Bong, came the sound of a powerful, high-sounding cymbal.

Asaph, the master of the cymbal was beginning. Everyone came to attention as the music began to play. Male and female singers began to sing, *"Enter into his gates with thanksgiving and into His courts with praise!"*

Shulamit recognized this tune as one her father had taught her, but it was quite different. It was way more majestic with the horn section's long, silver trumpets and large curved ram's horns.. The music added to the powerful feeling of the presence of God. It was an awesome experience full of the majesty within the tent.

Shulamit felt somewhat frozen in her place and almost unable to move. From her position, facing both the Ark and the audience, she could see that the people in the crowd were taken in by the awe and presence, much the same as she was.

Shulamit was overcome.

She found herself relieved when the song was finished, and she could sit in her seat before she lost her balance. She was always a sure-footed person, but the feeling of falling over was powerful.

While the music paused, Shulamit thought about how King David's worship and faith had produced his "Mighty men," and brought the surrounding nations to their knees. She knew that, if she were not following the cues of Bathsheba and Solomon, she would be on her knees right now. She prayed in her head, *I want this relationship with you, Yahweh. The same King David had in his worship.* Shulamit was aware of a spirit within her directing her thoughts, and she danced with the feeling of connection to the King of Kings.

A slower song began that interrupted her. A female soprano voice with much vibrato scaling up and down many partial notes rang out, *"Who shall ascend into the hill of the Lord? Or who shall stand in His holy place? He that has clean hands and a pure heart..."*

That was the very prayer she had prayed that afternoon.

Was the Lord confirming her prayer? She looked at the singer and wondered if this was Asaph's daughter Shira, just as Bathsheba whispered her name in Shulamit's ear. She was correct. Her name, Shira, which meant song, surely fit her. And there was a glory on Shira's face as she sang.

The whole tabernacle was glowing with glory.

Soon the choir with all ranges of voices joined the male and female singers, *"Lift up your heads, O you gates! And be lifted up you, everlasting door! And the King of glory shall come in. Who is this King of glory? The Lord strong and mighty, the Lord mighty in battle..."*

After the song was sung through once, Asaph invited everyone in the tabernacle to sing the song. Shulamit's soprano voice rang out in a similar, sweet sound as Shira. Queen Bathsheba sang a resounding mezzo-alto, blending in as if angels were singing through them. Joy overflowed Shulamit's heart as she could feel glory taking over her worship and singing through her.

She couldn't stop if she wanted to.

Solomon looked over at her and saw the glow on her face. He whispered to Zadok, "Do you see the glory on Shulamit's countenance. When I see that sparkle and joy on anyone, I know that the Spirit of God is on them. She is radiating from an inward glory as the Spirit of God moves upon her heart." He continued in a hushed tone, "That is what I noticed about her when I first saw her. Her eyes sparkled, and she had the glory of heaven. I could not take my eyes off of her."

"You still can't," the High Priest commented, "You are overcome in love my king. I have never seen you look at a woman the way you look at her. She will be good for you."

As a new song began, the congregation was taken deeper into the Holy of Holies. A deep baritone voice stood up and sang, *"One thing have I desired of the Lord, that will I seek after; that I may dwell in the house of the Lord all the days of my life, to behold the beauty of the Lord and enquire in his temple..."*

Solomon whispered again to his Priest Zadok, "You have to observe this. She will listen to this new song with her eyes closed. Watch. She is totally focused on the music. Now she will sway to the music, back and forth, gently catching the rhythm and taking in the heart of the song."

"I see that," the Priest observed.

"She as captured the feel of the music, now she will listen more deeply to the words. She loves poetry. She loves to hear the voice of God in inspired words," the king reflected. "Now watch her, she is beginning to sing slowly as she the is catching the tune. She is developing the tone in her voice as she gains a deeper understanding of what God is speaking through the psalm."

"Your observation is very keen, Solomon. You make me see it too."

"I can tell she wants to dance, but she won't operate outside of protocol. She will continue to sing. She knows the music is loud and she thinks she won't be heard. Watch her take a deep breath so she can hold the high note along with the sopranos. She is enraptured. Look at her mouth shape the words with exaggerated movement. Her throat is quivering like a songbird as she pushes the air up from her belly and brings her hands in front of her heart as she sings. When she finally opens her eyes, you will see every emotion she sings upon her face."

"How sensitive you are to your bride," Zadok acknowledged.

"Watch this Zadok," Solomon interrupted. "She can feel the song is coming to an end. Watch her calm down and open her eyes. She is suddenly remembering where she is. She has been flying with the eagles and now she is back. Watch her ground herself and remember her bearing. She is an adventure just to watch."

The High Priest whispered back, "I am amazed that you know her so well in such a short time."

"You forget. I grew up watching my father worship and write songs that he would lead in worship. I recognize the same quality of heart that makes a person a real worshipper. She is a gentle dove who can be guided in flight by the Spirit that surrounds her wings."

Another moment of Selah came upon the Tabernacle as the song ended. It was a holy, beautiful moment to meditate and bow before the Ark. The High Priest Zadok and King Solomon led the example as they bowed before the presence of God.

Bathsheba led Shulamit up to the front of the Ark to bow.

When she arrived, Shulamit fell to her knees and bowed her head to the ground. She petitioned before the Lord to help her be a good queen and representative of Him; that she would give honor to Him and Solomon. In that moment, a still small voice spoke inside of her, "You are *my queen*. I have chosen you."

A tingle went through her whole body as those words spoke into her spirit. She wiped a tear of gratitude from her eyes as she rose to return to her seat. Something transformed within her spirit that she could not explain. A confidence confirmed what she already knew. God had brought her to the King here at the palace, and she was in the will of El Shaddai, God Almighty. A deep feeling of humility came over her, knowing she had been chosen to such an awesome call, and she knew only Yahweh, God Himself could help her fulfill it.

As the time of prayer and petition came to an end, Asaph announced that there was one more song and all were welcome to dance.

> *You crown the years with your goodness,*
> *And the little hills rejoice on every side.*
> *They shout for joy they also sing …*

Shira came down from the choir and took hold of Shulamit's hand to begin a circle dance. Very quickly, more and more women joined in. The steps were easy, as the right foot stepped behind the left and the left foot stepped left, and the right foot stepped in front of the left foot. Over and over they leapt round and round. It was a simple melody and a simple dance to a simple song, but the glory in the dance was majestic and joy was abounding.

Afterwards, Asaph dismissed them with the Aaronic blessing. "The Lord bless you and keep you; The Lord make His face to shine upon you and be gracious to you: The Lord lift up His countenance upon you, and give you peace."

Solomon and his family were escorted back to his chambers where a late evening meal waited for them. As they partook of the food and drink, there was much laughter and rejoicing.

"The presence of God was very powerful tonight," Nathan remarked.

Shulamit began to realize that Nathan seemed to be different than Solomon and his brothers. He seemed to be the most interested in the Glory of Yahweh, rather than earthly glory. He seemed to discern the difference. To the other's the glory of their wealth was accepted as the blessing and glory of God upon their nation. But Nathan discerned Spiritual glory, and Shulamit sensed that. She also realized she was lightheaded from not eating all day. She picked up a piece of bread and dipped it in a sauce made with eggplant. She knew better than to drink the wine being poured on an empty stomach.

"What did you think, Shulamit?" Nathan asked.

With all eyes turned towards her, and knowing she was still overwhelmed with the whole experience, she stumbled through her answer, "I'm still overcome. I remember the same feel of the presence of joy when I was a little girl, but I was worshipping back in the crowd. Being up close to God's presence was more powerful than I remember. I could not help but sing and dance the same as I could not help myself as a child."

The High Priest, Zadok, now felt he had to ask, "There was a little girl I blessed as a worshipper in Israel some years ago. Are you that girl?"

Shulamit's eyes began to water anew. "Yes," she said. "And you are the Priest who blessed me with that prophecy. I have held that in my heart day and night since that time. It changed my whole life. I knew I could not marry anyone who could not be part of the fulfillment of that prophecy."

"Bless you child. The Lord has brought you here. Tonight. I saw the words come to life as you worshipped—a queen, full of the joy of the Lord, and worshipping with a heart of joy. We are blessed."

"*I* am blessed," Shulamit said, bowing her head.

Solomon held up his glass of wine, "To my queen, who brings joy into our kingdom."

After the meal, as everyone was saying good night, Solomon took Shulamit's hand and said he would escort her back to her quarters himself. He led her a different way, up a flight of stairs to a balcony overlooking the tabernacle. To Shulamit's surprise, the music of the tabernacle could be heard from there as it continued constantly. They sat down on a bench by the rail. It was a pretty spot with flowerpots all around and partially covered for shade. Part of the moon revealed itself from behind clouds, and a few stars shone in the sky.

"If you ever desire to come, be alone, and just listen to the music, you can come up here," said Solomon.

"It is lovely listening to the music here."

"You still haven't seen much of the palace, and I have a lot to show you. I thought I would start with this quiet place. Soon you will be known by everyone in the palace, and you will start looking for places to be alone. Tonight, many ladies of the court have seen you sing and worship in the Tabernacle. Stories will be circulating before dawn about my new bride. That is how it is here. You will find that being a queen makes you a public person. Everything you do, and say, and wear will be noticed." Solomon paused. "I haven't spoken to you about this before, but you know as a king I have other wives." Shulamit nodded, and he continued; "And when I tell you this, let me assure you, I did not choose any of these wives. They were marriages based on alliances with their countries for peace and business connections. You are the bride that I *chose*. I am deeply in love with you. The more I know you the *more* in love with you I become. When I saw you worshipping in the Tabernacle tonight my love grew yet deeper. No one compares to you." Shulamit closed her eyes, trying not to let tears escape. Solomon noticed and lifted her face to his. Her eyes glistened as he looked at her. "I need a bride who loves our God, Yahweh the way you do, and is from my own culture and country. My other brides have converted to Judaism, but they do not have the heart you have. Brides from the nations can never match up to marrying amongst the chosen people. You have much more than just beauty."

Shulamit sat there continuing to hold back tears. Solomon was saying that he chose her. And yet she did not know if, perhaps, the thought of him having another bride was hard to think about. She had to acknowledge that he had other brides, even though he had not mentioned it. She knew she would have to face that sooner or later. She could not really process it yet.

It had been an overwhelming night. Hearing the voice of Yahweh Himself; hearing Him say she was chosen—it was still echoing in her ears. She chose to focus on the most positive experience of this night—God had chosen her, and Solomon was saying the same thing. Her God was behind all that was happening in her life. Just knowing she was chosen by God was the most important thing. She knew she was in the will of Yahweh. She also knew that He had answered her prayer in giving her Solomon. She loved Solomon.

Yes, she deeply loved Solomon.

"You are quiet. Do you wish to share your thoughts?"

"I love you, Solomon. I love you deeply. I prayed for my husband to be all that you are. But I guess I did not really know what I was praying for."

Solomon could not resist giving her a gentle embrace before he quickly stepped back. "My sweet Shulamit. I know how you feel. My beautiful Shulamit, beautiful in all ways. I guess none of us know where life takes us," he said, smiling. "I never expected to be king. I had many older brothers. But Yahweh chose me, and I was overwhelmed. When Yahweh gave me a chance to choose what I wanted, I asked for wisdom. And then he gave it all to me. I see that you have wisdom within you. Know this. God will never call you to any place without giving you the anointing to go there."

He stood up and leaned on the railing, beckoning Shulamit to join him. "I saw a queen in you the moment I saw you. I envisioned you dressed as royalty with gold chains around your neck." Shulamit reached up, touching the finery around her throat. Solomon smiled. "My counselor and friend Zabud, who is son of Nathan the prophet, he saw it in you too. *Elohim*, our creator God, created you especially for me, and there will never be anyone like you."

A renewed peace came over Shulamit. She knew all that Solomon said was true, and she accepted it. Accepting the call of her God, overwhelming and challenging as it might seem, created that great peace within her.

"I feel a peace in accepting," she said to Solomon. "I accepted to be your wife. Now I accept to be your queen. I didn't know I had to accept that too to find peace, but now I do. I do."

14 KING SOLOMON'S VISION

Life was changing very rapidly for Shulamit as the king's new bride. Every day, Solomon sent her dresses and shoes, jewelry, scarfs, and new things to do.

One morning, as Shulamit was looking over the new gifts, she received a message. Solomon was coming to show her around Jerusalem. She hadn't seen the whole palace, yet he wanted to show her his work on the new temple. After her maidservants prepared her, Ahishan walked her to the outside of the palace where Solomon waited by a litter. It was carried by several strong guards. He greeted her with a large smile which she returned with a glow.

"I want you to see the big picture of all that is happening in Jerusalem," he said.

Solomon helped her inside the covered litter. The sun was shaded with sheer curtains, and she could see out without others seeing in. Solomon sat opposite her. Within moments, they were carried down steps and through the old quarters of Jerusalem. They passed by a large marketplace with many small shops and rows upon rows of decoratively displayed spices, food, clothing, and other items. Shulamit could vaguely remember walking in this market area with her mother and father as a child.

"Jerusalem is the center of world commerce. I have a treasure house in the palace with the best of everything that can be found but I will show you that another time," Solomon said.

"I look forward to it," she replied. She hadn't stopped smiling since she first saw him that day.

Solomon and Shulamit were carried across a bridge where they could see another side of the city. "I am expanding the wall of the city to accommodate all the plans I have including the temple."

Shulamit was amazed at Solomon's vision. Several ramps were built to carry large stones up to where the workers were laying the foundation for the outer courts of the temple. Other structures were being used to lift the large blocks of heavy stone for more precise placement. Shulamit stared as workers joined similarly sized stones on the streets so carriages would be able to drive over them smoothly, unlike the dirt highways outside Jerusalem. The guards carried the carriage up several sets of steps to a large, leveled area of white stone. In the center a higher platform was being built.

"This is Mount Moriah, where I am building the temple." Solomon

106

pointed toward the steps that lead to elevated groundwork. "Laying the foundation is the hardest and longest part of building."

"There are so many types you are using. How ingenious."

"All the stones come from quarries where they are rough pieces of large rock. Then the stones are hewn, measured, and shaped to fit before being brought to the temple site. The stones are laid in place without hammers or axe and fit perfectly."

Solomon went on to explain how the stones for the building of the temple would first be covered with silver by a skilled craftsman. After the walls were in place they would be covered in boards of cedar with carved figures of cherubim and palm trees and open flowers. Then they would be covered with gold inside and out. His face lit up as he described the various details of the temple. He was excited as he described the precious stones, vault beams and floor types, and doors of the temple being built with the same strong fir tree wood.

Shulamit concentrated hard to try to remember all the details, but the magnificence was more than she could retain in the first hearing. She studied the excitement on Solomon's face and the glory that shone on his countenance as he spoke of building and tried to visualize it all. Solomon explained that silver represented the salvation of Israel; gold symbolized deity and glory; and that the walls of cedar expressed royalty and kingship, because it was an imperishable wood. He started to explain about the jewels and precious stones that would go into the temple, but when he saw it was too much to explain at once, he offered, "I will explain more of these details at another time."

"I am fascinated by it all Solomon,." Shulamit admitted. "I don't catch all of the details, but I feel the wonder of it all. It is like poetry to me. As you speak of all the glory, I feel singing in my heart.

Solomon smiled. "I love sharing the visions God has given me with you, because I delight in seeing the sparkle in your eyes."

Shulamit perceived his earnest heart. It made her feel humble. "And God will give you more tomorrow. You will forever keep me full of wonder."

"Don't forget, our God, *Elohim*, keeps me full of wonder too!"

Suddenly a thought puzzled her. "Where will the ark of God be?"

"The Ark of the covenant will be placed in the Holy of Holies, as it was in the Tabernacle of Moses."

"When that happens will we no longer be able to be close to glory in the presence of God?"

"God's glory will be all over the Temple, but the Holy of Holies will be where the High Priest will go for the forgiveness of our sins on Yom Kippur. Right now, we have two temples," he explained. "The one in

Gibeon where we have our animal sacrifices, and David's Tabernacle here at Zion where we have worship. But they must come together. Otherwise, when people from all over the world come to see the glory of our God, they will only see part of the picture.

"That is true."

"Right now," Solomon said, "people see the glory and joy of worshipping in the tabernacle. That is good, but there is price to be paid for that joy. Our sins are forgiven each year by the sacrifice of the animals.

"Yes. Each year we can repent of our mistakes and start afresh."

"Exactly," said Solomon. "When people come to see the Glory of God in our Temple, we want them to know that we have a God who is merciful and forgives sins. We want them to see that our favor comes from our heart and our relationship with a loving God.

"I get it," Shulamit acknowledged. "The two tabernacles together point to a greater glory. They have always been separated since I was born. But as you say, we, as a people called of God, present God to the world," she said getting excited again. *Yes! They should see the whole picture.* "I will miss worshipping in the sweet presence of God before the ark of the covenant, where the Lord has spoken to me the two times."

"Never limit God," Solomon said with a quizzical expression on his face. "When God spoke to me, I was sacrificing animals at Gibeon, and remember how we both agreed God spoke to us up in the hills of your village."

"The heaven of heavens cannot contain God."

"I would certainly not wish to be king without his anointing upon me. The glory of God has been with you from the day your mother conceived you, preparing you for me and His Kingdom. The moment we were betrothed my covering fell upon you. God is with you, my love."

"I like what you said. I will not limit God. He is bigger than anything man would try to limit Him to. All my thinking is being expanded."

"God is always expanding our knowledge and our vision. Let me share more about our growing kingdom."

Before Shulamit could catch her breathe over the glory of the temple, Solomon began sharing his vision again, pointing out areas where he was building his new palace once the temple was built. Solomon planned large courtyards and civil buildings for holding court. They exited the litter and he walked her around, showing her where the large palatial quarters he planned to build for her within the future palace grounds. The plans were approximate, but in her new quarters, she would be close to the temple where she could easily go through a hidden passageway to a special woman's courts overlooking the temple worshippers. Solomon designed that passage for his queens to pray and worship. After the tour, Solomon helped Shulamit back and inside the litter.

"You are keeping your promise to give me my own home."

"That is what you desired is it not?"

"Yes," she said, overcome, "but a *palace*?!"

"What vows I signed in my marriage promise to you on the Ketubah, I intend to keep. You are favored above all my queens. Ask me whatever you want, and I will use all my power to make it possible. I admit that your dreams are most challenging, but that is why I like them."

Shulamit noted that there were many foreign workers. Solomon saw where she was looking and explained. "It takes a lot of laborers to do the work in the quarries, carrying heavy loads, and felling the trees in Lebanon. I have brought the best architects and skilled craftsmen I can find from Syria, Lebanon, Egypt, and our own people. Most of our people are overseers in the labor, but they are also being trained so we will have the best skills in our country. I also teach them the skills that *Elohim* gives to me."

"Jerusalem is truly blessed to have a king with such vision."

Solomon took her hand, about to share what he thought was perhaps his biggest vision. "People will come from the far ends of the world to see the wisdom that God has given Jerusalem. They will see our temple and then give glory to God. They will hear our music and our worship, with the best music orchestrated anywhere in the known world."

Shulamit was totally caught up in the grandeur of his vision. "It will fill them with joy."

"They will see our palaces, and buildings, our agriculture, our gardens, taste our good wine, and see all the blessings that God has given to us."

She had to laugh when Solomon mentioned tasting the good wine, despite the excitement she felt about his ideas. "For a moment there," she said, "I heard the voice of my father talking about having the best wine in Israel."

"Oh, really?" said Solomon, beginning to chuckle.

"He is the one who taught me to dream. He made me love dreamers. I realize now, being a king, you are the best of dreamers, setting the vision for our country to be the greatest in the world."

"A king likes to surround himself with dreamers and people who have ideas. I love to help people who dream become the best they can be."

"It takes a lot of work to carry a vision to completion," Shulamit said.

"Yes, and I know our Father in heaven feels the same way. He looks for people with good hearts, and He wants to help them develop their talents. People who carry Godly desires are those who build up countries."

"As king, I can feel that you carry the heart of our Father in heaven."

"Come," Solomon jumped out of the litter and held out his hand to Shulamit, "Let us walk around a bit more."

109

He led her over to the wall where his expanded city was being built. She could see the valley surrounding the city. She also saw the hills all around as they reached the top of the steps. It was a beautiful sight. Solomon pointed in the direction of Bethlehem, where his family came from. "I will take you there sometime. I still have family there. I can show you where my father David used to care for sheep. He often shared the lessons he learned while raising sheep because they taught him how to shepherd people."

"I wonder if it would remind me of my own shepherding experiences," Shulamit commented.

"Everything we do in life, we build upon. As we learn more, we grow from our lessons, and add more. It is like laying the foundation of a city. We learn to draw upon everything we have ever done or experienced."

They walked around the new part of the city for a while before Solomon led her back to the litter to return to the palace. They retraced their journey back to the palace across the aqueduct and past the busy markets. Solomon escorted her back to her quarters and said, "This has been a long day, but I will see you again tomorrow and show you more of the palace."

***

The following morning a messenger brought word that Ahishan would be escorting Shulamit to one of Solomon's government chambers. They walked through several large corridors and finally turned into an official looking room lit by oil lamps and sunlight.

The center of the room had one oblong cedar table standing off the ground. There were matching high back chairs adorned with purple seat cushions tucked under it. One side of the wall had a map of Israel and the surrounding countries. Each country was painted in different colors with their respective flags, rivers, and boundaries. The King's Highway, outlying towns and cities, and mountains were marked as well. Shulamit had never seen such a map, and stood studying it, trying to figure it out.

Around the rest of the room were cabinets containing scrolls and lattice windows. The wall opposite the map had a large board on a stand with large black letters of the Hebrew alphabet painted on it. Near it were papyrus, clay pots of ink, and reeds. Shulamit tried to see how many letters she could recognize and thought of how she hoped to learn to read and write soon.

Shulamit was still looking around the room as the High Priest Zadok and Asaph's daughter, Shira, entered the room.

Zadok introduced Shira. "You unofficially met her in the Tabernacle when you danced with her."

"It was fun," Shira added.

"Yes, thank you for drawing me into the dance," Shulamit replied.

"After I brought you into the dance, I felt I was following you, rather than leading myself."

"Oops," Shulamit said, putting her hands up to her mouth.

"I did not mind, your dance is a gift, and perhaps we can share our gifts together and create more dances."

"Yes, yes, yes, I would love that above anything else!"

The High Priest Zadok interrupted with a smile before saying, "Now, ladies, we are in the king's chamber on official business.

"What business, Father?" said Shira.

"A very important business called teaching you how to read and write."

The girls laughed and sat straight in their chairs facing the board with the alphabet. Zadok said, "I know you ladies already know some of the letters and some words, but we are going to have a review. He took a stick and proceeded to point to and pronounce every letter of the alphabet, directing them to repeat after him. After laboriously repeating the letters Shulamit asked, "Rabbi, is there a song to help us remember them?"

The Priest looked at her as if trying to remember if anyone had written such a song. He wondered how she came up with these ideas. "Maybe, but I do not remember," he said.

Shulamit looked at Shira with a big smile as she said, "Then we will write one."

Zadok became serious about his teaching, saying, "On your own time, ladies. Now I know why men do not try to teach women." The girls quit smiling at each other and respectfully turned their focus back to their teacher.

The High Priest's tone tried to remain serious as he gave them the history of their language. "We have the only vowel system of our time," he explained. "We have the Niqqud, thanks to Solomon, and we can now pronounce words without pictorial aides. We have a very accurate Torah because the scribes write each page perfectly from letter to letter, and word to word without any mistakes. If a mistake is made on a page, the whole page must be painstakingly rewritten." He began to pace a little as he spoke. "The Torah is our Holy Book and there is no room for error in the Holy Words of God. The songs of the Tabernacle are part of the Holy Book in our tradition. We are known throughout the world as *The people of the Book*. We have been given the responsibility of preserving the Holy Word." The two women looked at each other with serious expressions. "But this is not just any book," Zadok continued. "It is the *only* book in the eyes of God. Besides bringing forth the Messiah, it is the most important mission in our Lord's time. Kings and queens will come and go, but the Word of God will live on. Chronicles of our kings will be written and preserved for future generations to learn from by our scribes. What comes from our tabernacle and our throne is changing history."

Again, Shulamit and Shira looked at one another, this time with a deep fear of God. This was no longer just about them being given opportunity to learn to read and write. This was about something much greater than themselves. As they each considered what they heard within their hearts, they realized their desire to read was something put within their hearts from God. It came from their deep love for worship. Deep joy resonated in Shulamit's heart as this reaffirming insight came. Her desire was from God and showed from the wide smile that spread upon her face.

Zadok recognized Shulamit's smile and what it meant. "Yes, Shulamit," he glanced from one to the other, "and Shira, there is a great joy when you realize that something you have dreamed of doing all your life has actually been put in your heart from God. It is wonderful to know that you are moving in the will of God. It signifies that God himself will be with you and bless you as He quickens your heart to perform His will."

Shulamit felt a pure peace move within her spirit, a knowing of God's approval.

"Now, here is some papyrus paper, and small clay pots with reeds and ink. Choose a reed pen out of one pot, and dip it in the smaller pot with ink, and we will begin the practice of writing a few letters. The first letter is *Aleph*. It means ox head, power, authority, strength, Eternal God, and beginning. Once you master the strokes of *Aleph* the other letters will be easier. Go to the right top corner of the page and we will write the letter from the top down. Now watch the strokes that I make."

Shulamit dipped the reed pen into the ink and was exhilarated as she looked at her first letter. "Very good ladies," Zadok commented as he looked over their work. "Now write that letter across the row a few times until you feel confident with it. Writing takes practice." They concentrated intently on their writing and after a space of time, Zadok had to break the intensity to move on to the next letter.

"You can practice this more on your own but now we will learn *Beit*. This letter is easier to write. *Beit* means house. Together the two letters, *Aleph* and *Beit* mean the strong man of the house," Zadok commented as he showed them the strokes. "Now practice a few rows of this letter."

Silence dropped in the room again as the ladies gave their full attention to the movements of their hands. They were startled when Zadok roused them from their captivation. "Now, ladies, you know two letters, let's write a word. Go to a new row and write the letter *aleph*. He demonstrated this on his paper. Now write the letter *beit* two times, and another *aleph*: *aleph*, *beit*, *beit*, and *aleph*. I will show you the vowels at another time, but you have just written the word *Abba*.

Shulamit and Shira were delighted at writing their first word as they held their papers up in front of themselves. Shulamit simplified writing in her mind, "Letters are just symbols for sounds," she said, "and together they make words."

"Yes, and it is easy to recognize *YHWH* because we are familiar with the word, but it carries deeper symbolism. If you take the meaning of the letters, you realize that the strong man of the house is *Abba*. Our eternal God is the strong man of the house of Israel. The Hebrew alphabet is much more than letters and sounds. When you learn it, you also gain a deeper understanding of God." Zadok turned to the letters on the wall. "Each letter also has a number, and each number has a meaning. I haven't taught you the vowel sounds yet, but we will wait until we can read and write the letters of the alphabet." Shira and Shulamit were once again overcome with the joy of learning. "This will be the end of our lesson for today," Zadok said. "You have done very well. I have never seen such dedicated students."

The ladies were looking over their writing when they received a surprise visit by Solomon. He commented, "I told you they would be good pupils. Let me see what you have written."

Surprised and shy to show her work, Shulamit held up her paper to Solomon. He gave a large approval. "You ladies, with your delicate hands, are more precise than most men who write, and perhaps even some of the scribes. Rarely do you see such well written letters on the first attempts."

Both Shulamit and Shira's faces lit up. *What could be better than the king's approval? The king is the strong man over the house of Israel?* Shulamit thought.

"Bring your papers. Let us go to my chamber and celebrate."

As they walked down the hall, Shira began to sing, "*Aleph and Beit, and gimmel and dalet; Hey and Vav and Zayin.*" She looked over at Shulamit for help remembering the letters.

Shulamit sang, "*Chet, and Tet, and Yad, and Kaf.*"

Together they sang, "*Lamed, Mem, Nun and Samekh.*" They started to stutter when Solomon and Zadok helped them out with, "*Ayin and Pey, Fey and Tsade, Qof, and Resh, Shin, Sin, and Tov.*"

"We are getting it Shira, our alphabet song," Shulamit rejoiced.

When they got to Solomon's chambers, Shira played the harp and Shulamit picked up the tambourine to beat out the rhythm. Solomon and Zadok helped them remember the letters. Soon they could remember the whole alphabet. They made the rhythm fit and had a song. The laughter rang out again.

Solomon said to the High Priest, "I told you my Shulamit always makes me laugh."

The servants brought wine and food. Zadok blessed the wine, and they sang the song again. Solomon was happy to see Shulamit making friends and feeling at ease in the palace. He could also see that, with Shira and Shulamit together as women worshipping in the palace, the tabernacle would come to an all-time high for the women. He hoped his other wives would join in. Unity always made Solomon's heart rejoice.

After dinner, Zadok and Shira left. Solomon offered to walk Shulamit back to her chamber, but first he took a detour. "There is still light out, so I want to show you the palace garden. I bring extended family, leaders in our government, as well as foreign dignitaries here."

"I look forward to seeing it."

As the two walked through the arched entrance into the garden, Shulamit noted how exotic and masterfully created it was. Four walkways led to a center fountain with fruit trees lining the walkway. They walked past rows of trees with ripe apples and olives and dates. Solomon took her hand and led her to where some orange trees were beginning to bloom.

"I love the smell of fresh blossoms on a tree," she said as she picked a blossom and held it to her nose."

Solomon and Shulamit walked past the growing fig and pomegranate trees. They were just out of season and starting to lose their leaves, but the evergreen large pine, cedar, fir, and cypress trees were scattered throughout the garden, filling in the green. Solomon led her over to whether sweet smells from rows of roses and lily of the valley permeated the air. He picked a rose and placed it in her hair over her ear. "A woman's beauty is always enhanced with flowers."

Shulamit smiled at his loving gesture.

The garden was also enriched with the musky and spicy scents of spikenard, calamus, pepper, and turmeric and more. Solomon saw her delight in all the smells. "A garden must be known for its beauty in sight and smell. That is what nature gives us, and I put that in the design of my gardens."

"It is amazing!" Shulamit couldn't say more. Once again, she was feeling overwhelmed.

"I have arranged the plants in order of those that needed sun or shade, wet soil, or drainage," Solomon explained as they came closer to the center fountain. He named several plants and how they grew best. "Some of the plants I am growing here in Jerusalem are an experiment. I do not know if they will thrive here. But if not, I will see if they will grow in other places in Israel."

"It reminds me of how my father would experiment with growing different kinds of grape vines in the mountains. Not all of them thrived, but the ones that did made some of the best wine."

In the East corner of the garden was a tower with hyssop growing up the sides of the high walls. Solomon saw her looking at it and said, "I will take you up to the top of that tower after we are married. That is my secret place. There I have many pots of seed plants I am experimenting with. It is a quiet place where I can relax and study the nature of my plants, and other things. Only a few people know about it. So, it will be another secret between you and me."

"I am fascinated by your love of gardens and knowledge of how all the plants grow best. I always loved working in our garden at home."

"We were meant to live in a garden, so until we get back to our garden in Heaven, I am doing the best I can to bring it here."

They walked over to a bench near the fountain and sat down. Solomon saw Shulamit had a far-off look in her eyes. It was that special look on her face, the one that first captivated him. "Are you dreaming again?"

"Yes, I guess. I didn't realize it. I was thinking that after I know how to read and write, I am going to write about all these beautiful plants and scents in our story to describe our love. I want to share our joy."

"I will read your story and write a song from it."

"A song to our story," she laughed, "I would love that."

"Are you going to share what the Lord spoke to you when you worshipped at the ark in the tabernacle?"

"You want to know, Solomon?"

"I want to know everything about you. You really don't need to tell the secret between you and God to the world, but I am betrothed to you."

"Ok, I will tell you. But don't laugh," she sighed.

"You are funny, my bride, but I won't laugh at anything coming from deep within your heart."

"He told me, 'You are *my* queen, I have chosen you.'"

Now it was Solomon's turn to be serious. "I thought *I* chose you. But if God chose you for me, that is even better." Solomon looked deep into her eyes, feeling within himself a deep fear of God, and said, "And so you are, my chosen bride. I know there will never be another you. You are the song of my heart."

"You are the song of mine, I think," Shulamit said, smiling.

Solomon laughed, "You are fun getting to know. There is so much to you." He paused for a moment to ask, "Am I making your dreams come true?"

Shulamit bowed her head. "Solomon, you are my dream. I am realizing that the more I know you."

"I will not awaken love until it is ready, but I thank God that your love is beginning to awaken. You cannot know how much I long to make you mine entirely."

They sat by the fountain for a few moments in silence before Solomon said, "The sun is almost down. Let me walk you back to your chambers. Tomorrow is Sabbath Eve, and there are things I wish to do. I want to show you more of the palace and introduce you to my other brides." Shulamit looked curiously at him. "Always remember, you are my chosen bride above all. Even my mother chooses you. You bring more joy to my heart than I think I have ever known. Our journey is delightful."

"Yes. *Delightful*," Shulamit replied.

15 THE GROWING RELATIONSHIP

Solomon was always full of surprises. One morning he showed up unannounced, just after she had been dressed. He came with a servant carrying a large, covered gold tray. Meliba led the king and Shulamit to the low cedar table on the plush carpets of the antechamber. The servant took the lid off the tray and gently placed the contents of the tray on the table while Shulamit eyed the contents with amazement. With silent efficiency, the servant set a blue cup designed with gold lions and gold trim in front of Solomon as he sat down. Then she set a red cup with designs of golden crowns and a gold handle in front of Shulamit, who looked at Solomon and smiled. Not wanting to break the delicate vessel, Shulamit picked up the cup and turned it around in her hand admiring the handiwork. Solomon was delighted to see how pleased she was. The servant continued to set gold vessels on the table. Shulamit smelled cinnamon in the bread as the aroma wafted from one of the covered platters. Solomon smiled again as he saw the expression of anticipation and joy on his Shulamit's face.

Finally, the servant picked a gold jug of pottery with blue flower designs from the tray. She poured a dark liquid into the decorated cups. This fresh aroma caught Shulamit's attention anew, and she picked up her cup to take a deep inhalation.

"I have never smelled this kind of tea," she said, fully engaging the deep, roasted scent.

Solomon grinned, "It is not tea. This is a drink called coffee."

He took a deep drink and encouraged her to try it. She tasted it and immediately made a complex expression. Reading her face, Solomon signaled Meliba to come forward, "Pour in a little cream and honey," Solomon suggested. "It will take the bitterness away."

Meliba stepped forward and added a small amount of each to Shulamit's cup. Shulamit tasted it again and said, "This is much better," and smiled at Solomon. "Coffee is quite different from any drink I have ever tasted."

When Shulamit set her coffee mug down on the table, Meliba uncovered the bread platter. She then placed it in front of Shulamit. "Coffee," Solomon said, "is a drink best accompanied with pastry and food, rather than an empty stomach. Try one of the rolls. They are made with cinnamon and honey and walnuts and fresh from the oven. They are a particular favorite of mine"

"Mmm," she said, tasting the food. "This is delicious. I smelled the cinnamon. I have had it before. Papa mixed it in wine once." She smiled at the memory of her father. "He was always trying new things, but cinnamon was a luxury we only enjoyed at festivals."

Solomon was delighted to see her enjoy herself. "Cinnamon originally came from Egypt and the Far East, but now, with open trade, Israel enjoys many things we have not had before. I have found there are some kinds of cinnamon trees that can grow here. The trees add a delightful scent to a garden." He looked at Shulamit with a deepening gaze. "Just like a woman, a garden is about scent as well as beauty."

Shulamit smiled at his hidden compliment. Would she never stop smiling? She prayed not. "Where does coffee come from?" she asked.

"This drink is made from the seeds of fruit that grow on trees. The seeds look like beans. My tradesmen on the merchant ships brought them back from a country called Sheba below Egypt. I would like to try to plant a coffee tree in Israel, perhaps where it is warmer, but I am not sure we get enough rain and moisture for it to grow here. Some things are easier to import."

"I love everything you teach me," Shulamit said as she took another sip of coffee. "Drinking this coffee in these beautiful cups adds to its splendor."

"I like your curiosity about wanting to know where things come from. I will introduce you to my bride who paints them. She loves to paint pottery of all sorts and I encourage her to use her talents. I believe that everyone is always the happiest when they are developing their gifts and using them."

"Wow," Shulamit teased. "So, you are helping me develop my gifts?"

"That is what wisdom is," he said, chuckling. "It is creativity. But it is also developing the understanding and talents within yourself and those around you." Solomon stood up. "'By wisdom, the heavens were created', and God must give me wisdom to build the temple, but I am not building it personally. I teach my team leaders to look for talent amongst the workers and slaves so they can equip them. I choose the most talented people I can find in Israel, Egypt, and surrounding countries," he said, getting bolder. "I am putting them together in teams so that they can use their God-given talents to teach and train more teams of workers under them."

Solomon walked to Shulamit and took her hand. "Come, let us depart. Today I will show you around the palace." He led her from her room, and Shulamit felt as if she weren't even touching the ground. They walked, turning down a long hallway she had not explored before and stopping at a side entrance of the grand throne room. Here she and Solomon sat on chairs behind a see-through curtain, where they would be able to watch the proceedings and not be recognized.

Solomon's brother, Shammuah, was holding court. Two men were arguing over a stolen sheep. One man denied the theft, but there were two witnesses who testified he had stolen the sheep. Shammuah was handed the Torah and read where it said that seven-fold had to be repaid to the man who owned the sheep. The thief tried to protest, but there was more evidence, which proved that he was lying. *There is no argument to be made with laws written by God himself,* Shulamit thought.

Solomon whispered to Shulamit, "Shammuah holds court where the cases are cut and dry by the laws of the land. Most of the time, at least two or three witnesses can verify the truth of the situation. I preside over the more difficult cases where there isn't an answer specifically mentioned in the Torah."

"That is wise," Shulamit said.

"We are a land of laws, otherwise there would be lawlessness, and no one would feel safe or protected. The standard of the written Word gives people something to trust in, so there is always a copy of the Torah by the Throne for reference."

"Yes. That makes sense," Shulamit said. "Very wise indeed."

"A country is united when it has trust in the right place. Wise men come from other countries to observe our laws and gifts of governing."

"Can I come back and listen to the court at other times?"

"Of course, look up towards the balcony above," he said, pointing. "There are lattices the queens can stand behind. From there, they can look down at the court without being observed. You can observe the whole court better from above, but you are welcome to come in this side entrance and sit behind this curtain which is closer to the throne. That way, you can hear better. However, you must always be as quiet as possible."

"I will. I promise," Shulamit said, hoping their conversation wasn't heard.

"Let us go now." He said as he took her hand. "We can discuss more outside."

Shulamit nodded. They left the area behind the curtain and were met by soldiers just outside the throne room. Solomon nodded slightly to them, and he began walking with Shulamit. The guards walked a safe distance behind them, making very little noise. They continued walking down another large hallway. "I am very happy you want to learn to read and write so that you can study the Torah," Solomon said. "Of all my wives, you are the first to ever make such a request. You know our people are not to marry foreigners, but I have married foreign wives who have converted to our faith. They are required to observe our festivals, holidays, New Moons, and to keep our Sabbath. They circumcise their sons, eat our Kosher food, and observe our laws. But to make them hunger to know more and really learn the heart of our Father is not something that can be forced."

"True," replied Shulamit. "Faith is something that must come from the heart. I guess the seeds were planted in my heart in my earliest years. Sabbath evenings are my best childhood memories. Our family united in worship and prayer with my grandpapa or papa teaching from Torah. They prayed blessings over each of us individually and prophesied into our lives. I believed everything they taught me. I believed the words they spoke over me. Perhaps the foreign women need more time to learn of the goodness of God and desire it."

"As I told you before," said Solomon, "I need a bride like you with a heart after God who can be a spiritual leader in my queen's court. Your heart for worship might be what they need to know our Father in Heaven more."

Shulamit looked at him with a very shocked expression on her face. "Me? I'm just learning how to put the right clothes on with the help of my maidservants."

Solomon laughed softly. "You have the right clothes on. You are wrapped in a garment of God's Holiness. The purity of your heart covers you. When I first saw you singing and gathering grapes in the heat of the day, I saw a queen."

"You did?"

"Of course, I did, even then, with your servants singing along with you. Nathan the prophet taught me that when Samuel heard God choosing Jesse's youngest son, David, he said, 'Man looks at outward appearance, but God looks at the heart.' The day I first saw you, I visualized gold chains around your neck and royal robes on your body, but what I really saw was a beautiful woman full of a joyful heart."

Shulamit gazed at Solomon, touched by his words. Solomon spoke as a king directly into her heart and it made her faith in the Holy Father grow even deeper. She wondered if she was all the things he said, or if he was prophesying what she would become. In her dreams, she had always wanted to be like Shira, singing in the Tabernacle. Now she realized God was expanding her dream, giving her new friends, and aligning her in this new call.

"I accept what you are saying Solomon. It is amazing and overwhelming." There were tears in her eyes that she could not hold back. "I always wanted to be like Shira, and I still will be, but in a different way."

"Remember what I said before," said Solomon. "Never limit God in any way. Just keep your heart open to all that He has to give you, and He will keep giving you more and more." He turned to Shulamit, squeezing her hands gently. "As my queen you have only to ask, and I will give you all I can. My heart is yours."

Shulamit beamed with joy at his profession of love. Would she ever get used to the outpouring of constant love? Squeezing his hands, she looked away before the tears of joy came down her face.

Solomon and Shulamit held hands intermittently as they walked. The long hall turned and soon they were near the outer buildings of the palace complex. "Here we have workshops that supply items and services for the palace. Waving her on, Solomon said, "Come." He led her into a room where workers were mixing various distilled resins and spices with oils. Stopping at each person, Solomon introduced them by name. He knew each name without hesitation. Shulamit respected that he cared about his workers and took the time to learn about them and their families.

"I come in here when I want to relax sometimes," Solomon said. "I also experiment with various scents." He picked up a small container of refined olive oil and added some drops of myrrh and Frankincense. He held it up for Shulamit to smell it. Shulamit smiled as she inhaled the sweet, strong odor. "Now, let's give it some spice," he said as he added a drop of cinnamon oil and a few drops of rose oil. He let her smell it again.

"I love it," she said. "This is amazing."

"I am mixing you a special scent, but you can learn to mix your own."

Solomon let her smell many different oils, herbs, and flowers. He introduced Shulamit to Hananiah, the master in charge, who bowed to her as he handed her the small vial of scent Solomon mixed, "Welcome my queen. You may come any time and I will teach you all about the art of making perfume."

"Thank you," she said, "I would love that."

"Come," said Solomon leading her out.

They went to the next workshop, which was for wood working. Many men were busy building tables. chairs, beds, and other items for the palace. Some carved flower designs into the wood. One man sat, polishing a small table that stood off the ground. Nearby were a few chairs that went with it. Solomon led her over to where he was working. "You are doing fine work, Simeon," he said to the young man, who smiled broadly with pride. "Let me introduce you to the beautiful woman who will be using your masterpiece. This is my new bride, your queen, Shulamit."

Shulamit addressed Simeon, "Our king is right," she said. "This table is perfect. It is delightful to meet you, and all of you who labor from your hearts," she said louder, looking around at the other workers, who had stopped working to listen to her. "Thank you all for making this palace such a beautiful place to live in." The workers' spirits perked at her words. Solomon smiled at Shulamit, whose joyful simplicity so easily engaged those she encountered. He guided her out of the workshop so the workers could return to their projects.

As they walked a little farther, they could hear women talking and laughing. Upon entering the next building, the women who were busy sewing and embroidering suddenly stopped their work and stood up and bowed respectfully to Solomon. He acknowledged them and introduced them to their new queen. As they bowed to her, he said, "These are the women who make the curtains for our walls, and the covers for our furniture and litters. They even sew the beautiful dresses, such as the one you are wearing."

Shulamit looked down at her beautiful dress and expressed her deep pleasure with a big smile. "Thank you all so much. I so appreciate the fine work you do."

Solomon summoned Adah, the head seamstress, asking her to bring a dress he had just commissioned especially for his delightful love. Shulamit's eyes lit up as she took hold of the delicate dress with both hands, examining the handiwork. "This is perhaps the most beautiful dress I have ever seen," she said.

"It is designed for dancing," said the head seamstress, "and the lightness of the material will flow out in waves at the slightest move." The women nearby could not help but smile.

The head seamstress continued, "Your king designed the dress for you, my queen. And we were honored to make it."

Shulamit turned to Solomon with joy so full she was almost in tears. "I have never felt so special and loved in my whole life." Many of the women felt happy tears come to their eyes as they saw the joy flowing from the king and his bride. Their love was a contagious delight.

Shulamit thanked all the women again as they walked towards the exit of the workshop. In passing Shulamite took note of the large reams of silk and linen material stacked on various shelves, with containers of all colors of thread. Particularly, Shulamit noted large spools of gold thread such as had been woven into her dress. There were of course many supplies she did not recognize; but she would be sure to ask about at another time.

"I think the women enjoyed seeing your response," Solomon said to Shulamit as they exited; "And saying how you feel so loved."

"I meant every word," she replied.

"You have given them something to rejoice and talk about. Men often like to work in silence, but women can't work without talking and laughing."

"Yes," Shulamit said as she laughed. "We love to share our emotions and talk about love."

"And you will make me extremely happy by wearing that lovely dress this Sabbath evening. On Sabbath with my brides, we always dance." Shulamit did not even care that Solomon mentioned his other wives. "Your dancing is as delightful as Heaven itself," Solomon continued, "and I want everyone to share your joy of dance." She was just so happy at how covered in love she felt.

"I just love to dance," she said, heat rushing to her face. "Being around you makes me want to dance."

"We will dance. But come, I have more things to show you."

They walked past potters, metal workers, launders, and came to the jeweler's workplace. In this shop, the jeweler, named Aholiab, acknowledged the king and, on cue, brought a ring up to Solomon. Solomon took the ring and placed it on Shulamit's right ring finger. It was a large, sparkling clear stone embedded in intricately designed gold. Shulamit stared at it for a long time, turning her hand round and round to see how the light moved through and reflected off the beautiful stone.

"This is amazing," she said.

"Yes," Solomon said. "It is one of a kind, made for a queen." He took her hand and smiled. He was right, it suited her perfectly. "It's a diamond. My merchant brought this rare stone from the lands below Egypt. Diamonds are mined deep underground and skilled workmen from the East know how to cut and polish these stones. It is a very hard substance. I am studying its properties and plan to send men down on my merchant ships to mine more of this." He squeezed her hand. "As you wear this stone, everyone will know how special you are to me."

"Thank you so much for the ring," Shulamit said. She kept staring at it and shifting her hand. "The ring is majestic, but you're telling me how special I am means more to me. I think I am beginning to like it that you are a king."

"Awe, my bride is awakening," he said, smiling.

Shulamit smiled in return. Solomon was right. She was beginning to accept that he was not the shepherd she fell in love with, but something much more. She was entering a dream bigger than she had ever dreamed. And even more, it was happening right before her very eyes. Yes, her eyes were awakening to something wonderfully new. "I hope I can become a queen worthy of you."

"My sweet Shula. *Shula, Shula, Shula.*" He had never used this nickname before. Shulamit's face grew even hotter. A name used three times in their culture put emphasis on its importance. "You are worthy because I, the king, say you are worthy," said Solomon. "I am watching you step into the role of a queen, even today. It was evident by your gracious interaction with the servants of the palace. They were all delighted in you. I know you are concerned about meeting other queens, but you are the most beautiful rose of the field, and all others are thorns compared to you." Shulamit started to speak but quieted herself. "Just be yourself," he said, taking her diamond-ringed hand again. "Remember, God chose you."

They looked at each other for a long moment before Solomon turned, letting go of her hand.

"Believe it or not," Solomon admitted, "sometimes I doubt myself, and then I remind myself that it wasn't just my father King David who chose me. God chose me too. That brings me confidence. You will be a fine queen. Now I am going to take you back to your chamber so you can rest and put on that pretty dress for tonight."

16 DANCING SABBATH

Solomon's eyes lit up at the sight of his beautiful bride when he arrived to escort her to her first Sabbath evening in the palace. "You look beautiful," he exclaimed. Shulamit twirled around in her white dress. As she did, it flowed out around her like a flower opening petals in the wind. Solomon laughed, acknowledging that his new bride would forever be unpredictable. He stepped forward, surprising himself a bit, and took her hand. Laughing, he twirled her around several times. Joy flowed out of them both. Solomon stopped a moment to take note of the other details of his bride. Gently touching the light rows of gold as they grew in a semi-circle around her neck, he said, "This is how I visualized you when I first saw you—adorned with gold chains. It thrills my heart to see it now." Shulamit smiled at the idea. She was a real woman stepping out of her beloved's dream. *What other dreams does he have of me,* she thought.

Shulamit put on a delicately designed veil that covered her head and was held in place by a thin circlet. The veil highlighted her wavy long black hair as it cascaded down her back. Well-manicured hands and henna tinted nails set off her diamond ring. She wore gold bands on her wrists, and long dangling earrings offset her beautiful face. Solomon took in every detail of his beautiful bride, even the fact that she wore no makeup except a touch of red on her lips. He smiled then grabbed her hand and, like children at play, led her in a light skipping step down the hallway towards the woman's court.

Despite her lightheartedness, Shulamit felt slight trepidation as they neared the entrance of the court. She was simply too unsure of what she was walking into.

The thought of encountering real princesses who grew up in royal courts made her feel anxious. *How will they receive me? She thought. I am a simple country girl. I know this is my new home, and I want to belong. I want them to like me, and I want to be a blessing to my beloved king.* "Help me, *Abba*," Shulamite prayed under her breath as she looked down at the dazzling reflections from her diamond ring.

Solomon read her thoughts. "Trust me, my love. I know how to present you to the world. My other brides and ladies of the court will honor and respect you. You will be just fine. Remember what I said last night about just being your sweet self."

Shulamit wanted to believe him, but wise as he was, he wasn't a woman.

As the sun was descending, music could be heard coming from the women's dining court. The smell of rose, jasmine, and sandalwood incense, along with freshly baked bread, permeated the air. The women were all engaged in conversation and joyfully greeting the Sabbath.

The king entered the room with Shulamit. The priests, who were playing music, lowered the volume but continued playing in the background. She held Solomon's hand and stepped onto the polished marble floors as the court rose to greet them both. For a moment, Shulamit's mind almost went blank as she felt everyone's stares upon her. Solomon signaled the ladies of the court to be seated, which eased her tension, but only somewhat. She would have hidden her ring, but Solomon grasped that hand and displayed it as he led her across the floor. She thought she sensed jealousy for a moment, and she tried to put it out of her mind.

Instead, Shulamit took in the décor of the room. The polished marble floor was partially covered with several layers of thick, intricately designed carpets. They must have come from the Orient. Long tables were covered with gold cloths, weighed down by large candelabras in each table's center. The tables encircled the room with everyone facing inward, and the ladies sat comfortably or reclined on large decorative cushions surrounding the tables. There was a large open area for dancing in the middle of the room. Brass braziers lined the room's walls burning coals, keeping the atmosphere at a pleasant temperature on the otherwise chilly late fall evening in Jerusalem.

Solomon, continuing to hold Shulamit's hand, glanced first at her and then at the women.

"This is the heart of my kingdom," he announced." He proceeded to walk Shulamit around the room and introduce her to his queens.

"This is Gevira," he said. "This is the bride I promised to introduce you to who painted the beautiful vases and the cups we drank from."

"Oh, it is so wonderful to meet a lady of such accomplished talent," Shulamit said. "When I drank out of the red cup with crowns on it, I felt quite royal."

Sitting next to Gevira was another lady of the court. "This is Gevira's counterpart Malkah. She decorated all the tables you see here. She knows how to choose the right goblets, cups, platters, napkins, and flower arrangements that turn our meals into banquets."

"What a wonderful gift," Shulamit said as she bent down and gave her a hug. "I hope to learn from you, the art of the banquet." Malkah smiled back. She felt honored to be *artist of the banquet.*

Solomon walked down to the next table where another beautiful lady with flowers tastefully enhanced her pulled-up tresses. "May I introduce you to Kerem. She is our outstanding flower arranger. Many of the large pottery around the palace contain her flower arrangements. She can work wonders with flowers in every possible way, and that includes the beautiful flowers in her hair." Kerem gave a bashful smile to Solomon as he remarked on her flower-styled hair. Shulamit nodded to show her agreement with Solomon.

Rounding the encircled table arrangement, Solomon acknowledged another of his artisan brides. "This is Elisheba. She can take bulrushes, pine, willows, grasses, vines, and plant fibers of all kinds, along with gold threads and create masterpiece baskets to hold items in artful arrangements, including the flowers that Kerem arranges.

Shulamit stooped to hug her too. "I used to weave baskets while watching the sheep on the hills with my friends and family, but none as beautiful as yours. I would like to learn your techniques."

"It would be my honor," Elisheba humbly responded.

Solomon continued introducing Shulamit to the women of the court. Each responded graciously, making her feel welcome. Soon enough they came to the last table. "Let me introduce you to another of our talented artisans. This is Ilana. She is a very gifted weaver and embroiderer. She is responsible for many of the woven pictures on the palace walls and teaches my other brides. I love to display the work of their hands. I love beauty of all kinds. Royalty and beauty go hand in hand."

"So pleased to meet you," Shulamit responded. She was starting to feel overwhelmed by not just the beauty of these brides, but their excellent talents. She did her best to hide her anxiety.

But Shulamit was not blind to the fact that these women were staring at her. She could feel them eyeing every part of what she was wearing, her hair, her hands. She felt the envy from some who saw her ring. She sensed they coveted the adoration the king gave her, comparing her to themselves and wondering what makes the king attracted to this woman from the country?

Shulamit did not wish to compete with them. She just wished to be their friends in her new home., but she was still not fully aware of what it meant to marry a man with other wives. She tried to focus on loving Solomon and honoring this new life. She was blessed to be here, where she could worship and become a blessing to God and her country. The idea of such glory was something of a buffer to the jealousies she sensed in the woman's court.

After introducing his new bride to his wives, Solomon led her to a slightly elevated seating area. Everyone could see their table. It had cedar high backed chairs inlaid with red, gold, and purple striped cushions. This king's table had the same ornamentation as the others, along with a Kiddush goblet designed with a lion. As they approached, servants pulled chairs for them, per protocol of the court. Solomon held to the protocol in the seating arrangements as they weren't sitting alone at the table. A few of the women, pregnant or holding babies, were given higher honor by sitting closer to the king.

Bathsheba arrived at the main entrance.

The Queen Mother's entry signaled the servants to light the Sabbath candles as Bathsheba took her place at the head table on Solomon's right side. Solomon gesture for Shulamit to sit at his left, which was a sign of special honor. When Shulamit sat, Solomon held up his hands to silence the room. The ceremonial acts were about to begin.

Bathsheba covered her head with a delicate lace scarf. She lit the Shabbat candles at the head table and circled her hands over them three times. Bathsheba led the song, and the court joined in chanting as appointed ladies lit their candles at each table.

She sang:

> *Barukh atah Adonai,*
> *Eloheinu,*
> *meleck ha'olam*
> *asher kidishanu*
> *b'mitz'votav*
> *v'tzanu l'had'lik neir shel Shabbat.*
> *Amen*
> *(They blessed the Lord of the Universe who created light and commanded them to light the lights of the Sabbath.)*

Solomon stood up when the song was done and asked, "And why do we have the other two candles?" He knew the answer but asked to get the reply.

"Blessed be our king," the queen to Bathsheba's right stood up and said, "The Lord has given him a son."

Solomon stood up to honor her as he held out his hands. "Let me hold my new prince," he said, smiling. The happy mother presented her joyful bundle wrapped in a blue blanket with gold trim. Solomon picked up his son with utter delight and kissed him on his forehead several times. The baby boy wrapped his hand around Solomon's forefinger, and Solomon said, "My child is a strong, healthy baby."

The king held his baby up in his hands above his head and blessed him, "May you be like Ephraim and Manasseh. May God bless you and protect you. May God show his favor and be gracious to you. May God show you kindness and grant you peace." He held the baby to his chest for a moment and then handed the child back to his mother, giving her an affectionate hug. With a wave of his arm, Solomon called a servant who carried a pillow. On it was an intricately decorated circlet crown with a central red ruby encircled by smaller gems. Solomon picked it up and put it on his wife's head. He declared, "Bless my queen as a mother in Israel; fill her heart with joy as she cares for her new son."

Bathsheba whispered into Shulamit's ear so that she would understand the significance of what was happening. "When a bride has a baby, she is honored with a crown because now she is acknowledged as a queen."

"No longer just a lady of the court?" Shulamit said.

"Correct," replied Bathsheba.

Solomon turned to the bride on the other side of Shulamit, putting his hand on her belly. Smiling, he blessed the baby growing in her womb. Her face lit up with a brightness that only a woman pregnant with new birth can give.

Solomon said, "Bring me my harp. This calls for a special song of thanks. Once he received his instrument, Solomon began to sing:

> *Lo, children are a heritage from the Lord,*
> *The fruit of the womb is a reward;*
> *Like arrows in the hand of a warrior,*
> *So are the children of one's youth.*
> *Happy is the man who has his quiver full of them*
> *My wife shall be a fruitful vine,*
> *In the very heart of my house,*
> *My children like olive plants all around my table*
> *Lo, children are a heritage from the Lord.*
> *Blessed is the man who fears the Lord."*

Solomon put down the harp and said, "Little children belong to the Kingdom of Heaven. The king is blessed by his children."

As if on cue, other mothers began to bring forward their sons, and one by one, Solomon walked down the line and blessed them all. Each mother expressed her joy as Solomon blessed their dark, curly-haired sons.

While Solomon was blessing his children, a thought popped into Shulamit's mind, *"You will have a daughter."*

She almost dismissed the idea. *"Where did that thought come from?"* she wondered.

After blessing his sons, Solomon walked back to the head table. He held up the golden kiddush cup full of wine. Servants quickly went around the tables, pouring wine into everyone's cups. Solomon led the chamber with his strong voice as he blessed the sovereign God of the universe who created the fruit of the vine:

> *Baruck atah Adonai*
> *Eloheinu*
> *Melekh ha-olam*

borei p'ri hagfen (Amen),"

When Solomon sat down, the servants brought bowls and poured pitchers of water over everyone's hands in a ceremonial act of handwashing. As they did this, everyone sang a song blessing the Source of Life and the Holy Commandments. They dried their hands and sat down in silence as they awaited the blessing of the bread. A servant brought forth a large gold platter that displayed an elegant cloth embroidered with grapes and pomegranates which covered the braided challah bread.

Solomon now asked Shulamit to bless the bread.

Trying to hide her surprise, Shulamit removed the covering over the large platter of bread and belted out in her strong soprano voice, "Blessed are Thou, Lord our God, King of the universe, who brings forth bread from the earth, amen." Her voice was so strong that it easily carried across the whole room.

She then broke off a piece of bread from the challah and passed the plate around. The platter of challah bread went throughout all the tables. As it passed them, everyone broke off a piece. All the while, the music continued quietly in the background. Some hummed along with the sweet solemn melodies.

After the court partook the bread, Solomon signaled for the servants to bring forth the evening meal.

Meals were not hurried occasions in this culture, especially on the evening of the Sabbath. This special evening of the week was the joyful gathering of the families in Israel, and here it was wives and children around their king. Large festive dishes of chicken and kugel, noodles, grated potatoes and onions, and kibbeh (a lamb casserole with onions and bulger) were placed on the table. More courses came as the platters were emptied.

Laughter and talking infused the joyful meal. Mothers nursed their babies at the tables, and servants stood by to assist the younger mothers with fussy babies.

Solomon dipped a piece of bread into the kibbeh and grasped a large piece of lamb within it. He held it up to Shulamit's mouth. She was surprised, but accepted the food gracefully, delighting in its deliciousness.

Solomon poured wine. Shulamit noticed the bride beside her did not wish to drink wine nor eat much of her food. She whispered to Solomon that perhaps he should ask the servants to get her some milk. Solomon looked over to his queen to be with concern and asked a servant to bring her milk.

As the bride beside her gladly drank the milk, Shulamit said, "When my mama held my little sister within her, she sent me out every morning to milk the goats and bring her fresh milk. Papa said I had to look after Mama while he was away, and I learned what she desired to eat: cheese, curd, and bread, and lots of milk. If you have any questions about what to eat or need someone to help you when your baby is due, you can ask me. I helped my mother deliver fifteen babies, including hers."

"That is very kind of you. My name is Nikkal."

"Your accent is like one of my maidens, are you from Tyre or Sidon?"

"I am Hiram's daughter from Tyre."

"I am Shulamit, so happy to know you. We shall be friends." Shulamit knew that knowing someone's name in their culture was to tell that person something about who they were.

She tried to hide her surprise. Shulamit knew Hiram was the king of Tyre in Lebanon who traded with Israel and sent the timber to build the temple and the palace, she was living in. He had been a friend of David's and was now a friend of Solomon.

Shulamit was quick to discern people's origin, he noted. It was just as when she first met him and told him that he sang just like she imagined King David had sung. She was hard to fool, but again, he realized it was a useful gift to have in a queen when visiting dignitaries would come. He could depend upon his wife to help him discern various details when they visited his kingdom. He continued to be surprised at how his simple vineyard bride could ingratiate others. Solomon could see *Elohim* at work in his young bride's life.

Solomon, the wise, would always have something special to share with his ladies of the court. And they all looked forward to that wisdom or songs he would share. Now, he was going to introduce her officially and give her, the grand entrance into the reign of queens.

Solomon stood up and said, "Keep eating my brides, and while you eat, I will sing you a song of my Vineyard Queen:"

> *I heard a sweet song in the distance*
> *Calling out to me*
> *It is the song of the Vineyard Queen*
> *Singing joyfully*

> *Tall and stately like a Palm Tree*
> *Dancing delightfully*
> *Bearing a basket of grapes on her head*
> *Working cheerfully*

> *She carried herself with strength*
> *Intimidating me*
> *I sent my friend to inquire*
> *Of possibility*

"This maiden has many suitors"
He relayed to me
She is waiting for the right one
My thoughts were, "It's me"

I approached her with trepidation
She stood eye-catching and bold
Like a filly amongst Pharaoh's Chariots
I saw a queen wearing gold

When she saw me, her smile was inviting
I was lost within her glance
We both knew in that moment
As we began to dance

We danced and we couldn't stop dancing
And we are dancing now
Though I am a king with a kingdom
To my Vineyard Queen, I bow

Before any queen could feel less loved, Solomon proclaimed, "Queens of my court, I bow to you all. You are all deeply loved, but tonight, I introduce you to a worshipper. We are a country of worshippers, and our history goes back a long way. My father, King David, taught me to worship from when I was a child, and my happiest days were worshipping with him and my mother," he said as he made an honorable gesture with his hand toward his mother. "Just as we have done in the tabernacle, we shall continue to have worship all hours of the day and night in the new temple. My father, David, our recent king, saw in a vision of heaven when he got the temple's blueprints. The praise in Heaven never stops. Our Lord, *Elohim*, pours out His glory as He inhabits the praises of His people.

"Within our Holy Torah, there are many women worshippers, and tonight I wish to introduce you to the first woman worshipper in our history—Miriam, the sister of Moses. Miriam was about seven years older than Moses, and she was also a prophetess. When her mother was with child, Miriam prophesied. Miriam proclaimed that her mother would give birth to the child who would be the Israelite leader. That leader would bring about the Hebrew's redemption from slavery in Egypt.

"As history tells us, when the pharaoh, Ramses II, became distressed by the growing number of Hebrews, he ordered all the male babies of Hebrew slaves to be drowned in the river. Jochebed, Moses's mother, could only hide him for three months. In a desperate attempt to save her baby's life, she wove a papyrus basket for him and put Moses in it. Miriam, Moses's older sister, was only seven years old when she placed Moses in the Nile River and followed the basket, watching over her brother. She guided the floating basket down the river and hid in the bulrushes until the Pharaoh's daughter found him.

"Miriam then approached the Pharaoh's daughter and offered to find a nursemaid for the baby. So Jochebed was able to nurse her own baby and instill some Jewish heritage into him before the Pharaoh's daughter raised Moses as her own. Even at a young age, Miriam demonstrated her role as a leader with boldness, courage, strength, and ingenuity.

"Later in the history of the Israelite deliverance, we come to the Red Sea. The Pharaoh's army was chasing them, and they look doomed, but Moses stretched out his hand over the sea and the Lord caused the sea to go back by a strong east wind all that night. The waters were divided, so the children of Israel walked through the midst of the sea as on dry land. When all the children of Israel were safely through the waters, the Lord told Moses to stretch out his hand over the sea again. When he did, the waters drew back, and all of Pharaoh's army was drowned in the Sea."

Solomon looked over to the musicians to see that Asaph, his daughter Shira and his musicians arrived to play the next song. Solomon continued. "Then, Moses and the children of Israel sang the Song of Moses."

Asaph musicians began to play music as he led the choir began to sing.

I will sing to the Lord
For He has triumphed gloriously
The horse and its rider
He has thrown into the sea!

The Lord is my strength and song
And He has become my salvation;
He is my God, and I will praise Him;
My father's God and I will exalt Him.
The Lord is a man of war;
The Lord is his name

Solomon held his hands up for a pause while he spoke words from the Torah. "Then Miriam the prophetess, the sister of Aaron, took the timbrel in her hand (Shira handed Shulamit a tambourine) and she began to sing and dance."

Shulamit looked at Solomon briefly, and he whispered in her ear, "Sing with Shira and show how Miriam worshipped before the Lord." Shira began to sing the chorus. Shulamit began to sing as she took the tambourine, lifted it over her head, and began leaping circles on the strong beat of each turn with a loud ringing stroke.

Sing to the Lord
For He has triumphed gloriously
The horse and its rider
He has thrown into the sea

Asaph sang the voice of Moses with the male choir.

Pharaoh's chariots and his
Army He has cast in the sea
His chosen captains also are
Drowned in the Red Sea

Solomon held out his hands for a pause again, while a servant brought out several large baskets of timbrels. Solomon began to hand timbrels to his women of the court. Then he spoke words from the Torah again. "And all the women went after her with timbrels and with dances."

Shira sang out the chorus again as the wives began to follow Shulamit in dance:

Sing to the Lord
For He has triumphed gloriously
The horse and its rider
He has thrown into the sea

Shulamit led the women dancers in a larger circle, with each of them following her simple steps. They stepped out, first to the right, raising the timbrel over their head to the right giving it a strong beat, and then to the left, with the second beat of the timbrel. Then they leaped and turned a circle. All the while, they kept the beat while holding the tambourine over their head.

The male singers continued with the verses, and the women both danced and sang the refrain together. Solomon got up and danced center of the circle, twirling around with his hands outstretched majestically as the women of the court danced around him. They danced and laughed until the music slowed down momentarily for the last verse:

You will bring them in and plant them
In the mountain of Your inheritance
In the place, O Lord, which
You have made

For Your own dwelling
The sanctuary, O Lord which
Your hands have
Established
The Lord shall reign forever
Ever
Ever
Ever

The music's quick beat returned at a grand finale as everyone in the room sang while the women danced.

Sing to the Lord
For He has triumphed
Gloriously!
The horse and its rider
He has thrown into the sea!

Catching their breath, Solomon led them in great applause to the Lord, and, full of joy, laughter broke out again. Shulamit was both laughing and stunned at what had just taken place. Solomon had drawn her out, and though she was scared, Heaven had come through gloriously. She thought of the words from her father's song. "When you worship Heaven smiles upon you." Then she recalled the words of the Rabbi long ago—someday her worship would bless Israel. She had forgotten about it, but it seemed to her that it is only when prophecy is forgotten that it happens.

Several of the wives came up to Shulamit and told her how much fun it was, and that they could feel glory as they worshipped with her. Some of them asked, "Will you teach us to dance?" Shira looked over toward Shulamit and gave her a big smile. She and Shira had the bond of true worshippers, understanding how the joy of worship brought people together as nothing else could. Shira's reassuring smile was also a smile of victory, because the women of the court were accepting her. A breakthrough had happened with the dancing, and she had gained some favor. Shulamit responded to the ladies who asked her to teach them to dance with abounding joy, "Nothing would make me happier."

Solomon smiled at Shulamit and asked, "Are you ready to go to the Tabernacle and worship?" Asaph was already leading his musicians in the direction of the Tabernacle. Solomon shouted to his royal wives, "Come, my brides! Let us go and worship in the presence of the Ark of God."

Joyfully they skipped and danced over to the Tabernacle. As the queens took their special place toward the right side, Shulamit was full of joy to be in her favorite place—in the presence of God. It was even more wonderful to enjoy His holy presence amongst the other queens in the congregation. She would have stayed and worshipped all night had Solomon not come and whispered, "My bride, come, let us have some quiet time together as we end this Sabbath Eve. Remember, I promised you the Sabbath, my love."

Shulamit was so surprised at the thoughtfulness of Solomon, remembering all her heart's desires. Her love for the king grew even more. Shulamit's father had always affirmed her as a young woman, but now Solomon made her feel more like a woman coming to life. He took her hand, entwining her fingers with his as they walked back to a garden terrace near his chamber.

"You look so beautiful tonight," Solomon said in a low voice. "Your dancing lit up the room. You are contagious to everyone, but especially to me. Dancing with you tonight reminded me of the first time we met. I knew that I wanted to dance with you for the rest of my life. Did you feel that way?"

"I knew you were the desire of my heart. I dreamed of having someone to worship with. I would not let my heart love someone I could not worship with. Yes, I can dance with you forever. I never imagined the feelings in my heart that opened the day we met. I can't help but dance."

"Aww, my lovely one, I am so happy you are happy. I cannot wait until we are one but I'm giving you time to feel at home here in the palace, and you have only been here a short time. Tonight, the ladies of the court warmed to you through the dance. I was not surprised, but it was even more than I expected." Solomon paused a moment, then said, "I hope you don't mind that I had you lead worship without asking you first, but I knew you would dance more spontaneously if you did not have time to think about it."

"I don't really think about it. I feel it. Remember, both my mother and my sister are named Miriam, so my father taught us that story very well. We sang the song at home. Not exactly like that, but it always stirred up my heart to dance since I was a child. Just to hear about our Lord triumphing gloriously sets my heart into motion."

"Do I set your heart into motion?" Solomon asked.

"I told you, I can dance with you forever," she said in a sigh, as she twirled around.

"I guess I just like to hear you say it."

"Like your song for me about the Vineyard Queen? I shall write you a song too. I fell in love with a shepherd, and I fell in love with a king. You are my Shepherd King. Now all I want to do is dance and sing. How is that?"

Solomon's grin almost made her laugh. "That's a start," he said.

"A start? I look forward to knowing more."

"And you shall, my love, you shall."

17 FIRST DREAM WITH A PROMISE

Every night since her first Sabbath in the Palace, Shulamit went to sleep dreaming of Solomon singing *The Vineyard Queen* to her. She thanked *Elohim* for all his goodness and for Solomon's love. Shulamit prayed to be able to respond to Solomon's love song with one of her own. One morning she woke up from a dream where she was back on the mountain. Shulamit was in her secret place where she first met her shepherd-king. From her dream, song lyrics began flowing into her spirit, and she woke with words and the need to add music.

As the first rays of light came in through the high window in her chamber, she threw on her robe. Bursting with inspiration, Shulamit rushed barefooted into her dayroom to play her melody on the harp.

My shepherd-king plucked his harp
And the mountains begin to sing
Striking my heart like a cymbal
With an uncontrollable ring
Music moved on wings of wind
It was your voice drawing me in

I ran to the sound of your song
I was running after a call
Your voice led me to jump and leap
Like a gazelle over a wall
I sensed a profound mystery
And my heart wanted it all

I closed my eyes to worship
Desiring to take your song in
Your music, your words, your voice
Within me transforming
Feeling deep within my heart
The Presence of a king

The little hills danced for joy
At the voice of my shepherd-king
A window opened to heaven

That made the cymbals ring
Let me hear your voice again
Make my mountain sing

Oh, let me hear your voice again
Make my mountain sing
You make my mountain sing!

Shulamit's maidens were awakened by her voice and begin to sing with her in the dayroom. Shulamit struck the harp and Sheriti picked up the tambourine as she began to dance. Kiba began to sing harmony with Shulamit, her Egyptian accent adding a new beauty to the words.

Shulamit's bond with her maidens was so sweet and meaningful to her. They fulfilled their service with joy, even now, as they made music together.

After the song was over, Shulamit asked, "Do you think Solomon will like this song?"

Meliba replied, "Mistress, if you haven't noticed, our king likes everything you do." They all giggled at this truth. "You give him so much joy. You have conquered the mountain of his heart like no one ever has."

Kiba added, "And certainly the mountain you both stand upon shall sing and inspire all other mountains in this kingdom."

Shulamit pulled both of her maidens into an embrace. "I appreciate your words," she said. "I appreciate all you do for me. You are more than servants. You are friends to me, and if you ever have any need, feel free to come to me." She stood, sighing with contentment at her maidens, her new song, and her life. "I love Solomon, and I want him to feel proud of me. I want to be a good queen. Thank you so much for helping me to be a queen."

They all returned to Shulamit's quarters to dress her for the day. Shulamit wanted to wear something special for the Sabbath worship, something as joyful as her new song for Solomon. She always looked forward to the Sabbath and going to worship in the Tabernacle. There was nothing she loved more. In fact, her first desire *every* morning was to be dressed presentably and go to the Tabernacle to pray and worship.

She loved the way the psalms were expressions of David's emotional honesty. Her parents taught her to pray like David while growing up—by honestly presenting her needs and thanking *Elohim* with belief and hope of his blessing and answers. Since she had met Solomon, she felt so loved; it was as if all her prayers and hopes had come true. Her main prayer now was to ask the Lord to help her be a woman of God that Solomon would be proud of, and to help her learn all the things being taught her. Shulamit had always been a quick learner, but she was definitely challenged now, with so much to process in her new surroundings.

Going to the Tabernacle and the presence of God always helped her find peace. This morning the Levites were singing David's prayer for guidance.

Give ear to my words, O Lord
Consider my meditation
Give heed to the voice of my cry
My King and my God
For to You I will pray

My voice You shall hear in the morning, O Lord
In the morning I will direct it to You
And I will look up…

Shulamit loved this prayer.

David shared his troubles, but he also acknowledged the Lord's help and mercy and the joy of putting trust in the Lord's name. It was so joyful to sing with the Levites, and she couldn't wait to join them. For Shulamit, entering the temple was like taking a breath of fresh air.

As she bowed before the Ark, she also prayed for the Lord's help. She felt great peace coming from the Presence of God. Shulamit leaned into the feeling, and time washed away. It would have been easy for her to stay in the tabernacle all day, but a guard tapped her on the shoulder. At first, she resisted, but only for a moment. She was happy to leave when the guard told her the king was waiting for her.

Shulamit was escorted to Solomon's private garden, seeing a meal being set outside on the grass as she entered. Bathsheba was there, as were Solomon's brothers, Shammuah and Shobab, and their wives. Nathan, his counselor Zabud, the High Priest Zadok and his wife, and a few other high-ranking military officers were in attendance as well.

"It finally stopped raining long enough to eat outside," Solomon said as he joined her. "So, let's enjoy this sunny Sabbath as long as we can."

Shulamit and Solomon smiled at each other, and he escorted her to her seat before blessing the meal. There were sounds of laughter and talk and song in the air. During a quieter moment, Shulamit whispered to Solomon that she had written him a song.

"My bride has written me a song," Solomon said, quieting the conversations to silence. He signaled for a harp to be brought over from the musicians as they played quietly in the background. "Let's hear it."

Shulamit said, looking at him in wonder, "I expected to share this song secretly with Solomon, as a response to his lovely song calling me his Vineyard Queen. But it seems he keeps putting me on the spot, so I will sing it for you too." Shulamit took the harp when it was handed to her. "I wrote it this morning as I woke up after dreaming of the day I met Solomon on Baal Hamon. All of my feelings came flooding back to me, and I felt compelled to preserve them in song."

Shulamit sang her happy tune, and Solomon could not take his eyes off her. It was as if there were no other people in the garden.

But there were.

Love was radiating. The fresh scent of pine stirred the air, along with Solomon's Myrrh and Shulamit's spikenard. No one mentioned it, but everyone felt ringing in their hearts as their eyes watched the sparkle in Shulamit's eyes and the fixation in Solomon's.

Solomon joined Shulamit in the chorus as she sang it a second time, *"Let me hear your voice again, you make my mountain sing, you make my mountain sing."* Everyone sang the chorus a third time. As they sang, a gentle breeze blew through the Cedar trees. Solomon took her hands in his when she finished and put down the harp.

"This is my Vineyard Queen everyone. She makes me sing." He laughed and then added, "I hope this is only the first song of love you write. It is exciting to watch your love awaken like a flower coming into bloom. I can't wait for springtime."

Shulamit smiled, her eyes twinkling in wonder. The joy flooding her heart matched the warmth of the noonday. She felt accepted in the community with Solomon's family and good friends. Shulamit felt the developing bond with Solomon's family almost as a breeze in the garden. It was so affirming and put Shulamit at ease to sing her song, just as if she were at home. Her brothers, who had always teased her growing up, always honored her songs. She was one of those who spoke from the heart and put it to music.

Finally, the evening came, the Sabbath candles were blown out, and everyone returned to their individual quarters.

***

As the weeks passed, Shulamit's days became increasingly busy. The hardest part for her was learning the art of making herself look and dress like a queen. It was so different from her home and the way she did things there.

Every morning, her first desire was to go to the tabernacle, but it wasn't always possible. Two days a week, she went to her class with the Rabbi Azariah, those she enjoyed thoroughly. The High Priest's son was masterful as he taught her and Shira reading and writing. Shulamit practiced often, writing, and rewriting the characters until she had them down to an art. She placed papyrus around her room to help her identify words and associate them with objects. Often, she and Shira got together after their time with Rabbi Azariah to discuss what they learned, which also helped cement the lessons within her.

After their writing, Shulamit and Shira began to practice dancing and singing together. This new schedule became a joy to her. Shira helped her sharpen her skills on the flute, harp, and cymbals. She often brought her harp to join Shulamit by the center fountain. Many other brides met there during the warm part of the day. They engaged with their babies, created crafts, or just relaxed in the sun. Shira would play her harp as the women carried on their work.

One day, Shulamit sat beside Elisheba, who was teaching a few other brides how to weave a basket of reeds. Elisheba smiled and invited Shulamit to join the lesson. Shulamit carefully watched how Elisheba soaked her reeds in the fountain to soften them. Using grasses and gold thread, Elisheba wove the reeds into a large basket for carrying clothing.

"Hold the reed tight like this," Elisheba instructed, taking the thread in a tight grip, "while you weave the gold threads through it.

Shulamit listened and followed her instructions carefully, amazed to see her basket taking shape. "I love this," Shulamit said. "But I will need more practice for mine to be as fine as yours. I thank you for showing me."

Nikkal, also weaving a basket under Elisheba's instruction, smiled in agreement. She commented, "Isn't this fun? We can learn so much from each other." Turning to Shulamit, she asked, "So, when are you going to teach us to dance?"

"Anytime you like," Shulamit almost laughed. "Now, if you like. Shira is here to play music."

Elisheba jumped up, leaving her basket incomplete. "Let's dance! It is a good time to give our hands a break."

Shira began to play a happy psalm about King David lifting his hands while he praised. She sang, *"So I will bless you as long as I live, in your name, I will lift up my hands."*

Gevira walked away from her painting, and Ilana put down her embroidering to join them. They were soon joined by a few other ladies.

"I have no real way to teach worship." Shulamit said, "It is something that must engage the soul, or it has no meaning. So, let us first start by listening to the music to catch its rhythm." They were happy to try, listening to Shira's beautiful playing. A few closed their eyes. "Try to listen to the lyrics and really begin to feel the song," said Shulamit. "I admit, sometimes it can take a few minutes to feel like moving. I close my eyes and just listen, as some of you are doing." As she said this, Shulamit closed her eyes and began swaying to the music. "This song has a sweet melody for praise," she almost sighed. "Can you picture King David giving praise to *Elohim*?" She opened her eyes and looked around. The women were staring at her in rapt attention. "When I think about it, I see him raising his arms up like this." Shulamit began lifting her arms up and out into a V-shape form.

The ladies of the court lifted their arms out wide toward Heaven, imitating her.

"Now, let us form a circle, looking inward to each other. Imagine our Father, *Elohim*, in the center of the circle. Imagine He is smiling at each of us." She paused as they formed a circle. "We dance in a circle because we are sisters, and dancing brings us into equality and unity. We are the circle of eternity that has no beginning or end." Shulamit paused a moment so Shira could play a musical interlude. Then she said, "Now, bring down your arms, and we will step to the right facing inward. Right together, right together, right together, and then we will go the other way. Left together, left together, left together." Shulamit smiled at how quickly the ladies were learning. "Wonderful. Now release hands as you turn to the right. Walk in step to the rhythm of the music." She corrected one of the ladies, saying, "Stay behind the person in front of you. That's it. Right, left, right, left." They took several steps until the song's words returned, *'I will lift up my hands in your name.'*

"Now we can end," Shulamit said, "by raising our hands upward and outward toward Heaven. Turn toward the center, as at the beginning." They all laughed with joy as they finished the song. "I think that was easier than weaving and embroidering," she blurted out, "At least for me anyway."

"Can we practice some more tomorrow?" asked Ilana.

"Certainly," said Shulamit. "Nothing would bring me more joy than worshipping with you!"

As the days went on, Shulamit taught the ladies about prayer dances. Some included kneeling; others jumping and spinning for joy; some called for leaping and skipping; some were simply holding arms outstretched in surrender. Shulamit and Shira invited the priest to join them at the garden from time to time. When he did, he taught the women about King David and his struggles as he wrote the Psalms. Many ladies came to hear the priest teach, and others came just to dance. There was a change to the dance as each woman learned. As they began to understand and enjoy the feeling of God's presence, it seemed to bring more joy and anointing in their worship. Shulamit sensed the transformation of the ladies as they stopped merely dancing and began true worship. She and Shira would look at each other in wonder and amazement. *"What is this?"* Shulamit sometimes thought.

The favor of God came upon the group of women. Soon, more palace women joined her in worship. In time there was a core group of worshippers regularly praising *Elohim* in the garden. Happiness filled the atmosphere as they bonded in worship, and Shulamit began to feel more at home with her new sisters.

***

Over time, Shulamit learned her way around the palace and began to go more places on her own. She even watched Solomon conduct court from time to time. Her growing awareness of Solomon's wisdom created a hunger in her to want more divine wisdom in her life. Every little thing he shared with her was fascinating. Solomon overflowed with the knowledge of so many things and Shulamit desired to take it all in. Bathsheba often visited with her and took the opportunity to show Shulamit around as well, which was a great blessing. The day the two visited the kitchen was a special memory of Shulamit's.

Bathsheba announced, as they arrived at the door, "This is the belly of the whole palace."

She introduced Shulamit to the master chef, Shilshah, and the chief in charge of supplies, named Ashvah. You may ask Ashvah for anything," Bathsheba said, "and he will give it to you. We often bring our own yeast starter dough and have the kitchen aides mix in flour to make bread for us."

"You make bread?" Shulamit asked of the Queen Mother. Bathsheba nodded with a great smile. Shulamit looked over to the huge ovens on one side of the room. There, bread was baking along with meats on rotisserie. She could smell the large pots of cut meat boiling over the stoves. The walk-in pantries had a heady aroma of spices, dried foods and grains, and piles of fresh fruits and vegetables stacked with great organization. It made her hungry, but she didn't know where to start.

Bathsheba saw her wonder and replied, "The fresh items are delivered to the palace daily."

"It is like a marketplace."

"Yes," said Bathsheba. "You are quite right."

Shilshah, reached over to one of the many pastries and gave them each a small sample. Shulamit's mouth was blessed by such flavor, and she smiled, showing her great delight.

"Every tribe has its gift, and Solomon brings only the best to the palace," Bathsheba said. He is from the tribe of Asher. Shilshah beamed with pride as the queen mother continued, "Most of our cooks in the palace are from that tribe. It certainly fulfills the prophecy Jacob gave many years ago. 'Bread from Asher shall be rich, and he shall yield royal dainties.'"

"I would like to come and learn how to make such dainties. I could teach my mother what I learn here. She loves to display her cooking at the festivals."

"You might be able to charm him," Bathsheba said. "But these chefs like to keep their family secrets to themselves. They have a code of honor they call their royalties, and even in the royal family, we must respect that." Shulamit was almost ashamed of asking, but Bathsheba smiled at her, removing her concern. "Solomon honors the rights of creativity, and he wants each man's labor to be properly rewarded. It would be a great honor to have such a gift to share with your mother."

"I would tell my mother to honor the tribe of Asher for anything she learns from their gifting."

"You are funny, my daughter, but that sounds like a good idea. Always give proper honor to people and they will be much happier. Solomon calls creativity wisdom and encourages people to use their creativity."

"Solomon's wisdom makes our kingdom great."

"We are a great people because God has poured a lot of blessing through talent upon our people," Bathsheba said. "I'll explain more as I walk you back to your chambers. I suspect my son will be visiting you there soon, to ask about your visit to the kitchen."

Bathsheba was right. Solomon soon arrived at Shulamit's chamber. He did so regularly. Unknown to Shulamit, King Solomon went out of his way to smooth her transition from village life to palace life. Ahishan, Bathsheba, and Solomon's personal palace servants were all instructed to keep an eye on his new bride, in case she needed any help. Shulamit had the special blessing of growing up with those who worshipped with King David personally. Her greatest grooming happened before Shulamit ever met Solomon, and Solomon knew he was only adding finishing touches to something that *Elohim* had started many years ago, from the time she was conceived in her mother's womb. *"Thank you, Elohim, for making her perfect for me, she is my living delight and wisdom,"* he prayerfully considered as he walked to his love's chamber.

Greeting Shulamit with a warm smile upon entry, Solomon asked "I heard about your visit to the palace kitchen today. How was that? Do you feel you are beginning to know your way around the palace?"

"It was almost like going to a village marketplace," Shulamit related, "where the country people bring their fresh produce to sell to the local people and visitors. I know how much work it takes to load and unload food and cook on open fire pits and the smell of fresh bread. But the palace was another mighty example. I especially enjoyed tasting the delicacies of the skilled chefs, the best cooks in the country. That was awe-inspiring."

"It pleases me to hear of all your new experiences and that you are beginning to feel at home," Solomon asserted. "Come, let us go and sit in your secret place in the garden," he said as he asked Meliba to have some tea and appetizers brought to them. "I have something to share with you." Shulamit looked at him with that curious look she always got when he was about to take her somewhere new or share some of his wisdom. *She always seems to know things*, he thought. Solomon realized, in his concern to bare his heart, he had forgotten to affirm his love. "By the way, did I tell you how pretty you look right now?" Shulamit's inner peace seemed to return, yet she still sat gazing at him. Meliba came out and began to pour their tea. Solomon thanked Meliba, but neither he nor Shulamit noticed the tea. *Why is it*, Solomon thought, trying to avert his gaze, *every time I look into her eyes, I forget all my logical thoughts. Her beautiful eyes are too much for me.*

Shulamit opened her mouth to speak, but Solomon blurted, "The love song you wrote to me is still ringing in my ears. I wake up with, *You make my mountain's ring* reverberating in my mind." Shulamite smiled, and he could feel the air calming. Solomon had only to look at his fair bride, and it was all the affirmation he needed. He knew that she, being a woman, needed to hear adoring words. He too, was being affirmed every morning as he woke up to her song in his heart.

After a long moment, they each finally took a sip of their tea. Solomon said, "I need to go on a short trip to meet with other kings about business, and I wanted to make sure you are adjusting well to your new environment before I am gone for a while." Shulamit's face became momentarily concerned, but she quickly recovered. Solomon saw the hidden sadness as she acknowledged his leaving, but he was strong in his resolve that his leaving would be good for her.

I am perhaps too protective, he thought. *I don't wish to keep her from growing.*

Solomon concluded that his bride needed time away from him to process all her many feelings and experiences since she left home. A lot had happened to her, and fairly quickly. *Maybe if I am away for a while, she will have time to get to know her emotions and know if her heart is awakening to me.*

He would once again admonish his inner circle, especially Ahishan, the palace overseer, to look after her while he was gone.

While disguising her emotions, Shulamit immediately felt a longing in her heart. He hadn't left, but it reminded her of the feelings of emptiness she felt when he was not around. She kept busy learning things in the palace, making new friends, worshipping, and developing her worship group. But she knew it would be harder to be happy about it, knowing he would be gone.

Solomon kissed her hand as he departed from her secret place, and he added, "I will return as soon as I can." Shulamit forgot most of what he said at the end except the word *return*. Feeling distraught for a short time after he left, she prayed for *Elohim*'s comfort.

"Help me not to be sad, *Abba* Father. Help me to keep myself busy in his absence."

She resolved that she would make use of the time, and really get to know the palace and its people while Solomon was gone. They found her curious—a girl from the mountains living in the palace.

Shulamit had already realized that most of the ladies she encountered had grown up in palaces and spent little time in the country. While Shulamit felt she had so much to learn in the palace, she was glad to have her country upbringing. Even though the people of the palace knew makeup, clothing, jewels, and the finer things of a palace, their knowledge was in many ways quite limited. Raising sheep and animals was a blessed life—a life they had never experienced. Shulamit listened to the other princesses' stories about their lifestyles as she processed all she had now entered into. She really had no real time to miss her country life until Solomon left her. She had been so busy learning so many new things. Shulamit missed getting up in the morning to do chores about the vineyard and taking the sheep up into the green pastures. Singing in the hills was a special delight, and she missed it. It was all beautiful, but so was the palace. At home, she danced on the hills, but here she worshipped in the tabernacle in the presence of God. *Nothing is better than the living presence of God*, she thought. *For that, I give my all.*

As she thought about it the more Shulamit knew, in her heart, God had brought her here. She was stepping into a new identity and being given a new call. While she had some awareness, thinking too much about it was more than she could process. The call Shulamit was walking into was, in many ways, unprecedented. King David had paved the way as a warrior and worshipper, but Solomon as king was taking the country to new heights. He dreamed big. Shulamit had dreamed too, but now she was caught in a bigger dream. Solomon's dream. God's dream.

Yes, it made her anxious. Every time she took her eyes off *Adonai* and looked at her circumstances, she felt she would faint, especially without Solomon there. But she knew she had to grow, grow into this call.

One day, while dancing with her worship group inside the queen's court, the elaborately dressed Egyptian queen, Nefretari, joined them. Shulamit had heard about her, but now she was encountering the full display. Nefretari was followed by a whole entourage of servants. Her elaborate gold headdress covered long hair, braided with colorful beads. The black kohl on the sides of her eyes was elongated to a pointed wing, with her eyelids painted cobalt blue. Her face was beautiful, especially with her eyes like that, but it was her lips, painted a deep red, that highlighted her. Even the gold rings in her ears couldn't keep someone from staring at her lips. They looked like they held a secret—many secrets.

Queen Nefretari wore a gold collar necklace with multi-color stones. Fingernails red from henna, matched armbands around her elbows and wrists. She looked utterly fearless, almost haughty. The deceptively simple white dress she wore had a wide gold belt with two long tails in the front, like snakes dancing to a hypnotic tune. The queen's eyes locked on

Shulamit.

Her servants carried a large chair for her to sit in. It looked like a throne. They propped a stool under her feet, laid a gold tablecloth on a nearby table, and set down her plate and goblet. After that group finished setting her elaborate table, they poured wine while another group of servants brought her food that looked especially prepared.

The brides stopped the dance to show their respect, but the Egyptian queen gave her full attention to Shulamit alone.

"So," she said, "you are the girl from the mountains that Solomon has brought to court. I heard about your tambourine dance." Her nose almost wrinkled in cruel curiosity. "Your skin is dark for a Hebrew girl, is it not?"

Shulamit was shocked by this queen's blunt insolence and didn't know exactly how to answer her. Putting on her most courageous face, Shulamit blurted out, "My brothers were mad at me, so they made me work the vineyard in the heat of the harvest sun." Continuing to hide her anxiety, she added, "But if I had not been singing during the harvest, I would not have met Solomon." Just saying his name made her heart hurt with missing him.

"So, you really are a Vineyard Queen?"

"Solomon—"

"Isn't your family's vineyard truly King David's?" The Pharaoh's daughter interrupted.

"Both. My family's and King David's," Shulamit almost stammered. "But now it is my family's."

"The king has been generous, I see."

"My family sold some of our vineyard to King David so he would come and worship with them in the month of Elul when he came to visit his vineyard."

"Clever indeed," Nefretari said, almost bored.

Shulamit felt her face getting hot. "My family fed and protected King David. They fought with him before he became king. They loved him. He taught them how to become worship warriors. God protected them and King David won all of his battles because he sought the Lord about how to fight each one."

"Are you a worship warrior?" the queen mocked.

Shulamit didn't know what the queen was really asking, but she answered, "I am a worshipper. My greatest joy is to go to the tabernacle and worship in the presence of the Lord."

"And so, you are turning the other queens into worshippers too?"

Shulamit could feel her heart beating loud and quick as she kept her face from showing her many emotions. She was learning to walk with courage, even when she did not feel strong. This was just another form of battle.

Shulamit replied, "Israel is a kingdom of worshippers to our King of Kings, creator of the universe, Lord of Hosts, our protector and provider.

He deserves our worship. Solomon loves to worship with us."

"Is that so?" the queen replied. It seemed Shulamit said the right thing, as the mocking tone lessened a great deal. "I admire your joyful simplicity. Continue your worshipping. Who knows? I may want to worship with you."

Shira, who hadn't stopped playing the harp, finished the song. In response to the queen's comment, Shulamit demonstrated the final dance steps.

"We have finished this round of dance steps and will continue in a few days. You may practice, and then we will continue." Shulamit quickly, but politely, told Nefretari, it was a pleasure to meet her, and she excused herself. Shulamit rushed to her chamber, sat down on her low couch, and began to cry. She did not really know why she was crying, but no one had ever talked to her that way. Shulamit so wished to love and be loved in her new home, but Nefretari's words made her heart hurt. Solomon being absent just made the feelings stronger. She began crying all the more.

A few minutes later, Bathsheba came to Shulamit in her chambers. Bathsheba already knew everything that had just happened, as the gossip was quickly making its way around the palace. She was thoroughly upset with the Pharaoh's daughter. Trying to be friendly, Bathsheba asked Shulamit for her perspective of what happened.

"Do not take Nefretari seriously," Bathsheba counseled as she put her arms around Shulamit. "She thinks she is superior to everyone in the court, even Solomon. Nefretari was forced to marry Solomon by her father. She feels she has been exiled to a kingdom inferior to her own. Solomon has done everything he can to make her happy, including giving her the whole palace in Hebron to live in, but nothing makes her happy. She was supposed to return to Hebron a few days ago, but she has stayed longer. I suppose it was to meet you." She gave Shulamit a gentle squeeze. "I'm sure she was not happy hearing about your worship dance of the Pharaoh's horses drowning in the Red Sea. I think she still likes to think of us as former slaves, rather than God's people." Pausing a moment to allow Shulamit to process what she said, Bathsheba added, "But you need not be too concerned with Nefretari. She will never live in the palace with the rest of the queens and ladies of the court. She considered herself above everyone and has refused to accept our One God of Israel. Nefretari denies the faith of Abraham, Isaac, and Jacob. She will always have to live in a separate palace. She will never be admitted to worship in the Temple because only believers can go to the Temple. For now, she will stay at the palace in Hebron, until such a time as Solomon builds her a palace of her own in Jerusalem."

"Oh," Shulamit said simply. But at least her tears were no longer falling.

"You might as well know now, there are few secrets in this palace,"

Bathsheba explained, as she continued to hold Shulamit in her arms. "People like to talk. You are the new person to talk about right now." Bathsheba looked directly into Shulamit's teary face, "God has given me such a love for you," she said, as she patted her arm with her hand.

"Thank you, Queen Mother," Shulamit said.

"I will tell you what I do. Every morning when I wake up, as I dress and groom, I pray, and I put on my crown. I put on the royal crown, but I also put on the spiritual crown. My spiritual crown is the crown of authority given to me by God. Only I am called to fulfill the role that I have as Queen Mother. Right now, you have a circlet crown as a queen to be and it is still a call that you are walking into, but God gave you the authority to fulfill that role, and you must claim it. Come," Bathsheba said, rising and bringing Shulamit up with her. "Let us go to the Tabernacle together and worship. You will be seen with me, and it will be known that you have my favor." Bathsheba looked at her and smiled. "I do love you, isn't that wonderful?"

Shulamit wiped a tear of love from her eye and responded, "I love you too."

Hand in hand, as promised, Shulamit and Bathsheba walked to the Tabernacle. Shulamit's heart was still heavy, but the priests were singing, which helped. She listened to the words, making them a prayer of her heart.

> *Hear my cry, O God*
> *Attend to my prayer*
> *From the end of the earth, I will cry to You*
> *When my heart is overwhelmed*
> *Lead me to the rock that is higher than I*
> *For You have been a shelter for me*
> *I will abide in Your tabernacle forever*
> *I will trust in the shelter of Your wings...*

Shulamit found herself crying before the Ark, not remembering that she'd even walked there. She identified with King David, singing amid battle. Shulamit sang along, her heart acknowledging the worship. She, too, needed her *Elohim*, her shelter and strong tower. Shulamit felt she had been in the midst of a storm while arrows were being shot at her. But as she prayed, she felt the arrows were miraculously missing her. Shulamit needn't fear. She was protected by the shelter of *Elohim*. She began praying for the Lord's anointing to fall upon her, to protect and keep her safe too. "Thank you, *Abba* Father, for the wonderful legacy of worship that King David has given us, that enables us to enter into a closer relationship with you. I am so blessed. Bless you, *Elohim*, for being such a loving Father, as King David has called you. I want above all else to have a relationship with you as our

David. Lord give me his heart for worship."

The days went by, and Shulamit began to miss Solomon even more than she thought possible. At first, she was busy and excited with everything around her, especially worshipping in the Tabernacle. But then she began to think about what a joy it was to be in Solomon's presence. Just watching him standing, looking out over his kingdom from the palace, was thrilling. As she stood in his presence, he always made her feel like such a beautiful woman with his affirmations, and she liked that part of her being drawn out.

She liked his strong, masculine presence as she sat by him or walked with him in the palace and gardens. She loved worshipping with him. When he held her hand or kissed it, she felt weak as he told her how much he adored her. Shulamit began to realize that she wanted more of him. They were not the same feelings of worshipping in the tabernacle in the presence of God. Still, they were feelings that made her think of how God had a heart for man and woman when he created them for each other. She realized she had feelings of love for him. Her love for Solomon actually made her love for God deeper.

Shulamit knew that her Father in Heaven had answered her prayer and brought Solomon into her life. Only a good God who really knew about the longings in her heart could bring the man, for whom she had waited and prayed, into her life. She could never doubt God's love for her, but the feelings she had for Solomon were not something she knew now how to readily express. Shulamit sat in her chambers, thinking about how Solomon described the building of the Temple. Salvation was given to the people by the sacrifice of the people in the outer court. Communion and prayer were made in the inner court by the priests.

But something much greater existed in the Holy of Holies.

That was what she wanted with Solomon. It was a powerful love she would never know until she fully knew Solomon. She thought of it as a dance. Dancing in worship brought her expression of her feelings for the Lord. There was more, though she did not understand it. Shulamit had to admit, she was growing curious. The longing for her lover became so strong that it entered her dream with a song.

In her dream, she wandered through streets, crying out her poetic prayer, "Have you seen the one I love?"

By night on my bed
I sought
The one I love
I sought him
But I did not find him

The Worshipper and the King

The one I love

I will rise now I said
And go about the city
Into the streets and squares
I will seek
The one I love

Have you seen him?
Have you seen him?
Have you seen the one I love?

To the watchmen who
Go about the city
I said have you seen
The one I love

Scarcely had I passed them
When I found
The one I love
I held him
And I would not
Let him go

I have found him
I have found him
The one I love

He held me
And he told me
He will never leave me
And he will never let me go

And I held him
Yes, I held him
And I would not let him go

Shulamit did not know that she was crying out in her sleep.

"Have you seen him? Have you seen him?" she kept calling out as she turned restlessly on her bed. Meliba was concerned at her cries and went to find Ahishan. He knew Solomon had just returned to the palace and sent his guard to bring Solomon to her chamber.

Her dream shifted to a new scene as Shulamit saw the full moon, high in the sky with light reflected on her lover. He wore a bright white robe with a gold sash, but a shadow covered his face, so she saw only a form. She saw only an outline of wavy hair just past his shoulders, but it was the same as Solomon. A cloud covered the moon as she ran and grabbed hold of him. She would not let him go, and he spoke peace over her heart. The voice said, "You are precious to me, and I will never leave you or forsake you. I will love you forever and ever."

The sun came up and shown so brightly upon her beloved's face that Shulamit could not distinguish it as the face of Solomon, but as the bright sun moved from his face within her dream, Shulamit opened her eyes. There was Solomon, in reality, looking down on her.

Shulamit flung herself into his arms. "Oh Solomon," she said, "I know you will never leave me or forsake me. I have found you again, and I never want to let you go."

"You have been dreaming, my love." He embraced her. "Your maiden said you were calling out for me in your dream, and she was concerned. I just arrived at the palace and came as soon as I heard, but as I arrived, I saw you dreaming. You had the most peaceful look on your face, and I did not want to awaken you. Are you sure it was me in your dream?"

"It was a real person visiting me in my dream. I thought it was you. I wanted it to be you. I did not see your face, but the man in my dream had the same hair and size in his shadow as you."

"Amazing!"

"I have missed you so much, Solomon. I felt myself being held, and I really hoped it was you. So, you haven't been holding me? I felt you! And I felt a desire for all your love, forever. You were holding me, and speaking such soft loving words to me, I knew I could not let you go." She summoned her courage and said, "And I wanted to kiss you."

"Do you still want to kiss me?"

Shulamit sat up in her bed. "Yes," her face went hot, "I feel I want to kiss you, and hold you like we did in the dream. I love your sweet soft words of comfort and your promises of love."

Solomon replied, "Then we must begin to make preparations for marriage as soon as the winter rains are over. I am a happy man. I can't remember when I have ever been so happy."

18 PREPARATIONS FOR THE WEDDING

"Call a meeting," Solomon commanded Ahishan. As he left, Solomon called out, "Bring my chief council! Be sure to find Benaiah, Zadok, and his sons. Notify the heads of the palace and my most skilled artisans. I am going to honor my bride Shulamit with the grandest wedding Israel has ever seen. Make sure the head seamstress sees me immediately. Only Adah will do!

Benaiah spoke to his military officers, upon hearing the summons. "I hope we are not being called to a war council. Never are we called in such haste otherwise." The head palace guard nodded to Benaiah, wondering what it was all about also.

As heads of state crowded into King Solomon's private meeting hall, they were surprised to hear the king announce, "This wedding will require a lot of organization for protection. We will have a procession displaying our military might under the leadership of Benaiah. Ah," he said as Benaiah entered, "there you are. We will have trumpeters going before you in the wedding procession." Benaiah's relief was short-lived. There was no war council, but a military procession was still a huge undertaking.

"A procession, sir?"

"Of course! You and your main guard will go before glorious carriages and palanquins. I'll have those designed by the daughters of Zion, under the Adah's and my design. Where is she?" Solomon turned back to his many ideas, saying, "Pillars of myrrh and frankincense smoke will be prepared by Hananiah in the palace perfumery." Solomon continued detailing his plans and asking for. Solomon knew how to champion enthusiasm and it was growing as they caught his vision.

"I will make the grandest cake I have ever made," Shilshah, the chief chef, announced.

"Bring my bride, Shulamit," he called out to Ahishan. "She needs to participate in all this."

Before too long, Shulamit was escorted into the council room. She entered in starry-eyed surprise as the most powerful people in Israel stood up to acknowledge her. Her face flushed at so much attention.

Solomon eased her anxiety, as always, by standing up and coming to her. Taking her hand in his kingly, gracious yet authoritative manner, he soothed her, while exciting her at the same time.

"This is my beloved bride," Solomon announced. "She is the woman I love above all. I adore how she loves to worship *Elohim*, but still somehow loves me." The crowd laughed quietly.

Shulamit was still so overwhelmed she could hardly hear all Solomon was saying.

He continued, "My bride has a few unusual desires we have not practiced in Israel. She wants to be wed before the Ark of the Covenant. I know it is an unusual request, but my bride says the presence of God is the best place to honor him and his gift of marriage. It is also an opportune time right now. Soon, the Ark will be in the temple, and we won't be able to spend so much time this close to God's Holy presence."

Shulamit heard enough of what Solomon said and thought, *I did not realize I was asking such an unusual request. I see the people are surprised too.*

The members of the council did not know how to react to such a wedding before God, as wedding in Israel had generally been secular events with a priest's blessing. However, Solomon was their sovereign king, and they could all see how happy he was. They all knew that when a king is happy, everyone is happy.

"She is indeed a beautiful woman in spirit and body," someone said quietly. Murmurs echoed. One of the priest's sons said, "Solomon may have more than one wife, as King David, but there is always one above all others in a man's love." Whispers continued as the honored participants processed the revelations from the king and queen-to-be.

King Solomon loved these types of meetings. He loved discussions of grandiosity and beauty, just as he did discussions of designing and building. Drawing the best out of his people, giving them opportunity to dream, along with all the materials to create their ideas, was to everyone's benefit. Solomon knew great talents in people continued to arise in Israel, making the country even greater.

The chief carpenter came up with an idea of building chairs designed as thrones. His idea was to hold the thrones up, so those who came to the wedding could see the happy couple share their adoration and songs to each other.

"So be it," Solomon said, putting his royal approval on the young man's idea. "I have chosen the bride of my heart, as God chose Israel! Marriage has been ordained by God through His love and desire for us to know happiness. There has never been a wedding like this and perhaps never will be until our Messiah comes. We are just forerunners of the glorious days in Heaven. I wish to show my happiness to all Israel. Shulamit is to me as Israel is to Yahweh."

When all discussions of wedding plans were placed on the table and agreed upon, the meeting was adjourned. The palace would be busy for a while designing and creating for the great day ahead.

But Shulamit was overwhelmed, and she knew it.

She left the meeting in a stunned state, unable to process all that was happening. It was all so fast. Shulamit was in love and that was all that counted to her, but a *king* loved her, and a king showed his love in ways few other men could. The day passed quickly, with her mind full of questions. She went to bed praying for the heavenly Father's help.

Abba, she prayed in her heart, *I don't want to say this is too much for me, but I do need your help. I know you called me to be here. That, I do not doubt, but help me.* She tried to relax after her prayer, but it was no use. Her mind refused to calm down. Tossing from side to side, she lay awake thinking of all she had heard that day. Finally, Shulamit prayed in her spirit, *Abba I surrender all this to you, give me strength, and wake me up refreshed. My heart is open to hear from you, and to be all you have called me to be.*

As if in response to her prayers, the Lord sent her sweet dreams. Shulamit rose the next morning, dressed, and went directly to the Tabernacle to seek the Lord. She drew strength from His presence and needed to pray before the Ark of the Covenant. King David prayed, "Early will I seek You," and Shulamit followed that example. She found great comfort by participating in the thanks and worship, pouring her heart out before God.

She thanked *Adonai* for his comforting dreams, as well as bringing Solomon home to her. She thanked him for awakening her heart to know how much she truly loved Solomon and how she now had a real desire to know Solomon as a wife. But she had to admit her nerves were still there.

"But Father," she sighed, "a wedding before all Israel, I never planned that. I trust Solomon always does the right thing for the throne and country, but I have only just begun to know how to go out and come in. And now he and I will wed in the spring. He wants me to make such a grand entrance. I don't want to say I can't do it, for I know you brought me here; You called me to be a queen. But *Adonai,*" she said, sighing again, "my Lord, it is scary. I am in over my head, and I can't do it without you. I ask for your anointing to help me carry out this plan." A thought came to her, and she asked, "Do I need to be anointed?"

She heard within her spirit, *"Did I not say I am with you and will never leave you nor forsake you?"*

"I thought that was Solomon in my dream," she replied aloud.

"SOLOMON IS MY ANOINTED," came the voice again, *"AND I DO SPEAK THROUGH HIM. I SPEAK THROUGH HIM PERSONALLY TO YOU. SOLOMON DOES ANOINT YOU BY HIS PRESENCE AND LOVE FOR YOU, AND HIS DESIRE TO SEE YOU BECOME A GREAT QUEEN. I WILL NOT HOLD BACK THE DESIRES OF YOUR HEART. THOSE DESIRES ARE FULFILLING MY DESIRES. TALK TO SOLOMON; HE WILL DO WHAT IS RIGHT."*

Shulamit bowed before the Ark. She realized, as she was bowing, that her Lord heard her heart, and He really cared about her desires. *Elohim* answered her prayers so many times to bring her where she was, and she still barely understood how much her Father in Heaven loved her. She began to feel a song arising in her spirit, so she hastened back to her chambers and grabbed her harp. Excited and inspired, Shulamit walked to her private gazebo, her secret place in the garden, to sing a special composition.

She named it, "Crown me with Your Presence."

Crown me with your presence, O Lord
Rest upon me
That I may walk worthy
To fulfill your call
Through me
Place upon my head
An ornament of your grace
And a crown of glory
That when people see my face
They see your beauty
Flowing through me
Guide my steps
To walk before you
Righteously and Holy
That I may come before your throne
Uprightly
Clothe me with your love
Embrace me
Never let me go
Keep me in your mercy
I am awed by your majesty
It overwhelms me
Strengthen me, O Lord Almighty
To fulfill this awesome destiny
I thank you for your favor
And that you trust me
With all of my heart, and the joy within
I have never been so happy
I pray that you preserve me
With your presence crowned upon me
I know I can be your bride and queen
As long as you are with me

Light drops of rain fell outside of the gazebo as Shulamit became lost in her song. She was still singing when Solomon walked up behind her. Shulamit had been so caught up in song she did not realize he was there.

"That was a beautiful song," he murmured into Shulamit's ear.

"Ooh," she said, almost jumping. "I did not know you were there."

"Keep on singing. I love it."

Shulamit found herself a little embarrassed. Her song was more of a prayer to *Elohim* and not one she meant to share with anyone else. Solomon noticed her shyness and responded, "Since when have we kept secrets from each other? I love that in your heart you have a fear of God and always ask for his help and guidance. As your king and beloved, you must know that I am here in any way I can be, to help you walk into your full destiny. I thought you understood that from the very beginning. I want to share all of our prayers and dreams together."

"I need *Elohim*'s help to be married and crowned before all Israel. Do you think I need to be anointed to do this? I went to the Temple to pray about it. The Lord said many comforting things. One of those things was to ask you."

"My love," Solomon said as he gently lifted her face toward him, "I have always thought you were called and anointed, but I understand your concern. I can arrange for you to be anointed in private. The High Priest Zadok and prophet Zabud can do this." Solomon smiled at a budding idea. "My father and I were both anointed before we stepped into our positions as king. My father was anointed by Samuel, in private, many years before he became king. God works that way." Solomon turned, motioning for a servant. He said something quietly, and the servant walked away. Turning back to Shulamit he said, "An anointing is, in many ways, a prophetic seed. The seed grows with practice, time, and walking with God."

"That is true, and well said," replied Shulamit, marveling at how Solomon seemed to know every detail of his palace and how it worked.

"I know that God never calls us to any position without giving us the authority and anointing to carry it out. Know this too, sweet Shulamit; you share my name from the root word *Shalom*. Have you studied what the meaning of those letters in the word Shalom are?"

"Not yet," she replied. "What does it mean?"

"A strong man armed keeps his house," Solomon said. He took her hand with an affectionate squeeze. "Peace always comes with a cost. We must battle to enter into peace. Do you know the letter *Shin*?"

"Yes," Shulamit responded, "I can write my name, and *Shin* is the first letter. I thought my name just meant peace."

"Shin means sharp, mighty, devour and teeth; depending upon the context it is used. The symbol that goes with shin is two teeth. I'm sure you have seen that."

"Our language is so full of meaning. But as I learned to read and write, I see there is much more than I ever imagined."

Solomon nodded. He said, "Hebrew is full of prophecy and enlightenment."

"It is a language that teaches us more about our Heavenly Father."

"You are right, my love, and the next letter in your name is about the anointing you are asking for. *Lamed* is a staff, a symbol of authority. So far, we see a picture of a strong ruler with sharp teeth carrying authority to carry it out. Yes, we need the anointing and authority from God to do our job. As a nation we learned from Saul that without the anointing we can't carry out our mission."

"My brothers reminded me of that as I was leaving. They said my beauty and talents may be what brought me to the palace, but I should never start to trust in myself, or all will be lost. It is only God."

"You have a healthy fear of God, my love, and I admire that quality in you. I feel you always drawing me toward God. You are already more of strength to me than you realize. I also know you are growing stronger into your call." Shulamit's face grew hot with the compliment.

"I am happy to know I bless you. That my name blesses you," she said.

"The next letter in your name—"

"In *our* names," she corrected.

"In *our* names, is *Vav*. It is the symbol of a nail, which means to attach. A nail holds things together and connects things. It goes with the next letter *Mem*.

"*Mem* is water," said Shulamit.

"That is correct," Solomon said, smiling. "But it also means mighty chaos. Connecting the words from the letters we get this sentence: *A strong ruler will destroy the authority attached to chaos.*"

"A strong ruler will destroy the authority attached to chaos," Shulamit repeated.

"You see my love," Solomon said as he took her hand, "there is a lot more to peace than meets the eye. To keep peace, I must stay prepared for war. I keep a strong well-trained military that other nations are afraid to attack. We have the best weapons, horses, and chariots so no one will try to attack. None dare challenge our authority which is really from God."

"My father always taught me about how the men in the village trained to protect us. They practiced with swords, slings, and arrows for any attack," Shulamit continued, "But what you do is on a much grander scale."

"It is amazing that the name your family gave you carries a call to rule. You have an innate understanding of warfare."

"I didn't consider it that way," she said. *He is so wise*, she thought.

"You do," said Solomon. "And as my queen, you shall share my authority to conquer evil as you walk into a room."

Shulamit bowed her head, overcome by the loving words of her betrothed. Solomon sensed her bashfulness and once again, lifted her head.

"My love," he almost cooed, "you are amazing. You have always carried an authority when you worship. As you sing and dance, the presence of God has always come so strong upon you that nothing evil could ever get near you. The power of your worship destroys chaos. Your lovely smile lights up a room and the darkness leaves. Your sweetness and love spread the authority of kindness and joy, and darkness does not live in that atmosphere. You already have this authority. As a king, it is to my glory to have a strong queen to stand beside me, and rule with me. You are already strong, but we will anoint you for more."

Shulamit's face grew quite hot. "You are making me remember my childhood," she said. "When I was pretending to be David, I would yell out his battle cry to Goliath. My brother quit playing because he said a girl shouldn't play David. But my uncle, Jether, told my Papa of another side of David. One I *could* be. That was when my father wrote the song, "When you Worship." It carried the seeds of prophecy. Later, the high Priest also prophesied that I would bless Israel with my worship. Now I see it." Shulamit began filling with a deep, bubbling joy. She also felt the weight of a great calling. One she knew she was meant to step into. "I have worshipped before God but worshipping as a queen is another anointing. I feel I am about to make a big shift in my spirit.

Solomon laughed, "You never stop amazing me. Your worship has always enlightened me, and I love that. But now, you will step into double anointing as prophetess and queen, like King David. You shall be anointed, and you will grow in the call that was already yours. We were born to be our call, we step into our call, and we keep growing in our call to become more." Solomon stepped forward and kissed her forehead. "I must go tend to some things. But I shall see you again, soon."

Solomon left Shulamit in her secret place with a lot to ponder. One side of her wondered if she really understood what she was getting herself into. The other side was excited to be with Solomon as his wife, bride, and queen. She would do whatever it took to be the woman he needed in his life.

Shulamit began considering the vows she would write for her wedding. This, too, was a new thing. Every time the weight of responsibility hit her, she also thought of the joy of her calling. She knew how much *Adonai* loved her, and how much Solomon loved her. Her faith was growing, giving her new ideas.

The following morning, Shulamit couldn't wait until her class with the Priest and Shira to share her heart. They were finishing the last few letters of the alphabet. Shulamit could write and read them, but they were taking on greater meaning as started stringing the letters and words into sentences.

Shira and the priest were happy to hear about Shulamit's spring wedding joy. Shira was betrothed to a Levite priest soon after Shulamit's wedding date was announced, and she and Shulamit began sharing their marriage dreams together. "What greater dream does a young woman have than to love and be loved," Shulamit remembered her elders saying.

Shira's and Shulamit's shared joy increased the joy of their worship individually, with each other, and together among the core group.

"Joy creates joy," Shira said one day, as they were dancing. "Songs create more songs, and songs are always bubbling up from a happy soul."

A few weeks later, Bathsheba accompanied Shulamit down to the seamstress shop. The head mistress, Adah, showed Shulamit reams of material. There were even a few dress designs the king had drawn for Shulamit to choose from. Shulamit had learned to design her own, but this was her wedding dress, and she loved the idea of Solomon being a part of the creation. The deep, royal colors in the seamstress shop sparked her imagination and heart.

She chose a design Solomon drew and found colors for it, then studied the length of the train. The vibrant reds, blues, purples, and golds were the colors of queens, Bathsheba pointed out. Then Adah showed her a long ream of sheer white silk. Unrolling it with the help of other ladies, Adah held it for Shulamit to examine. "We can embroider this with delicate threads of gold in flower designs," Adah explained as she showed her samples of designs to choose from.

"How long will it be," Shulamit inquired, "and how many maidens will it take to carry it?"

Unrolling more of the material, Adah said, "It would take 10 or 12 bridesmaids to carry the train." Shulamite took a moment to visualize herself in the dress, followed by so many people. In her mind, she expected to be in the Temple with a ceremony that was much more intimate. The air was filled with the scent of incense floating upward to the Heavens. Things were different, but she knew it was a gift from the Lord, to be so displayed.

"I see glory in it," Shulamit said. "Let me look at the design one more time." She added a curved line between the flowers. Adah nodded, respecting the keen eye of her queen-to-be.

Next, Shulamit, Bathsheba, and Adah discussed the bridesmaid's dress. Together, they decided on blue. It was the same color as the blue in her wedding dress. Her gown, however, had the additional royal colors of red and gold.

Everyone was excited, and the work started in haste.

The daughters of Zion, specially called to serve in the courts of Jerusalem, sewed new clothing for all members of the wedding. They took months to carefully craft each piece, embroidering purple cloth for the king's palanquin, chariots, royal seating banners and covers, as well as the throne.

Shulamit visited them in their workshops throughout the chilly winter. The warmth in the hearts of servants who loved their work and their king contrasted with the cold snow outside. Shulamit followed the example of Solomon in offering thankfulness and encouragement for all their work.

"I am so honored to have such skilled artisans creating in my presence," she often said. "If I ask you questions about how you do what you do, it is because I wish to learn from you. I wish to understand as much as I can all the skills that go into making something so great happen."

Indeed, though she learned wisdom from her king, her own earnest admiration could be felt by the artisans of the palace. Her genuineness made them feel honored, a part of something great. The royal wedding would be remembered by many for years to come, and everyone involved wanted to be a part of history. But all the preparation and choices kept Shulamit drawing upon her imagination. Solomon, Bathsheba, Ahishan, Shulamit's trusted lead attendant, Meliba, and even head dressmaker Adah were happy to advise. But Shulamit always prayed and considered her decisions rather than just relinquishing her own responsibility to choose.

As the days passed, she tried to worship as much as she could, which was its own work. Shulamit had a large group of dancers now. They joined in the Sabbath Eve worship dance regularly, many times with new worship steps. Shira officially joined the team of musicians, so Shulamit didn't see her as much as she used to. But Shira taught her the songs of the tabernacle, and on special worship occasions, they worshipped together. People who came to worship at the Tabernacle saw the worship dances, and knew they were especially blessed. The visiting worshippers often wanted to learn the dances and take them back to their villages.

Shira taught some of the other priests' daughters to dance, and it soon became a phenomenon. The dances were worship. The worship brought joy. Joy spread like wildfire. Even Shira began to create dance steps of her own and Shulamit loved learning from her when she had time.

The High Priest was always delighted by new songs and new dances. He declared, one Sabbath, before the whole congregation, "The Glory of God is here! There is no worship like the worship from the Tabernacle of Israel, no music in the world like the songs that come from the Spirit of David and the Priests, and the beautiful dances. When the Holy Spirit's presence falls upon people, creativity arises. Hear our symphonies and acknowledge God's chosen people! Our great worship inspires me to minister before the Lord and teach the statues of the Lord to Israel. Indeed, we have so much reason to praise the Lord."

Though he sometimes did not speak about it like the High Priest,

Solomon was very aware of how well his father planted the need for worship within the power structure of Israel. The foundation for worship throughout the day and night was a seed that was growing quite well in the kingdom. Solomon was also aware of his Vineyard Queen's effect on the worship in the Tabernacle and joyful song in the palace.

Solomon loved the worship and found his own inspiration as he worked late at night on his building plans. He put down his pen as he realized the connection between worship and presence like never before. Shulamit was a source of more divine power than even she knew. The sincerity in his bride's desire to have the power and purity and anointing to worship and be a queen carrying glory would bless Israel for generations. And their children…

Solomon stood, smiling broadly with hope. Now that his plans were in place, he was ready to surprise his beloved with, yet another dream come true.

He surprised her, indeed.

In the quiet of the night, as Shulamit was about ready to dress down for sleep, Solomon came with one musician on flute and two others playing lyres. They arrived quietly, then began dancing and making beautiful music. She was surprised awake to the sounds of the intimate serenade.

Shulamit opened the door of her chamber and the king held out his hand.

"Follow my lead," he said and began to skip and sing.

> *Come my bride*
> *And skip with me*
> *Down palace halls*
> *To destiny*
> *I choose you*
> *Our Father too*
> *Let us rejoice*
> *And follow through*
> *My bride of mountains*
> *And rivers deep*
> *Grab hold my hand*
> *And let us leap*

Yes, leap they did.

They performed a dance as they traveled, performing steps Solomon quickly taught Shulamit through their travel. Shulamit was enthralled, but still picked up the few steps with ease. They started at the same time, each one taking a high leap in the air. Solomon would catch Shulamit as she landed, twirling her around before setting her down. Then they returned to skipping down the palace hallways. After a few feet, they would start again.

Shulamit noticed there were rose petals strewn on the floor. Before she could speak a question, Solomon began a song. As they went through the candle-lit halls dancing, she joined in the song with him. They weren't quiet, but the song wasn't meant to be loud.

> *Through fruitful vineyards*
> *Rose blossoms galore*
> *Dancing through paths*
> *To the throne room door*

They arrived at the palace throne room after a few minutes. It was empty except for a few guards at the doors, as the court was not assembled this late. Well-lit with candles, especially around the throne, Shulamit caught her breath at the intimate, powerful setting.

Still holding her hand, Solomon slowed his rhythmic steps. He began walking at Shulamit's right side, holding her right hand up and out toward the front of the room as he sang.

> *We step into glory bright*
> *Illustrious candlelight*
> *Behold the kingdom throne*
> *I extend my invite*
> *I shall share my kingdom*
> *But before I do*
> *As your devoted king*
> *I now anoint and bless you.*
> *Before my throne*
> *Bow on your knee*
> *While I bestow upon you*
> *New identity*

Solomon bent his knees with her briefly, signaling her to stay before the throne when he stood. The high priest's son, Azariah, and the Prophet Zabud appeared from behind the grand fixture carrying a small golden vial of perfumed oil.

Azariah moved to the front, facing Shulamit. He poured the oil slowly, in a circular pattern, around the top of her head. As he poured, Zabud gave Shulamit a prophecy.

"Blessed you shall be in your beauty upon the throne," he began. "You were born to be a queen. And you shall bring strength to the king through your worship. You shall stand as a warrior beside the king in times of need."

As Zabud finished speaking, Solomon placed a small golden crown with jewels upon her head. Solomon had been singing very quietly as the anointing took place, but at the end of Zabud's prophesy, he began to sing in a stronger more intimate voice.

> *The sweet ointment that makes*
> *Your face to shine*
> *And crown on your head*
> *I make you mine*
> *My bride, my queen*
> *You may now stand*
> *Heaven witnessing my heart*
> *Now take my hand*
> *I now share with you*
> *My God-given authority*
> *To sit at my right side*
> *And reign with me*

Solomon took Shulamit by the hand and led her to the throne. As he sat, he led her to join him on his right. The musicians moved to the side of the room, playing quietly.

Solomon looked lovingly at Shulamit and said, "You look glorious. I see the anointing shining upon your face." He paused, "Your eyes are sparkling so. How do you feel?"

Shulamit brimmed with peaceful power as she said, "I feel crowned with your presence and glory upon me. I feel so loved by my Father in Heaven. And you." The emotions they felt were overpowering, blooming poetry from deep within their hearts. Shulamit sighed, content. "I feel my anxiety fading away," she said with wonder, "and now I feel I can enjoy my wedding day because of so much love coming out of me. I am overflowing. And I will continue to overflow with love. From God. From you. From all the people of the kingdom. To them. I feel honor. I feel peace. I feel strength coming from you. I feel...joy. I want to share with them my joy."

"My love," Solomon said, proud to almost bursting, "you shall be the most beautiful queen Israel has ever seen. Beauty and sweetness radiate out of your smile. They are like shorn sheep come up from the washing, every one of them bearing twins and nonbarren. Your lips like a strand of scarlet. The joy of your presence lights up the atmosphere like the dawn of a new day."

Shulamit wiped a tear from the corner of her eye. She realized she had been carrying a lot of tension and anxiety within her. Now, she was beginning to let it go, feeling more relaxed in Solomon's presence all the time. Solomon knew how to make her forget her fears in his song and dance. He knew the keys to what moved her heart and spirit.

Looking out from the throne, Shulamit remembered, *Song is what I heard when I first encountered Solomon singing upon the hill and dance was my response. Solomon makes me dance. He knows how to lead. He knows how to lead me. How to love me.* That night, he led her to where kings and queens reign. *God is leading my life to His seat of authority,* Shulamit thought. *I feel highly honored and deeply humbled at the same time.*

Solomon seemed to read her thoughts.

"Yes," he said, "other kings and queens will come to Jerusalem and bow before this throne, because we are heaven's light to the world. Out of all the nations of the world, God has called us to share His glory. It *is* an honor." Solomon shared with Shulamite, "When God first came to me in a dream, I felt overwhelmed to govern such a great people. So, I asked the Lord for wisdom and understanding to judge and rule. After I was anointed with the Holy Spirit, God's wisdom came over me and I became aware of Him shifting me to a higher level. I began to do and create things I never imagined. Learning to listen to Him and trust His leading was well worth it. My faith has grown to where I believe nothing is impossible. The wisdom given to me by God made me into the king I am. You will see and experience this too."

"I have heard about God granting you wisdom," Shulamit replied. "But when you tell me from your own mouth it is so much more exciting."

"I always watch the response of people when I offer them positions of authority in my kingdom. If they do not respond by feeling humbled by the great task before them, I reconsider giving them the job. But I also expect them to want to serve in that position, with faith that they are called and thankfulness for the opportunity to use their gifts."

"You are so wise," Shulamit confided. "How can I not think about the awesome responsibility of ruling upon the throne? But you know my key. You danced me here to the throne, you sang to my heart, and you spoke poetry about my beauty. Your actions took away my anxiety," she said and paused a moment. "I realize that, right now with you, I feel like I can conquer the world. That is what you pull out of me. You make me feel strong and courageous enough to command armies."

Solomon laughed a bit, then became serious. "You make me feel weak," he confided. You have conquered me."

Shulamit started to laugh. It started softly, but grew louder, like a song rising from with her joy. Trying to speak during her laughter, she said, "I laugh sometimes and don't know why. Remember how we laughed on the mountain when we first met. Maybe on the mountain, I felt so happy and somewhat overwhelmed by surprise when I first saw you," Shulamit's laughter became a giggle. "That time I was full of joy. For the first time, I felt I knew what love was, and was overcome with the laughter of a fulfilled dream." Shulamit's laughter erupted out of her again. After a pause, she tried to contain herself and speak. "Now I am sitting on a throne, overwhelmed again at where God has brought me. I did not dream this, but it is a dream." Having said what she wanted to say, she burst into belly laughter.

Suddenly an inquisitive expression came across her face, and she laughed as she spoke, "Is it proper to laugh while sitting on a throne?"

Solomon laughed at her question, realizing he was caught up in Shulamit's joy. He laughed like he did on the mountain, so hard he couldn't seem to stop. "Laughing on the throne?" He doubled over. "We're doing it right now, aren't we? I suppose God sits in the heavens upon his throne and laughs sometimes. He made us in His image, so if we are doing it, He must do it too. Perhaps he is up there laughing with us." Solomon burst into laughter anew.

They laughed together for quite some time. Every time one of them tried to talk, they laughed. Finally, Solomon and Shulamit just resigned themselves to enjoying the laughter until it stopped on its own.

"My love," he forced himself to say, "you are such a delight. I can hardly wait until our wedding night."

"I'm going to write you some wedding vows," Shulamit spoke to her own amazement. This seemed to shock them both, stopping the laughter in the best possible way.

"Wedding vows?" Solomon said. "We already have the Ketubah. That is vow enough."

"Yes," she said with a shy tone, "but the Ketubah is about laws of agreement and covenant. Wedding vows are about the heart. I want to speak a vow from a deeper level in my spirit," she said, becoming bolder "one where it touches heaven and takes love to that higher level." Shulamit could see Solomon thinking about it and continued. "A wedding vow is my heart speaking to your heart and not just saying my duties as a wife. I know how to run a home, raise kids, and care for a husband. But my vows will talk of what I will do to keep our hearts alive and burning within us.

"I want to keep the love between us alive forever and ever," he said.

"This is the sacred love where God meets us in the Holy of Holies. This is the great covenant created by the Passover Lamb, to love the land of Israel forever," Shulamit said. She stood, twirling around him in a dreamy stroll "It is the river of life flowing from the throne of God," she spoke, "where we jump in and stay refreshed."

Shulamit grabbed his hand and they twirled around. Soon it became a dance, where they circled each other and then backed off, lifting hands up to a throne in heaven. "It is a spring in the mountains that bubbles up, overflowing with joy," Shulamit said as she jumped.

Solomon leapt also. He caught her as he had when they were dancing down the hallway.

"This is the promise of keeping," Shulamit continued. "This laughter in our lives and the kisses of love, they will never stop." When Shulamit said the word kiss her mind stopped abruptly. Sometimes she never knew where she was going when she spoke. Whenever it happened, her heart took over.

But Solomon knew what was happening. He also knew not to awaken her love too soon.

"Thank God our wedding is not too far away," Solomon replied. "I look forward to hearing your heart in your wedding vows.

19 BETHLEHEM

"My bride is too perceptive," said Solomon. She knows too much about all the wedding preparations for me to make the wedding a surprise. What should I do?" he asked his brothers and mother.

"I suppose you are right about that, she is perceptive," Shammuah replied.

"Well," Solomon paused, "I need a solution."

"You can do the old trick many mothers and fathers have done with their daughters," Shammuah said. "To distract her, you should take her on a short trip. Perhaps for a week while the final wedding preparations are being made. When she returns, she will be surprised by her family greeting her and everything decorated for her great day."

"Great!" Solomon said. "Have her servants secretly prepare her belongings for a surprise trip to Bethlehem. I have promised to take her there, so she will not suspect anything." Giving it a few more thoughts Solomon said, "Call Ahishan, Zadok, Banaiah, and Adah. I need to go over a few final instructions before I leave. And yes, Nathan," he said as he turned to him, "I need you to come with me, so she believes we are going to the annual sheep shearing in Bethlehem."

***

The next morning, Solomon made his way to surprise his bride outside the lattice of her chambers. Shulamit had already awakened to the sound of birds singing in the early dawn. She dressed to go out into her courtyard. She liked taking that quiet time to breathe in the blossoms of the newly bloomed almond tree and smell the aroma of the first signs of spring. Solomon's singing outside her window was a welcome change of plans.

Rise up my fair one and come away
For lo, the winter is passed
The rain is over and gone
The flowers appear on the earth
The time of singing has come
The voice of the turtle dove is heard in the land

Shulamit knew by now, the tone in Solomon's singing and joyful melody meant he had a surprise. Throwing on her outer robe, she hastened to greet him in the courtyard, still barefoot.

> *The almond tree has blossomed*
> *Its fragrance fills the air*
> *The fresh sweetness of spring*
> *Is blowing everywhere*
> *The time of dancing has come*
> *For lovers without a care*

Shulamit joined Solomon in the chorus again:

> *For lo, the winter is passed*
> *The rain is over and gone*
> *The flowers appear on the earth*
> *The time of singing has come*

Solomon took hold of Shulamit's hand as they walked to the outside corridors to the south palace gate. Sheriti and Kiya, carrying bags and a pair of shoes for their queen, followed closely behind them once they began walking again. Palace guards carried chests of Shulamit's personal belongings. As they reached the gate, she saw soldiers on horses were waiting to escort them. Before Shulamit could think about what was happening, the door guards opened the carriage door and Solomon assisted her inside. Shulamit's maidens were assisted into a separate carriage with some of her personal effects, and other wagons carrying supplies behind them. When all was loaded up the King gave the sign to move forward.

Shulamit was again a part of a royal entourage, such as she had seen as a child looking down from her mountain on the king's Royal Highway. As her mind flashed back on that scene, she realized she was no longer an observer looking at a dream from above. She had truly stepped into another dream that was happening in her waking life.

As they exited the South gate of the city, Solomon turned toward Shulamit with a smile and announced, "I promised you I would take you to see my family village and the hills my father, King David grew up in. We are now on the road to Bethlehem. I know you have an adventurous heart, and I promised to share many adventures with you."

Shulamit smiled as she peered out of the pulled back curtains on either side of the carriage. She loved the rocky rugged Judean mountains around them, and smiled as they continued winding around the curved road. Bethlehem was only slightly higher than Jerusalem.

Solomon interrupted her thoughts. "We are now on the main trade route that leads through Hebron and down to Egypt." As he spoke, he pointed out landmarks and green mountain ranges on their journey. "Don't you love the way everything is so green after the winter rains. I love to look out and seeing how the flowers dot the hillsides with their various colors. And," he said pointing, "see the way the olive trees line much of the rugged road?"

The horses trotting casually over the curved roads when the back end of the chariot hit a bump, due to the occasional large rock still embedded into the road. Their carriage bounced up and Solomon reached over, grabbing Shulamit to make sure she was ok. He called the driver to slow the horses down to a walk.

Shulamit inhaled, smelling groves of fully bloomed almond trees and cherry trees which were just beginning to bloom, their sweet perfume enhanced the air. Shulamit took another deep breath and remarked, "I have always loved the way early spring always opens by the fragrance the trees and the grape vines. It makes me anticipate the fruits and grapes that will follow."

Her comment sparked another verse from Solomon in his Song of Spring:

> *The fig tree puts forth her green figs*
> *The vines with their tender grapes*
> *Give a very good smell*

Shulamit knew the expression was becoming common, since the country was living in peace under Solomon's reign: *Judah and Israel dwell safely, each man under his vine and fig tree.* Inspired she added to the verse:

> *My Beloved,*
> *You are the fruit of the vine*
> *In time*
> *I will drink of your wine*

Solomon replied to her, singing,

> *And you, my Love*
> *Are the fragrant blossom*
> *Without you*
> *Would no tender grape come*

Together, they sang,

> *For lo, the winter is past*

The rain is over and gone
The flowers appear on the earth
The time of singing has come

They laughed together. "There is no sweeter spring fragrance than you," Solomon confessed. "The morning suits you well, with your hair blowing in the breeze."

Shulamit began combing her fingers through her hair realizing her maidens had barely combed a few strokes of her hair before she had run out the door.

Solomon noticed her hand movements and touched her shoulder, putting her at ease. "I see your maidens have been teaching you the ways of palace grooming," he said. "But remember, I fell in love with a woman who danced with me on a mountain. And her hair flew about her in all directions like goats running down Mt. Gilead."

"Did you fall in love with me at that moment?" she teased.

"The moment I first saw you, I was in love. Everything within me came to life."

"And I fell in love with a singing shepherd who came from I knew not where. Nor at the moment did I care. But I believed in a God who answers prayer."

Solomon laughed deeply, "You too, are the answer to my prayers. God is good. We have a good, good Father."

The caravan ascended another hill and saw shepherds tending sheep scattered on the distant hills. On one hill, a doe with a bell around her neck could be seen leading the herd out to pasture. Shulamit knew the country instinctively; the hills around Bethlehem were not so different from her village home in the mountains.

"Are any of these the hills where David shepherded his sheep, and where he learned to play the harp, wrote songs, and communed with God?"

"I'm sure he kept his sheep on many of the hills around where we are now, but we are not there yet. Tomorrow I will take you on a tour of our village and hills, and you will see David's favorite hill and watering hole. You speak of my father as a legend. Through your eyes, I get a different perspective of him. I understand people need heroes to strengthen their vision of how God can work through man. I suppose, since I knew my father as a man who was not perfect, I saw him differently. Still, I was fully blessed to know how he loved and trusted God. He knew, without God's anointing, he could not rule a nation. I too am a king, and I ask daily for the wisdom to be the king that will lift the heart of God's people to accomplish great things."

Shulamit took a moment to think about what he said before she responded. "I love you as a king, a man, and a shepherd," she finally said,

172

"and I honor the anointing you carry to rule a land. But mostly, you will always be the Shepherd King who sang and danced with me on the mountain."

The sun was bright above them as they finally came to the crest of the mountain where they could see Bethlehem. Solomon ordered the drivers to stop their carriage so they could step out and enjoy the view. A servant soon arrived, offering water mixed with wine. Solomon said, "You will soon drink water from the well of Bethlehem. Do you know the story of David's mighty men breaking through enemy lines to draw water from the well because he wanted the fresh water?" Solomon explained that in the hills near Bethlehem were aquifers. Cracks in the fissures of the rocks created springs of fresh cool water like the clear, clean water that comes up from the well of Bethlehem. "There is no need to mix this water with wine to make it refreshing to drink. David's men loved him so much, they were willing to risk their lives to bring him this fresh water. But he would not drink water that could have cost the men their lives."

"I would like to drink some of this water from the well of Bethlehem."

"You shall, my love," Solomon said. He took her hand, leading her up a hill to a shaded place under a large oak tree. "Soon, you shall drink of the water from the well my father loved to drink from." A sudden insight came to his mind regarding the heart of his bride, "They are big footsteps to step into, my love. I know."

"Yes," Shulamit replied, "I get that. I am stepping into your footsteps of wisdom as I walk with you. I wish to receive all I can from you. I wish to be like you, because I love you. I love God's anointing upon you."

"My Love, you honor me. You see glory in me that perhaps few do. I hope you always do. Kings like to be honored and kings respond to honor with favor. Maybe it is why you are my favorite. Love is wonderful that way," he said as he gave her a hug. "Come, let's return to the carriage," as he began to lead her back down the hill.

Feeling the heat of the day, Shulamit asked, "Are there any places to swim in these fresh waters?"

"Yes. I know some secret places where you can swim with the women." Suddenly he stopped as an idea came to him. "Someday, I will build pools near the aquafer in the south of the village. My brides, and the ladies who serve in the palace, may swim there."

Shulamit watched her betrothed. Solomon got a certain sparkle in his eyes when a creative idea came through his mind. "I am starting to know you," she said. When you get that look, you are dreaming of great things."

"I thought I always have a sparkle in my eyes around you," he laughed.

"So, I put a sparkle in your eye?"

"You help me dream, you make me sing, and you fill me with wonder."

Shulamit suddenly had a funny memory. It was something her mother said about her father. "My mother always told me that when people got around my father, they started dreaming."

"And so you are your father's daughter."

"My mother saw my father's dreams as more work that she would have to help him carry out."

"Dream on, my love. I love work and have plenty of workers. We are the people of God and should be the most creative of all people. I also do my best dreaming when I am standing on a mountain looking out at the view. My father often quoted our tribal forefather Caleb when he had a battle before him. "I will take my mountain," he said, slightly imitating his father. "Caleb was a legend to my father. He was strengthened by Caleb's faith. Great men before us set examples that help us take our own individual mountains.

"I know about Caleb," Shulamit said, turning toward Solomon's face. "That is why my father gave my brother that name. He wanted his sons to be strong mountain men. Conquerors."

"The more I know of your father, the more I see the man of faith behind you. I understand why my father was his friend. Solomon paused briefly, and then said, "There are many kinds of mountains. And everyone is born to conquer their own; be it family, faith, music, government, business, educating future generation, even creative arts. Together we will go to the heights of Lebanon, and the tops of Amana, Herman and Senir. There is always a great future for dreamers. And you are made for more, Shula, for you have conquered me."

They reached the carriage and traveled up and down a few more small hills before they came into view of Bethlehem. It was beautiful to behold in the distance, situated alongside the limestone hills from which they built their city walls and high towers. The procession descended into the village, creating a spectacle as they passed through the large, fortified city gates. People waved and greeted the king and soldiers as they entered. Shulamit noted their curiosity about the special occasion that brought the king to his family home. Solomon whispered in her ear. "The villagers love the family of Jesse in Bethlehem. David retook the village from the Philistines when it was conquered during the time of Saul. David conquered the enemy. It was a happy time in Israel, and my family was honored. Now they honor me for keeping the peace.

Solomon directed his carriage driver to the center of the town square. When they stopped, he escorted Shulamit down from the carriage, leading her to a large well. Solomon drew some water into a bucket and ladled a drink for Shulamit. She swallowed the cool fresh water and sighed.

"Do you like it?" he asked.

Her face answered him clearly, but Shulamit said, "As I drink this water,

I see how great stories are made. I understand why David would desire this water and why soldiers would risk their life to obtain it from this well."

"You are truly a blessing to me," said Solomon.

From the well, Solomon led Shulamit on a short walk through the village to the house of Jesse. They came to a sizable dwelling. The rooftop had short stone wall sidings for safety, while plants sat on the rooftop walls creating beauty. The outside staircase to the roof had vines growing up the sides, creating more serenity in the landscape. Shulamit knew, without seeing them, that clothes would be drying in the sun on the roof and tools and supplies were often stored in a storage room on the roof. The animal stall was not attached to the house as in many country homes, but behind the house. This layout kept the smell of animals at a distance. But she did smell something. Behind the house, a lamb was being roasted on a large open pit. Shulamit thought, *Word must have gotten out that we were coming. People are fast to spread news in the country, and we do love to show hospitality.*

Members of his family came out to greet them. "Welcome, welcome," they said in greeting while embracing everyone with warm hugs. They escorted Solomon and his bride to be, into the central courtyard.

Shulamit expected to see a dirt floor and could not hide her surprise as she looked upon glazed tiles beneath them. Solomon read her expression and explained, "I can see that you expected to see a dirt floor. As I explained before, when my father had to reconquer Bethlehem from the Philistines it was in shambles. What I did not tell you was how David took my grandfather Jesse and my grandmother to Moab for their protection as Saul sought to kill his family. The town that had been unprotected now had to rebuild their homes.

"Oh." Shulamit said with a concerned expression, "I did not know all that happened to your family."

"So," Solomon continued, my father tried to make it up to the town by providing the means for them to rebuild with a few amenities," he said, motioning with his hand, "like the glazed limestone tiles in place of a dirt floor. He gave them new furnishings too. Remember the low cedar tables you can also see in the courtyard?"

"I do," said Shulamit. The tile design is very pretty, and I see it keeps dust down, and is cleaner, like in the palace. I hope someday all the farmer's homes can have clean tile floors."

"You always think of other's needs," Solomon said. "I hope to make everyone's life better in Israel."

Solomon began introducing her to members of his large extended family. "Most of my family now lives in Jerusalem, leading in the government or military. But since all tribes must keep their original inheritances, we never give our land away. Some members of the family must always maintain it. It is nice to return to your family roots from time to time."

Shulamit looked up to see another familiar face. Nathan bowed briefly, and she smiled. Nathan gave a warm smile in return. Solomon noted his presence and, smiling himself, said, "Nathan has always been fond of our country home, is that not so?" he asked Nathan.

Nathan was different than the rest of this ruling family, Shulamit noticed. He seemed more like a man from the country. More spiritually inclined, like the prophet he was named after. He also truly enjoyed worshipping in the tabernacle and through that, they had become friends. Despite his natural preferences, Nathan was obedient and loyal to whatever governmental assignments his brother, the king, gave him. She could tell they were a very close family, and loyal to one another. Shulamit noted the authority that Solomon had as king was a shared authority in his lineage as a ruling family. There was an honor in their character to give their lives to a greater cause then themselves. *They are like soldiers who would lay down their lives in battle to save their families and country,* Shulamit noted within herself.

The evening meal was laid out before them. The men sat at one side of the table, talking of agriculture and what was happening in Jerusalem. They remarked on how well the temple construction was coming. Shulamit sat at the other side of the table with the women holding babies and children. She loved talking to everyone. While this family carried authority as extended members of the king's family, and did indeed behave as ruling class in Jerusalem, here, in the country, they were completely ordinary people. They were just like her family.

She loved it.

Like her family, they were shepherds and vineyard keepers. Like her family, they loved to drink wine, sing and laugh, and tell stories.

Shulamit's mind wandered in the presence of these joyful people. She realized how great God was, who lifted ordinary people up to greatness as they answered their call. She realized that Solomon and his family were actually very unaware of themselves and their influence upon others. Observing their humble nature, she better understood why Solomon was surprised when she spoke of his father as being a legend. David's mighty men were indeed a legend. They were strong fighters who did great things in moments of destiny. But even their anointing resulted from King David's leadership and his ability to instill great faith in his followers.

Abba, please keep my heart open to You. May I continually receive from Your heart through Your anointed people and the psalms You poured into the heart of David. Solomon told me he felt unprepared to be king when he accepted Your call. But You have been faithful to give him great wisdom to rule. Lord, I want all this too. I want to be like this sweet, humble family. She realized, in agreeing to step into something, the "yes," within her spirit allowed God to work through her. *Yes, yes, yes,* she continued to say within her spirit.

That evening, as Shulamit and Solomon climbed the winding stairs up to the rooftop to sit out under the stars, she shared her heart with him. She talked about how she realized that people who did great things for God were just ordinary people who said, "yes," to God.

Solomon smiled in amazement at the insight of his bride to be. "God has given you wisdom, my love" he told her. "I write about wisdom, and I tell people to get wisdom and understanding, but everyone has to come to that awakening themselves and be hungry to accept it."

Shulamit looked into his eyes with amazement.

"I asked for wisdom," Solomon said. "And God gives me wisdom continually. But it still has to really become part of me, planted deep within my heart. My mind can grasp things, but it is a process of doing and life experiences that makes us become this wisdom."

"I never realized that you are learning too."

"Of course, we all learn together as we go through life. We learn to love each other better as we share our hearts. You grew up freely sharing your heart with your family, and I grew up guarding my words; you are helping me express myself more clearly," Solomon said, as he pulled Shulamit's shawl up over her shoulder.

"So we are really growing together?"

"You are my beautiful one, Shulamit, and you are becoming. You are like a beautiful star shining in the heavens. Look," Solomon pointed at a group of stars in the heavens. "See that bright star?"

"Yes."

"That star is called, *Hamal,* and in a line below it *Mesarthin*, and below is *Arieta*, they form the horn of the constellation *Aries*."

"You mean the ram."

"Yes, the ram. So, you know something of the stars?"

"A little, my father always told us that when certain stars arose in the sky it was a new season, and it told us the most important thing to do in that season."

"Yes, a star can point to many things. In Jerusalem when we see the constellation *Aries* we know it is time for Passover, and we remember the Passover lamb that had to be sacrificed to save the first born male child in Egypt."

"And Papa told me how *Elohim* provided a ram so Abraham would not have to sacrifice his own son. But someday would sacrifice His only son. It makes no sense to me, but I remember Papa taught me the Torah the best way he knew it."

Solomon said, "That is a bit of a mystery, but here in the country when we see the ram horn picture in the sky we know it is time for the barley harvest."

They laughed.

"Heaven speaks to earth," Solomon laughed. "I do love mysteries, but I have learned to wait until our Father in heaven reveals them to us." They laughed again. "My starry-eyed bride, we could sit out here all night, but I have a long day prepared for us tomorrow."

***

The next morning Solomon called to her outside of her lattice window, "Rise, my love. The birds are singing their morning songs of joy, and the shepherds are leading the sheep out to pasture."

Dressing herself quickly in clothes for the country, Shulamit's maidens gave her sturdy sandals for country hiking. Solomon was dressed in shepherd's clothes, complete with staff and lyre slung over his back. He had a wineskin strapped across his shoulder and a short sword in the sheath of his girdle. Shulamit took the food pouch Solomon offered her, carrying it over her shoulder. She giggled when he gave her a small sling then tucked it into a pocket in her vest.

He grinned as he said, "Just in case we need it." Then he took her hand to begin their adventure. They first ascended a steep rocky hill. A fresh breeze blew from the west, carrying the smell of the fresh blooms. Solomon and Shulamit walked through olive groves filled with star shaped flowers in white, yellow and purple.

"These are lovely," she said.

"Yes," said Solomon, "but you are more so."

"In our village, we call these flowers the star Bethlehem."

Shepherds were leading their herds, driving sheep and goats as they continued out into the farther hills. They rounded a hill, and Solomon said, "We are getting close to David's spot." He pointed to a large oak tree besides a hill where water cascaded down into a large pond.

Walking up to the large tree, the two collapsed under its shade. "This was his favorite spot," Solomon almost panted. "He had shade here, and lots of green grass for the sheep and water to refresh them. He composed many songs sitting out here under the trees."

Shulamit imagined how it was and could see King David singing right where she was. She could see his soul being restored by the still waters, and she could feel the peace.

"Do you know the song about the Lord being his shepherd?"

"Who in Israel does not know that psalm," he commented as he reached for his lyre and began to play the psalm.

The Lord is my shepherd. I shall not want.

He makes me to lie down in green pastures
He restores my soul. He leads me besides still waters…

Shulamit sang with him. Their voices blended together with a lovely timbre. His voice was deep and masculine sounding, while hers was high pitched and soft. Individually, both voices possessed a beautiful tone.

Shulamit traced her fingers over the grass. "Here I am," she spoke with wonder, "where David wrote his psalms. And I'm with you singing as if he were here. I can feel him here singing through you as if we are there with him as he wrote this song. You carry so much of his heart."

"I think you bring out that worship side in me. When I watched you sit peacefully down, leaning on the trunk of the tree. It is almost like I saw you enter a dream while we sang. Your great sense of wonder allows you to become part of every story you hear. Your sense of intuition and knowing shows you have made a connection with the heavenly realm. Sometimes I can feel angels around you. Your sweetness is beyond anyone I have ever known." Solomon looked into her eyes for a moment, and words began to come. He picked up his lyre and began to sing.

In the stillness, she knows
She knows, in the stillness
As she lies beside the still waters
Her tender soul is restored
As her heart rests in peace
She knows, she is adored

She knows, in the stillness
In the stillness, she knows
The peace in the paths
Where righteousness flows
She's a picture of calm
Where the gentle breeze blows

In the stillness, she knows
She knows, in the stillness
Aware the good shepherd is near
She bears no want or fear
Her sweet tranquil smile reveals
Goodness and Mercy is here

She knows, in the stillness

The Worshipper and the King

In the stillness, she knows
The heart of the writer's psalm
In wonder she enters the story
So serene is her graceful body
Reflecting the peace and the glory

In the stillness, she knows
She knows in the stillness
Beauty rests on her presence
Drawing her king to come near
Who through words in a song
Describes his delightful pleasure

She knows, in the stillness
In the stillness, she knows
As she lies beside the still waters
By love's song her soul is restored
Her trust is assured
She knows she is adored

A sweet shyness overcame Shulamit as her cheeks blushed, and then she responded, "When I was a young girl, I dreamed that someone I loved would write a love song for me. You never stop."

"You make me sing. The very essence of who you are is love. You make songs flow out of me. I want to never forget these moments as our hearts are growing together," Solomon confessed as he took hold of her hand.

Shulamit felt a warmth inside her body, and another flush coming over her cheeks. Even being in the shade of the tree could not prevent it. She knew she was safe with Solomon, but she began to understand why her culture never let men and women be alone together. Not that they were completely alone. She was aware that there were guards just beyond her sight. Shulamit was aware of her own temptations. And while no words were spoken, she knew Solomon felt it too. The constraint was becoming difficult to maintain as their emotions for one another began burning inside.

Shulamit was first to break the overpowering mood as she walked over to the pond. She sat upon a rock, unlaced her sandals, and let her feet dangle into the cool water. Solomon walked over a little further and stepped into the water, throwing handfuls of water over his head to cool off.

Solomon ended the silence as he burst out, "We need to marry soon. Are you ready?"

"I think I can't spend any more time with you alone unless we marry," Shulamit admitted.

They both laughed. They stopped for a brief moment, but then laughed again.

Solomon said, "You are making me laugh again. Now I know we sometimes laugh because we were trying to hide our feelings of being overwhelmed with one another. This laugh is freedom; this laugh is joy; this laugh is hiding our overwhelming feelings. This laugh is love rolled into its many emotions. This laugh is the sound of lovers excited in each other's presence. This laugh is a sign of a lifetime of laughter to come." Noticing the lengthening shadows, Solomon said, "Let's return to the village before sunset. I want to take you up to the tower and show you the sunset across the Judean desert."

Shulamit tied the laces of her shoes together and slung them over her shoulder. She wanted to feel free like she was in her own hill country. They partly walked and ran down the hill. Solomon led the way as he knew the path, but Shulamit was right on his track. "You are probably the only woman in the world who can keep up with me, and I know the trail."

At one point, Solomon stopped and pointed toward a mountain. He said, "This is where the spring feeds water into Jerusalem. It also trickles down the hill into a small lake near the outskirts of Bethlehem. You can swim with the maidens and ladies in the village."

"I would love that," Shulamit affirmed.

It was nearing dusk as they returned to the village. Solomon led her to the tower on the wall above the gate of the city. Surprised, Shulamit looked out and saw bright yellow sunlight covering ranges of golden mountains. As the sun came down, and the sky started turning shades of orange and pink the mountains turned from brown to purple in the distance. It was an amazing sight. Never had she witnessed the desert part of the country.

"It is absolutely beautiful. It is how I visualize the Shekinah glory over mount Sinai when Moses received the ten commandments. Isn't that why he covered himself with a veil so they could not see the glory fade?"

"Moses had a reflected glory, from being with God. We often reflect God when we are carrying his glory," Solomon explained.

"You mean like that sparkle you get in your eye when you are coming up with a new idea? Or when you are writing a song?"

"Or looking at you?"

"Looking at me?" Shulamit asked.

"Yes, that overpowering look you get in your eyes when you give me that admiring look sometimes. I have to turn away because it can be overpowering."

"I didn't realize I did that."

"You do, my love. I realized the moment when you realized you were really in love with me, when you admitted you really missed me, and didn't want to be apart from me. I saw the deep love. Your eyes light up, and they carry a gold radiance of glory."

"Hmm," Shulamit admitted, "I didn't know that."

"I have also seen a glory in you when you dance. A glow comes all around you."

"I have seen a golden radiance around the Ark at times in the Tabernacle during worship."

"That is it. Sometimes the glory we see is obvious, but other times we must grow into the glory to learn to recognize it. It is like it is hidden from people who are not seeking to see the glory."

"I am always seeking to feel the glory when I worship," Shulamit said as the realization came.

"Your glory in worshipping grows stronger as you are more closely relating to the Spirit of God."

"Sometimes when I am dancing, I feel so much energy that I can dance forever."

"That energy is also glory, my love. Glory can be presented in many ways. Sometimes we see it, sometimes we feel it and sometimes we are just overflowing with energy. Sort of like the sun. I would like to discover it someday, but I watch how plants need the sun to grow and I know there is energy."

"Amazing, I never thought so much of glory."

"Glory is everywhere. Remember last night looking at the stars. David wrote a song about, how the heavens declare the glory of God; they are telling a story. Each month is part of a sequence in God's redemption plan, and it will be revealed in God's time. Our father in heaven showed the pictures to Adam and their meanings so he would know there was a redemption plan for man so he would not lose hope. Adam taught this science of astronomy to Seth who taught it to his sons. They needed to know the times and seasons of the year for seedtime and harvest as well."

"How good our Father is, to never leave us without guidance and hope," Shulamit expressed with great wonder. You have opened to me an understanding of glory that I was never aware of. It gives deeper meaning to life."

"Yes, and now, on earth, you have seen the big view of the sunset from Bethlehem towards the desert in the distance." Solomon pointed South. "About a day's journey southwest by horse, is Hebron, the city where my father was crowned king. It is our nation's oldest community, where the Tomb of our Patriarchs is located. Abraham purchased that land. Abraham, Isaac, Jacob, Sarah, Rebecca, and Leah were buried there."

"I'm gaining greater understanding of our nation's history. I love learning about it," Shulamit declared.

"Look over there toward the olive trees. That is village of Tekoa. It produces the best olives and olive oil in Israel."

"The chief cook in the palace told me our olive oil came from Tekoa."

"You are learning about our culture too," Solomon smiled.

Then Solomon pointed over toward the southeast, explaining how it was the direction of the Dead Sea and En Gedi, the oasis where his father hid from Saul.

Shulamit nodded as he pointed, but thoughts were running in her head.

Turning Northeast, Solomon pointed toward Jericho. "Jericho is possibly the oldest city in the world. It is situated on one of the main trade routes of the world. It is at the edge of a ford where at the right times of the year it was easy to wade across. Jericho is the entrance to the Judean Plateau from the East, and the route North across the country. That is why it was an important place for our forefathers under Joshua's leadership to conquer upon entering the Promised Land.

Shulamit, being her usual adventurous self, made her petition to her lover, "Is it possible I can visit these places someday. In particular, I would like to visit the places where King David hid from Saul. Then my understanding of his psalms of crying out to God for help might become deeper."

Solomon responded, "I believe you have a deeper insight into the king's prayers than you think. But I saw the look in your eye when I pointed out the locations to you. You know I can never deny you anything. In God's time, I will take you. It is several days ride. You may have to learn to ride a horse to make long trips."

"I know how to ride a donkey," Shulamit answered, "but I have never considered riding a horse before."

"As queen, your worldview will expand. Many nations and lands come to our palace. Understanding where they come from is always wise. I still ride a donkey in steep places. But in long distances, when possible, I ride horses because they are much faster. I will teach you."

"Ok," Shulamit agreed. *New visions and dreams I never thought of. Lord, you are full of surprises.*

As they headed to the house of Jesse, Shulamit pondered more. *The house of Jesse, City of David, Temple of Solomon,* Shulamit thought. *These are all names from one family and I am now part of this family.* A holy fear came over her.

Entering the villa, they joined the rest of the family around the large table for the family meal. There was lots of laughter, song, and wine. Solomon stood up and gave a toast, "Today, my bride walked where David walked, and she has drunk from the well of Bethlehem. She has become part of our family, is she not beautiful?" Shulamit blushed. Then Solomon began to sing the song he wrote that day. "In the stillness, she knows"

"The king is in love. Let us cheer," a cousin shouted as he made a toast with another goblet of wine."

As the evening was ending, Solomon announced, "Tomorrow, Nathan and I will join the rest of the men in the town in shearing sheep. My bride-to-be has expressed a desire to swim in our nearby lake. She misses her secret place to swim in on her mountain. Our country's natural lakes are better than any man-made mikvah pools within the palace, though I have designs for pools here and in the new palace after the temple is built. I trust some of you ladies will join her when she goes swimming. Let all the pretty women have a day of cleansing. If any of you need to learn to swim, ask my Shulamit, I've heard she is an excellent swimmer."

The next day Shulamit, her maidens, and several of Solomon's female relatives swam in the lake. Most of the country women knew how to swim, but Shulamit taught those who didn't how to float by paddling like a dog upon the water and bringing their heads up for air. "The most important thing is to learn to float and be relaxed in the water." Sheriti and Kiya had never swum and were afraid, but Shulamit prompted them by holding them upon her arm to float until they felt comfortable. Then Shulamit surprised them all as she climbed up a high rock and dove in. They laughed as she came up grabbing hold of her undergarments.

One of the village ladies shouted, "I can see why the king loves you so much. You are full of fun and laughter."

Shulamit replied, "I used to be embarrassed when people laughed at me. My brothers always teased me. But I finally accepted that it is part of who I am." She continued treading water as she expressed, "I have so missed swimming."

Towards the end of the day, Sheriti and Kiya had learned to float. Kiya shouted out in joy, "This is one of the most fun days of my whole life."

It dawned upon Shulamit that servants needed to be able to find enjoyment as a reward for their labors. She started considering ways those who served in the palace could be happy in their labor.

That evening her maidens fussed over her even more. They massaged sweet oils into her skin and rubbed her hair with scented oil, brushing it until it shone. "We love to make you beautiful for your beloved," Sheriti declared. They filed and painted her nails with a soft red henna. Then they all rested before the evening meal as they were tired from their exercise and being in the sun.

Unlike the ladies, rising from their rest smelling like roses, Solomon and Nathan came back smelling like sheep. The contrast made them all laugh at dinner. One woman said in a laughing voice, "This is why we women do not mind eating at the other end of the table."

Shulamit could now compare life in the country and in the palace. *They are quite different, but there is good in both.*

Judy Pendell

20 THE WEDDING PROCESSION

The town's people waved goodbye as the king assisted Shulamit back into their carriage. "Blessings, to our king and his bride to be!" they shouted as they walked behind the carriage to see them off. Shulamit felt so loved and honored by his family.

"What a lovely family you have. I feel part of it already," Shulamit said.

"You are a part of it, my love," Solomon responded. "If sometime in the future you need a break from the palace, I will arrange protection for you to visit them in secret. My family will always protect you too. They have been through a lot, and they know how to protect themselves. Now, they are just like soldiers."

"Thank you for bringing me to meet them." Shulamit said. She tilted her head, changing the subject. "You didn't talk much about shearing sheep last night, at least not across the table." Shulamit smiled at the memory, "But did you enjoy it?"

"Oh, yes," Solomon said, returning her smile. "Nathan and I as a team held our own, but we were not the quickest. These country people do it all the time and they are very skilled. It is fun for me though, to get away from the palace and be an ordinary citizen from time to time. Keeps me in touch with everyone, and that is important for a leader."

"Do you think living in a palace will make me forget my country origins?"

"You my love," Solomon said, taking her hand briefly, "I don't think so. I realize you are learning the ways of the court, but it is your humble origins that make you so adorable." He squeezed her hand. "The natural sweetness and beauty inside of you does not need to be so highly adorned as other queens in the court, because they don't have what you have."

Shulamit smiled. "You always know how to make me feel good, and comfortable to be myself."

"Now I will show you how to retrace your steps back to the city. Do you remember that large tree?" He let go of her hand, pointing out of the carriage.

"The oak tree we sat under?" Shulamit laughed. "How could I forget? I see the cherry trees are fully blossomed now, and the olive trees remain a healthy evergreen. From this direction I can see more of the purple and red flowers stand out."

"Now you know it is a sign you have reached Bethlehem."

Spring is so beautiful here," she commented.

The horses picked up a trot when they passed the rocky roads. As they traveled, Solomon pointed out more landmarks. Soon they had traveled enough to overlook Jerusalem on the horizon. In the late afternoon, the mountains and hills surrounding Jerusalem on all sides were breathtaking.

The caravan had to wind down a curved road around the city before ascending to enter the gates of the city. Soldiers on horses met them at the gate, escorting them through the newer part of the city where the Temple was being built. Across the aqueduct toward the City of David, Shulamit noted the elegant brass lanterns hanging from poles. They were just being lit, and they glimmered along the newly partitioned city roads from the new Temple to the City of David where the palace was.

"I never noticed the lanterns before."

"It is because they are new," said Solomon. "The lanterns bring light to the city at night and give protection against crimes in the dark."

"They add beauty," Shulamite said acknowledging how the new palm trees, stone planters with flowers, and grasses edged the road. "I love the arrangements of roses, and lilies and the, umm…" she faltered, forgetting names.

"Tulips, and lisianthus," Solomon pointed out. "We are beautifying the city for special occasions."

"Oh," Shulamit said. She did not want to ask what the occasion was, and she knew Solomon liked surprising her.

As they got closer to the palace, she saw poles draped with golden ropes. They created a walkway from the tabernacle to the palace. In the distance, she saw a large tent in front of the palace. Before she could think about what she saw, her family came running toward her from the side entrance. The carriage began to slow, and Shulamit waved excitedly.

"Rebecca!" Shulamit shouted, "You are here!"

"I would not miss the wedding of my best friend," Rebecca responded, tears in her eyes.

Shulamit was ready to break protocol, open the door of the carriage, and jump out, but the guard quickly moved to open her door and helped her. Solomon followed behind.

Embracing her lifelong friend, she turned to look at Solomon. He gave her a proud smile. She knew he was enjoying her surprise. Little Miriam came tugging on her robe, "Isn't this exciting? We are going to have a big wedding. Twirling around in her new dress she giggled and said, "Don't I look pretty?"

"Yes, Mirriam," Shulamit said and grabbed hold of her waist. She attempted to lift Miriam up, as she always had, but then said, "You are too big to lift anymore, little sister."

Joshua and Caleb escorted her mother over. Shulamit embraced her and then her brothers. She could not hold back the tears of joy at seeing her family. Solomon stepped forward and embraced Joshua and Caleb.

"Ima Miriam," he said as he kissed her respectfully. Solomon picked up little Miriam, swinging her around. "I guess it is no longer a surprise that we are going to have a wedding. Come. Let's go in and dine with the rest of the family."

They were escorted into Solomon's private dining hall. Shulamit's uncle, Jehiel, was already there with her aunt and cousins and they all rose to greet the family. Bathsheba walked over to Ima Miriam, taking her to sit by her and the other women. The room soon filled with laughter and loud, excited speeches.

Solomon stood up and silenced them. "I will make introductions." The brief moment of silence and respect for the king's introductions reverted back to many talking at once. "If you have never spoken to someone here," he said over everyone, "now is your chance."

Shulamit could not wait to spend more time alone with her best friend Rebecca. Turning to her she said, "I can't tell you how happy I am to see you, Rebecca. My friend, with whom I shared all my childhood dreams, I have so much more to share with you."

"Me too," said Rebecca.

Servants came and served the food and wine greeted by laughter.

"How did you all manage to get away from the farm at barley harvest?" Shulamit inquired of her brothers.

"We live in a village full of people who help each other," Joshua said half-joking, "but the king did send a few servants to help while we are gone."

Shulamit turned toward Solomon, "Your surprises always amaze me. You don't miss the details."

After a short time, someone arrived at the dining room door. Solomon signaled him to come in. "I want you to meet Emrah," he said to Shulamit. "He will be our new master of ceremonies. Emrah will be working with High Priest Zadok, planning arrangements within the Tabernacle to seat our honored guests. He needs to prepare details for Asaph to compose special worship music. and work with Ahishan and Benaiah as well. So tonight, we will all retire early. The next few days will be extremely busy."

Shulamit bid her family good night, glowing with happiness. Afterwards, Solomon walked her to her chamber. He gave her a kiss on the cheek and said, "Sleep well my love, tomorrow will be a big day."

Sleep? Shulamit thought. It seemed impossible. As her maids prepared her for bed, she asked Meliba to be sure all her wedding garments were set out and prepared to dress in a moment's notice.

"I assure you all is ready," Meliba consoled her. She showed Shulamit where her wedding dress lay protected yet on display. All her wedding effects were in sight.

Finally, Shulamit gave in to her exhausted body, and within moments she fell asleep.

***

The next day was a whirl to Shulamit.

She was not sure when exactly the wedding would occur. Solomon was keeping that a surprise to everyone. Everyone was on standby, practicing their individual parts.

The following morning Ima Miriam, Rebecca, and little Miriam came to her quarters early. They spent the day grooming each other. Shulamit laughed as she saw how shy her mother and best friend were about others grooming them.

Miriam was not timid. She was enjoying it all. She did, however, need considerable help to learn how to walk down the aisle in the Tabernacle.

Kiya tried to explain stateliness. "You stand straight," she said, "and you walk slowly down the aisle, right behind Rebecca, in front of Shulamit and your mother. Drop flower petals slowly first to one side, then the other," she said. "Not so quickly you run out before you make it up to the front. And remember to smile, and don't look too serious." Miriam was enthralled by Kiya's accent.

Little Miriam did not realize she was trying so hard to remember everything that her face was extremely serious. She forced herself to smile. When she did, everyone laughed. Miriam looked like she was going to cry thinking everyone was making fun of her.

Mama made light of it. "Shulamit, she is your little sister and so much like you."

"She hugged her little sister. "I remember how easily I got my feelings hurt when people laughed at me. But now I just accept it. It is who we are, but it has never stopped us from doing anything, right?" Miriam took a moment, then gave her big sister a genuine smile.

"That is my girl," Mama said. "If it makes you feel any better, I am trying to remember all I have to do, too."

The air lightened as Rebecca said, "Me too."

"I hope I don't forget my wedding vows," Shulamit said. "I've been practicing them for weeks, but sometimes I get anxious and forget things too."

They all laughed.

"We haven't had this kind of wedding before, so it is new to all of us," Meliba admitted.

Other ladies of the court began to arrive in Shulamit's private court. They came to practice carrying the long wedding veil into the Tabernacle. The goal was to keep it off the floor. The 12 women took several practices to learn how to work together, and little Miriam laughed, knowing she was not the only one who had to learn things.

Shulamit brought her mother to where she kept her special jewelry collection, showing her necklaces to wear to the wedding, but her mother was reticent.

"Oh," Ima Miriam said, "the last time I wore all my gold jewelry was at my own wedding a long time ago, and this is much more jewelry."

Bathsheba had just quietly entered the room. Hearing the comment, she spoke, "Your humility is a blessing to us all. But you are the mother of a queen now, and by wearing these, you are displaying the glory of the kingdom." Bathsheba's face softened at Ima Miriam, and she said sweetly, "This is a rare day, and you won't always have to wear so much. I only wear my royal jewels on special occasions myself. But remember, as you walk your daughter down the aisle, you too are being honored for the wonderful daughter you brought into the world and raised so delightfully." The two women smiled at each other. "As mothers it is such a delight to see our children enter into such joy."

"That is a wondrous perspective," Ima Miriam said. "Thank you."

Shulamit could see her mother was still unsure, but with the Queen Mother being so kind, it certainly helped to ease her mother's concerns.

The women spent the day sharing stories of love and enduring friendships. Shulamit hoped to remember these moments forever. She could see her thoughts mirroring the women around her.

***

It was during the middle of the fourth watch that trumpets could be heard outside the palace.

Ahishan arrived at Shulamit's chamber and said, "Prepare yourself quickly, for the bridegroom is arriving."

Meliba, Sherita and Kiya were already awake, moving about the chambers with efficiency. They helped Shulamit into her white silk wedding dress, delicately embellished with gold threads and precious stones. Her outer robe of scarlet, purple and sapphire was also lined with gold trimmings and scents. Myrrh, frankincense, spikenard, saffron, calamus, and cinnamon enveloped her as she moved. Shulamit's gold necklaces stacked up her neck making her head feel a strange disconnection to her body. As Meliba attached the gold chains from her nose ring to her right ear she began to feel the queenliness of the day settle in her mind. She began to breathe slowly as the long gold chains hung down from her neck, arms, and wrists. There were even small gold chains around her ankles. Black Kohl for her eyes, lips touched with red, and for her cheeks, a dash of pink color. How this went so quickly was beyond her, but as the golden slippers were placed upon her feet, she knew she would soon be ready. They combed her long bouncing curls of hair, sprinkling it with gold dust. The final touch was her long lace veil, anchored with a thin, gold band containing precious jewels.

As they placed the tiara on her head Meliba assured her, "You are the most beautiful bride we have ever seen. You will make all Israel rejoice."

There was a knock on the door.

It was time.

The guards were stoic as they escorted Shulamit to the outer wall of the palace. There she could be seen by all with the help of the lanterns hanging from the wall. She looked out at the city lit up with candles, lanterns and men carrying torches. It was dazzling. Looking down, Shulamit saw the most majestic picture. King Solomon, her bridegroom, wore a royal robe of purple trimmed with gold. He was sitting on a majestic white horse with bejeweled golden bridles.

Surrounding him were the trumpeters and joyful instrumentalists. They were followed by sixty mighty men on foot. Each man had a sword on his thigh to protect from any attempt of ambush in the night, being experts in war.

The bridegroom proclaimed in a loud voice, "I have come for my bride!" Solomon reached for his lyre and began to sing, as other musicians on flutes, organs, and harps joined in:

> *I have come for my bride*
> *Before the Holy City*
> *Let my bride say, "Yes"*
> *And everyone agree*

Shulamit shouted down from the palace wall, "Yes, yes, yes!" The people gathering around shouted, "We agree!"

> *Let Heaven and earth*
> *Be a witness for me*
> *I the bridegroom say, "Yes"*
> *When you say, "Yes" to me*

> *Come my bride, come my bride*
> *Come and walk with me*
> *All Heaven came to earth*

The Worshipper and the King

When you agreed to marry

You are my bride forever
Abba is in the midst of us
Our whole world changed
The moment you said, "Yes"

"Yes, yes, yes!" Shulamit sang.
"Yes, yes, yes!" Solomon proclaimed.
"Yes, yes, yes!" The people celebrated.
"Come my bride, we are blessed!" The bridegroom sang.

Trumpets sounded and the crowd shouted, "Come and meet your bridegroom." Shulamit was escorted down the palace steps by her bridesmaids, dressed in the royal blue dress she designed. They carried her long veil as she walked to join her bridegroom. Her bridesmaids moved beautifully, never letting the veil touch the ground.

Joyful music continued to play, and the chosen people sang:

The King has come,
The King has come,
He's come gather his bride.
Her Joyful week as now begun
And the whole kingdom rejoices.

Solomon jumped off his horse and dashed over to his bride. Shulamit was trying to hold the veil across her face where only her eyes were seen but the wind blew the veil away from her face as Solomon approached.

"I know it is you," he whispered as he embraced her openly. "And you are your most beautiful. I give you permission to pull your veil to the side and let the people see you, only cover it in the Tabernacle so I can uncover it again."

People shouted, "Bless the king and his queen!" as Solomon walked his bride over to the bridal carriage where her mother had just arrived. This cedar wood carriage was ornately designed, gilded with gold lions to represent the tribe of Judah. The cushions inside were royal red with golden embroidery designs of crowns and flowers. Shulamit's bridesmaids gently folded the veil beside her in the carriage. The elegant red mare wore golden bridles studded with emerald and rubies. The horse was driven by a soldier in royal military attire. Shulamit took a short moment to appreciate how brilliant everything shone on her carriage, even in the lantern light hours before dawn.

Another carriage of equal elegance pulled up behind them with Queen Bathsheba and Nathan, who was her escort for the procession. Emrah, the master of ceremonies, directed the carriages into position, waving the next carriage into place. This one held her brothers, Rebecca, and her little sister. Miriam, beaming with excitement, waved at all the people.

Before Solomon could climb back on his horse to join his place in the pageantry, Bathsheba signaled the master of ceremonies to bring Solomon over to her carriage. When he arrived, she held out a wreath of flowers. The king bowed, allowing her to adorn him.

"I present this for your espousal," Bathsheba proclaimed. "On this day, may all of Israel see the gladness of your heart." Solomon bowed again to his mother as a soldier walked his horse over to him. Smiling, Solomon jumped on the horse, ready to join his brothers in their place of the procession.

By the time the master of ceremonies had everyone in their place for the parade, the sun was beginning to rise. They could now march through the city and let all Jerusalem participate in the joy of their marriage.

Shulamit watched the sun begin to capture all the gold and jewels in the morning glow. "I never expected such a big event," Shulamit said to her mother, full of nervous energy. "Solomon told me a royal marriage is about the kingdom. I knew it would be quite spectacular, but this is still quite a lot of people and jewels and gold!"

"That is true my daughter," her mother replied with calming assurance. "Once you are part of the royal family, you are no longer just your own. You are now a servant of the people, part of the royal emblem of all their dreams. Your wedding *should* be a public display for the kingdom. But the king is very much in love with you, and he wants to share that joy with everyone as well.

"I love him, too," Shulamit said, beaming.

"As a mother, I am pleased to know this. Seeing you marry reminds me of all my own happy memories with your father, and we need reminders of our lives' happiest moments."

Before they could go deeper into their conversation, trumpets began to blow, and the horse began to pull them forward.

The trumpeters marched in the front, followed by the soldiers from the twelve tribes of Israel. They rode on highly decorated horses carrying the flags of their tribes. Judah's soldier rode in the front with the banner of the lion, then Issachar and Zebulon, followed by soldiers carrying the banners of the other tribes. The priests were next, carrying large smoking censers of frankincense and myrrh. Young maidens carried baskets of rose petals behind them. Some held large baskets of flowers to throw out into the crowd. Behind the maidens came the flute, organ, and lyre players. Women dancing with tambourines carried the beat of the marching. Then came threescore mighty men holding swords. Each was dressed in royal purple with gold dust sprinkled in their long black hair.

Behind them, Solomon rode his royal steed with his purple robe cascading over the horse. Riding beside him were his brothers, dressed in their royal apparel with their swords.

Shulamit followed in her carriage as the central feature of the parade, holding a large bouquet of myrtle, lily-of-the-valley, and rose lilies. Her mother sat beside her as her escort. She was calm in her support role which was quite a blessing to Shulamit. The crowds roared as the bride passed by. Soldiers had to prevent the thronging crowds from advancing to get a glimpse of the highlight of the parade. Shulamit couldn't help but be overwhelmed.

The other carriages followed. The crowd also pushed in as closely as they could to see the Queen Mother and the rest of Shulamit's family. More musicians followed the carriage and more valiant foot soldiers with swords across their thighs made up the end of the parade and provided protection. They slowly made their way through Jerusalem into the City of David. As the streets narrowed, the parade formation had to squeeze closer to get pass the onlookers. People were everywhere, on the streets, in their porches, and on the rooftops, waving with joy and excitement. It was as if the wedding were for every one of them.

Solomon rode stately on his horse. He waved at his people, the people who loved him, as he preceded his bride in the carriage behind him. Everyone was interested in Shulamit's wedding finery. She waved intermittently to the crowd as she passed. Two carriages behind her, little Miriam was thoroughly enjoying being part of the procession. Shulamit could hear her, waving and laughing at the same time.

It was late morning when the long procession finally made its way to the entrance of the large tabernacle tent. Solomon dismounted his horse to a loud cheer. He walked to his bride's carriage and escorted her out to an even louder cheer as her bridesmaids rushed to hold the wedding veil. Emrah was right on the spot directing all the parties of the wedding to their right places at the grand entrance of the Tabernacle.

The doorkeepers had set up large cedar benches, leaving an aisle up front in the middle where the families of the bride and groom were led to sit on opposite sides. The other queens and ladies of the court sat behind them. Next to be seated were the high-ranking soldiers and their families, and other officials; leaving the back of the tabernacle for standing room to as many people as could fit.

After the people were settled in, the music shifted to a joyful, stately melody. High Priest Zadok, in his glorious attire, walked in with Asaph the temple music director. Bathsheba escorted Solomon, followed by his best man, Zabud, and his three brothers as attendants. While Shulamit's bridesmaids were arranging the veil, Shulamit's brothers entered. Behind came Rebecca, the maid of honor, carrying a large bouquet of flowers. She was followed by Miriam, who was happy to be a flower girl throwing rose petals to the ground.

The High Priest took his place before the ark where incense clouded much of the view of the cherubim. Solomon stood before the Ark with Bathsheba at his left, his best man, and his brothers. Shulamit's brothers, Rebecca, and Miriam took their place to the right.

Flutes began playing the introduction to a new song. Shira began singing, "Behold the bride comes. The bride comes to meet the bridegroom. Let all rejoice before the throne of heaven! Let all rejoice…"

The crowd stood and turned toward Shulamit as she walked slowly beside her mother. Her bridesmaids did their job well, holding the long veil which nearly filled the whole aisle of the tabernacle.

"Awe," some said, "the bride is so beautiful." Others in the crowd whispered, "Look at the love in Solomon's eyes."

And they were right.

"This Shulamit queen was special," one soldier's wife whispered to another woman beside her. "No one, ever before, had a wedding vow been made in the sacred Tabernacle before God."

"Truly. Look at the king."

When Solomon looked at his approaching bride, it drew his breath out of him. As Shulamit drew closer, it was as though light radiated from her. Solomon overflowed with joy that ignited a fire throughout the crowd. This was their king, their wise and stately king, standing before the ark of the covenant and showing a side of himself never before publicly witnessed in Israel. The people knew that the presence of God was in the Ark and over it, between the cherubim on the mercy seat. But Solomon was a glowing manifestation of a Heavenly King. Eternity had stepped in, and Solomon stood, foreshadowing a glory to come.

Shulamit and her mother found their places in front of the ark and the bridesmaids behind little Miriam. As Shulamit turned to face Solomon the love between them seemed to attract angels. Heaven was clearly there signaling approval.

The High Priest raised his hands for all to be silent.

Then he began, "We are gathered here before our Heavenly Father and the Ark of His Holy Covenant. This Holy Covenant was made with Moses as a contract of marriage between God and our Holy nation. Likewise, marriage is a symbol of the closest expression of joy in the relationship between bride and bridegroom in Holy Matrimony.

"In the first wedding ceremony when God created male and female in His Image, He declared man shall leave his mother and father and cleave to his wife, making them become one flesh. Our king has chosen a bride and they will declare their vows before our Creator and these many witnesses."

Solomon turned and bowed before the Ark. He whispered a prayer and then stood. He prayed aloud, "Lord, and Father of all creation. I honor You, and I thank You for all the blessings of heaven and earth. You look into our hearts and are mindful of our desires and needs. You care for our happiness. I thank You with all my heart for this beautiful bride You have given me."

Solomon turned toward Shulamit and said, "My love, you are my heart's desire. I could not ask for more. You are my crowning joy. As your bridegroom, husband, and shepherd king, I promise to do all that is within me to love you as you deserve to be loved and support your happiness. I shall assist you as you walk out your destiny. I will push you toward your dreams. I will help you be the queen you were born to be. I am enraptured by you. Thank you for waiting for me. I promise to protect and keep you as long as we both shall live."

Solomon stood, gazing into the eyes of his bride. Her eyes were locked into his, like the dove that mates for life. So entranced was Shulamit that the High Priest had to tap her on the shoulder and cue her to speak.

Shulamit bowed before the Ark. She spoke her vows solemnly.

"I honor You my Father in heaven," She began. "I am awed by Your presence and all You have done for me. I want to worship You before Your throne forever. My heart is humbled that You have chosen me as a bride to your chosen king. By your grace, I will give You my all and fulfill this awesome calling. Thank you for answering my prayers. You have given me a king, but You are my King of Kings forever."

Shulamit turned to Solomon, and for a moment, she felt almost faint, like she did in the country when she first realized her shepherd was a king. Her mind almost went blank, and she took a deep breath to regather her thoughts. But as she looked into his adoring eyes strength came to her. She said, "Solomon, from the first moment I looked into your eyes, I became aware of how much God loves me. You are an answer to my prayer. The first time I heard your voice and saw your face, I could not stop dancing. You made me discover a joy I never thought possible. I want to dance with you forever. I want to love and care for you and meet your heart's desires until the end of my life."

The High Priest joined hands with the Bride and Groom, He wrapped a prayer shawl around their joined hands as he declared, "What God has joined together, let no man put asunder. Before God and man, I pronounce you man and wife. May you be blessed with joy and gladness."

Solomon did not wait for the High Priest to grant permission for him to kiss the bride, as kissing was rarely done in public in their culture. He reached over and caught his bride completely off guard as he passionately pressed his lips to hers.

A shocked and surprised crowd sat silently for a moment, then broke into a hearty applause. The High Priest gave the crowd time to applaud. Cutting his speech short by the display of happiness he announced, "No covenant is complete without the breaking of bread. As Abraham walked between the sacrifice and cut covenant, so the king and queen will walk down the aisle between the two families to show the joining of families in Holy Covenant."

The people turned to face the bride and groom as they walked out of the Tabernacle. Crowds gathered outside, anxious to see the happy couple.

Emrah directed soldiers to bring the royal palanquin, made of gold and silver with supports of gold. The embroidered purple seat was lovingly created for the king by the daughters of Jerusalem, and Solomon sat with the curtains open so all could see them. Flower garlands draped the outside of the carriage, which had been scented with incense of frankincense, myrrh, and all the merchant's most fragrant powders. The palanquin was lifted into the air by guards carrying them with silver poles upon their shoulders. This elevation allowed the crowds to see them as they made their way.

Soon after, the rest of the bridal family members walked joyfully behind them as they made their way to the large tent in the front of the palace.

When the newlyweds arrived at their large wedding tent, the king and queen were escorted to a roped off area. There they could safely step out of the lowered palanquin and greet people one by one as they walked by. Music played softly as Shulamit stood beside Solomon, greeting their chosen people for what seemed like hours. Men bowed their heads and greeted them with "Shalom, your majesty," and they responded in kind. The women curtsied and said "Shalom." Some were bolder and more talkative expressed from their heart things like, "We are so honored to come face to face with you, and we wish you the best."

Shulamit engaged some with kind words and occasionally kissed the little girls on the forehead.

At one point Solomon whispered in her ear, "Greeting our people makes them feel honored too, and more in unity with us. A king cannot have a kingdom without people who honor and obey him. Nor a queen. We need each other."

Those who came to greet the king and queen were given raisin cakes and small amphorae of wine as part of the celebration. Soon enough, the master of ceremonies came out as the crowd dispersed and announced that the banquet was prepared. The guests were waiting for their bridegroom and bride.

Holding her hand, Solomon walked with Shulamit through the palace doors into the large dining hall. Tables were arranged around a large dancing area. Lovely flower arrangements and golden candelabras were set up on every table. Ahishan had organized the seating arrangements for the families and people invited to this occasion. Hundreds of people attended, representing the nobles of Israel, and visiting ambassadors from other nations. For the people who had joined the parade before they had time to find their best apparel (and poorer family members), robes had been made especially for the occasion and given as gifts.

Solomon and Shulamit were escorted to the prominent elevated table in the center as musicians played. Everyone was led to their place. Little Miriam escaped her family and ran over to Nathan. She whispered in his ear, "I want to marry you. Please wait for me."

Nathan smiled as Shulamit's mother came and took her hand. She excused her daughter's behavior, and announced they were going back to their table.

Nathan looked at little Miriam and smiled, "When we attend a wedding, romance fills our hearts, and we think of love."

Everyone found their seat and looked to King Solomon to take their cue. Solomon broke off a piece of bread, dipped it in spiced oil and offered a bite to his wife. Shulamit repeated likewise to Solomon. As they took their first bite, the people around them clapped and cheered.

Solomon stood up and shouted, "Bread has been broken, the covenant has been made. Let everyone enjoy this covenant meal."

As servants carried trays of food and wine to the tables, the High Priest stood up and gave the first of several blessings. "Blessed are thou," he started, "Lord our God, King of the Universe, who created all things for His glory.

Azariah, the High Priest's son, stood up and gave another blessing. "Blessed art thou Lord our God, King of the Universe, Fashioner of the Man."

Asaph stood up and gave another blessing. Shamau gave one following Asaph.

At last Solomon's best man Zabud stood up and spoke. "When two people meet, they each carry a light. That light connects with another flame from God when they come together."

Laughter was loud in the room as the people talked and enjoyed each other. At the end of the meal Solomon stood up and held a goblet of wine. The servants refilled everyone's goblet at his cue. "This is the second cup of my marriage covenant with my glorious bride. As you drink this cup with me, let us remember this day of joy and gladness and this wonderful banquet confirming this great day before all." Solomon and Shulamit shared his cup of wine.

Shouts of "Mozel Tov," reverberated throughout the echoing walls.

The music began to play again and this time it was Shira singing a special song she had written as a surprise and gift to her bride-friend Shula.

Let joy arise
The king has found his queen
She's his crowning glory
He's her everything
Our Father in Heaven
Looks down to say
Let everyone rejoice
On this fulfilling day

Let everyone share
In the joy of the king
Come on rise up
Let us see the dancing

The bridesmaids jumped up into a circle and began to dance and sing.

We delight in our king
And the queen of his choice
For the love that they share
We dance and rejoice

The king's groomsmen leaped forth into a circle and began to dance

We honor our king
His lovely bride we bless
It is this great joy we share
That we dance to express

Solomon grabbed Shulamit's hand and led her to the dance, singing as their gazes locked.

With my bride I take hand
I lead in the dance
We circle each other
Without losing our glance

Then Solomon swung Shulamit in a wide circle around him. It was amazingly fast, yet delightful, graceful. It was just as before when they danced on the way to the throne room. He released her hand again, and they twirled around each other in a figure eight form. As the music slowed, they gently came to a halt. Solomon and Shulamit stood, gazing into each other's eyes with waterfalls of love.

When the dance was over, Solomon's personal servant came and informed him that his chamber was ready.

Zabud announced, "And now it is time for the married couple to enjoy their rewards of love."

Everyone stood, shouting for joy as they waved to the couple. And, with Zabud following behind, Solomon led his bride toward the royal chamber.

21 THE KING'S REWARD

Solomon grabbed Shulamit's hand and led her running, practically flying down the palace corridor toward his private chambers. Zabud and his private guard were left trailing behind. As they approached Solomon's outer chamber, the fragrance of frankincense, myrrh, spikenard, and rose flooded the atmosphere.

Two guards standing stepped forward and opened the double doors from opposite sides. Expecting to walk beside her bridegroom through the doors, Shulamit had instead been lifted her off her feet.

"Our loving Father in Heaven spoke of Israel," said Solomon. "He carried his bride on eagle's wings and brought her to himself. So, I shall carry my bride to myself."

Feeling her heart skipping beats, Shulamit was thankful he did not immediately set her down. She glanced at the bridal chamber, abounding with beauty. Flowers in colorful vases and golden candlesticks were scattered around the room. There was a table set with wine and delicacies atop a royal red carpet. And, of course, the enormous bed of a king. But her emotions were overpowering in the presence of her beloved.

Solomon felt the trembling of his bride as he held her in his arms. He began to comfort her with loving words. "I have waited so long for this moment," he voiced as he gently set his bride down. "I cannot take my eyes away from your beauty." He sighed as he continued holding her. "Behold, you are fair," he uttered in absolute amazement. Shulamit blushed beneath her veil. Her bridesmaids had taken off the larger one, leaving a short veil in its place. For the moment, it eased her transition into the deep emotions of the sacrament about to take place. Solomon continued to describe her beauty, knowing instinctively that even fair women need to be told they are beautiful and adored by the one they love. "You have dove's eyes behind your veil. Your eyes are full of love. They sparkle of love."

Shulamit was somewhat unaware of how her eyes expressed the love she was feeling at that moment. She felt good listening to Solomon's compliments. Drawn into his words of love, she began to focus less on her own emotions.

"Your hair is like a flock of goats going down Mount Gilead," he said.

Mount Gilead, she thought. She knew her long black curls bounced as she ran in the hills. *That is where the goats go to be sacrificed.* But she didn't feel as if she were in any danger. Quite the opposite. Shulamit trusted her husband

and knew she could give herself to him, heart and soul and body.

Solomon could always read her mind. "My love," he said, "you are now mine. Trust me, as your shepherd, to care for you as a shepherd for his sheep." She smiled at him, and he caught her face in his hand, lifting it to him. "Your teeth are like a flock of shorn sheep, white from the washing and evenly matched. Your smile is bright, beautiful, and joyful to my gaze." As he spoke her smile grew. "Your lips," he continued, "as Rahab's scarlet ribbon, speak with mercy and grace, full and refreshing like an oasis." They stared into each other's eyes, heady in the moment.

He has always genuinely listened to me and valued who I am, Shulamit thought, *and my desires and ideas. He values my soul and spirit as much as he adores my beauty. How many years had I waited for someone to look inside of me and see more than my appearance? When we met, Solomon was handsome and charming, but his kindness and caring way were what made me love him.*

She recognized the divine in him.

"I see your cheeks are blushing behind the veil, like halves of a pomegranate showing me your tender meekness." He touched the veil and it danced against his fingertips. His eyes roamed downward to the stacked golden necklaces upon her. "Your long thin neck is like a tower. I see your inner strength stately and strong as you turn your head in all directions to observe all that is going on around you. You watch carefully and your powers of observation are excellent. The gold necklaces around your neck remind me of the shiny armor of shields and bucklers that David's mighty men hung on the palace armory to declare their conquests before the nation. You have conquered me. As my bride, you shall conquer many kings and nations. Thousands of famous soldiers shall surrender to your beauty." Solomon realized that as he studied his bride's beauty, the words were coming in a prophetically poetic way. He adored his bride, but there was more to her than even he realized. Or was he speaking into the future of his nation or a bride in a time to come? These surprising moments happened between them all the time, overwhelming them both.

"I'm so honored," Shulamit gasped. "I am so honored," she repeated.

"I too, my love. I too, am honored. You shall forever remain a mystery to me."

Solomon could go no further. He lifted the veil and embraced her in a kiss full of soft sweetness. Their souls melted together. Solomon lifted her up and carried her to the bed, gently laying her down as they continued to kiss. He removed the veil and gently unhooked the gold necklaces encumbering her neck. Between them, their outer robes disappeared while as they continued to kiss and embrace. Solomon began roaming over her body with his hands, and she trembled beneath his touch. Solomon melted her with impassioned words between their fevered kisses. "Your breasts are like two fawns," he moaned. "Twins of a gazelle, feeding among the lilies."

He gave her a nuzzle. "Love rests over your heart to be a wife and mother who nurtures those in her garden." They continued to embrace and kiss, exploring each other. Solomon rejoiced as he touched her. "You are all fair, my love, and there is no spot in you. Come, I will take you to the highest mountains, through the archway of trust."

At last, Solomon laid her down on the royal bed. As she lay down, he was gentle with her. Soon enough, they had reached a rhythm. "Come with me from Lebanon, my spouse," Solomon said. "Look down from the top of Amana and the top of Senir and Hermon. Together we will wage war from the lion's den and the leopard's lair."

Their desire reached its peak. Solomon exclaimed his passion. Shulamit joined with her own exultation in an exquisite moment, full of divine feelings. As the peak ebbed, Solomon ruminated on the moment. "You have ravished my heart," he said, "my sister, my spouse. How much better than wine is your love, and the scent of your perfumes. Your lips, oh my spouse, drip as the honeycomb. Honey and milk are under your tongue."

He leaned over her, praising Shulamit's most intimate parts as he described her garden. "My virgin bride is a garden enclosed, a spring shut up and a fountain sealed. Your plants are an orchard of pomegranates with pleasant fruits; fragrant henna with spikenard and saffron, calamus and cinnamon. All the trees of frankincense, myrrh, and aloes, with all the chief spices—a fountain of gardens, a well of living waters, and streams from Lebanon."

Shulamit was once again aroused by Solomon's words, sweet embraces, and kisses. Her fountain never stopped flowing; she was fully surrendered in her love as she invited Solomon to enjoy her again. As he did, Shulamit felt a song within her spirit.

Awake, O north wind,
And come, O south wind,
Blow upon my garden,
That its spices may flow out,
Let my beloved come to his garden,
Taste the fruits of your life in me.

Solomon fell into the gentle embrace of his bride. "I have come to my paradise garden, my sister my spouse, I have gathered my myrrh with my spice. I have eaten my honeycomb with my honey. I have drunk my wine with my milk."

Zabud awakened out of his daze to the sounds of joyful ecstasy coming out of the royal chambers. He moved a bit away and sat down, allowing them the tiniest privacy, as he was closest to the bridal chamber. Then he heard Solomon calling for him. He got up and rushed to the door when he heard Solomon shouting, "Eat, oh friends! Drink. Yes, drink deeply! Be Merry!

***

After a long while, they lay embracing. Solomon's head rested between her breasts as the sun sailed across the sky. They were wed. They had partaken of the marriage covenant. It was a new worship, a divine delight. But it was so much more. Unable to fully contemplate their act of love, Shulamit took a moment to observe the grandeur around her. "This is the biggest bed I have ever seen," she said, acknowledging the bed's high beams and rafters covered with curtains. The lace was designed with leaves, apples, and small white flower buds embroidered throughout.

"I designed it for you, my love. I made you this bed of green just like the one we sat under in the green hills by your village. It is something I hold in my memory and hope you do too." Solomon kissed her gently. "I hope it makes you feel at home."

"It does," she said. "I love the smell of the cedar and fir." Solomon sat up pointed out the headboard. There was a large, carved lion's head and flowers inlaid with gold. Awed by it, she turned to admire her king, saying, "I have been enraptured in a king's bed, by my beloved king."

"And I have brought the queen of all queens into my heart and my bed. I am honored to share my whole kingdom with you. There is no one like you, perfect in all your ways." He kissed her again, and they began again. Again, and again, until the next evening, time having been forgotten. Realizing they had hardly eaten in all that time; Solomon rang for food and ordered a bath to be prepared.

Shulamit noted the heavy woven tapestry spread across the bed as she rose. It was the Tree of Life. All the matching pillows had the same design. Solomon saw her note the design and commented, "When I think of you, I think of the Tree of Life. To lay hold of you is to eat pleasant fruits that fill me with life, happiness, and peace. I have never felt so full of life as I do now." He gave her another passionate kiss.

"I feel full of life too," Shulamit responded as she stood up. She put on a robe placed beside the bed and twirled around, gathering up her hair to fasten it in place with a large ivory comb. Solomon took her hand and led her across the soft red carpet to his bathing chamber.

In the center of his bathing room was a large, sunken bath with blank white tiles intermixed with other lotus flower designs. Solomon guided her down two steps into warm water with rose petals floating on the surface. The scent of rose mixed with almond oil and warm water made her muscles feel decadent. She lay back in the luxurious bath with Solomon beside her, watching the renewed pleasure on her face.

"I delight to see all your responses to love and joy," said Solomon. "Your face is transparent, expressive. Nothing is hidden with you, and I love it."

"I am the rose of Sharon, and the lily of the valleys," Shulamit said, teasing Solomon.

"Like a lily among the thorns, not a simple rose crocus flower from the Valley of Sharon but much more. There is none like you among the daughters."

"Like an apple tree among the trees of the woods," Shulamit said, running her hand over his bare chest, "is my beloved among the sons. I have sat down under your shade in our bed of green and your fruit is sweet to my taste."

A servant came with coffee, fruit, and raisin cakes with cinnamon that Solomon knew were Shulamit's favorite. Taking a bite of the fresh sweet bread, Shulamit continued, "You brought me to your banqueting table, and your banner over me is love."

"We have written another song, my sister, my spouse," Solomon said. "This time, the song is your response to my love. I want to remember how you look right now for the rest of my life."

"I want to remember all the wonderful things you have said about me now and on our wedding night and how you have made me feel. I can write now," Shulamit declared, "and I am going to write a long romantic song to keep it in our memory forever."

"Aww, my love, you are as smart as you are pretty," Solomon said as he began to play with a rose petal. "I love the way your eyes light up when you speak out of the depths of your heart. Your eyes entice me to love you again right here." He kissed her. "But I have another surprise when we finish bathing." He reached for a washing cloth and gently cleaned her body. As he moved the cloth over that special area, he expressed his joy over her beautiful garden. When he finished, she returned the favor and washed his body while telling him how handsome he was. The sun poured into the windows as their joy poured over each other.

Shulamit noted that they had been in the bath for quite some time. "The water is still warm," she said. "Is it our love working a miracle?"

"No," he said, smiling. "The bath is set upon pillars below the floor, and hot air flows between those pillars from an outside furnace. I have plans in my next palace for my brides and concubines to have large pools to bathe in." His eyes twinkled as he taught her something new. "Did you notice? I put in scented bath salts from the Dead Sea. I will take you there sometime. In the Dead Sea, it is possible to float on the water and never sink because of all the elements in the water which are extremely healthy."

"You amaze me," Shulamit said, a dreamy look in her eyes.

"Come," Solomon said, rising. "Dry off and get dressed. I want to take you to my secret garden. No one has seen it but my personal servants." He handed her a thick cotton towel after helping her out of the water. Shulamit wasn't sure if she was walking or melting across the floor. She felt so relaxed, yet they managed to get dressed quickly with the help of servants.

Solomon led her through her wing of the palace to his garden tower. Her extravagant relaxation was tested as they ascended the several flights of rounded staircases to his garden. Shulamit had been told Solomon's garden was off-limits whenever she inquired about it. In the palace, the women did not wander around everywhere without permission, even queens. And now she was being escorted by her shepherd king to his private garden. Shulamit was enveloped by the beautiful scents of jasmine, gardenia, and rose long before entering.

The rooftop was a personal retreat like she'd never seen. Solomon's taste was unrestrained but still intimate here. It was magnificent. A large pavilion with stripes of royal purple and gold shaded half the roof. Beneath it, carpets woven to resemble gardens blanketed the marble stone. Large pots of roses surrounded the pavilion. These were not the common roses seen in Israel, but roses imported from countries to the North and East. Behind the pavilion was an arbor entryway of potted jasmine. Lavender, mint, lemon balm, and many more herbs seasoned the air. Shulamit walked around the garden, admiring all the plants. Solomon told her the names and origins of each plant, and she enjoyed smelling them all as they walked.

"I love experimenting with new flowers and plants and studying them," he said. How much water and sun they like, or if they need shade. I let them grow here until I am satisfied, then I transfer them to other gardens."

"It must take a great deal of time and intellect to maintain such a magnificent garden," said Shulamit.

"This is also where I come to pray and think when I need to make decisions."

"Ah. So, if I cannot find you in the palace, this is where you will be."

Solomon took her hand and walked her to the wall. From that low wall, they could see all around Jerusalem. "We can see everything," Solomon told her. "Look, there is the Kedron Valley," he said as he indicated its location. "And there," shifting his hand, "there is the Garden of Gethsemane." He moved about as he showed her landmarks and monuments of the kingdom. "There is the South gate we departed from to Bethlehem. Over there is Mt Moriah—"

"Yes," Shulamit interrupted gently, finishing his thought. "That is where the temple is being built."

"Correct," he said, brushing his lips against her forehead. It made her body feather with heat from that spot on her forehead, all the way down to

Judy Pendell

her toes. Solomon, too, began to burn. It thickened his thoughts and made it hard to continue speaking. "It is starting to get dark now. See the lights in the houses going out? The stars are coming out, and soon they will be very bright. But right now, is my favorite time of the day." They looked at each other. "Your eyes are full of the light of stars." He leaned over and kissed her mouth, reigniting their marital fire. "I cannot stop kissing you. You are so beautiful. I just want to experience you, my beautiful rose."

"I love to kiss you too," Shulamit sighed. "I am so happy."

Solomon grabbed Shulamit and pulled her to the cushions under the pavilion. "Tonight, we enjoy love under the moonlight." Her response to Solomon's touch invited him with no words, and her sweet scent spoke of her readiness for his love. The joy of experiencing each other's love was exhilarating. Solomon was impressed by his new bride's enthusiasm. "My bride, you have a desire for love that is unquenchable."

Shulamit, too, was impressed. What first took words of love and kisses to arouse her now took only slight touches and shared looks. Shulamit was flooded with heightened sensitivity. She was now a flower in full bloom. Solomon knew this was only the beginning. And it would only get better. Sweet Shulamit was delighted and fully expressing her love to her beloved.

A while later, Solomon reached for the harp, and she responded with her own sweet words. Together they wrote a new song called, *Your Kiss is Sweet.*

Solomon began,

Your kiss is sweet
Your smile is sweet
Your song the sweetest of birds
Your dance is sweet
Your lips speak sweet
Sweet honey and kindness, your words

Sweeter than wine
Your lips touch mine
You're moving the bowels of my soul
So pure in heart
My other part
Together as one we are whole

And Shulamit replied,

My song flows through
My love for you
It is you who opened the fount

Your gentle kiss
Aroused my bliss
And led me with you up the mount

You made me sing
The bird took wing
Connecting like doves through our eyes
Our songs gave birth
Over the earth
Our love could not help but arise

Your warm embrace
Called me to chase
I will always run after you
I won't let go
Or lose my soul
My beloved, your love's so true

At the end, they sang together,

Our kiss is sweet
Our love is sweet
Our song will forever be told
Our embrace glows
Our blessing flows
To those who have eyes to behold

"Now we have a song to sing when we return to our wedding party," Shulamit said.

"Our love is a song. You are my best song. My mother told me that. We shall write many songs together." Their love led to song, and their song led to more love.

And so, their night went on.

***

On the last day of their week of love, Shulamit felt she could fly. She jumped, twirled around, and shouted out, "I feel like a woman, yes, yes, I do. I feel like a woman."

"You are a woman," Solomon said, admiring her beauty.

"I'm so alive! I'm overflowing with joy bubbling up inside of me!"

"You are a fountain of life!"

"Fountain of life," Shulamit repeated. "Yes, I feel the fountain. Something has happened to me, something deep within me. I love you

Solomon. Still I feel a love that has begun to flow much deeper. I feel as though I have stepped into a heavenly realm, and I will never be the same again."

"Mountain top experiences are like that. Your sight is expanded, your ears keener, and your feelings perceive and discern more. Your senses are heightened. The moment you become one with your lover, you can't help but cry out to God because it is as close as we get to experiencing heaven on this earth."

"Oh, I went to the mountain top with you," she said with earnest. "But I brought back a piece of heaven with me. Did you feel it too? Have you ever felt that way before, Solomon?"

"Hmm, not like I have felt with you. Except when the Lord answered my prayer for understanding. He said, 'See I have given you a wise and understanding heart, so that there has not been anyone like you before, nor shall any like you arise after you.'"

"Did that inspire your *Tree of Life* tapestry?"

"No, my love. *You* inspired me to design that tapestry. But perhaps there was a prophetic purpose in it."

"That must be it," Shulamit discerned. "When we consummated our love, and I invited you to come into my garden, I was in ecstasy. But I also felt a supernatural love flowing through you. I can't fully explain it," Shulamit said as she blushed.

"I can't explain it either, but I do believe you. Marriage with God in it is a threefold cord. It ties us together, and what is mine becomes yours. Our beautiful union of love enabled some of my God-given peace and gifts of love and wisdom to be imparted to you. Just accept it and thank our Father in heaven for it. I also receive from you fruits from the Tree of Life. The love of God is the source of all wisdom, from which come all gifts of imagination and creativity, and the understanding to create."

"Tell me again, what do I impart to you?" Shulamit teased.

He smiled. "You impart love to my heart. I am full of love for you. I have never known love before like I have known it with you. I have never known how good God is until I partook of your Tree of Life. I feel complete," Solomon said, relaxing. "Our path together is sweet and full. Everything in heaven and earth is ours. Together we have it all."

"Yes, together," Shulamit said as she kissed him.

"You are wise, my love. God is male, but he has a female side. He is the Lord of hosts, but he is also *El Shaddai*, the many breasted one. He is a mighty God who also nurtures." He took a moment. "Yes, my love," he said, "God has given you wisdom. Sweet Shulamit. Your love and wisdom shall make you a great queen."

"I accept His gift of wisdom and love, my beloved," Shulamit said with quiet joy.

"As husband and wife, we draw this wisdom and gold from each other. These gifts of the Tree of Life have an amazing power that creates life everywhere it goes. Solomon began to sing,

> *Happy is the man who finds wisdom*
> *Love her, and she will keep you*
> *She will place on your head a crown*
> *Her ways are pleasant ways*
> *Her paths of peace guide your days*
> *She is a tree of life*

> *She is a fountain of life*
> *She is a flowing river*
> *To those who love and embrace her*
> *She brings them delight and honor*
> *Sweetness flows from her lips*
> *From her, the honeycomb drips*
> *She is the tree of life*

Solomon gave her another deep kiss and Shulamit could feel love within her flowing again. To Shulamit, the real kingdom was this man, Solomon, her king. From their union in God's presence flowed all the graces of love and wisdom to create greatness. *Love is a gift that opens many fountains*, she thought.

***

When the time came for them to return to the wedding party, they wore clothing designed for dance, groomed to enhance each other as a matching pair. Shulamit's dress was gold. The precious metal itself was weaved into the fabric. Over her dress, she wore a fringed vest of indigo blue, which tied at the waist. The fringes hung down to her angles. Shulamit knew that Solomon had designed it for her, as he was dressed similarly in indigo and purple. His beard was neatly braided in kingly fashion. They were a walking love story in every way.

As they returned to the wedding party, they were introduced with a happy instrumental prelude. It was the beginning of an old traditional wedding song about love being complete. No one knew where it originated from, but they danced to at every wedding:

> *Let's rejoice, let's rejoice*
> *Let's rejoice and be happy*

Let's rejoice, let's rejoice
Let's rejoice and be happy

Let's sing, let's sing
Let's sing and be happy
Let's sing, let's sing
Let's sing and be happy

The king is happy
His joy is complete
The queen is happy
Her joy is complete

They repeated the stanzas, then added a new verse spontaneously in between about the bridegroom and bride. But something untraditional happened.

King Solomon and his Queen Shulamit were seated on chairs designed as thrones and then lifted up for all to see. A long sash was given Solomon at one end. The other end was given to Shulamit, connecting them in their chairs as they turned them around within the circle. Concentric circles formed around them, with the men in one circle and the women in another. In this pattern, they danced, holding hands or interlocking arms behind their backs or shoulders. They stepped to the right with the left foot, then followed with the right foot. Repeating their pattern, they circled the king and queen, lifted as they were on their chairs.

The song went on for quite some time with many adding verses. Finally, the wedding party called out for the king to sing over his bride. His voice was clear as a bell.

My Love is a rose
The lily of the valley

Amongst the daughters
She is perfect for me

The crowd sang the chorus's again and then pointed to Shulamit to sing:

Like an apple tree
Among the trees of the woods
Is my beloved
Amongst the sons

The Worshipper and the King

> *I sat down in his shade*
> *With great delight*
> *And his fruit was sweet*
> *To my taste*

The Bridal party cheered, and Solomon responded:

> *Behold, you are fair,*
> *My love!*
> *Behold, you are fair*
> *You have dove's eyes*

> *You have ravished my heart*
> *My sister, my spouse*
> *One look of your eyes*
> *And I am overcome*

Wanting more, the crowd looked to Shulamit:

> *Behold, you are handsome*
> *My beloved*
> *My eyes are locked*
> *In your love*

> *Your love is*
> *Better than wine*
> *Your name is ointment*
> *Poured forth*

Never had the people remembered a wedding like this, as King Solomon and his bride, Shulamit, sang their words of love. It set precedents in the hearts of the people.

The king and queen were eventually set down so they could enjoy the celebration from high-backed chairs on the podium. Guests brought reminiscences, jokes, magic tricks, poems, other entertaining gifts, always with a happy heart. Ambassadors from other countries bowed before her and the king with exotic presents from faraway lands. Some of Solomon's mighty men began a dance of jumping and kicking to a song honoring their king as laughter rang out throughout the great hall. The wedding celebration days went on with music and blessings from all who came. Shulamit met the wives of the mighty men, and they spoke blessings over her for great joy and many children.

Shulamit met a merchant who had just returned from a three-year trip to the Far East. He brought huge tusks of ivory which Solomon said he would use to make his new throne. When people asked how the king and Shulamit met, Solomon sang *Keeper of the Vineyard*, to which he added, and now my bride can keep my vineyard. When he said that, the people laughed. Shulamit responded to that by announcing, "My beloved is mine, and I am his." Many other gifts were exchanged. Solomon gave gifts to all who attended the wedding.

The last night of the festivities, Solomon said, "My mother wrote a beautiful song when I told her about my vineyard maiden. I would love the Queen Mother to sing it."

Bathsheba looked reticent, so Solomon picked up the harp and said, "My bride knows it and will sing it with you." And so, Bathsheba sang and Shulamit harmonized to the joyful words of the song, *The Presence of the king*.

There is peace
There is pleasure
There is joy
Without measure
In his presence
That I treasure
I delight to be his queen!

Many knew Bathsheba was referring to her love for King David, but also knew it was a song Shulamit could take to heart as well. It was for everyone who worshipped in their heart before the King of kings.

After Bathsheba finished singing, Solomon said, "I would love to hear Shulamit's family sing the song her father wrote about her when she was a young girl. Surely, I have seen her worship, and her heart is sincere before our King of kings." Shulamit's singing family, including little Miriam, who seemed unafraid of anything, got up. Once they gathered for a brief moment, they sang *When you Worship*.

When you worship.
Heaven smiles
Upon you

Our Father delights
Your countenance lights
And you shine

When you dance
Heaven dances with you
Our Father's heart is touched
He says,
"You're mine!"

The High Priest stood up and said, "There are five voices we must hear at a wedding: The voice of joy, of gladness, the voice of the bridegroom and the bride, and finally the voice of praise. We have heard them all during this week of celebration. But now, as a High Priest and spiritual father in the land, I have another blessing. Another song. Written by the Levites and other fathers of the land from the heart of our Heavenly Father, who gave us the gift of marriage. We are blessed to have Asaph to sing it."

Asaph was from a family divinely appointed by King David for leading worship. Not only that, his voice was strong and deep, the most powerful in the land. An anointing flowed from his half chanting, half singing style. It was as though the heavens open and our Heaven Father himself sang with the voice of thunder.

Our Father Speaks
To His bridegroom and bride,
"Be to each other a flame protector
Be to each other a flame ignitor
You are both part of my trinity
Don't smother each other
As you reflect me

"I created this passion
This consuming fire
That you cannot get enough of
If you are burning with me
Then you are burning with love
I gave for you to enjoy
To guard and let nothing destroy

"I am the fire in your heart
And that love that you have
For each other
I made you sister and brother
I made you groom and bride
I made you partners in love
When woman came out of man's side

"I made you to rule together
I made you for synergy
That your flames together grow high
Like a pillar in the night sky
Keep this fire alive
Eat of the fruit of my tree
That is how you glorify me

"You are my heart and my body
Love sensitively
Help each other burn free
Love the gift of a partner
Relationships are from me
When the world sees you love one another
They will know you belong to me."

There was a moment of deep silence followed by cheers from the party attendees. Shulamit thought to herself, *If I could ever imagine my Father in heaven offering his son to a bride and rejoicing over them, it would be God singing over Adam when He gave him Eve and commanded them to be fruitful and multiply, ruling over the earth.*

"Thank you, Father," she said under her breath. "I promise to be the best bride I can be."

***

Shulamit hugged her family tightly on the last day of their visitation. The wedding celebration was over, and they would be returning home. It would be a long time before she would see them again. She gifted them with many presents for Rebecca's upcoming wedding back at her beloved village.

Her quiet friend told her, "All week long, I have been asked to tell stories of our childhood friendship; I am not funny like you are, but people laughed at the stories I told."

Shulamit's bubbly little sister Miriam said, "Nathan showed me all around the palace garden. We worshipped in the tabernacle. And he even took me to the royal stable and showed me all the horses. He helped me groom one, too." Shulamit knew her little sister had hardly known her father, yet she carried so much of him in her life. Deep in her heart, Shulamit knew Miriam had a special call upon her life too. Maybe it was something very meaningful which she herself could not do. *God only knows*, Shulamit thought. She kissed the top of her sister's head, smiling at Miriam's unknown destiny. Shulamit had already said goodbye to her brothers and thought parting with them was quite difficult.

But nothing was as hard as saying goodbye to her mother.

Ima Miriam and Bathsheba had become friends. Shulamit knew her mother had so much love that she was a healing balm to anyone she encountered. Bathsheba welcomed Ima Miriam's honesty, too. Anyone could talk to her mother from their heart, and it would be kept sacred. Such was the wonderful family Shulamit came from, and where much of her character had been formed. Shulamit knew she would prove to be a strong asset to the king, but she would miss the people God used to help make her such a blessing.

22 JOPPA AND HIRAM OF TYRE

Shulamit was returning to the palace from early morning worship in the Tabernacle when she heard Solomon come up behind her on a horse.

"Hop on," he said, reaching down his hand.

Attending to his king and queen, a nearby servant came over. He held his hands together for Shulamit and with the help of the servant, she found herself sitting behind Solomon on his horse a moment later.

"Hold on to me," Solomon said. "We are going to the stables. I want to show you some of the horses that just arrived."

"Wonderful," she said, wrapping her arms tightly around him.

They rode slowly through the horse gate, then trotted until she could see the majestic animals running in the nearby pasture. Solomon pointed to an elegant sorrel horse with a long, flaxen mane and tail. "Isn't she lovely?" he said as he ordered a young stable boy to fetch her.

The boy brought the young mare over to the stable and began grooming her. Solomon asked the boy to show Shulamit how to brush such a large animal. Shulamit could tell the horse enjoyed being groomed by the way it responded to her touches. After the horse whinnied with pleasure a few times, Solomon helped Shulamit feed the mare some barley, after which Shulamit lead it over to the water trough.

"This horse reminds me of you," he said. "She is a young mare, almost a filly, like you were when we met. She is high strung and would be anxious, but she senses you mean her no harm." He stroked the horse with a calming touch. "Look at her magnificent body. She is an impeccable combination of muscle and build. Also, elegant and graceful, like you."

Shulamit blushed at his description. And he was right. The horse's long, slender legs were perfect for running with great speed. Long, thick neck muscles held up the sorrel's elongated head. The animal seemed perfectly made. Solomon had an excellent way with animals and Shulamit loved to see it. *He understands their nature*, she thought.

"Many stallions would follow her to battle," he said, "like soldiers following a warrior queen." It was as if Solomon was speaking Shulamit's thoughts just as she thought them. "I know you have ridden donkeys," he said, "but horses are more easily managed, and fast, even if they are not as sure footed as donkeys."

"We want the speed that we can get from horses, then?" Shulamit asked.

"Yes. We want to get places faster, and get messages sent quicker. We want watchman on the wall to ride quickly and warn us of enemies coming. Not only that," he said with a smile, "enjoying the speed of riding with the wind blowing upon us is a thrill, one we can only get from riding horses. But first we must master them."

"I see," said Shulamit.

The stable boy brought a bridle and Solomon showed her how to put it on.

"You sit without leaning forward and hold the reins. Like this," Solomon said as he showed her. When Shulamit was sitting firmly on her horse, looking confident and unafraid, the horse master, Megiddo, brought Solomon's horse over. Atop his own mount, Solomon looked at Shulamit with pride. "Ok," he said as his horse began moving, "let us go for a short ride."

"Yes," she replied with excitement. Shulamit was nervous, but quickly became accustomed to the calm mare. Solomon taught her more about handling the reins as they rode out. Eventually, he led the horses into a gentle trot. "So how do you like riding?" he asked.

"I will get used to it," she responded. It was hard to keep the trembling out of her voice.

"You are doing very well."

"That is good to know."

After a short trot down the road, they turned around. "This will be enough for today," Solomon said. "We will come and ride from time to time, until you are prepared to take a short trip. I want to show you more of Israel from horseback." Solomon helped her down from the horse, and then asked, "Do you like this mare?"

"I love her."

"She is yours," Solomon declared. "Do you have a name for her?"

"Yes," Shulamit said after a small pause. "I will call her Sorrel. I love her copper color."

"Good," Solomon laughed. "Just don't love her more than me. I can see she is already bonding with you."

That was the first of many rides. And Shulamit loved morning rides with Solomon more and more as she gained confidence. She never knew what Solomon was going to do next. Riding Sorrel gave Shulamit a refreshing respite from all the duties of court. The court had some rather rigid protocols as far as her behavior and appearance that she was still getting used to. She had learned all the court secrets of being well groomed and prepared to present herself before dignitaries. And though she had neglected her personal "vineyard" before, she married Solomon, now she was always excited to make him proud of her when he presented her to others. Solomon sent her new dresses and jewels when he invited her to join him at royal dinners with kings and dignitaries so she could wear them.

He seemed to enjoy her readiness at court, adding glory to the customs of their culture. Shulamit spent hours selecting her wardrobe and jewelry, combing her hair, and choosing perfume to match. Love had the most transformative power over her, and it extended beyond herself to others around her, and most of all her beloved king in their most intimate moments.

"We are building up a nation, and fulfilling our call given to our father Abraham to be a blessing to the world," Solomon once said as he was teaching her the justice and wisdom in his proverbs.

"How you keep track of so many things, amazes me," Shulamit confessed. "I cannot follow it all, but I am determined to try."

"I am aware of your determination. I like that about you, but don't be anxious. It will come with time. Remember I was raised in the palace. This is new to you, but you my love has everything you need to grow into a great queen."

She glowed with joy at his compliments.

The latter rains of spring were coming to an end and Shulamit was happy to see her worshipping dance team continued growing. She had a faithful inner core of dancers who showed up regularly and were quick to learn the dance steps. They practiced throughout the weeks and regularly presented their dance before Solomon on Sabbath Eve. Her most faithful dance partner, besides Shira, was Nikkel. Nikkel learned quickly and had a beautiful grace in her dance, even though she was becoming very much with child.

One day Shulamit noticed her timing was a little off. "Are you ok, Nikkel?" she asked.

"I have been having these very small contractions off and on now for two weeks now, but I can't really tell if it is not just some cramping."

"Hmm," responded Shulamit. "Just let me know if they get worse."

"I just don't want to miss worshipping and dancing with you," Nikkel exclaimed, "as it is the brightest part of my day."

"Mine too," Ilana said as she joined their conversation. Several other dancing queens added how they loved their worship time. Nikkel wanted to continue, so Shulamit agreed to let her. "Please, just be careful," Shulamit said.

They had finished most of their dance on the voice of the Lord, His majesty over the waters, and nature bringing forth life and birth. As they danced through the final lines of song, "The Lord will give strength to His people; The Lord will bless His people with peace," a pool of water rushed down to Nikkel's feet.

As the women noticed the water, Shulamit announced, "We are done for today! She turned to a nearby servant and said, "Call the midwife, have servants deliver the birthing chair, and help me accompany Nikkel to birth her child."

They walked as quickly as they could across the courtyard to Nikkel's chamber, stopping a few times as contractions became stronger.

"The Lord will give strength to His people," Shulamit quoted as she admonished Nikkel to take measured breaths.

Nikkel begged Shulamit, "Don't leave me, I want you with me for the birth, as you promised."

"Don't worry," Shulamit said as she comforted her, "I will be with you through your whole birth."

When they arrived in Nikkel's chamber, Shulamit instructed her to sit at the edge of the bed. "Let me see how close you are to birthing." Shulamit was surprised to find that the baby was already crowning.

"The baby is coming now," Nikkel grunted.

The next contraction brought forth the baby's head. The following contraction brought forth a screaming baby boy. His cry was loud enough to be heard down several palace hallways. Shulamit did nothing but catch him as Shiffrah, the midwife, arrived.

"What lungs you have," Shiffrah said as she began to wash the baby and rub him with salt. While she did that, Shulamit turned back to Nikkel.

"You're almost done," she said to Nikkel as she assisted with the next contractions, which brought out the afterbirth in one piece. Nikkel went limp after the last push, and her servants made her comfortable on her bed. Shulamit took the screaming baby from Shiffrah and put him on Nikkel's breast. He immediately began a strong suckle and calmed.

"I have never experienced such a quick and easy birth," Shulamit laughed.

"I am so glad you were here with me," a tired Nikkel replied.

The midwife said, "I'm sorry I missed this, my queen. But you are going to heal nicely, Nikkel. And what a beautiful baby," she said touching his thick, black curls. Your baby has a strong body."

Solomon arrived moments later. Great joy spread over his face as he was handed the swaddled baby.

"He will be a strong prince and warrior, Solomon said as he looked all over the baby. "He already has a strong grip."

Solomon took Nikkel's hand and kissed her forehead. "I am proud of you," he said. "I know you have been through a battle, but you still look beautiful, my newest mother and queen. We must send a message to your father, Hiram." Solomon paused a moment, thinking. "Perhaps I will deliver it myself."

Shulamit tried to quietly exit the room, but Solomon called to her and thanked her for her for being a good sister to Nikkel and helping her bring his son into the world.

All Shulamit could say at that moment is, "The voice of the Lord brings birth."

"Your wisdom is a blessing," Nikkel said as Shulamit left the room.

Shulamit returned a few hours later. As she tiptoed in, she saw Nikkel asleep. The young prince was in the baby bed next to her. He was on his stomach, which he apparently did not like, as he was pushing his head up with his strong arms and trying to look around. Shulamit gently picked him up and put him on his back. He stopped whimpering and began to look around. Shulamit said to the maiden looking after them, "This is the strongest baby I have ever seen."

***

When it was determined that the rains of Spring had finally come to an end, Shulamit went out to enjoy the sunshine with Sorrel in the stable yard. Solomon found her there. He rode his horse over to join her.

"You are becoming quite an equestrian," he said. "Do you feel comfortable enough to ride Sorrel on a short trip? I've sent word to King Hiram in Tyre that he has another grandson, and I've invited him to meet us in Joppa."

"I would love to," Shulamit said, "my heart is always open to new adventure."

"That is my bride, always eager to experience more."

"I have vaguely heard of Joppa," Shulamit said. "Is that the seaport?"

"Yes, it is our biggest port on the way to Tyre and Sidon in Lebanon. I must go to check on my new merchant fleet and see how the cedar timbers are faring. They are being floated down from Lebanon to Joppa for the temple."

Shulamit enjoyed being with Solomon as often as she could. Yet, she found herself becoming ever more fascinated with this kingly side of him. "This sounds like quite the adventure. How long will we be gone so I know how to prepare?"

"I have already ordered your servants to pack, for we are leaving early tomorrow morning."

If Solomon had already given orders, there really wasn't much she would need to worry about. "I look forward to joining you." She spent the rest of her day resting and wondering about the trip.

They left early in the morning. For security, there were soldiers before them and a rearguard behind them. Once the packed horses were in their proper place before the rearguard, they started their trip. The caravan moved down the hilly Judean Road at a trot until they reached a less steep road from Jerusalem. Once reached, they sped up to a gallop. Shulamit could feel Sorrel's power underneath her as the horse moved her muscles. It was more fun than Solomon described. Soon the wind got into her eyes and Shulamit laughed as tears streamed down her face. She was so caught up in the excitement she did not even feel her body until they approached a strange looking town at the edge of the Judean hills, and they began to slow down.

"We will stop here for a while and let the animals rest," Solomon commanded. He dismounted his horse and came over to help Shulamit down from her horse.

"Where are we?" Shulamit asked.

"This is Gezer," Solomon explained, "the half-way mark to Joppa. It was a dowry gift from the pharaoh of Egypt upon my marriage to his daughter. The town of Gezer had been burned in war, and now I am having it rebuilt as a military outpost to protect the trade route along the coast. Come, I'll tell you more as we take a small meal."

Stable boys came and walked their horses to the newly built stables. Shulamit's legs felt wobbly under her, as riding used her thigh and calf muscles differently. She realized she would need soothing balm rubbed on them or she would be sore later. Solomon helped his bride regather her stability and balance. "You have done incredibly well," he said, "and you kept pace amazingly. Let us go rest for a while before we mount up for the rest of the trip."

They were led to a private chamber to wash off the dust. Once their feet were cleaned, the attending servants massaged their tightening muscles with warm aloe oil. Solomon and Shulamit relaxed a bit and ate. It was a short rest, but the horses seemed renewed by the brief respite. Soon the guards, camels, and horses were moving on, continuing the last half of their journey.

As they began to trot, Shulamit looked out over the fertile Ayalon Valley and saw the ripened wheat harvest. Reflecting the afternoon sun, the fields shone like gold. She thought of how blessed Israel was, to have such a bountiful land.

Evening was upon them as they approached Joppa. From a hill in the distance, Solomon pointed toward a magnificent stone fortress on the sea's edge.

"There she is," he said, "the *Bride of the Sea*. It was originally built by Japheth, the son of Noah. My father conquered it from the Philistines, and now I am going to make Joppa into a major seaport. We are going to build large ships and develop trade throughout the world."

"You are a marvelous dreamer, and you bring these grand dreams to life," said Shulamit.

By the time the kingly procession arrived at Governor Abinodab's beautiful mansion on the outskirts of the town, the stars were coming out.

The watchmen opened heavy wooden gates under large arches that allowed access to the dwelling behind fortified stone walls. The cobblestone pathway crunched under their feet after Solomon and Shulamit dismounted their horses. Edged with palm trees, the guarded entry path led to Governor Abinodab's palatial mansion. Shulamit's eyes widened in appreciation at the elaborate, high-beamed home. Stately pillars stood guard of the main entry and decorative vases full of plants also seemed to stand guard. Walls painted with scenes of the ocean caught her attention. She noted how the wall murals went all the way to the beach.

Once they cleaned up, Solomon and Shulamit joined the governor at a relaxed dinner by a fire. It was a light meal of grilled fish and roasted eggplant, with bread they dipped in spiced olive oil. While they ate, Solomon and Abinodab discussed the building of the temple, and how the trade of meat, drink, and oil was going in exchange for cedars from Lebanon.

Shulamit was glad she had learned how to behave with dignitaries in the palace as she sat in on this very private conversation with her husband and other dignitaries. She listened with fascination as Solomon and Abinodab exchanged visions of world trade. While they were talking, a ship-captain arrived and was introduced as Javan. Shulamit did not recognize him until she heard his eloquent voice. When she did, she remembered him from her wedding ceremony. He told fascinating stories of his travels. Solomon and the governor were apparently financing his continued explorations of trade into far flung countries. But he was the one who knew the countries and how to accomplish good trade business. Shulamit could tell Solomon was impressed with this man.

"You are more than a tradesman as we send you out," Solomon said, lifting his glass, "you are my ambassador representing the crown, our God, and the nation of Israel. The adventures you shared at our wedding caught my interest, as well as my bride's. If you speak with such elegance in other king's courts, you are honoring our kingdom and our trade will be blessed." Solomon looked at her, smiling as he silently encouraged her to speak.

"I would like to hear more of your travels to foreign lands," she said. "Your stories are most interesting; and the new products you return with enhance our lives."

"Happily, my queen," Javan said, bowing. "I am honored by such a request."

The light of the full moon reflected upon the water where large sea faring vessels were anchored. It was the perfect backdrop for Javan's tales. He started talking about a land in the South named Sheba. "Sheba is rich in spices, jewels, and gold, but ruled by a female warrior class with a queen who drove a hard bargain. She kept two of our men there to teach her our language, as she wished to know more about our wise king and our God. I have to return there to get our men back."

"She sounds wise," Solomon said to Javan.

"Why?" asked Shulamit.

"We have an alphabet and a business language that everyone who trades with us must learn." Solomon turned to Javan. "Be sure to offer to teach her."

"We Israelites keep accurate written records and just balances," Governor Abinodab said to Shulamit, "so no one can cheat us, or accuse us of cheating."

Solomon elaborated Abinodab's thought. "I learned the importance of written records," he said, "as many people have brought cases to our courts of being cheated. Many times, I would ask for the records. They had none. That was the problem. It was hard to make a judgment without evidence."

"But multiple witnesses can help," Shulamit asked him quietly, "correct?"

Solomon answer in her ear. "Even witnesses can be false." He turned to the dinner guests and spoke louder. "So now, when our ships go out to sea, our governors or princes look over the ledgers. There is a uniform record of all the merchandise going out, and when the ships return, those ledgers are once again reviewed."

"The importance of proving ourselves honest in business builds a reputation that makes others trust in us," said Shulamit. "'Trust is good for business', my father would say." She felt proud of her husband, even as she was learning even more from him in this new area.

"A quick profit of dishonest means does not guarantee profit in the long run," said the governor.

"Yes," said Solomon, "A good name is to be chosen rather than great riches."

"That is a wise saying, and needs to be passed down over the generations," said Abinodab.

"I am putting that in my book of proverbs. It has been passed down by mouth, but when written, it will have God's authority and seal upon it."

When they finally ended their meeting, Shulamit was very tired from the long day. Still, she was anxious to wade out on the beach. Solomon laced his fingers in hers as they walked together. Wading in the gentle waves, Shulamit gazed out the sea.

"This water just goes on and on," she told Solomon. To Shulamit, the sea was both enlightening and startling at the same time. The water was warm, and it felt good to wade in the calm sea. They walked out deeper into the water and embraced each other.

"Isn't this wonderful?" Solomon asked.

"Yes," she replied. "And the salt in the sea water feels so comforting to our bodies after a long day." Solomon pulled her close. "It is so peaceful," Shulamit said, sighing into his embrace. "I have always been a mountain woman, but I could learn to enjoy living by the sea."

"The horizon out there," Solomon said, pointing, "is where the blue water turns into stars. In the day, you can see where the sea meets the sky, but at night the sea becomes a part of the heavens."

"Yes," Shulamit gave him a gentile kiss. "Heaven meets earth." She confirmed.

"Yes, my love," Solomon giving her a deeper kiss. "This is where Heaven meets earth."

***

The following morning, Solomon bade her sleep if she desired and enjoy the day with the Governor's wife. "I'm off to inspect the wood that has been rafted down from Lebanon," he told her. "I will join you at dinner."

Shulamit was happy to continue her rest. She went back to sleep thinking, *Solomon has so much energy. How can anyone keep up with him?*

The day passed with calmness and comfort. As did the next. Shulamit enjoyed the lovely, sunny days and gentle winds on the beach with the governor's wife and local ladies.

Meanwhile, Solomon kept quite busy, even as he was relaxing. A few days after their arrival, he received a note from Hiram, inviting them to visit his palace in Tyre. Hiram added to his note that he wanted to hear about Nikkel's son, the newest addition to "our family."

"Our family," Solomon laughed as he read it.

"Why is that funny?" Shulamit asked.

"Hiram was a great friend of my father's and has been loyal to us for many years in supplying craftsmen and fine woods. He built my father's palace, and I have many more plans for his skilled workers. Hiram is valuable to Israel, and our relationship is very important. I am pleased he works as if we are family."

"I am as well."

"It is also good that you helped deliver Nikkel's baby. It gives you opportunity to ingratiate yourself toward him. Just don't give any indication that you are more special to me that she is. This is where we all learn to take a low seat and consider the feelings of others."

"Nikkel, Shira, Bathsheba, and my maidens have been my first friends in the palace. Nikkel *is* a close friend to me. Besides Shira, she is my best worshipping partner. I can honestly tell him of the value she is to me."

"Loyalty is one of the strongest of all virtues a person can have. One of the reasons you are of such value to me," he teased.

"But not the most important reason," she teased back.

***

Early the next day, they began their journey up the coastline to Tyre. Shulamit was most impressed by the beautiful scenery. Olive, apple, and apricot trees grew along the sides of the highway like soldiers and countrymen, guarding the way. Large pine trees could be seen further inland, and high mountain peaks covered in snow stood in the distance.

As they did on their way to Joppa, they stopped to rest the horses at the halfway point. This time, they found themselves on a beach. Shulamit and Solomon walked along the shore. Scattered along the beach, half buried in sand, were Murex shells. Solomon picked one up and pointed out to Shulamit.

"It is a special shell," he said, "found only on the Phoenician coast. It takes about 1,000 shells to make a small amount of purple dye. That dye is worth more than gold and has thwarted many wars. Israel has been trading with Tyre and Sidon through many kings using these shells."

"Wonderful," said Shulamit. "And so beautiful."

"King David saw more value in trading than conquering. The men have intermarried with the daughters of Dan, adopting to our God, and teaching our people a great deal. "Let us take some back to the palace," he said, handing her one.

"I will keep this one as a remembrance."

That evening, as they came near to Tyre, Hiram rode out with a group of his soldiers to greet them.

"Welcome my friend!" Hiram said, full of joy. Solomon jumped off his horse with a huge grin and the two men gave each other a warm embrace. "I was happy to receive your message about our new son."

Solomon's pride glowed through his smile. "Yes," he said, "our family has grown indeed." It was understood that sons were considered the strength of their culture. "He is very strong and handsome," said Solomon. "He will make a good warrior and prince."

Hiram looked over at Shulamit and the soldiers behind her, still sitting on their horses. "I see you only brought one wife with you."

"I left in a hurry to deliver the message and had no time to arrange a caravan. Let me introduce Shulamit," Solomon said, walking over to her. "She is the one who delivered your grandson, and she has a story to tell. Shulamit is Nikkel's good friend. She can fill you in on everything, as women always do, you know."

"A story?" He looked at Shulamit with a curious, lusty look. It was clear he noticed her beauty. "Well, let's go to the palace and relax," Hiram said, "then we can talk about my son some more."

Solomon who noticed everything, especially Hiram's lusty look at his wife. He gave a gentle shake of head to Hiram, as if to say, "Hand's off." There was no malice, but the loving rebuke was clear. Hiram smiled, receiving it with humility.

The two kings rode together in front of Shulamit, talking about business, specifically the launching of a new ship on its maiden voyage. Shulamit was glad to let them talk, as horseback riding during the trip was starting to make her inner thighs ache. The discomfort was making itself known and she didn't feel like conversing.

They came to a causeway built of large stones that led to an island city surrounded by large walls. Homes were all built inside of the walls themselves and overlooked the sea. *So many pillars*, Shulamit thought as she saw arches leading to a monumental palace seven stories high with large pillars on the palace porch. Shulamit's legs began to ache anew when she saw how many steps led to the entryway.

It took less time than she thought, but it was still a lot of steps. Her legs were crying out in pain by the time she reached the top. They entered an enormous room with cedarwood floors and purple textiles. Tapestries covered cedar walls with beams held up by pillars throughout the high room. The beauty of the palace was a pale second to the burning exhaustion in her thighs and calves.

Hiram saw her discomfort and looked to Solomon, who seemed none the worse for wear. "My servants will take you where you can rest and bathe before we meet to dine," Hiram said.

That was music to Shulamit's ears. Even Solomon seemed happy, though his face stayed stoic.

Having bathed and rested, Solomon and Shulamit were escorted onto a high terrace overlooking the sea. "Welcome," Hiram greeted them again. "I trust you found your accommodations satisfactory." Servants led them to the low table where Hiram sat with several of his wives on his left. He invited the king and his bride to sit on his right, the place of honor. Servants on the nearby terrace filled wine cups, plating fish and other appetizers fresh from the grill.

"Our families go back a long time," Hiram said. "Our nations have been at peace and doing blessed business for generations." He took a deep drink of his wine. "I first heard about your father David when I was a child. The story of how he killed the giant Goliath with a sling shot was told as far from Jerusalem as here, in our country. Even his battle cry was repeated."

"I know the battle cry," Shulamit broke in, clearing her throat. "You come to me with a sword, with a spear, and with a javelin," she cried out. "But I come to you in the name of the Lord of hosts, the God of the armies of Israel, whom you have defied."

King Hiram and Solomon joined in the battle cry with Shulamit. "This day the Lord will deliver you into my hand," the exclaimed, "and I will strike you and take your head from you. And this day I will give the carcasses of the camp of the Philistines to the birds of the air and the wild beasts of the earth, that all the earth may know that there is a God in Israel. Then all this assembly shall know that the Lord does not save with sword and spear; for the battle is the Lord's, and He will give you into our hands."

All three shouted, "Yea!" as they finished the battle cry.

Hiram continued his story about King David. "When I heard of all the nations he subdued from Syria," he said, "Moab, Ammon, and from the Philistines from Amalek, I realized I did not want to make war with him." Solomon laughed with understanding and Hiram continued. "I sent emissaries to him, "letting him know I wished to do business with him and offer my skilled laborers to build his palace. After all, I am fond of having my big toes and my thumbs." They all laughed.   "And you, my lady," he said to Shulamit, "I have never heard a woman speak a battle cry before. What made you learn that?"

"I come from a family that protected David in his flight from Saul," Shulamit said boldly. "They took him food. My grandfather even volunteered to fight with King David, knowing the Lord was with him and that he would win. My grandfather trusted in the Lord, so he was not afraid.

"David gave everyone courage around him," Hiram added.

"But my Saba—"

"Your grandfather," Solomon said to Shulamit, who seemed distracted by her tired muscles. Her face never betrayed the pain, but Solomon was, once again, paying special attention.

"Yes, my Saba said that David's battle was more about worship than the actual encounter with the enemy. David would not make a move without enquiring from the Lord in worship. So, David's army began to play their instruments and dance until David heard the voice of God with His mighty instructions. Then, with every move they made in battle, it was like angels were fighting with them and protecting them. Very few men were harmed. My Saba committed to being a worshipper after that, which is how my family became worshippers."

"Really," said Hiram. "What a marvelous legacy."

"After David became king," Shulamit continued, "he came to visit us, to thank us for all we had done to help him. He loved our vineyard, and we sold him a small part of it, with the promise that David would occasionally worship with us and teach us his new songs. I learned to love David while I was still in my mother's womb. I wanted to be like him. I wanted to become a warrior, but my uncle Jether said it was more appropriate that I become a *worship* warrior. Now I worship in the Tabernacle and Nikkel is my best worshipping partner besides Shira, the priest's daughter."

Hiram's wife, the older woman seated next to him, wiped a tear from her eye saying, "Nikkel always loved to dance."

"So, tell me, your majesty," Hiram said, staring into her eyes, "what does my grandson look like? Does he look like me?"

Not being used to being called your majesty, Shulamit tried to evade the question in a pleasant way. "He is a most handsome baby," she said, "with a thick head of black curly hair, and a strong face. He was born to command, but he looked like a newborn baby so, only time will tell. However, he is the strongest baby I ever saw."

"And the birth?" Hiram's wife asked. "How was my daughter?"

"Your daughter danced up to the very last minute. She said it kept her mind on God and not the pain. In fact, we were singing a Psalm about the cedars of Lebanon and how the voice of the Lord makes the deer give birth when Nikkel's feet were soaked by her water. I ended worship right then. By the time we walked across the yard to her chamber, the baby's head was crowning, and the servant handed me a clean blanket. All I could do was catch him. I never saw such an easy birth in all my life, and I used to help my mother in the country."

"So, my daughter is in good health."

"She and the baby are in perfect health."

"I think I remember that Psalm," Hiram said. "It was after David, and I made an alliance to build ships and trade together. He sang of God's glory over Lebanon and how God's voice planted the cedar trees in Lebanon. I will never forget the power of David's worship. I knew he worshipped before we launched a ship to sea. And I saw the blessings of our alliance together such as I had never experienced before. His sailors that went to sea with our men would sing His songs when a storm came near. His Psalms calmed fearful hearts. I do believe in your *Elohim* as creator of Heaven and earth."

Solomon handed Shulamit his lyre to sing the song that she and Nikkel had learned and created a dance to before she gave birth. Shulamit began to sing,

Give unto the Lord, O you mighty ones
Give unto the Lord glory and strength
Give unto the Lord the glory due to His name
Worship the Lord in the beauty of holiness

The voice of the Lord is over the waters,
The God of glory thunders,
The Lord is over many waters
The voice of the Lord is powerful

The voice of the Lord is full of majesty

Solomon reached out for the lyre and handed Shulamit a tambourine. As Solomon sang, Shulamit got up to dance, the tambourine adding strength to the beat. She welcomed Hiram's wives to dance, and they joined her. She taught them steps while keeping time in the center of a circle they formed around her. Holding hands up towards heaven, they praised the Lord who gave strength and peace to his people.

Hiram got up to dance and Solomon joined in while playing the lyre, much as his father had done. Glory came down upon them in joyful unity. They came to the end of the song after repeating several verses for emphasis and gave each other hearty hugs as they came down from the experience.

When they sat back in their various seats, Hiram looked at Solomon and said, "It was as if David himself was here worshipping with us. You carry so much of your father in you, and your young bride is a compliment to the worship, without which, some of David would be lost." Looking at Shulamit he announced, "You are a true worshipper, and I am glad my daughter worships with you."

"You must come to the dedication of the Temple and enjoy their worship," Solomon said.

"And *you* must build a palace in our mountains to bring your wives during the hot summer months in Jerusalem. Please bring your son with Nikkel to visit her family too," he laughed.

"We will discuss this later," Solomon replied, looking at Shulamit. "I can see my bride is very tired from the journey."

"Yes, we shall definitely discuss it. Let us retire after such an engaging evening."

Later, as Shulamit fell into their bed, Solomon took her tired body into his arms. She said, "I don't know what came over me when I interrupted and spoke out the battle cry of David. I love how you cover my mistakes so gracefully."

"With another king it might have been a mistake, but Hiram is special," Solomon said. "He knew my father and they shared hearts. You showed him what a *worship warrior* is. And you were right to speak it. *The Lord will give strength to His people,*" Solomon said as Shulamit gazed into his eyes. They shared a kiss. "Hiram is thankful that his daughter has such a friend. And I, I am thankful for you," he said, as he kissed her again.

23 Dream Two

Two more winters came and went, and the time for the dedication of the temple loomed. The golden, holy place stood on Mt Moriah, shining in the bright sunlight as final details were put into place. Solomon planned sacrifices from the upper tribal territory in Dan to the Southern Judean territory of Beersheba, and even near the border of Egypt. He spared nothing for the glorious temple and dedication, working hard to complete everything on schedule. Everything had to be made to glorify God, so Solomon was a king obsessed with beauty and perfection.

Working so hard at this time, Solomon began to visit Shulamit later and later in the evening. She found herself challenged and busy showing visitors around the palace, her worship group, her writing, and her other royal duties. As a wife, she was working so hard to do her best, but she was beginning to miss what Solomon really needed. In fact, she had begun to mix up her priorities, placing the royal duties and things she liked to do before her husband. Shulamit would find herself very tired at the end of the day, so when Solomon came to see her, it was more difficult for her to stay ready for him. Shulamit would fall asleep waiting, and over time she started to feel taken for granted. Solomon was beginning to feel the same. If only she knew.

One-night Shulamit slept, but her spirit was awake, and she had a dream. In it, Shulamit was in her bed chamber, weary of waiting for Solomon's promised visit, so she bathed her feet, took off her garments, and blew the candles out. Later, in the wee hours of the morning, she heard a knocking at her door.

"Open for me, my sister, my love, my dove, my perfect one; for my head is covered with dew, my locks with the drops of the night."

Shulamit called back, "I have taken off my robe and bathed my feet, how shall I soil them?" Despite her hesitation, she got up and put on her robe and slippers. As she prepared, Shulamit started getting excited that her lover was there. His hands had touched the latch of the bolted door, leaving behind traces of liquid myrrh, but by the time she got there, he had turned and gone. *My heart leaped when he spoke*, she thought. *I sought him, but I could not find him.*

Shulamit realized how she had failed responding to her lover's call with compassion. She longed in her heart for him. Feeling despair and sorrow for her attitude she thought, *if only I had watched for him a little longer and not fallen asleep.*

Shulamit threw on her outer robe, shoes, and wrapped her veil around her head. The dream changed scenes as she went into the streets of the city searching for her lover. The dream's watchmen beat and bruised her, thinking she was a woman of the night, and the keepers of the walls tore her veil from her head.

Shulamit cried out to the daughters of Jerusalem. "I adjure you, O daughters of Jerusalem, if you find my beloved, that you tell him how much I love him and want him."

The daughters of Jerusalem called back, "What is your beloved more than another that you should command us to find him?"

As Shulamit began to answer she was caught up in a new dream, a vision of her beloved's glory. She became an observer, watching as her dream self-described her beloved's glory. Words flowed out as she expressed the vision. Shulamit decided she would write the vision down when she was awakened from her dream. *I don't want to forget this,* she thought. *I shall make it a poem, and I'll call it:* My Beloved's Glory.

White and ruddy
He stands above all others
Chief amongst tens of thousands
On his golden head
A crown of glory covers
In pureness of sight

He understands
His raven curls
Tumbling on his shoulder
Letters written in black
On a background of glory
Proclaim the Word

In white flames of splendor
His dovelike eyes
Pools of revelation
His gentle face
Reveals fullness of emotion
Fragrant spices flow
From his devotion
And his kisses
Like lilies dripping myrrh
His kind voices
Speaks to reassure

His strong hands
Rods of gold set with beryl
Hold unlimited power
Never used in anger
His body is carved ivory
The work of a sculptor for glory
His legs are pillars of marble
Set on bases of fine gold
His inner and outer strength
Magnificent and noble

He stands tall
Like a cedar in Lebanon
He is steadfast
No one can rival him
Most sweet are his kisses
He whispers love to me
He is altogether lovely
That is why I love him
This is my beloved
And this is my friend

The Sisters of Jerusalem, her dream's brides-to-be, sang out,

Where has your lover gone?
O rarest of beauty
We will follow you
We long to see

***

The dream scene changed again. Shulamit started running, climbing up the many stairs of the king's tower. She remembered Solomon was in his secret garden. It was where he went when he needed to be alone and seek the Lord within the palace. And she was right. Shulamit saw Solomon in the garden, bowed in prayer under a tree. He was sweating huge drops of blood saying, "Not my will but thine be done."

She cried out as she ran toward Solomon. "Oh Solomon" she said, "please forgive me. I did not mean to hurt you. I would never do that. I realize that I have been selfish. Thinking of myself and what I am getting out of our marriage. I wasn't aware how much it costs you to do all you do for our kingdom and country. I guess I never considered the cost of my calling. Please forgive me. Please forgive me!"

Something shifted in Shulamit's heart as she asked for Solomon's forgiveness. She realized Solomon had gone out of his way to make sure she was challenged. He wanted her to be happy in her life at the palace. But she had begun to neglect her most important part of being his wife. He needed her to just be there for him, to love him, listen, support him, pray for him, and help in his battles. He was her lover and friend, and she valued what they had. When the maidens asked her why there was no lover like him, it had awakened in her heart how special he was. Shulamit wished to guard and protect what they had and never let anything come between them.

Shulamit awoke from the dream with her heart on fire with love. She knew she needed to go and seek out her beloved. As in her dream, Shulamit knew instinctively where her husband would be. When Solomon had much on his heart, he was in his secret garden where he would not be disturbed. She felt the Lord's call to go to him. Shulamit threw on her slippers robe, dashing off to the hidden stairs leading up to Solomon's secret garden. She ran as fast as she could around the curved staircase. As she took the last steps, there was Solomon, leaning forward at his table. He was writing into a scroll.

Solomon looked up to his love with delight. "What a surprise," he said, pleased to see her. "I was just finishing my dedication for the temple, and wanted to come and see you, but did not wish to wake you up at this late hour." Solomon held his arms open to her and Shulamit ran into his embrace. As he held her, she shared her dream.

"My heart sank at the thought that I or anyone could cause you so much pain,." Shulamit said, beginning to sob. "I had not waited and watched even an hour for you. I felt so convicted! You have done so much for me, and I have done so little to help you carry your burdens. I promise to think less of myself and more of the vows I made to be your wife and helper. You are fully mine and I desire to be fully yours."

"Awe my sweet love, you are completely aglow. You are as radiant as the City of Tirzah, lovely as Jerusalem, and awesome as an army with banners." He kissed her forehead. "You ravish my heart. The love in your eyes melts me. I am held captive by your love, which is your most yielded sacrifice. I can see how your love has grown for me. You have become part of me."

"You have become a part of me too." Shulamit said just before Solomon kissed her.

"Others see your beauty and sing of you" he said. "You make song wherever you go. You are shining so brightly right now in the glory you carry; I see you now arising as the dayspring of the dawn, fair as the moon, bright as the sun." He kissed her again, quickly. "Yes, I see you clothed with the sun, the moon under your feet, and a garland of twelve stars surrounding your head."

As Solomon described her glory, once again, her spirit opened into a vision. "I see us," Shulamit said, "sitting in the chariots of the noble people and being lifted up together in the glory realm. I see us raised up in glory together." As she described her vision to Solomon, he was spiritually aware of the power of Shulamit's vision.

"I can feel the glory cloud around us," he said, full of awe.

Shulamit continued to describe what the Lord showed her, "We are inside of a chariot of fire that is full of light. It is so beautiful here. I hear music I have never heard before and I see colors I have never seen. I feel we are being taken up into a glory so great we might not come back."

"You are in glory my love. My father told me of a Zion in heaven that he wanted to create on earth." He squeezed her to him. "But you must come back," he moaned into her hair. "You see me in glory with you, but I am here for you to come back to. I need you. Your worshippers need you. Look down and see those of us who need you to return. We need to share this glory with our nation."

Shulamit obeyed Solomon and looked down. From her vision, she saw the daughters of Zion calling out to her, "Return, return, O Shulamit. Return, return, that we may look upon you."

Shulamit responded without thought, "What would you see in the Shulamit? The dance of two camps?"

Solomon spoke to her then, "Yes, the dance of two camps. I see the dance of Mahanaim, of heaven and earth connecting. You are bringing the glory of heaven back with you as you return. He began to interpret her living vision, "Everyone wishes to see your dance."

"My dance?" Shulamit said, starting to release and return to the reality of her beloved.

"Yes, my love," Solomon replied. "You dance so gracefully, as though you dance with angels. I see a day when your dance will bring Israel and all the nations together into one new man."

The vision ended and Shulamit found herself in her beloved's arms. "We have been in glory," she said. "The glory has taken us into new visions near or far in the future."

"Both, my love," Solomon said as he continued to interpret his understanding of Shulamit's vision. "I feel a song coming out of this," he said, and began to sing.

Return, return
O Shulamit

That we might look
Upon you

What would you see in the Shulamit
As it were, the dance of two camps
Because you dance
So gracefully
As though you dance
With angels

"I am humbled before my almighty God. And I do feel like angels dance through me sometimes."

"So true, my Love, angels always dance through you." Pausing for a moment Solomon said "I believe I have always seen you in that glory, from the first time I ever heard you sing in the field and sought you out. Our God, *Elohim*, is in the process of taking us to greater glory. He gives us glimpses of this now, as well as greater things to come."

"I see the dance," Shulamit responded. "I see myself dancing with my sisters, the queens, princesses, concubines, and maidens in the court." She almost giggled, "We are like an army with an angel behind each one of us as we dance."

"Yes, Lord," Solomon declared, "In accordance with my Shulamit's vision, send a host of angels from heaven to earth to dance at the dedication in unity and glory. Bring your glory, Father God. You are preparing our hearts to move with You. Draw your people into greater intimacy with you and fulfill the dream you put in my father David's heart. Let Your Glory come!"

"Amen," she replied with joy. Shulamit's eyes lit up as another revelation overtook her; "Oh Lord, I realize that my dream of always wanting to worship in the Tabernacle was a dream King David imparted into my family in worship. It was divinely placed within my heart at a youthful age. And now the dedication of the temple is the greater fulfillment."

"We are both fulfilling the dream *Elohim* put into David's heart. You to worship, and me to build the temple. Do you see why God has brought us together?" Sparks flowed between them as Solomon fixed his eyes upon his love, and she mirrored his gaze. They stood immobilized at the profound awareness in their spirits, feeling it drawing them closer together than ever.

Moments went by before either could speak, but it was Solomon who talked to his bride of her true depth and nature.

"My love," he said, "you are a dreamer of dreams. It is a gift, and your dreams are prophetic in nature. I believe there is more to your dream, even

I cannot understand it all. Your encounter with God when you saw me in the glory is still a mystery to me. Perhaps when we each see the glory in each other we are having encounters with God."

"Perhaps."

"It is hard to imagine God as a man. But I have always wondered what is meant by the phrase, *Angel of the Lord*. Since no man can see God and live, perhaps he comes to us in our dreams or other ways. My father, said some thoughts are too high for us though they are prophetic, and we can't figure them out. He put them in his Psalms anyway, so future generations might have the prophecy revealed to them."

"I hear what you are saying. There are many psalms that prophesy into the future, and we don't clearly understand them. But if it, wasn't you in my dream, it was a very real man."

Solomon smiled. "I believe you. You are simple in spirit and heart and easy to love. But you are a woman of more mystery and depth than any other I have ever met. I love the dreamer in you and your worship of *Elohim*. That is what I need most, not your royal duties. You draw me toward the spiritual kingdom and keep the world from pulling me away from God. When I see you, when I kiss you, when I know you are mine, I am forever reminded of how good God is."

"Me too!" Shulamit added.

Solomon smiled. "The timing of you coming to my garden has been needed. I know God sent you here as I was finishing my speech and plans for the dedication ceremony. Your dream and your spirit of glory has lifted me out of my anxious thoughts about God consecrating the Temple. You have confirmed that God's Presence will be at the dedication. I met with Zadok, and we discussed the scriptures and highlights of the temple dedication to be given before the people. Would you like to hear it?"

"I am honored."

"I long to hear your thoughts. But the sun will be up before we finish."

"This will not be the first time we stayed up all night together," Shulamit said. with a smile.

"But this for a different reason."

Shulamit sat quietly at Solomon's feet as he read the dedication. She only spoke yes and amen as he declared how the temple he built was born in the heart of his father David. She was in awe as Solomon declared of God's glory. "Even heaven and the heaven of heavens could not contain all of God's glory."

Shulamit's mind flashed back to when first met Solomon, and she had to ask, "Remember when we first sat on the grass together in the hills and I said, 'I can feel the presence of God with us?' We agreed God was everywhere, and not just in the Tabernacle."

"Angels must be drawn to lovers," Solomon laughed. "But He will be drawn to repentant hearers wherever God's children find themselves in need of His help. They can turn toward His holy place where God keeps His name. And when *Elohim* hears their prayers, He will forgive."

"What a wonderful promise," Shulamit rejoiced. "The people need that promise of hope."

Finally, as Solomon reached the end of his proclamation and prayed, "O Lord God, do not turn away the face of Your anointed. Remember the mercies of Your servant David."

Tears welled up in Shulamit's eyes as she saw the sincerity and desperation of Solomon for the favor of God. "The world always looks to a king for strength and favor. Your dedication touches my heart," Shulamit responded, "and it will touch all the people. You have shared the promises of God given through Moses, and the great forgiveness God gives even when we sin. The people shall understand that they have sacrifices they can bring before the Lord to obtain this forgiveness. What a great and loving God we have. It will be an amazing dedication."

Solomon embraced his queen. "You have been a great strength to me tonight, my sister, my spouse. Within your heart is a warrior like Deborah who could lead an army to battle just as you lead dancers. The tribe of Judah has always had to lead in the battle, and it takes such a heart of a lion to lead out in war. You, my little lamb, are also a lion."

"I hope I do not have to have many dreams like I had tonight. You were sweating drops of blood."

"I believe that some of your dreams are prophetic in nature and speak of times in the future of another king. That future king will have to fight a far greater battle for the redemption of our people."

"You, my king, always know the interpretation of riddles and puzzles beyond most of our understanding. It seems no one can share a mystery with you that your heart does not discern on some level."

"Look toward the east," said Solomon, yawning. "The rising sun is shining brightly on the temple."

"We have battled through the night and won."

"God has given us dreams, visions, and heard our prayers. I know now that the glory will fall on the temple dedication. I learned from my father, a great warrior, most battles are won in prayer long before an army will ever go out to fight. Come," Solomon said, leading Shulamit to the stairs, "let us go down to my chamber where we can shut out the daylight and get some sleep. We can think about love in the morning."

Shulamit laughed, "I am so happy. I'm happy you have gotten to know me as a lion."

"O, come my lamb, the battle is over, and you need to be tenderly embraced."

Judy Pendell

24 GROWING IN GLORY

Shulamit woke up before dawn the day after her dream of glory. She could not wait to go to the Tabernacle to worship and open her heart to the Lord. Her amazing dream from God overflowed her spirit with joy and she just had to express it in prayer. This was one of those special times when she just wanted to bow before the Ark and soak in the presence of God. A soft melody played as she meditated on the dream of her eyes being opened to Solomon's Glory and the glory they experienced together. She kneeled lower, touching her forehead to the ground, and poured out her heart to the Lord.

"Heavenly Father," she sighed in joy, "I thank You for the new glory You have brought me into with Solomon, and how we come together in You. I feel our shifted love and attraction growing together through You. You have united us to fulfill a greater purpose, serving each other and your kingdom." Shulamit's heart was so full and overflowing she could not stop. "Father, I love You so much," she began to weep, "for all You have done. I am honored and humbled by all You have brought me into. I still feel like I am walking on a cloud, and I cannot come down. I have newfound courage from You." Her words became unintelligible as Shulamit's heart poured worshipful prayer and praise. Lost in worship, time drifted like a river.

Zadok came into the tabernacle for his morning offerings, and was joined by King Solomon. They were surprised to see Shulamit bowed before the altar surrounded by a shining glow.

"Your bride is full of the glory of *Elohim*," said Zadok."

Solomon replied, "Last night, she had a dream about seeing me in glory. It must have really blessed her."

"She is lost in the presence of God," Zadok said in awe. "I have never seen her worship like this. I wonder how long she has been here praying."

"Shulamit loves God," said Solomon. And she loves me. She sees me in glory, but sometimes I sense she sees me as more than I am."

"You are the symbol of a Heavenly Kingdom," replied Zadok thoughtfully, "and she is not wrong to see that.

"To see her praying now with that glow, she draws me in, like her dream did where I felt us lifted in glory together. But then again, we are in love, and love does that, does it not?

The High Priest laughed. "Love does funny things, that is true. But I believe God speaks into Shulamit's dreams with a prophetic voice."

Zadok moved away from the main area, where they could speak more freely. Solomon gave Shulamit a long look, then joined him. It wouldn't be long before he had to complete his work, and Shulamit was too enthralled to be interrupted.

"Shulamit sees into the spiritual realm," Zadok said, "which is a very great gift to you. God has given her to you as a joyful lover as well as a blessing of strength."

Solomon confessed, "I came to join you this morning, but I too feel this need to thank God for His blessings. I also will thank Him for speaking to me through the dream of my wife, and the comfort of knowing He has blessed us with glory for the dedication. I shared my speech with her last night. God is going to move and I am excited. The affirmations she gave increased my confidence and must have been from *Elohim* himself."

"The Lord is drawing you closer together in Him for His service," Zadok answered. "You know, I sometimes share the temple messages God lays on my heart with my wife. Hearing her say how it blesses her, and will bless our people, is always affirming."

"Bless me Zadok, and I will return to my balcony where I can hear the worship and pray from there," said Solomon. "I do not wish to distract you or my bride." As he exited, he was surprised to catch his mother entering the tabernacle so early. He changed course, walking over to greet her.

"It seems as if something is in the air," he said to her as he greeted her with a kiss. "Everyone is arriving for the early worship this morning."

"Indeed," said Bathsheba. "I must confess, one of my maidens was returning from prayer and told me she saw Shulamit praying before the Ark with an amazing glow surrounding her. I wished to come and see. I thought I might catch some glory of my own in the atmosphere."

Solomon laughed quietly, "Ima, you have always been a seeker of Godly glory. I remember you grabbing my hand to take me to the tabernacle when Father wrote a new song from his latest experience with God. It was you who taught me to discern God's presence when Father spoke."

"It did you good, my son," she said, a joy in her voice, "How else could you have followed in his footsteps to become such a king?"

"I do appreciate that. Perhaps if Shulamit does not pray all day, you might wish to invite her to dine and share some of your glory experiences with her. She is always receptive to know more about God."

"We shall see," said Bathsheba. She nodded a loving farewell, then entered the tabernacle to worship as the hourly shift of priests was taking place.

As the song ended, Shulamit felt her prayer time over, so she rose from her prostrated position, extending her arms in worship with the final notes. The presence of the Lord had not dissipated in the slightest. Asaph was now leading worship with a peppier melody and faster beat.

Bathsheba made her way over to Shulamit, saying, "I would love it if you would come and dine with me. I see you have been in the glory, and I would like to share this moment with you, if you don't mind."

"I am honored," Shulamit agreed.

Bathsheba took Shulamit's hand as they walked to her private chambers. "It's a beautiful morning," she told her, "Let's sit outside in my garden."

***

The Queen Mother's pavilion was surrounded by climbing roses and colorful pots filled with grasses and flowers in fall hues. The two set on low, pillow covered benches while the servants brought them tea, sweetbread, and fruit.

"You were so aglow this morning. Many people in the Tabernacle observed the glory imparted to you from sitting in the presence of God."

"I was unaware of my glow."

"You are still glowing," Bathsheba shared her observation, "but it is beginning to fade. You must have been there for quite some time."

Shulamit smiled, excited to share. "I had so much I wanted to talk to my Heavenly Father about," she explained as she lifted a fragrant cup of tea. "Sometimes I feel a need to pause and meditate, so I can process all the Lord is doing in my life. I want it sealed within my heart and not lost."

"I understand," Bathsheba said, "King David used to spend a lot of time meditating before the Lord. It reminds me of lyrics in one of his psalms," Bathsheba commented and then sang, "I will meditate on the glorious splendor of Your majesty, and on your wondrous works."

Shulamit put down her teacup and sang the lyrics again with her. A servant came to pour more tea, and the Queen Mother signaled with her hand for the servant to continue. Bathsheba was focused on their sharing hearts; she did not want the flow disturbed.

"David drew much strength from meditating and pouring out his heart to the Lord. He listened for the Lord's instructions with great intent. The greater the battle or decision he had to make, the more time he spent in the presence of God. This was one of his many secrets to success."

"Yes," Shulamit agreed. "Last night I experienced a dream of glory. I went to Solomon and shared this dream with him. Solomon called me a mighty army with banners and we both sensed we were being drawn into a holy chariot toward heaven. Then he read his dedication of the temple to me. I listened, and I prayed with him. He said he felt me as a warrior, united with him giving him strength for the battle ahead. He said he saw me like a lion."

"Today you were praying with the kind of intensity David had."

Shulamit bowed her head, humbled by such a compliment. "Because Solomon confirmed my dream about being an Army with Banners, I asked the Lord to help me make my worshipping dancers bless Solomon mightily at the dedication."

"That is a beautiful request, young queen."

"So far, we have learned the lyrics and expressed our feelings for various psalms through dance—"

"I have seen you dance for Solomon on Sabbath Evenings," said Bathsheba.

"But never have we had occasion to demonstrate our dance before a large crowd at a festival, let alone a dedication of people coming from all over the world to Israel.

Bathsheba had a sudden insight, and her face became serious. "An Army," she said, "Hmm, an army is organized into troops and teams with captains. I know you have an inner core of dancers who have been with you since you started your worship team with Shira. Can you not divide your worshippers into teams and put your best worship leaders over groups of five to seven ladies?"

"We kind of have been doing that in practice."

"As the daughter of a warrior," Bathsheba spoke with authority, "I heard about war strategy all my life. The Lord had the various tribes organized for battle camped around the Tabernacle. Judah always went first."

"Throughout my childhood, my grandfather taught us about war on Sabbath Evenings. His happiest days were fighting with David before he became king. My grandfather's stories made me desire to be a boy and fight. But God had other plans," she laughed. "My father transformed that desire by calling me a Worship Warrior." Shulamit stood up, "There are times when David sings about war and I make stomping steps, like this," she said as she demonstrated her dance. "I imagine myself trampling upon the enemy, as if he were a snake under my feet."

Bathsheba laughed too. "God surely knows how to change our plans." Sipping her tea, she changed the subject slightly. "Do you know why the lion is the king of all the animals in the hills? He is not the strongest of animals." Bathsheba answered her own question, saying, "Courage. A king must know the source of his strength during risks and then surround himself with those who see his courage and come into agreement with it.

"Courage," Shulamit repeated.

Bathsheba continued, "Solomon has the anointing and call of God upon his life. But even kings need to be surrounded by those with their own courage."

"I hope to be such a person," Shulamit confided.

"You are, my dear," Bathsheba said, smiling. "Courage comes from God and His overflow into your life. When I saw you worshipping in prayer this morning, I sensed God's anointing and strength upon you. Great anointing leads to great courage."

"I believe my dreams of Glory was about having courage for the mission we are walking into."

"God has been preparing you both for what He is about to do in the next Holy Weeks. Both King David and the High Priest Zadok, who had anointed Solomon with oil at his inauguration declared, 'God would never call a person to a position without giving him the gifts and anointing to fulfill the call.'"

Shulamit sat silently for a few moments. Then she reached over to Bathsheba and gave her a loving embrace as tears of joy came down her face. "I know you are sharing with me from your experiences with King David," she said. "I am so blessed to have you, and the other wonderful friends God has given me in this palace. Sometimes I feel unworthy, but I do feel courage and glory have come upon me through last night's Godly dream encounter. It is hard to explain, but Solomon discerned it. I have promised in my heart to give my all-in support of our king and the kingdom."

***

As Shulamit pondered Bathsheba's advice about how to organize her army, she walked to her own secret place under the stars, considering how she could best present her vision. She remembered Bathsheba laughing and saying, "God changes his plans." And then she remembered how she had loved David's battle cry in her desire to be a warrior. Before her father shared a new idea of her becoming a worship warrior, it burned in her like a joyous fire. Suddenly she thought, *a worship warrior can have a battle cry too. I must write a worshipper's battle cry.*

Through the night Shulamit thought of her dream, her worship, and what Solomon said about an Army with Banners. Her grandfather had taught her songs from David that were battle cries. He said the psalms were written during the heat of war as he prayed before leading his soldiers to battle. As David's soldiers fought with him, they knew they would win, and it caused them to fight more valiantly.

As she processed all those thoughts, she wrote her battle cry. This time of creation was not like her love songs, flowing from her with ease. Shulamit struggled writing it. It made her understand how Solomon had struggled writing his dedication of the Temple. He had searched the scriptures with the High Priest to find the promises made to Israel for obeying the commandments. She realized that declaring the Word of the

Lord before the people, with expectation of fulfillment, took faith. *That is what kings and leaders do,* Shulamit thought. *They give courage to their people. That is what I must declare to my army of worshippers. They look to me to lead them in worship.*

Looking up to the stars as the sky faded from black to grey, Shulamit prayed, "Heavenly Father, I turn this over to You, I trust that You have spoken and will honor this declaration."

She felt the morning dew upon her skin. Venus appeared in the sky. Dawn was approaching. The thought of Solomon calling her a lion came to her mind and she laughed as she returned to her chamber.

Later in the morning, as her worshippers were coming together, Shulamit noticed many more worshippers showed up than their usual.

"We saw you glowing in the tabernacle, and we know something new is happening," Queen Karem excitedly announced.

"Yes, let us in on your secret," Nikkel added.

Shulamit was surprised, although Bathsheba said she had seen the same. Shulamit really had not fully understood how this breakthrough and newfound courage was observed by others. *Now is the time to declare the vision the Lord has given me,* she thought.

Using hand signals to draw the women close to her she began to cry out,

"Come ladies of the royal court
I have a vision to share
You have all been faithful to prepare
And now with God's grace I declare

Like an Army we shall dance up the stairs
At the temple's dedication
A glory shall come upon us
And there shall be great celebration

As an army fights strong and mighty
To honor the King of Glory
We shall ascend the hill of the Lord
And worship majestically

Angels shall dance with each of us
With our bodies as light as a feather
Wings on our feet moving swiftly in flight
As we gracefully move all together

Our Heavenly Father shall smile on us

245

Our worship is His delight
Our joy shall draw people together
And nations shall come to the light!

As she finished her declaration, the ladies, clapped their hands and shouted, "Praise God, Hallelujah!"

Solomon had been standing outside the door listening and came walking in with her friend Shira. Shulamit's joy was tripled at seeing her love, and her dear friend, and at the shout of God's war cry.

"Let us applaud that," Solomon said. "You shall indeed be an Army with Banners, as the Lord gave Shulamit in a dream. There is spiritual power in the atmosphere. It is reminiscent of David's mighty men. Worshippers are to be honored, for you bring the presence of God."

Solomon escorted Shira to Shulamit and joined their hands. He whispered into her ear before walking away. "Keep leading from the heart my love, it is no longer you but the Host of Heaven taking over. And take courage."

Shulamit thanked Solomon with a glowing smile as took his exit.

"And look who is here," she called out to the ladies. "It is Shira, who helped create this Army with banners."

Shulamit ran up to embrace her friend who held a young baby boy. She kissed her cheek and then bent to kiss the baby on the forehead. "What a surprise! How long are you here?"

"I'm not sure," Shira replied, "But at least through the end of the festivals. After hearing your declaration, I simply could not miss participating in the worship at the dedication."

"Hear that, ladies? Shira is going to worship with us." The women made cries of delight, then began fawning over her son. Shira managed to draw her baby away from the women adoring him. She handed him over to his nursemaid and said, "I am ready to worship now."

Together they all practiced some of the halal dances. "I can already feel a lightness in my feet," Elisheba shouted.

"Me too," Karem rejoiced, "I feel light as a feather. God is good."

They all laughed as refreshing joy came upon them while they worshipped. After the dancing, Shulamit brought Shira to her private chambers. Shira had been living North in Naphtali with her husband, one of the governors responsible for gathering palace taxes and food supplies each month of the year. Shira was no longer singing in the tabernacle as the priest's daughter, but she had married well and was incredibly happy.

"I have missed you very much," Shulamit confided. Looking down at the baby boy, she asked, "And this handsome prince must be Ahimaaz." she bent down and kissed him on the forehead again. Sitting at the low table and drinking tea, Shulamit stared at her friend with her baby. "It seems like yesterday we were young girls learning to read and worship together. And now, here you are a mother. May I hold Ahimaaz?"

"Of course." As Shulamit picked up the baby and met his steady gaze, she smiled broadly at his gurgling baby sounds. Something in her heart softened. A feeling came over her that she had never felt before and a tear dropped from her eyes.

Shira observed the tears and caught the longing look. "Do not worry, your time will come to have a little one. I believe God has called you to a different calling for now. You must worship and dance to glorify Him at the dedication of the temple. But you will have a baby soon."

"Until this moment," Shulamit said, sounding fragile, "I have never thought of having a baby. I have been too busy to even think about it. Ahimaaz is so endearing. The way he looks into my eyes and even smiles at me. Oh, my heart," Shulamit said as she choked back more tears, "my heart just opens to him, and I realize I am ready." She paused, then spoke again, boldly, "Yes, I am ready to have a baby."

Shira nodded, offering her an embroidered cotton cloth to wipe her tears. "Yes, you are ready, my dear friend."

"You were my first friend my age in Jerusalem. You became to me like my childhood friend, Rebecca. I missed her terribly, but you took her place in my life."

"You miss your friend Rebecca," Shira mentioned.

"Friends will always be friends., That is for life, no matter what direction or distance between us. Our lives are changing, but Rebecca will always be in my heart, the same as you are. My brother, Joshua, just delivered wine from the harvest to the palace, and I learned that Rebecca has had their second son and is with child again. It gladdens my heart to know my brother now has plenty of sons to help maintain the vineyard and animals, and that my mother was going to be well cared for by grandchildren."

"God is so good," Shira said. "He always looks after us. You know Shulamit, I have missed dancing and worshipping with you. I am overjoyed to worship with you at such a special time."

Ahimaaz begin whining for his mother, and Shulamit handed him to Shira. "He is hungry. We should go."

Walking Shira to the door, Shulamit thanked her again for encouraging her hope for a child. "I believe what you said," Shulamit told her, "I will have a baby after the dedication, and I accept that as coming from God. It rings true in my Spirit."

"But first, the Temple dedication," Shira said, smiling.

"Yes. First the Temple dedication."

25 THE DEDICATION

Waiting for the new year, Shulamit felt like her anxious mind seemed to wander through the whole city. Crowds of people poured into Jerusalem in the late afternoon, admiring Solomon's Temple. It was shining like gold in the bright sun. Shulamit shared the fullness of her heart with Shira, who had come to visit while her son slept. They stood together on the palace wall, looking down at the excited crowds.

"I know in my heart," Shulamit said, "these are going to be unforgettable feast days. God is going to show up in greater glory than we have ever experienced in our lifetime. My joy is over full."

Shira replied, "The Priests are cleaning, repenting, fasting, and purifying themselves like I've never even heard of before. They all want to make sure they are fully prepared for God to bring His presence."

"Solomon and I have been preparing for these Feasts as well. My ladies of the court are excited to worship in His presence. I cannot wait to see the tiny sliver of new moon tonight and hear the trumpet blasts that will herald in the new year.

"*Rosh Hashanah*," said Shira with solemnity.

"This my favorite time of the year. I love the progression of all the *High Holy Days*—

Shira interrupted, a smile on her lips, "beginning with the *Feast of the Trumpets.*"

"Yes," Shulamit said, also smiling. "I love the way *The Ten Days of Awe*—

"Or *Repentance*," Shira interjected.

"—draw us all together to forgive each other. That forgiveness helps us draw closer to *Elohim*. And I love *Yom Kippur, the Day of Atonement,* when we can feel God's grace as He forgives our sins, so we get a whole new fresh start for the year ahead."

"So true," Shira agreed. "Who understands the power of forgiveness better than *Elohim*'s chosen people?"

"New chances and new beginnings in life, yes."

"We understand beginnings and new beginnings. *Rosh Hashanah* represents the day *Elohim* created the earth."

"*Elohim*, our creator. Praise be to Him," Shulamit said, noticing a little boy's face down near the wall. His face glowed, full of wonder as he looked around. "And someday He will return and create a new Heaven and earth. We are his people, and we have such a beautiful, unique covenant with

YHWH. He will honor our sacrifices and forgive our sins until the day He makes all things new forever, and we can have joy to celebrate the Feast of Tabernacles forever."

Shira's smile widened, "We need to go now and join our families to enter the Tabernacle, before sundown."

And she was correct. Solomon had just arrived, sharing a look of holy love, joy, and excitement with his wife. He took her hand and led her to join the others. Solomon was there to escort his queens, princesses, and ladies-in-waiting to the Tabernacle.

Everyone was specially adorned for the occasion. They entered with thanksgiving and praise as always, but with more reverence on this Holy Day. As the sun set, the trumpets would blow in the Tabernacle to call forth the New Year. Doorkeepers escorted the various royals and nobles to their respective places in the front as the Tabernacle became crowded. There was no room to sit.

Shulamit stood there, about to consider her past year. But before she could get too deep in thought, the trumpeters began to blow the many ram's horns in unison. It was uplifting to hear the glorious thunder of Heaven roaring through the horns.

The first long blast vibrated her body with its loudness, and awakened Shulamit's spirit to the mighty triumph of God. After that came three short, broken blasts that almost sounded as if the horns were weeping. Shulamit felt a deep sadness for her sins (and the sins of the nation) that needed to be forgiven. But once again, the horns' sound shifted, and nine short, staccato blasts created a tremoring feeling of alarm within her.

Shulamit had been taught, like all Hebrew people, that during the *Feast of Trumpets*, the book of Judgment was opened in the Courts of Heaven. During that time, the deeds of every believer in *YHWH* went under review. It was not a time to be taken lightly.

This *Day of the Awakening Blast* had clearly enthralled Shulamit's spirit. She did not like to think about judgment, preferring to focus on the *Days of Awe* as a time of opportunity. Every Israelite, including herself, had time to examine their hearts, see if they needed to make amends to anyone they hurt, and if necessary, show kindness and charity, righting their heart with others and *Elohim*. Renewing love for one another; that's what Shulamit considered the *Days of Awe* to be about.

At last, the appointed men lifted their shofars to blow 99 long, loud blasts. The final blast was held as long as each man blowing the shofar had breath. It was such a long, loud sound, the people were overtaken by a fear of God and awe.

Holy quietness and prayer followed the end of the trumpet song. In the Tabernacle, musicians played soft, solemn music. Israelites bowed before the Ark in an attitude of repentance. Many whispered prayers like, "Lord forgive my shortcomings and let me not be blotted out of your book of life." Their earnest prayers were another form of holy music reverberating in the Tabernacle.

Shulamit was taken up in a vision, finding herself standing before God himself, her Heavenly Father. *Elohim* appeared as a very bright light, surrounded by angels as He sat upon His heavenly throne. Shulamit walked up a glowing flight of stairs and bowed before His presence, overcome by His glory. Shulamit couldn't even open her mouth to ask forgiveness. As she lay prostrate on the ground, she felt light wrapping around her. It took her hand and lifted her up, helping her to stand. Great love, warmth, and calm emanated from the light as it came from *Elohim's* throne. Though Shulamit heard no words, she knew she was fully forgiven by her creator. The blissful feeling of love took her breath away.

When she came out of her vision and found herself bowed before the Ark, it took her a few moments to realize she was back in the earthly Tabernacle.

Shulamit whispered, "Thank you, Father, for Your vision. I shall never forget your love. I know I am not blotted out of your book. And I pray, right now, as all Israel prays before You, that we *all* have clean hands and pure hearts to be blessed in the coming year."

Shulamit focused on the song starting in the Tabernacle. The atmosphere shifted with the singers' new lyrics. They spoke of light, strength, and fear breaking off of broken spirits. The priests began to play her favorite Psalm, and her heart leaped anew at the words.

The Lord is my light and my salvation; whom shall I fear?
The Lord is the strength of my life, of whom shall I be afraid?"

This was a psalm Shulamit had sung since she was a child. The vision she'd just had reminded her of how she felt when she sang that song in her youth. Perhaps she had not realized the profound peace she always received when she sang as a young girl. The psalm removed any fear that she would not be in the *Book of Life*. Shulamit joined in the song, full of the joy from her childhood. As she sang, she was enlightened by the fact that she had always been very blessed. *I guess I have been more fortunate than many,* Shulamit thought. *More loved, more protected, and raised by parents who always watched over me. The thought that I would ever be blotted out of the Book of Life by my loving, Heavenly Father never made any sense to me. My heart has always desired, and been able, to please Elohim.*

She smiled at the end of the psalm, sighing the last lyrics as it was finishing.

Judy Pendell

I remain confident of this
I will see the goodness of the Lord
In the land of the living

Wait on the Lord
Be strong and take heart
Wait, I say, on the Lord!

After the Tabernacle opened the *Feast of Trumpets*, Solomon led his queens, princesses, and ladies-in-waiting back to the grand dining hall of the palace. There they were joined by the city's officials and nobility for a traditional late-night feast. Bowls decorated with rose blossoms were full of pomegranate seeds with rose water and lavender. They were set out, along with the fare for the *Feast of Trumps,* formally known as *Rosh Hashana.*

King Solomon dipped apples into a center bowl of honey declared, "Thank you, Father for your sweetness in our year to come."

Pomegranate seeds always spoke of fruitfulness and promises to be birthed, and as she ate one, Bathsheba cried out, "Many promises will be birthed this year."

The servers set out fish heads on large, gold platters. The priest spoke of how the fish heads symbolize the head of the year. But it was also *Elohim's* way of declaring to Israel that His people are called to be *the head and not the tail.*

Shulamit knew that being the head came with a cost, but it came with great honor and blessing too.

Round Challah bread, a traditional part of communion on Sabbath and feast days, came next. Challah bread being round had special significance. The priest announced, "The bread is round on this special day because it represents the circle and eternity of life." He looked over to Solomon, as head of his own house, to bless the bread.

Solomon acknowledged him, stood, said his blessing, and then lifted the wine and shouted, "*I'shavah Tovah!*" which meant, "good year." Cheers were great in response. The room was full of talk, laughter, and happy thoughts. At the end of the night's meal, as they headed to their various resting chambers, people turned and blessed each other again and again.

"May you be written in the *Book of Life!*"

***

All too quickly, the *Days of Awe* were coming to an end and the great *Day of Dedication* arrived.

Priests sacrificed the last of the sheep and oxen families of Israel had brought to receive forgiveness of their sins. Prayers and atonement were finished, and the atmosphere shifted from solemnity to joy. The people, who came from all over Israel for the Holy Festivals, gathered on Mt Zion in the City of David.

Each person's heart was focused on the Ark of the Covenant.

Levite Priests, specially blessed for the holy duty, placed staves into rings on the four corners of the Ark and lifted the staves onto their shoulders. They began their travel to the Holy of Holies. Following behind them were 120 priests. Those priests blew trumpets, leading unified singers and an orchestra with resounding cymbals, psalteries, and harps. Other priests worshipped as they came behind them, dancing with palm branches.

King Solomon led the elders of Israel, tribal chiefs, mighty warriors, and the men of the noble families. As they walked up the steps to the temple, they sang the songs of ascents.

The queens and ladies of the palace were escorted on litters and in golden carriages to the base of the broad stairs leading up the Mount to the Temple Entrance. Each woman was arrayed in royally colored robes and elegant headdresses. Priests, proud of their placements, stood on the steps as they played the songs of ascents in the traditional order.

Shira sang, her voice strong and clear, at the forefront of the ladies who danced, carrying banners up the steps. Shulamit sang as well, leading her dancing warriors with arms flowing in free movement. Special dance routines took place as the group reached an elevated platform at the top of every 15 steps.

"I cried to the Lord in my distress, and he responded to me...," the women twirled, rejoicing with their movements until the song was complete. They moved in unchoreographed dance up the next 15 steps.

"I will lift up mine eyes to the mountains..."

"I was glad when they said unto me let us go into the house of the Lord..."

"To you who sit enthroned in heaven, I lift up my eyes..."

"Our help is in the name of the Lord, the maker of heaven and earth..."

Crowds of people rushed to catch a glimpse of the dancing sequences. Glory shone in their worship as the queens, brides, and maidens of the court continued to move in rhythm up the stairs singing, "How blessed are all who fear the Lord as they follow in His ways."

They danced their way up the last 15 steps, arriving at the final platform. Here, the dancers separated into concentric circles, singing, "Behold how good and how pleasant it is for the brethren to dwell in unity."

Shulamit saw women from the crowd staring in awe of the dancers, and she invited them to join. Dancing was a great unifier in Israel. It made the feast days so joyful, and Shulamit didn't want anyone left out.

After the last dance, the temple gatekeepers took the women of the palace to a staircase hidden behind a wall. The stairs led to the Queen's Court on the walls of the temple. From this spot, they could look down upon the inner court to see the priests and hear the music. Once there, Shulamit and the other women joined in the song of praise, which was led by the oracle, who directed the priest's choir.

Oh, give thanks to the Lord,
For He is good!
For His mercy endures forever.
Let Israel now say,
"His mercy endures forever!"
Let the house of Aaron now say,
"His mercy endures forever!"
Let those who fear the Lord, now say,
"His mercy endures forever!"

The queens looked down from their vantage point to see the priests carrying the Ark through the outer courts into the inner courts of the Temple. They saw the priests enter the Holy Place, but from where they were, only the curtain was visible as the priests passed through. Zadok and Solomon had told them about the chosen Levite priests who carried the Ark of the Covenant into the Holy of Holies. They would set the ark down, draw out the staves, and the holy Ark would have a new home.

The Glory of God would remain in the Temple forever.

As they waited for the sign that the Ark was now at rest, the women noticed a thick, black cloud that must have come from the Holy of Holies. It flowed throughout the entire temple. Music stopped as priests fell prostrate on the ground, and no one close to the black cloud could see to stand or serve while God's presence filled the house of God. Shulamit was overcome with joy and awe as the cloud diffused through the temple into the outer courts. Everyone fell to their knees, quiet reigning as everyone waited on the Lord.

The dark mist thinned as it rose and, to Shulamit, looking down from her vantage point was like looking through a veil. Eventually, the dark smoke dissipated. But the presence of *Elohim* was still a heaviness, and everyone remained still.

After a long moment, King Solomon walked up the steps to the brazen scaffold and stood facing the altar of sacrifice. He declared, "The Lord has said that He would dwell in thick darkness." Solomon, overcome, held a long pause after that statement.

Shulamit was still kneeling on the ground in the Queen's Court. She tapped Shira, who was next to her, on her arm. When Shira looked at her,

Shulamit's questioning look seemed to ask, "What does that mean?"

Shira whispered, "The priest taught us that we humans are incapable of seeing all the fullness of God's glory and living through the experience. So, when God wants to come close to us, He dwells in darkness for our sakes."

Ah, yes. I remember, Shulamit thought. "Like Moses in the thick cloud on Mt. Sinai," she whispered. Her eyes flashed like they did when she gained insight into a hidden mystery.

Bathsheba recognized the spark in Shulamit's eyes. She had come to recognize it over the years, and whispered, "God's presence resting here is going to draw people from all over the world to know the glory of God."

"I see," Shulamit said. "That is Solomon's desire." She turned her eyes toward Solomon. They began to shine with love and pride as King Solomon began his dedication speech.

Solomon turned toward the Temple and declared, "I have built a house of habitation for You, and a place for Your dwelling forever." The king turned his face to bless the congregation. Israel, as one, stood to receive his blessing. "Blessed be the God of Israel whose hands fulfilled what he spoke with his mouth to my father David." Solomon proclaimed, and his voice rang throughout the temple. "The Lord had said that, since the day He brought Israel out of Egypt, Jerusalem was *Elohim's* chosen place for His Name and His Temple. It was in the heart of my father David and has now been realized by his son."

The king kneeled upon the brazen scaffold and extended his hands toward heaven as he began to pray, "Oh, Lord God of Israel, there is none like You in Heaven, or in the earth, which keeps covenant and shows mercy unto your servants. Heaven and the heaven of heavens cannot contain Thee! How much less this house which I have built. Hearken therefore unto the supplication of Your Servant, and of Your people which they shall make toward this place. Hear therefore from Thy dwelling place, even from Heaven; and when You hear, forgive. If the people be put to worse before the enemy because of sin and return and confess, you will hear and forgive. When Heaven shuts and there is no rain because of sin against You, yet if they pray toward this place and confess their sins, You will forgive."

Solomon continued, mentioning pestilence, treatment of strangers, and captivity. If *Elohim's* people would only return with their heart and pray toward this land, *Adonai* would hear and forgive. "Arise, oh Lord," he continued. "Let the priests be clothed with salvation and the saints rejoice with goodness."

When Solomon's prayer ended, a bright column of fire appeared from Heaven, full of red, orange, yellow, white, and hints of blue. It descended to the Holy of Holies, dividing into flames that consumed every one of the burnt offerings and sacrifices within the Temple. The sweet scent of burnt meat and fats perfumed the air, and those in and around the temple were warmed from the holy fire.

Over the Holies of Holies, a new blaze began. But the fire on the offerings rose as if called, meeting with the fire descending from heaven. As they met, they exploded in yellow, amber, and gold light. The fire dancing between heaven and earth continued even after the embers of the sacrifices began dying out. This new, golden glory filled the whole temple, spreading like a rushing wind. The women's court and the court for foreigners also felt the renewed and burning presence of God. The presence changed its expression, becoming a thick, flowing mist which covered the whole of Mt Moriah. It could be seen for miles around.

The people in the mist bowed their faces to the ground.

Shulamit tried to capture the mist in her hands, but it could not be caught. Shira smiled as she said, "I tried too. We can't capture it. But it is real. I feel the power in it."

While Shulamit continued lying on the pavement she began to pray for Israel, her beloved Solomon, her family, and even a prayer for herself to have a baby. With a jolt, she felt a warm tingling flow throughout her whole body, overcoming her with strong internal peace.

God heard my request.

She was not sure what the feeling was, but she began to thank God for His answer to her prayer. From her high view, Shulamit envisioned the people in the outer courts face down on the pavement. Their children were around their families, full of the joy of the Lord and playfully trying to grab the golden mist of glory.

"We are all childlike in wanting to capture the glory," Shulamit said. Shira quietly laughed in response.

As the weight of the glory began to lift, there were great shouts of joy. People began to jump around, declaring healing miracles.

"I can see!" and older man shouted.

"I can walk!" a child yelled as he threw down his crutch and began to dance around his weeping mother."

"I can hear!" an older woman cried out.

Many more began shouting for joy as they worshiped and praised the Lord. They sang, "He is good, for his mercy endures forever!"

Solomon stood on the brazen scaffold and held out his hands for a moment of quiet.

"Today," he began, "the Lord has consecrated this location as the place where His name will dwell forever. Not since Mt Sinai, when God made covenant with us four hundred years ago has such glory been seen. God has accepted our sacrifices. Our sins have been forgiven on this great day of atonement, and the covenant He has made with us is confirmed. We are the most blessed nation on the earth. Rejoice! Eat, drink and be merry on this great day!"

A sparkle of holiness shone in the eyes of the people and gold dust appeared on their skin, clothes, and in their hair.

"We must remember to tell our children and our children's children," a father announced to his sons."

Many of the inner court's orchestra priests broke into divisions and moved from their posts, bringing worship with them. The music rang out all around the temple mount. Strangers visiting Jerusalem could hear the powerful temple worship and watched the people in the streets of Jerusalem dance.

Shulamit and her worshipping warriors rose from the ground, so overflowing with glory they could not help but dance. Solomon looked toward his bride and the dancers, waving for the guards to protect the royal ladies as they came down from the woman's court and joined in the citywide dance.

Shulamit divided her dancers in the inner circle, sending them in small groups to join the dancing in the outer circles. She charged them to demonstrate the new dance steps to the worshipping women. Little girls wanted to dance too, and Shulamit invited them into her circle to teach them the steps. They learned faster than their mothers and older sisters. Within moments, Shulamit realized she could not control the move of the Holy Spirit, so she stopped trying to teach and danced with the flow, praying others could follow.

It was an amazing day.

Levites carrying torches gave them light as they danced late into the night. The glory seemed to give the people energy they had never experienced before. It was as if time stopped as all Jerusalem enjoyed their communion with *Elohim*.

This celebration of the dedication of the temple continued for an entire seven days. During that time, the king sacrificed 22,000 oxen and 120,000 sheep, from the entrance of Hamath in the North to the Brook of Egypt.

After the dedication of the middle court and brazen altar, they kept the *Feast of Tabernacles* another seven days. The meat from the sacrifices were apportioned to the people, with raisin cakes and flagons of wine. The people ate well, then slept in their sukkots. *Elohim's* command to celebrate this feast by living in their sukkots under the open sky was for them to never forget how He delivered them from Pharaoh and slavery, brought them through the wilderness, provided them with water and manna, and protected them from their enemies.

For Shulamit, this was her happiest time since she came to the palace. She went to the woman's court and danced new dances, becoming known as the Worshipping Queen in Israel. She was so called after the manner of Miriam, who led worship when the Israelites came through the Red Sea.

Day after day, Shulamit danced, singing to happy Hallel songs:

Praise the Lord!
Praise, O servants of the Lord
Praise the name of the Lord!
Blessed by the name of the Lord
From this time forth and forevermore!
From the rising of the sun
To its going down
The Lord's name is to be praised
The Lord is high above all nations
His glory above the heavens
Who is like the Lord our God?
Who dwells on high?
Who humbles Himself to behold
The things that are in the
Heavens and in the earth?

When Israel went out of Egypt
The house of Jacob from a people
of strange language

Judah became His sanctuary
And Israel His dominion.

On the first morning of *Sukkot*, and every morning of the eight-day *Water Libation* celebration, the priests danced through the woman's court. They carried golden pitchers of water from the Pool of Siloam, pouring them on the middle court's brazen alter for the daily sacrifices. It was a joyful event and the people danced along with the priests while leaving way for them to pass through them.

Each day, Shulamit and the palace women were escorted daily by priests to the Queen's Court to watch the Holy events take place.

After each outpouring of the *Water Libation*, the people shouted, clapped, and women beat tambourines in joyful applause. Shulamit would lead her worshippers down to the woman's court to join the celebration. At one point, the High Priest proclaimed, "Thank you, Heavenly Father, for sending the rain that brings us life. We are grateful for the bountiful harvest. We bless you Lord God for giving the early and latter rain that amply supplies all our needs."

The glory of this *Sukkot Celebration* was so great, Solomon extended it for two weeks. Dancing and feasting continued in the Streets of Jerusalem and throughout Israel. Shulamit greeted everyone during the days of *Sukkot* by saying, "*Chag Sumeach*," which means, "Happy Holidays," in their Hebrew language. She was happy to be out of the palace, amongst the people and teaching dances in this *Feast of Tabernacles*.

At the peak of this great celebration, Solomon brought Shulamit to his sukkot in the secret place. He poured a glass of wine, then they each broke a piece of the round Challah loaf and prayed, "Thank you Heavenly Father for answering our prayers."

They sat for a while, just holding each other, looking up to the stars through the sukkot.

After a long while, Shulamit looked at Solomon and said, "Isn't God good? He honored your prayers in the most amazing, confirming way. He blessed the Temple you built for Him, and the animal sacrifices for the forgiveness of all Israel's sins. I will never forget these days for as long as I live. Nor do I think anyone else in Israel will. My faith has grown in leaps and bounds during this time. I could never have imagined all of the amazing things we have experienced together."

Solomon looked into Shulamit's eyes, "You still have the sparkle of glory in your eyes from the other night, when you dreamed."

"So do you, Solomon. I remember feeling the glory all around as you spoke from the large platform, I can imagine it now. You, with your arms spread out toward heaven. I knew that heaven was smiling down upon you. I keep that moment treasured in my mind."

"When I saw you leading all the great women of Jerusalem in dance," Solomon replied, "I flashed back to the time I saw you dance at the harvest festival with your family. That day, I envisioned you leading the women of my palace and the tabernacle in dance, and what I saw then came true over these past weeks. You were truly *in* the glory of God during the Temple dedication. You have become the beautiful queen I first saw when I met you."

"I was living my dream, dancing with the women in the golden temple mist. It was as if I was dancing in heaven, even as my feet were on the earth."

"*Mahanaim!*" said Solomon.

"Yes," Shulamit said. "The dance of two camps."

"Heaven came to Earth, and your dream come to life, before all the people. Women will return to their villages all over Israel, teaching the dances you taught them. King David would be happy to see worship so joyful." Solomon embraced her tightly as they shared a sweet, affectionate kiss. "I love you so much," he said, kissing her again. "My lovely bride." They felt the presence of *Adonai* with them as they made love.

A while later, Shulamit whispered to her beloved, "I think we just made a baby."

"A baby?" Solomon said, surprised. "How do you know?"

"I just have a feeling," she said, full of peace.

"Oh, my lovely Shulamit, if I didn't know you so well, I would say wait and see. But with you, I have learned that your intuitions are right. So, yes! We are having a baby! You never told me you wanted a baby. We have been incredibly happy, have we not? I have been completely happy with you. We do not need a baby to be happy, do we?"

Shulamit sensed Solomon's concern. "Solomon, I am as happy with you as our first night together. I will never forget that first night, when you were so gentle and patient. We kissed and we kissed, and we kissed."

He looked into her eyes, seeing confirmation of her forthcoming motherhood. "I suppose every woman wants to have a child, eventually. And now we will. Our baby will be special." He looked in her eyes. "If it is a girl, I hope she looks just like you."

Solomon reached over and handed her a lyre as he felt a song coming on. Understanding him without a word spoken, she made music to his lyrics, and she later named the song, *We Kissed*.

We kissed and we kissed
And we kissed and we kissed
Like birds we flew high
In the sky
Through the rain and the storm
The oil on our feathers
Kept us dry

We kissed and we kissed
And we kissed and we kissed
I trembled as we flew
Covered from the fierceness of nature
Our hearts were protected and pure

We kissed and we kissed
And we kissed and we kissed
Tingling moved through my body
With ease
A gentle wind flows in and out
That stirred stronger and deeper
As I breathe

We kissed and we kissed
And we kissed and we kissed

The night turned to day
As we fly
Radiant shades of pink
Color the morning sky
And I sigh

We kissed and we kissed
And we kissed and we kissed
We flew through changing seasons
From cool into hot to a
Burning fire
We flew close to the sun
In heated desire

We descended to earth in a
Gentle Mist
And we kissed and we kissed
And we kissed and we kissed."

Shulamit smiled a glowing smile and joined the song, "And we kissed, and we kissed."

He laughed, "You were so beautiful that day, I just wanted to smother you with kisses, and I still do.

"I always love your kisses, Solomon." She touched her still flat stomach. "I am very happy."

Solomon's hand joined hers over her stomach, just before he kissed her again.

26 A SEASON OF BUILDING AND GROWTH.

The baby grew in Shulamit's womb as Solomon began a great building campaign.

After the glory of the Temple dedication, the people's spirits were high, and they were of a mind to build up their kingdom. Solomon loved this divine sense of unity in purpose and started working with gusto. First, a new palace near the temple would be built. Then he would create a palace for the Egyptian Queen in Milo. Once that was completed. other military stations would be built throughout the country. Shulamit enjoyed hearing about each day's plans and pitfalls as Solomon talked to her in his secret place.

Along with a few of Solomon's other wives, Shulamit was privileged to attend the meetings where Solomon shared his royal building plans. There, he would work out what seemed like millions of details with his chiefs of staff, chiefs of tribes, governors, brothers, and trained artisans. On occasion, even Bathsheba would join the men at the table. During one such meeting, Solomon, in his usual display of catching people's attention, had servants come into the room with a large scroll. They rolled it out on the table before everyone as Solomon encouraged them to gather around.

"See here, I have the architectural plans for the whole palace complex. The Forest of Lebanon is just here." He pointed to the plans where Forest of Lebanon would be. The image of the forest displayed large gold shields on the scroll. "And here," he said, pointing at another area, "is the Hall of Pillars." His hand danced all over the map, calling out different items. "Here is a hall for the throne, and an elaborate judgement hall."

"It is amazing," said Bathsheba.

Shulamit knew Solomon's plans were grandiose. He was a visionary with wisdom and just being around him expanded everyone's vision. *I love even this part of him*, Shulamit thought. *I am so blessed to love such a man and have him love me. Everything about him is exciting.*

"Incredible," Hiram of Tyre admitted.

"Thank you, Hiram," said Solomon.

"I see how much you have grown to be able to design a palace complex with such detail and beauty. Your God has certainly given you wisdom to create."

"Truly, it is the favor and blessing from God for seeking first His Kingdom. I plan also to expand royal roads, build storage cities, and build cities for my chariots and cities for my calvary and horses. I am also designing a large palace in Lebanon. There, my wives can enjoy the cool air in the high mountains instead of being in Jerusalem during the hot summer months. Solomon returned to the plans, continuing to explain an updated layout of the water supply system to Jerusalem.

"Since the walls were already expanded during the building of the Temple, and an existing water supply had been designed by the Jebusites before David conquered the city, we are incorporating their hard work. Building upon their foundation, we will be adding a water aqueduct from the pools in Etam. It shall bring more water into the city for irrigating the gardens and trees. Jerusalem is where God chose to dwell. And with the Lord's wisdom, Jerusalem is going to be the world's most beautiful city. Here," he pointed, "are the large palace baths and mikvehs I have designed for ritual cleansing." The leaders in the room tried to keep up, but they were clearly in awe of Solomon. Shulamit could see they wondered how it was all going to come to fruition.

Solomon sensed their confusion. "What do you think?" he asked one of the artisans. "Can we make it better? Can you help me create designs that will help beautify it?" To another he asked, "Do you have suggestions? Are the fountains and gardens in proper places?"

Shulamit knew, even with Solomon's wisdom as an inventor, designer, and master organizer, he thought about the people involved. She smiled at his thoughtfulness, rubbing her growing stomach. Solomon's ideas were complete from the beginning, down to the smallest detail. But he knew to honor those involved by asking them questions and seeking their opinions. Solomon had taught her that, if she engaged people in her vision, they would be happier to carry it out. He had encouraged her to involve her worshipping team during dances by asking them if they had movement ideas. Now she watched the king do this very thing on a grander scale.

Solomon had always said, "Without counsel, plans go awry, but in the multitude of counselors they are established." It was clear the leaders in the room were excited to help him fulfill his ambitions for Israel. As Solomon asked questions, lively discussion ensued, and others began inquiring about how to engage the work force, what types of stones and wood in the infrastructure.

"Where will the servants live?" Asked one tribal chief causing a breakout conversation.

"What is the design of the interior military barracks?" asked another noble, causing another.

"Where will the horses on the palace grounds be corralled?"

Solomon loved and anticipated their questions. "Those are great questions," he replied. He answered some questions but realized he needed to draw a more detailed map for some of their details to flow into the grand plan. "I will call another meeting in a few days with more answers to those questions. Please, think of more."

That evening Solomon had a private dinner with Zabud, Shulamit, Bathsheba, and his brothers. At dinner, he explained some of his plans with more personal expression. "I answered many of their questions, and I can provide more detail. But even so, not everyone can understand every detail of my vision."

Zabud listened intently and then came up with a solution. "I think you are going to have to teach."

"Teach?" Solomon asked, taking a sip of wine.

Shulamit interjected, dipping her flat bread into eggplant sauce. "Yes. We here have all been honored with your private teaching. It makes sense that, yet again, you will be an even bigger blessing, to more people at once."

Nathan added, "Like the rabbis teach the young men how to read in schools on Saturday mornings."

"Schools," Solomon surmised. "I have much to think about."

In a few days, Solomon called another meeting of artisans, engineers, military captains, and administrative organizers to discuss details. At this meeting, he offered to teach them. "Listen closely," he started, "for today I am going to do some teaching. To produce this vision, we will need to educate a great many people. In time, I am going to organize schools. But for today, I will explain our water system as it lies at the foundation of our city."

Shulamit watched, adoring her beloved Solomon's wisdom. He was truly a man of God, and a leader of leaders. *He has a gift for creating wealth wherever he puts his mind and hand,* Shulamit thought. *His visions expand everyone's life. He helps people to dream.*

Solomon taught with care, taking his time, and answering questions with confidence. He shared how stone pipes were needed to carry water through aqueducts from elevated water towers and cisterns. "With a good supply of water, we shall be able to plant forests of trees and gardens, but I will teach on gardens later. Laying the foundation of the newly dedicated Temple took the longest time, and so will building the foundation for the new palace. Not everything can be built at once, but we shall start with the palace for my growing family."

"Growing family," caught Shulamit's attention. She laid her hands on her stomach, and though there was no outward evidence, she could feel the joy of a baby birthing within her.

It was the most prosperous time in Israel's history, and to Shulamit, everything seemed possible. She went to her secret place in the garden to reflect upon the changes happening in her. Recalling her dreams, she had as a young girl, Shulamit touched her stomach, knowing there was new life inside her. "*Abba* Father," she prayed, "I realize You had to send me a king, because only a king could have fulfilled all my grandiose dreams. Being with child is another amazing surprise. I thank You, Father God for giving me such an amazing man to love me, besides You. What more could I ask?"

During this time of building, Shulamit also observed Solomon's wisdom in knowing how to recognize and position talented people so their talents could be maximized. Shulamit had watched Solomon interact with many men when they were invited to his table. Even when she traveled with him outside of Jerusalem (before she became too pregnant to travel), he was a magnet for talented men. When they were meeting people across the country, Shulamit loved watching Solomon talk to a person for a short time, divinely perceiving their heart and gifts.

But now Solomon was going to use these skilled architects and artisans he had brought from Egypt and Tyre to help him in his schools. Some of the brightest and best of Israel's own people had been brought to Jerusalem to train under stone cutters and architects for building the temple. Now they would now be used to teach their own people. Solomon taught them how to be good teachers and leaders. overseeing great projects. Jerusalem was becoming a centralized city just as Israel was transitioning into a unified world-renowned kingdom.

Solomon's schools were soon quite popular. Even the common farmers attended as the king himself taught on ways to grow more crops and build hillside terraces for beauty and water conservation. He taught skills for improving animal care. Solomon also designed new tools for plowing. His wisdom just kept flowing out of him into new innovations all the time. The news of his wisdom went out and soon everyone wanted to come and learn.

Shulamit, who had a hungry mind to learn about everything, loved going to his classes. But as she was approaching her seventh month of pregnancy, it was becoming harder for her to sit for long periods of time. She would shift her position from side to side to find comfort but eventually had to relent to less time in her husband's schools. Their baby moved in her womb all the time (she thought) and did a lot of kicking. But today Solomon was teaching on designing gardens, which was something she loved to do, so Shulamit forced herself to sit and listen. As Solomon was explaining about where to plant different vegetation for the best advantage of sunlight and water, Solomon noticed his wife having some discomfort. She was his most attentive student and looking at her always inspired him while he was teaching. Today he wanted to acknowledge her continuous interest in learning, "My bride is my best student, she is always hungry to learn more. I love that about her."

Later that evening, Solomon came to her chamber, and said, "I love you in my classes. Your face is so beautiful and glowing with expectancy, but I am concerned you might be overdoing it and straining yourself. These classes are going to go on for a long time, so can you rest for now and come back after our baby's birth?" Solomon placed his hand on Shulamit's belly. He is a real kicker. Maybe he needs you to lay down more and give him and you more room to breathe from all the pressure he is putting on your heart and lungs." Solomon laid down beside her, placing his head where he could hear the heartbeat. "There is something so exciting about hearing a live heartbeat, especially a baby growing in the womb."

Solomon began to gently massage his wife's back, helping her to relax. He soon stopped, rising to give her a sweet kiss on her mouth. His kisses moved on to neck, then her breasts, and down her body to her belly where he kissed her navel over the womb of his baby. "Bless our baby, Father God, make him strong and healthy." Solomon took some rose scented olive oil and rubbed it over her stomach. He said, "Make sure your maidens are rubbing your belly often with oil, to prevent leaving stretch marks as the baby grows. Your ankles are beginning to swell. Do they hurt?" He rubbed them with lotion and put a pillow under them. "You must keep them elevated as much as you can now, it keeps swelling down."

Tears ran down the side of Shulamit's face, touched by Solomon's tenderness. His sensitivity to her needs was so full of love. Solomon saw her tears and kissed them.

"I must be overly emotional right now," Shulamit confessed.

"It is natural, my love; a part of what happens with a woman having a baby. You need nurturing love, and it helps you release that same nurturing to the baby inside of you. The baby is part of you right now, and love is growing inside of you, for your baby. My love, your beauty is like the holiness in the temple, you glow with life. You reflect the Holiness of God to me, and my desire is toward you. You are irresistible.

"Even with this big belly?"

"Especially with your pregnant womb, you are more beautiful than ever. Sometimes during the day, I must make hard decisions judging on the throne, or doing business. But when I come to be with you, my heart becomes full of softness. You remind me of the Holiness of God, that we must approach tenderly."

Shulamit reached over and pulled Solomon toward her with a firm, but caring kiss. She surrendered to the vulnerable emotions rising inside her. Solomon responded with equal gentleness and vulnerability, feeling her mood. He felt her deeply. They took their time with sweet lovemaking, every bit as fulfilling as their most impassioned moments together. Shulamit's heart found a new level of love with her beloved; and he joined her in that deeper love.

"After being in the presence of your beauty," Solomon said later, "when I teach, I must remind our people where the source of our creativity comes from, and about the beauty of Holiness."

The next day, as pupils came into Solomon's class from all over Israel and other nations, he started by giving glory to God.

"As we build and create architecture, we must always remember the source of creation behind it. Our *Elohim* loves beauty. He created our beautiful world and said it was good, then created humans in His image. He said our creation was *very* good. Because we are made in the image of our God, we have His wisdom to create. Keep this in mind as you work to do all to the glory of our creator. Take glory in everything you do. Enjoy and praise God in your work as a worship to our Heavenly Father." The people felt the honor King Solomon bestowed upon them. They felt the weightiness of being part of something great and they internally vowed to labor with love and honor. "I want everyone to work with joy and have pride in their accomplishments," Solomon continued. "Remember too, as you are surrounded by regal beauty, you will grow to understand more of how you have been put on this earth to influence the world in a magnificent way. You are blessed by the being within the inheritance of the great kingdom and God's chosen city of Jerusalem." When Shulamit heard of what her husband said, she stopped to praise the Lord for all she had been given in such a man of *Elohim*.

Shulamit came closer to the birth of her baby and was thankful for her husband's admonition to rest. Every day, her maiden's and sister queens came to bless her, along with Shiffrah, the palace midwife. Solomon sent her regularly to check in on her, easing Shulamit's discomfort in various ways each day. They brought her fresh goat's milk, massaged her sore feet, and often rubbed her enlarged belly with scented oil. Queens also brought her baby gifts. Ilana, the queen who was an expert in tapestry and embroidering, taught the other queens to make baby clothes and blankets. They took care with special embroidering, using many colors in case it was a girl or boy. Solomon designed a baby crib and helped the palace carpenter build it. The palace had midwives, but the queens, brides, and maidens of the palace all wanted to be present at the birth. They wanted to honor the Worshipping Queen by participating in her child's birth, no matter the task. Rubbing her body, distracting her from pain, offering her sips of water, positioning her in the best way for birth, no offer was too great or small. They had become her sisters, and she felt so loved by them.

Shulamit kept dancing until the end of her pregnancy, though she turned more leadership over to Nikkel and Kareem. Nothing deterred her from worship, but she did rest more and more. Every time Solomon came to see Shulamit, he put his hand gently on her stomach and prayed, "Lord bless the fruit of your womb, and keep our baby healthy." He would kiss her stomach and listen for the sound of the heartbeat, laughing when he saw or felt the baby kick in her womb.

"Your child is happy to see you," Shulamit would often say.

"I can't wait to see my baby," he always replied with joy. "Make sure you let me know if there is anything you need. You can take a pillow to sit on in my classes if you want. But please don't stay if you are too tired." Solomon always paid attention to the smallest details in his love for her.

"You are such a good king, yet you still have the heart of the shepherd I fell in love with," Shulamit reminded him. "I am so blessed by you."

***

Winter turned to spring, nearing the Feast of Weeks, and Shulamit's baby was due. The birthing room was ready, and Solomon ensured everything was prepared properly for his wife to give birth. He consulted regularly with Ahishan, his trusted palace overseer, and priests who taught from the Laws of Moses in the Pentateuch, on cleanliness, having regular mikvah's for personal cleanliness, and especially before going near a mother giving birth. The palace priests kept all clothes and items that would touch the mother sterile. Protecting mothers, babies, and children was a top priority.

To Shulamit's surprise, when her brothers came to Jerusalem for the Holy Day, her little sister Miriam showed up with them. Miriam was now a young budding woman of 13. "I insisted they bring me," she said. I told them I was coming to help my sister with the birth of her new baby."

Shulamit smiled, wondering what kind of behavior her insistence included. "I am happy you came," she said, "and you will be with me at this important time." She hugged her not-so-little sister. Shulamit knew Miriam had been helping Rebecca with her three children and had learned all the birthing skills of the countryside women from her own mother. Shulamit also suspected that her strong-minded Miriam had other reasons for wanting to be in the palace, probably to do with seeing Nathan.

When Shulamit was able to get a moment alone with her older brother, Joshua, she found him at his wit's end.

"Another worthy man in the village wants to be betrothed to Miriam," Joseph told her. "And she told me she cannot make that decision until she saw Nathan. We agreed to bring her, as long as she behaves herself and doesn't walk up to Nathan and say, 'I want to marry you,' as she did before."

Shulamit laughed a little. "What can we do? I see she has grown from a rambunctious child into a more reserved, rather shy, and down to earth young woman. I will ask Solomon to arrange a private dinner, with our families and give them opportunity to connect."

Shulamit spent the next day with her sister, helping her to prepare for the dinner where she would see Nathan. For all her reserve, Miriam changed her clothes five times, fussing over every part of her hair and jewelry. Fortunately, Meliba, Shulamit's most fashionable attendant, knew just what to do. She advised Miriam to wear a simple, royal blue dress with a gold sash around her waist. It showed off her pretty young figure. Shulamite gave her a pair of gold earrings inlaid with pearl, with a matching pearl necklace. Meliba combed Miriam's long, beautiful black hair with a spray of scented oil to make it shine and smell of rose and sandalwood. Nervous and excited together, Shulamit escorted her sister to Solomon's private dining room. There, the royal family was already seated around the table waiting for them.

Sure enough, Nathan looked at Miriam and froze in surprise. He could not take his eyes off her. Throughout dinner, Nathan pretended not to look at Miriam, and she pretended not to return his look. Everyone else at the table pretended not to look at either one of them, yet all knew what was happening. It was meant to be.

Solomon whispered into Shulamit's ear, "Does this remind you of anything?" Shulamit could not help but laugh to herself. Solomon smiled and couldn't help but give a low, "Hmmmmm?"

Joshua and Caleb retold a similar scene with Shulamit years ago, when she almost caused Joshua to get in a fight with Solomon. Everyone laughed.

Finally, young Shammuah asked his mother why everyone was laughing.

"Years ago, when Nathan was sitting next to me at Shulamit's and Solomon's Ketubah, he asked me if Miriam was going to grow up as beautiful as Shulamit. It never occurred to me when I said, 'Wait and see,' that I would witness what is happening here now."

"Why are you laughing Joshua?" Shobab asked. Joshua recounted the whole country dancing scene, where Solomon ran past everyone for Shulamit to grab his hand, how Joshua threatened him, and how they almost got into a fight.

Now Solomon was laughing and said, "I was not sure I was going to win."

Zabud, Solomon's best friend started laughing, "I was there to fight with him, and I looked at Caleb and thought this is going to get bad."

"How did it stop?" Shammuah asked.

"My sister started crying," Joshua answered.

"Crying?"

"Yes," Shulamit interrupted, "Because I realized how much my brothers loved me. They were going to fight for me, and my shepherd was willing to fight for me too. But now this is not about me, this is about my little sister and Nathan. It is clear they cannot take their eyes off each other." Miriam's face went hot with embarrassment and Nathan looked in his drink. "My sister is like me," Shulamit said, "When her mind is made up, she will never change it. So here we are. Family, are we going to approve them to get to know each other, choose one another, and put our blessings upon their choice?"

Solomon spoke up, "Nathan I apologize. We have all put you on the spot."

Shulamit said, rather loudly, "You know the family you are marrying into at least." Everyone laughed.

"Do you wish to pursue Miriam as a bride?" the king asked.

"I do," Nathan said, in his quiet manner, but the intense, loving gaze in his eyes said it all.

Now all eyes turned back toward Miriam, and she had tears flowing from her sparkling eyes. She was in a daze. Shulamit reached over to her and hugged her. "Tears, from the girls of my family, means *yes*."

Solomon lifted a glass of wine, "Bless our bride and bridegroom to be."

As the dinner ended, Nathan could hardly wait to take Miriam's hand and walk with her around the palace gardens. Shulamit heard him say, "You are so beautiful Miriam, I am so glad I waited for you to grow up. I had so much fun with you when you came for your sister's wedding."

"Me too," Miriam replied. "I think we were in love back then and didn't know it," she said while holding his hand as they walked under the torch lit lamps in the palace garden. "But we do now."

Yes, you do, Shulamit thought. *Praise Elohim, you do indeed.*

***

Miriam being at the palace turned out to be a great joy to Shulamit for many reasons. Miriam took it upon herself to examine the birthing room. She walked in, acting so in charge that Ahishan, Meliba, and Shiffrah, the palace midwife, just let her carry on. They found her very humorous.

"We haven't seen the likes of her since Shulamit came to the palace and ingratiated everyone with her worship," Shiffrah told Shulamit.

"Yes," said Ahishan, "but Miriam has taken over midwifery jobs."

Shulamit laughed as she told Miriam, "You are so much like Mama. You know she is the one who managed our family not Papa. You were so young you didn't know. But Papa was a dreamer who loved to worship. I loved Papa, I loved our family worship, but Mama grounded us."

"Mama always said you were more like Papa," Miriam said, "But, I can see that your dreaming made it possible for me to meet Nathan. We are all different. But I love worship too, and so does Nathan."

"Nathan yes, he is quiet and methodical, but I have always noticed his worship is much more prayerful, and private, than outward. I have always loved him as a brother in spirit. And now—"

"We should go and worship," Miriam said, interrupting. "Do you want to go to the Temple? I long to hear the music and dance."

"I am too far along in my pregnancy to go the distance. If I went, I might possibly go into labor. Please, let Nathan take you tonight. but, if you like, you can come to my worship group in the woman's court and then to our Dancing Sabbaths."

"Dancing Sabbaths?"

"Yes, Solomon always comes on Sabbath Evening to the woman's court to be with his private family. Priests come and play music, we have our wine and challah bread to introduce the Holy Day there. Solomon blesses the children and mothers, especially mothers with child and those who just gave birth. We eat, then Solomon gives a Word from what God has laid on his heart. If he doesn't speak, he has the Priest speak to us. Then we listen to more worship and dance. So, we call it our Dancing Sabbath. Those who can, go to the Temple afterwards to worship. It is a very joyful time."

Miriam joined Shulamit with her worship group. She fit right in as if she had always been part of the worshippers. Miriam danced and clapped and played the tambourine, like her namesake Miriam who played the tambourine at the Red Sea. The women laughed with her, just as they laughed with Shulamit when she first came to the palace. They still did.

"We can tell she is part of your family," Queen Gevira said.

"It is because my family knew King David personally," Shulamit replied. "They worshipped and fought with him and knew him intimately. He bought a portion of our vineyard which we willfully sold on the condition that he came to our home to worship in *Elul*. He got into our blood. Now he is in our blood," she said as she patted her stomach.

"Yes, we will never forget the vineyard bride, but we did not know the depths of your connection with King David."

"Now I am the wife of Solomon, a worshipper, but a man of peace and builder of an international kingdom. It is different. But I am glad Miriam brings back my family joy of worship. It refreshes me. And now she is part of our royal family," she reminded the women, "for she and Nathan are betrothed.

They all clapped, "Welcome!"

After worshipping with the women, Shulamit and Miriam returned to her chamber where she lay down on the cushions by her dining table. She stretched out her body and took some deep breaths. Miriam asked Shulamit's maiden, Sheriti, to bring her sister, milk, and bread, which Sheriti was already preparing. Miriam liked taking charge and looking after Shulamit.

"I am so glad you are here," Shulamit told her. You get so tired at the end of pregnancy and preparing to give birth. Lately, I can only think of wanting the baby to come. Your coming has cheered me up. You have helped me get my mind off myself and my body. I love Solomon's classes, but I can't sit there very long. I am glad you came to my worship dance today. We all had a lot of fun."

"I can see that you are very near to birth. Take heart, dear sister. I won't leave you until the baby is born. I want to help deliver it."

"You are so, like Mama," Shulamit sighed. "You know I miss being able to just get up and walk with a guard privately to the Tabernacle. Now I must be part of a caravan with other queens, and often with Solomon, and we are waving at people on the way. My life is no longer private. Once you marry a king you are on public display. You will see.

"Oh," Miriam sighed, as though it dawned upon her. In her zeal for Nathan, she had not realized that part of being married to him. Shulamit read Miriam's thought. *No one in love really thinks everything through.*

"I am weary and don't mean to complain, do not take me very seriously right now." Shulamit said. "Being a queen has its good points, too. I get to meet so many interesting people—mighty warriors, honored guests, kings of nations, talented artisans. And I enjoy being close friends with the High Priest and Bathsheba. But my best time is when I am alone or with my beloved Solomon." Returning to her unfinished thought Shulamit expounded, "I look forward to being in the new palace which will be near the Temple, but it will be some years before it will be built, and we can walk through a secret hallway to the queens court."

"Solomon is building a secret hallway from the palace to the Temple?"

"The palace is full of secret hallways," Shulamit said. "It is so Solomon can visit his different wives without others knowing. It prevents jealousy."

"Are they jealous of you?"

"I don't know. We don't talk about it. Solomon forbids. But if they knew how often he visits me, they probably would be. I never want them to feel bad. I do have my favorite sister queens, and I don't want any bad feelings between us. We have much fun together."

"I'm sorry you missed the Tabernacle and that we can't walk there now. But now, at the Temple there is the huge women's court, and I have heard women from all over the country say, "I have danced with the Shulamit, Queen of Worship."

"They said that?" she asked her sister. Hearing such praise, Shulamit's voice cheered up. "That is encouraging to hear. I am missing what the people are thinking. I need to get out more and visit. Ooh," Shulamit said as she felt a small squeeze in her womb.

"What was that?" Miriam asked.

"I felt a contraction," Shulamit replied.

"Well, sister, you are very near to giving birth, no wonder you are feeling so weary," as she asked Sheriti to hand her the scented oil to rub on her belly. Another contraction came. This time Miriam felt it. "This baby is coming quickly. Kira, go tell Ahishan to let Solomon know his wife will soon be having a baby."

Solomon came running and assisted his wife to the birthing room, halting between the starting and stopping of contractions. He held her hand and wiped her sweaty forehead with cool water, assuring her he was with her. Shiffrah stood, quietly observing Miriam very carefully in case she needed to jump in and help. But Miriam appeared to have no concerns, having seen the birth coming quickly and without problems. Shulamit's contractions intensified rapidly and soon the head was crowning. Within just a few hours, the baby was out of the birth canal.

As Miriam held the baby, she let out a great cry. Clapping and tears, "It's a girl," Mirriam said.

"It's a girl," Solomon cried out, "My first daughter, a princess."

"I remember the Lord speaking to me in the Tabernacle," Shulamit panted, exhausted. "He said I would have a girl. I guess I heard right."

Miriam cleaned the baby, wrapped her in a blanket, and handed her to Solomon. He looked at his beautiful daughter, delighted when her hand grasped his. The infant princess had black curly hair and big, beautiful brown eyes with the longest lashes he'd ever seen on a girl. Solomon, elated, took his baby into his arms, and kissed her.

"I shall name her Basemath," meaning *beautiful fragrance.*

He then looked at his battle-weary bride and told her how beautiful she was. "Now you are a mother queen in Israel. I am so proud of you. You deserve a rest now. You have lots of help. Enjoy and love our precious baby girl."

Shulamit was happy to have Miriam with her during her two months of purification. She did not realize how much she had missed her family. Every morning, Miriam would come, full of joy, and sing over the baby,

Her fragrance
her sweet perfume
and all the scents of heaven
such sweetness
she brings to the air
in all her beauty fair...

For Shulamit, her time with Miriam was a time of true connection. They sang and danced with Basemath in their arms to comfort her.

"Mama sang over us all the time," Miriam said. "I think that is why we love music and worship so much. She said *Elohim* sings over us and so must mothers."

Shulamit laughed. "Thank you so much for being here, Miriam. You have made me remember the goodness of how I grew up, and all the joy of our worshipping family. I know Nathan loves to worship, and you shall have a very happy union."

Before Miriam returned to their family village, Shulamit made sure she sent Mama the rare spices she liked for cooking. Nathan was escorting her back with loaded mules of dowry for their Ketubah gathering. Miriam had no extensive list of dreams like Shulamit had, other than to be with Nathan. Nathan had living quarters within Jerusalem near his brothers. But he wished to have a home where he could have vineyards and keep animals across the valley that surrounded Jerusalem. "Deep in my heart," he told Miriam, "I knew you would be my bride, and I wanted to make you a home that was a little like your country home."

***

After Basemath's birth, Solomon could not wait until the days of Shulamit's purification were over to be intimate with his true love again. Shulamit was fully absorbed with her new baby, and she almost did not think about missing Solomon until towards the end of her purification time. Then, as the time approached, she began fretting about her appearance. When she dipped herself in the water at her cleansing mikvah, she asked Meliba, over and over, if she looked as lovely as before. Meliba assured her that she was still the most beautiful woman ever. "But will Solomon think so?" she asked.

On the day Shulamit's purification ended, Solomon arrived. He could not take his eyes off Shulamit and his beautiful baby. Shulamit was nursing a very hungry, healthy girl. Her breasts were full and seemed bigger than ever. Solomon liked to see mother's feeding their babies, but mostly his eyes were focused on his bride.

"Your beasts are soft and full of milk for your baby, but now you are a mother in Israel who will nurture many children in the kingdom." Solomon sat down beside his nursing bride a watched her for a few moments. Eventually, he commented. "She is one hungry baby. I wonder if she will be that hungry for knowing everything about life like her mother." Shulamit looked at him, her love clear. "Yes, my bride, there is no woman so hungry for life as you are. I'm hungry for you too."

Shulamit smiled. Solomon was saying he wanted her. *I hope I still look pleasing to him.*

Meliba took the baby when Shulamit was done nursing. As soon as the door closed, Solomon took Shulamit's hand and helped her to stand up. "Let me see my bride," he said admiringly. "You do not know how much I have missed you. Ah, you are as beautiful as ever."

Shulamit's eyes lit up. Solomon looked up and down. As he saw her feet he laughed. "How beautiful are your feet in sandals. Your feet are beautiful out of sandals too, as they were when I first saw you dance in the field. But they were rough and not scrubbed then." He bent down and kissed the top of her feet and caressed her soft heels. "Now they are soft and beautiful and stand out with the jewels, and sparkling bracelet around your ankle. You are not a servant without shoes who cannot leave the palace, but you are free to carry the good news of the goodness of God wherever you go."

What will he think when he sees my thighs? Shulamit thought feeling a jolt of fear. Solomon caressed her legs under the dress, gently moving up to her thigh as she began to feel a familiar excitement. "The curves of your thighs are like jewels, the work of a skilled workman." *Childbirth did not take away this feeling* Shulamit realized as her anxiety turned to thoughts and feelings of love. *Thank you, Elohim.*

Solomon loosened the sash around her waist as he moved lifted her dress and kissed her navel. Shulamit had been told that the navel in culture was considered the center of the soul and emotions. Now she knew, as she could feel her blood rush within her creating small bumps and tingling on her skin. "Your navel is a rounded goblet," Solomon spoke softly. "It lacks no blended beverage." His hands surrounded her small waist on both sides. "Your waist is a heap of wheat set about with lilies." She was losing focus, but she still visualized how farmers tied the wheat in the middle. Gently removing her dress Solomon returned to her breasts as he gave them each a gentle kiss, "Your breasts are like two fawns, twins of a gazelle." Full of milk they were, and soft for nurturing not just her baby. She had to press her hands to them to prevent milk from squirting out. Solomon laughed. But he was still intent on admiring her whole body. "Your neck is like an ivory tower. Still long and slim. You hold your head so beautifully like a queen who wears the crown. I look forward to showing you off with your new crown. Shulamit knew she would be part of a crowning ceremony as a new mother when she returned to their Dancing Sabbath. "Your eyes like the pools of Heshbon by the gate of Bath Rabbin. They sparkled and flowed with life. Shulamit responded by looking directly into his eyes knowing it was the Middle Eastern way of saying, "I am ready to give you, my love."

Still, Solomon insisted on describing everything he saw in his queen's new elevated status. "Your nose is like the tower of Lebanon which looks toward Damascus." She had a long Middle Eastern nose, "you are very discerning and know where to keep eye in the direction of danger. You are my private watchman, always aware of what is going on around you. I always know my heart can trust in you to pray and protect my best interests."

"I will always protect the one I love," she said, "The same as you protect me. We fight for each other's love together."

He gave her head an affectionate touch. "Your head crowns you like Mount Carmel, and the hair of your head is like purple. A king is held captive by your tresses." Now that she had a baby, she was truly a queen, and he acknowledged her crowning glory of royalty. Her beautiful, thick tresses curled down past her waist. They were surely her crown of glory. "How fair and how pleasant you are, O love, with your delights! I truly delight in you."

All Shulamit's fears that she would not still be so beautiful after having a baby were put to rest that night. He still called her his love of delights. Solomon found great joy in loving his wife and she found great joy in return. Nothing had changed except their love had grown deeper, and their love intensified after their absence from one another.

To their surprise, the unexpected happened, in their first night of love; a few weeks went by and Shulamit began to feel the same wheezy feelings of pregnancy again. While Solomon was laying the foundation of the new palace, and Nathan and Miriam were planning the final details of their wedding, Shulamit was confirmed to be pregnant with another baby. Solomon was delighted. "I felt that when I kissed your navel, that I was kissing another harvest within you."

"I could not think of that while you were kissing my navel, but something inside me told me afterward that we had done it again." They laughed.

Solomon then told Shulamit that he had to take a trip down to Ezion Geber, near Elath on the Edom shore of the Red Sea. He would be gone a while. "Remember when we were in Joppa and discussed a joint merchant enterprise with Hiram to send ships out into the world to create commerce. Well, now I will be going down with Javan, and some of his seamen will be sending ships to Sheba and Ophir and other ports in the South and East. Our goal to find more diamonds like the one you wear on your hand, along with spices, mineral wealth, and gold. I must put my seal on Ezion Geber to develop it into a port and examine how the sea faring ships are coming along. We will also breed camels for bringing merchandize along the King's Highway and up through Ein Gedi to Jerusalem. I am going to build Inns and a residence for us to stay in when you can travel again. Remember, I promised to take you to the caves where David lived when he fled from Saul. I want you to experience the whole country, so you know what we are reigning over."

Shulamit smiled when Solomon said, "What *we* are reigning over."

"My mother is getting old, and you are the one who is slowly taking her place as my favored queen. You are growing into that position."

"I am honored. But is it my becoming a mother that is making all this happen?"

"Being a mother is the most important thing a woman does, besides loving their husband," he said as he gave her a deep, tender kiss. "I will be back as soon as I can."

When the time came for her next birth, Miriam was preparing for her wedding, and Solomon was occupied with business outside of the palace in Jerusalem. This time, Shiffrah, the palace midwife, was there for her delivery. She was a very calm woman whose peace kept the delivering mother calm.

"One more push," Shiffrah said, and another baby girl was born into the world. She was cleansed, wrapped, and suckling on her mother's breast when Solomon appeared.

"I came as soon as I heard, but your babies come so quickly. Look at her, my amazing princess with reddish brown hair, and those brownish-green eyes. She is absolutely beautiful," Solomon said, overjoyed. Shulamit looked at him with inquisitive eyes as if to say where did the red hair come from?

Solomon read her mind and said, "I think my great-great-grandmother Ruth had red hair."

"I love my beautiful baby with red in her hair, what shall we name her?"

"I shall call her Taphath, for she is a distillation and a drop of fresh water from heaven. She shall prophesy like the rain, bringing drops of refreshment from Heaven."

After Solomon left, Shiffrah stayed with her during her days of purification. Shulamit and Shiffrah became close friends during that time.

"I hardly knew you were there when Miriam was helping deliver Basemath. But you are a strong presence."

"I was watching everything Miriam did with a sharp eye just in case I had to jump in and help. But I knew God was bringing your child forth, and we were just his helpers. it was the same this time. Observing you and Miriam after the birth, I enjoyed how you both were so joyful when singing over your child."

At that Shulamit burst forth with song:

Oh, dew from Heaven
Sweet distillation
Comes fresh revelation
Eyes and ears open
From words to enlighten
And joy to hope in

"That is beautiful. I would love to create a song like that," Shiffrah professed.

"You just did, in a way. Your desire gave me faith to draw it out. Solomon said I often do that to him. I am always hungry for what he says. People who believe in you inspire the good within you to come out," Shulamit replied. After a short pause to reflect, she said, "There is more than one way to be a midwife. A hungry heart also draws life out of a deep well and brings forth life."

Shulamit soon discovered that Basemath was as sweet as sweet-smelling perfume, with a very calm temperament. Taphath, on the other hand, was a strong-willed, fiery, temperamental baby, always demanding a lot of attention. As they grew, Basemath stayed quiet and seemed wise beyond her years, much like Solomon. Taphath challenged everything, always wanting to do what she was not told. She wanted to do everything her brothers did and always wished she had been born a boy, like Shulamit once felt. Now Shulamit understood why her brothers had often been frustrated with her. She had been blind to her own personality and its effects on others. But when she saw it in her daughter, it was hard to deny.

While Solomon was away, Shulamit continued to worship with the women of the court. Over time, her young daughters joined in the singing and dancing. Basemath was gentle and very graceful. She danced out of a desire to please God and others.

Bathsheba told Shulamit, "She is so much like Solomon was as a child, calm and obedient, always a quiet joy. He sat at David's feet and listened whenever he could. He was a great listener and never said very much. But he observed everything."

Taphath was not like her sister very much at all. She talked continuously and danced out of the sheer joy of dancing. She too was graceful, but she enjoyed all the leaping and twirling movements. Solomon loved coming to watch his daughters' worship, receiving great joy from them, and he complimented their worship and dance all the time. Solomon always brought them gifts when he visited them. But they also enjoyed showing him their new accomplishments. Taphath made a basket from reeds and presented it to her *Abba* king. Solomon treated it as if it were round Challah bread. She started making more baskets. Solomon asked her what she was going to do with the baskets, and she said, "I'm going to sell them at the marketplace."

Solomon laughed, and asked Shulamit, "Have they gone to the marketplace?"

Shulamit said, "We did occasionally talk the guards into stopping at the marketplace on the way to the Temple. Taphath begged them, and they let us stop for a few minutes.

"Taphath is an entrepreneur, continually thinking of ways to buy and sell." Solomon shook his head.

Basemath also loved to make presents for their *Abba king*. Basemath learned to make beautiful tapestry. When Solomon asked if she was going to sell them in the marketplace, she said, "No. I am making them to hang all over the palace and make it beautiful. I am also going to give them as presents to my friends."

Shulamit encouraged her girls to play music and develop in the arts along with other women in the palace. The women shared their skills with great joy. Some were good at making jewelry, some at perfumes, others at painting ceramic vessels or making delicate pastries and teas. Solomon said, "My wives are bringing a renaissance in the culture of arts in our kingdom." Basemath and Taphath learned from them all.

Solomon took great joy in his daughters, encouraging them to be soft and gracious as they presented themselves to people in court. The girls excelled in learning how to read and write. The princesses learned much more quickly than most of the princes, who mostly preferred to learn to ride horses and fight.

Taphath was aware that every young prince, as soon as he was old enough, was given a pony and taught how to care for it and ride it. She asked for a pony, but King Solomon denied her request. She kept begging her father to give her a pony until he acquiesced. It took months.

"As long as you promise to be quiet, I will include you in events with my sons."

Taphath learned how to be quiet when she wanted something.

Shulamit had thoroughly learned the lesson her father taught her as a child. She would indeed do more for God as a worship warrior than by trying to compete with boys in their strength. But trying to show this to Taphath was useless. Since Shulamit herself had learned to ride a horse, she understood it as a skill that gave her liberty to travel with Solomon at times. Shulamit began to ride alongside her young daughters as they trotted their ponies in the fields near the palace. She saw it was good for her daughters to learn how to care for an animal and to enjoy being outside.

"One of these days we will visit my family and you will learn more about care for animals and riding in the open field," Shulamit announced.

"I look forward to that Mama," Taphath responded. They bonded in time together.

"Your life has been quite different from mine, but it will do you some good to spend time in the country."

Shulamit realized the country was changing rapidly under Solomon's reign. It is like they were both caught up in a whirlwind of things happening quickly around them beyond their own control. At times while Solomon was traveling and building, and Shulamit was raising her young daughters, she found time to reflect upon her life. Shulamit wrote about the special love story between her and Solomon. Writing about their love kept it fresh and alive, as well as reinvigorating her writing skills. She was blessed to have an appointed scribe who helped her but with all her practice, she was becoming quite accomplished.

One evening, when Solomon came to visit, she was writing. When he asked her to share what she was working on with him, she read him some of their songs, and her wonderful moments of love with him. She read about her first meeting him, and how he had always been the love force behind her learning to live within the palace and lead worship with the women of the court. She read about their trip to Bethlehem, and their wedding vows.

"These are treasures," Solomon said after listening for a while. "I would rather read our story than the chronicles of the kingdom and all the proverbs I am working on. My heart is deeply moved. You have captured our feelings of love in the most amazing way," he told her. "I need to take the highlights of all you have written and put it into a song that tells our love story.

Shulamit was surprised. She was writing mostly for her own private memories and felt vulnerable about sharing her deepest feelings. Still, she discovered a deep joy as she shared the story of their love together. It did bring them closer and refreshed their marriage bond all the more. She was surprised to know Solomon wanted to hear it all, and they sang some of the songs together as she read.

"You express your heart so well," he said.

"I'm a reflection of you, and how you make me feel," Shulamit responded

"We need to go on another trip and re-kindle all these wonderful feelings of love."

"I would like that, as I was riding beside Basemath and Taphath on their ponies recently. I missed being out in the countryside."

"The girls are big enough now to stay with Bathsheba and your maidens. We need time for us. I will arrange a trip to Ein Gedi as soon as I can," he said as he kissed her. Soon, they began to bring physical expression to their feelings of love.

27 THE SHULAMIT SPRING

As soon as the High Holy days of Fall were completed, Solomon and Shulamit mounted their horses one early morning. Solomon was taking her on a long-desired adventure with a whole procession of protection and pack horses. Shulamit rode her Sorrel with confidence. Since she had been riding alongside her daughters, she and Sorrel had become grown closer, and riding was more of a joy than ever.

"You are a natural on a horse," Solomon declared as he admired his beautiful bride. He stared at her legs, which sometime showed the high boots hidden under her long purple robe.

"Thank you," Shulamit responded excitedly. "I love adventure and have always wanted to explore all the wonders of our land and see all that my king and lover is doing around the country. She was determined to keep up with the soldiers and not slow down the caravan, so she gave Sorrel a squeeze with her thighs.

"My love, you can do anything," Solomon said. Instead of joining her, Solomon slowed his own horse as they reached a steep enclave. Shulamit joined him as he said, "You have already ridden with me to Joppa and proved yourself a good horse rider. This trip will be just a little longer, and you will be challenged to know what you can do. But, I promise, we will rest when we need to. I love you, my adventurous wife."

The caravan began their descent through the Kedron Valley towards Jericho. As they circled past the Mount of Olives, Solomon stopped the horses for a moment. "Take your last look at the temple mount," he told Shulamit.

She turned back and caught the morning sun reflecting like gold from the temple mount. "Amazing," she acknowledged.

The group skirted past Bethany and proceeded down a steeper trail. The landscape changed from lush green to barren desert. And the weather transformed from the mild weather of the Western Sea to the warm weather of the South. In the afternoon they arrived at a junction surrounded by red rock. Solomon ordered the soldiers ahead to travel more slowly so he could describe the scenery to Shulamit.

"Look how the towers are spaced periodically along the road," he told her. "The road to Jericho can be treacherous. Mountains surround it, giving robbers many places to hide. This is a main road that caravans come through, and I want to make sure that all traders are safe in our country. So,

I built towers for military to be posted along the roads. Once completed, I assigned watchmen to look for any robbers or enemies that might attack traveling caravans. They are watching over us right now. If they see danger, they will blow a warning trumpet sound."

"That is a wise choice, and beneficial to our allies," Shulamit said.

Solomon heard the strain in her voice. They had been riding for a while, and though she didn't complain, the travel was starting to take a toll on her. "Look," Solomon said, pointing, "there is an Inn beside the tower below. There we can rest, eat something, and water our horses. We will not stay long. I want to reach Jericho before nightfall."

"Lovely idea. I thank you," Shulamit said, feeling numb in her seat.

He gave a command to one of the soldiers, and the caravan seemed to shift in anticipation of the rest. It was a brief respite, and they were soon moving again. Solomon continued to explain how he wished to expand the roads for travel. "It is good that the pilgrims who come to Jerusalem for the Holy Days do not come during the rainy seasons. And it is good that they come in groups where they can protect each other. I know *you* know that, but do you see how God designed our holidays to fit our seasons?"

By late afternoon the procession could look down the road and see Jericho, an oasis in the middle of the desert. "There it is," called Solomon. "Jericho, the city of palms and copious springs." Shulamit looked to see the beautiful trees lining the route to the city. "There you see the first city our forefathers conquered with the miraculous hand of God. And the key entrance into the Judean wilderness."

"It was one of Papa's favorite stories that he taught, how the people walked around the city seven days and then blew the trumpets and the walls fell down. Papa always wanted us to know how great our God is," Shulamit expressed with wonder.

"Surely, no country has a history of as great a God as ours."

"Thank you, *Abba* Father," Shulamit said.

"I have another memory of Jericho," Solomon said, turning serious. "My family was fleeing from Absalom, who was trying to steal the kingdom. We went towards Gilgal to cross the River Jordan into the forests of Mahanaim. Everyone covered their heads and there was much wailing. The women were very afraid. I was a young man then. Though I was very scared, I remember acting brave for the sake of my mother, sisters, and little brothers. They would not let me fight as I was too young, but still I was ready to protect our family."

"Solomon," Shulamit said. Her heart felt the fear and anger of her husband's memory. "I led a much-protected life, compared to you running from your own brother, Absalom. But now I understand you better. It explains why you take such precautions to protect your family and see that there is safety in the land. It was part of your preparation to be king."

"We all go through preparations for our destiny. You too were being prepared all your life. You are still on the journey of your destiny as we ride now," Solomon stated making light of a rather serious conversation.

The final ride into Jericho was very tiring, and Shulamit was fully exhausted as they reached their destination. Embracing Shulamit gently as she lay down to rest for the night, Solomon applauded his love with gentle kisses and soft words. "Sleep well until you wake, my love. You have been very brave today and need your rest."

Shulamit was asleep before Solomon finished speaking.

***

Shulamit awoke the next day to a beautiful breakfast with her husband. Servants brought them a tray of coffee and a delicious display of stuffed Medjool dates. Some were stuffed with fluffy goat cheese and dusted with pistachios. Some had goat cheese with pomegranate seeds. There were other flavors as well, and she devoured them all. "Delicious" was all she could say.

"Glad you like them. I think I will bring their cook back to our palace."

"You never stop searching out talent," Shulamit said and then laughed.

The rest of the day, Solomon showed her the orchards of date palms and balsam shrubs he was cultivating in Jericho, pride resounding in his explanations. The balsam produced resin for making perfume and medicine. Solomon was very happy to see how well his imported balsam were thriving in this temperate climate. "There is a balm in Gilead," Solomon said, "used for medicine and southing wounds. But this balm also makes delightful perfume and ointment, which is much desired in Tyre and by other merchants around the world. I am pleased to see it growing so well here."

Shulamit breathed in the woody sweet smell with a long, satisfied, "Mmmmmm."

Solomon smiled at her appreciation. "God has shown me how to extract the resin from the plant. When I am sitting alone with God up in my secret place, I find my thoughts move me, guiding my hands to do things."

"You, my beloved, are a marvel. You go to your secret place and invent things, and design buildings. And you build tools like no one else. God continues to bless you in the realm of the mysterious."

Solomon laughed. "It is the glory of God to conceal a matter, but the glory of kings to search out a matter."

"Amazing," Shulamit said. "You need to remember what you just said and put it into your book of Proverbs."

"You remember better than me," Solomon said with a chuckle. "You write it down and please give it back to me when we return home. This is another reason why I love having you with me. It is more than just to make love to you." They both laughed. "That might be the best part," Solomon continued, laughing, "but you are fascinating in so many ways. All these years have passed, and I am still discovering you as if I only met you months ago. You are deep, hungry, and always want more." Before he could get too passionate, he stopped himself. "But back to resin," Solomon said, "that is a secret that is not to be shared. The enemy would love to steal information and income that belongs to our people."

Shulamit put her hand over her mouth to show her love that the secret was safe. Solomon laughed again, then took her hand. "Come," he said. He crushed the balsam, pressing with olive oil. "Making perfume is a very time-consuming process," Solomon said, "but well worth it. Especially when I smell the beautiful fragrance upon my love," he rubbed some balsam onto her wrist.

"So precious," said Shulamit, responding to his touch.

"You are very precious to me." Solomon said, smelling her wrist. Once again, he changed the subject. Tomorrow, we have a long journey, but it will not be as arduous and steep as yesterday's ride. We will be continuing south along the Dead Sea to Ein Gedi, but we will be able to ride faster.

The next day, as they galloped along the West side of the stream leading to the Dead Sea, Shulamit was awed by the intimidating limestone mountain ranges filled with caves. "So many caves," Shulamit observed. "It is amazing."

Solomon ordered the horses to slow to a walk while he explained, "Rains flow through caves on the western side of the Judean mountains in the underground limestone passages. They reappear on the eastern side as springs."

"Amazing," said Shulamit, still trying to understand how it worked. "It certainly gave King David many places to hide. Seeing the caves helps me envision some of the psalms he wrote while fleeing Saul. She broke into a song she remembered,

In You, O Lord, I put my trust
Let me never be ashamed
Deliver me in Your righteousness
Bow down your ear to me,
Deliver me speedily.
Be my rock of refuge,
A fortress of defense to save me…

Solomon smiled to himself. He said, "It was all a part of his training to become king. My father taught me that it was in all his narrow escapes from Saul that he really learned to trust the Lord."

"His trust grew into a beautiful intimacy. Knowing how much our Father in heaven loved him sustained him. That is what I see. Not just victory of winning wars, but the broken moments that were transformed into beauty as King David continued to praise *Adonai*."

"Wonderful insight," Solomon concurred. "You must have a truly intimate relationship with *Adonai* just to understand that part of my father. He would tell me, 'The Lord will fight for you, and you shall hold your peace.' He said, 'You have to have that peace to do battle and reign. So much of war is fear and fighting fear within ourselves. And it is the biggest part of any battle. But we *overcome* by holding our peace.'"

"Holding our peace?" Shulamit asked.

"Yes, holding our peace is all about trust, and faith. That level of trust doesn't come overnight. It grows within us through our victories and when we think of all God has brought us through. Remember how anxious you were when you first came to the palace? Look how much you have grown."

"I have grown?" She gave him a questioning look, hoping for more explanation.

Solomon looked at her with desire before he said, "Do you think I would be in love with a weak woman; a woman who could not hold her peace in all the crises it takes to reign? You are so brave. I love the strength I draw from you. I sometimes feel you have some of the temperament of my father. He had the nature of an artist and a warrior, hypersensitive and impulsive. Sometimes it took all his energy to calm himself and control his emotions. My father told me that, in all the years he ran from Saul, his biggest lesson was learning to control his emotions and hold his peace."

Shulamit reached out to her husband. "I am blessed to have you," she said. "I am beginning to see that, while you have a lot of your father in worship, you have a natural peace. Your name matches you perfectly, *Solomon*. You are not a shadow of your father. Oh, no. You are a ruler who creates peace around you by your very nature."

Solomon squeezed her hand, gently kissing it. "My love, we complement each other in so many ways. I love the way you abandon yourself in worship, and in love."

"In love?"

"Yes, my love. You excite me."

"I do worship and adore you, as well as I worship and adore *Elohim*."

"A worshipper *is* a lover, and you cannot separate it. God wants us to love each other like we love Him. Marriage is the closest expression we have of the joy He wants us to know in Him."

"In his presence is fullness of joy," Shulamit spoke forth another psalm.

Abruptly Solomon ordered the horses to speed up into a gallop. Before he pulled away from her, he said, "I can't wait to ravish you as soon as we can be alone!"

***

A few hours later, they came to a side road with a market, with a place to water the horses. Sprinkling cool water on themselves was such a refreshment from the heat and dust on the road. Shulamit had become quite achy from riding and dismounted Sorrel. She tried to walk around and relax her stiffened muscles. She did not wish to complain or appear weak, but she was very tired. The caravan remounted their horses, continuing on the side road and her body screamed in protest. Shulamit said nothing but couldn't wait to stop and dismount again. Soon enough, they came to a small tent set up beside two trees, a jujube, and an acacia, she saw what looked like a pool made of rocks encircling it in the distance.

"What is that?" she inquired.

"It is where we are camping tonight. I wanted to surprise you. Those rocks surround a hidden warm spring, perfect for relaxing your aching body. I know you are not as used to riding for long hours like I am. I want you to enjoy our journey, not endure it."

"How nice of you to plan all this."

"I had soldiers ride ahead to set things up. I have stopped here before on the way to Ein Gedi. I knew you would like this area. Not only that, but the horses also need to rest; and there is another, larger pool down the road for the soldiers. I try to make sure they are taken care of too. Now, shall we go change and then soak in the warm water?"

Shulamit looked at Solomon, and suddenly she didn't feel so sore.

The minute they entered the tent and tied the door, they were in each other's arms, covering each other with embraces and passionate kisses. They could not get their clothes off fast enough. It surprised them both how excited they were for each other. The aches of the day meant nothing in comparison to the joy of being together.

Afterward, Solomon breathed deeply and sighed, "I warned you I was going to ravish you."

"I thought you were just teasing," she said as she snuggled deeper into his arms.

"Teasing? My heart was speaking out. You don't even know what you do to me."

Shulamit looked at him in wonder. "Whatever I do, it's because of you."

"There is no other woman with the power over me that you have. I am a king. I am supposed to be calm and in control. You make me so vulnerable it frightens me at times."

"I do?" Shulamit questioned. But then she said, "But isn't that what love does? Is it such a risk to really open your heart?"

"Perhaps opening one's heart is easier for women. I think that is one thing I love about you. You take risks. You are bold and courageous."

"Only because of what being in love does to me."

"Yes, love brings wisdom. There is a wisdom women carry, and they teach it to men, just reflecting their love. I see my love for you reflected back to me. It is beautiful. You are beautiful," Solomon said as he picked up a pitcher of wine and poured it into a large gold goblet. He offered his love a drink before taking one himself. "Let's relax in the warm water and communicate more."

Pink and white streaked the sunset sky as they sat down upon a stone lining the pond. They slid in, and warm water rose to their shoulders. "Oh, this feels so relaxing," Shulamit sighed. "I was so excited about making love with you that I forgot about my aching body."

"Oh, I hope I wasn't insensitive."

"No, not at all. We couldn't help it. Love does that. Our emotions overwhelm us, and our feelings of ecstasy move us."

"Interesting."

"I liked being ravished by your passion," she said as she threw out her arms wide beside her in an expression of surrender.

"If you keep doing that you will be ravished again," Solomon said as he gave a playful smile. He took another sip of wine and offered her drink.

"I love this moment," Shulamit said. She looked up at the sky. There was a full moon and stars scattered across the now night sky. She looked back at Solomon, seeing the moonlight in his eyes, and then she broke into song.

I wish this moment
Could go on forever
The stars looking down upon us
Like jewels delighted to crown us

Solomon started to sing with her.

I love this moment
My sweet bride beside me
Communing our hearts with eternity
Open and honest and free

They began sharing poetry, dancing together with their words.

This moment, this moment

Completely connected
Body, spirit, and soul
Like Adam and Eve in the garden
Uncovered, surrendered and whole

A moment, so present
Embraced in the moment
Thoroughly choosing our love
Drinking our cup of bliss
Transforming our hearts as we kiss

I wish this moment
To be sealed in our hearts
So, overflowing with fun
You are mine; I am yours; we are one

They ended their new song together.

In this moment
In this moment
Living only in this moment
Our hearts are on fire
We are wedded together - in love

They sang and laughed and ravished each other by the warm spring.

The next day continued their short journey. By the afternoon, the sight of Ein Gedi gave Shulamit a fluttering heart.

The village was truly an oasis in the desert, and a delight to see after her long journey. Palms and other trees, shrubs, and plants grew up into the mountains. Wild goats, called ibex, could be seen on the high peaks while birds of all sorts were flying all around. As they rode, Solomon pointed out the acacia trees and their yellow flowers. He showed her the Sodom apple, the poplar, the Jujube red dates. He was most excited to see that, in the warmer climate of Ein Gedi, the balsam plants were thriving just as well as they were in Jericho.

Shulamit noticed a delightful odor in the air. "Where is this sweet smell from?" she asked her husband.

"Ah," he said, "you are smelling the henna blossoms. They are a very fragrant plant."

"That is what you are to me," Shulamit teased, "my own special blossom."

They arrived at a small inn but before they could dismount, Solomon pointed to a nearby a building under construction. "That is where I am building a palatial estate for when I come to visit. It will also be for the merchants to use as they are passing through from Eilat, and of course, for my overseers and soldiers to use. I will be building more workshops for processing perfumes and products from the Dead Sea salts. Tomorrow, I shall take you on a hike and we will see it all. But come let's go and take our rest, for the adventures of this day are not ended.

"You are an adventure, she told her lover, "Everything else is just added blessings."

Arising, Solomon took her hand and gently pulled her up from the bed. "It is time for you to experience the delight of the dead sea."

A short ride down the road turned onto the beach by the Dead Sea. Royal tents were set up which allowed them to walk privately into the waters. They found, after a few steps into the water, that they could lean back and float. The couple laughed with each other. Lying on their backs with no effort Solomon and Shulamit floated, looking up into the sky as it began to change colors.

"My love," he asked, "did you ever imagine you would float beside me in the Dead Sea?"

Shulamit laughed. "Yes, when you first suggested bringing me here. I love this feeling of weightlessness. If I close my eyes, I can imagine I am an angel floating on a cloud. My friend Rebecca used to talk about what it would be like to be floating on clouds.

"Is that how you got your head in the clouds and dreamed so many dreams?"

She laughed again. "I wonder if Joseph the dreamer looked up at clouds. He ended up in a palace helping to rule an empire."

"Well, I suppose having your head in the clouds can have a good purpose if it stirs up your creativity to think of things that will do earthly good."

"I love you so much, my beloved. We always have so much fun together."

"We do, my sweet love," Solomon said. He reached for her hand, so they did not float apart. "We can come back again, but let's go, wash off the salt and get something to eat, then prepare for tomorrow.

Early the next morning Solomon led her up a trail to what the locals called *David's Waterfall.*

"This is the biggest waterfall in Israel, and you can swim in the pond below," Solomon said as Shulamit looked around in wonder. They continued up the trail to where they came to large caves. "Imagine," he said. "Saul was chasing my father with 3,000 soldiers and never could catch him. My father had opportunity to kill him and refused. He would not touch the

Lord's anointed."

"My Grandfather used to tell me stories about his experiences with David before he became king. He taught me about the importance of loyalty and trusting God to fulfill our destiny."

"He taught you well, and I can see it in our children. I like to believe that many such loyal men exist in our kingdom; men who fear God and are loyal to Him over their own promotions."

They continued up the mountain and came to a bend where they could look out over the Dead Sea and other streams. But Shulamit looked upward at the wild goats and asked, "What is the name of the stream above?"

"That is quite a way up, and I confess, I do not know the name," Solomon admitted.

"Shall we go, and see?"

"We have not yet reached noonday, my love, so we have time. I appreciate your adventurous nature, but I am also glad we have soldiers behind us to keep us safe."

"Remember, I am a mountain woman," Shulamit replied. "I have climbed many steep hills in my youth." She pointed at some broken branches on the ground. "They will make good walking sticks."

It was a steep trail upwards, with many ponds beside the stream to cool off from along the way. Finally, they came to where water flowed out from the side of a rock. The water formed a pool of water around its base.

Solomon said, "We shall call this spring The Shulamit Spring."

He ordered his soldiers to pile rocks to mark the spot where they could post a sign.

"Shulamit Spring," she said to herself. Shulamit was very excited by her discovery.

"Yes. Now, my love, you have a spring named after you. But we can't linger here as we must beat the sun going down the hill."

Using their walking sticks, they found balance going down the steep hill. At times they had to get down on hands and scoot down. It was dark by the time they got to where the hill was not so steep. Soldiers had lit torches, and they had the light of a full moon showing their path. At last, they made it to the main road. Solomon took Shulamit's hand and led her where the servants at the inn had created an outdoor fire for roasting lamb. They sat around the fire joined by the brave soldiers who had offered their protection on the long hike.

"She is a strong, courageous queen," Solomon said to the soldiers, acknowledging his bride before them. "She is fearless and helps me rule with strength. Honor her, for she will also help protect you in her reign." He held up a glass of wine in cheer, and they cheered with him.

Then Solomon sang a song in honor of his love:

My love is a life-giving spring
She turns the wilderness green
She's a delight to her king
She causes his heart to sing

My Shulamit Spring
My Shulamit Spring

My love is a desert oasis
Her touch makes flowers bloom
They reflect her joyful praises
The sweet perfume pleases her groom

My Shulamit Spring
My Shulamit Spring

My love is a waterfall
Full of love and overflow
Dancing over the rocks
Bouncing with sparkling glow

My Shulamit Spring
My Shulamit Spring

My love is an underground river
Full of life-giving water
Breaking through hard rocks
My love is heaven's daughter

My Shulamit Spring
My Shulamit Spring
You make your king sing
My Shulamit Spring

"Can a woman feel more loved than I am?" Shulamit said in response to the song and the cheers. "This is another journey I will never forget," she said with a sigh as she reached for Solomon's hand.

Before Solomon engaged in business the following day, he arranged for Shulamit to have a mud bath massage and an escorted walk through the gardens near the Inn. The king was negotiating with camel traders and purchasing camels so he would be too busy to join her. He was planning on planting more balm plants and developing more distillation projects for the growing perfume demand.

As Shulamit was escorted through the garden, she realized she was beginning to think like Solomon about whether these plants from the south could thrive in Jerusalem or even in the mountains. She remembered how her father brought in new vines from afar and tried to see how they grew in his village. Her father enjoyed experimenting. On another day, Shulamit busied herself collecting various plants to make flower arrangements for the inn based on beauty and fragrance. Queen Kareem had taught her well, and she had learned to gather plants wherever she was.

When Solomon came in to dine, he noticed the beautiful arrangements and the matron of the Inn addressed him answering his perplexed face.

"Your majesty," she said, "the queen is very talented with an eye for beauty."

The king responded to the matron, "You are a wise woman. My Shulamit learns and applies what she has seen and been taught. You can learn that from her."

Shulamit joined the two, adding, "I've been blessed to be around the king intimately and observe his ways of doing things. But I believe I am beginning to think like my king."

Solomon, looking first to the matron and then to Shulamit, said, "Gifts are imparted to special people around me who listen with an eye for creativity and beauty. I have queens raised in palaces and my Shulamit, you have already passed them up." He took her hand, then he looked to the matron of the Inn. "I see you and your husband are wise people that I can trust to promote over more of my business here in Ein Gedi."

During their last evening meal together, Solomon explained the business he conducted to Shulamit. He added, "Israel will need camels for exporting our products through the desert."

"Ein Gedi will not be small for long," she replied.

Business accomplished; they began the trip back to Jerusalem. As soon as they arrived at their palace, the winter rains came down in torrents.

"You always bring the rain, my love," Solomon acknowledged

***

When Shulamit returned to the palace, she found herself feeling more tired than usual. At first, she thought she was still needing rest from the long journey. But then she realized she was with child again. Miriam came to visit her with her own young son, Mattathiah, meaning *gift of yah*. Miriam was also well along with child again.

Shulamit perceived immediately that Miriam's son was special. He was always happy and gentle in manner, yet very intelligent, healthy, and strong.

He was very musically talented also, and Miriam was overjoyed to teach her son about worship.

While Shulamit was visiting her sister Miriam, her dear friend, Shira, whom she hadn't seen for a while also came to visit. She brought her son Ahimaaz and her two younger children, whom Shulamit and Miriam were meeting for the first time.

"This is so great," Shulamit said as she greeted them. She ordered tea and snacks, "We have a lot of catching up to do. While they visited, Ahimaaz ran around the palace gardens with Shulamit's daughters. Ahimaaz came in and whispered to his mother, "Basemath has a pretty voice, and she sings like an angel." He ran back out to play, and Shira shared that with Miriam and Shulamit what he whispered. Shulamit brightened. "I have an idea," she said. "If my daughter married Ahimaaz, then she would become a Levite, as I once desired. Wouldn't that be great?"

"And we would be family," Shira agreed.

"If they like each other when they come of age" Miriam added.

"They will," both Shulamit and Shira said spontaneously.

"Then you can arrange it." Miriam interjected."

"Agreed," Shulamit assented. "We are creating the next generations already. And I am with child again too."

"How exciting," Miriam said.

"Wonderful," Shira said, "Just think only recently we are all young girls. Now we have families, and families that are becoming truly extended families. "I remember how surprised I was to hear Miriam was marrying Nathan. Now your family is growing too. You both must come and visit me on the beach one of these days."

"We will," Shulamit said. "But now I would like to take you around the palace grounds and show you what has been done. It is not all finished. Solomon has finished building the main palace, but it is only part of the whole compound. Many quarters, set apart from the central palace, were still under construction. When the king discovered I am with child again, he has shifted his focus, and is putting immediate emphasis on completing my palace quarters. Solomon wants my new home finished before our baby is born, I'm hoping this time I will have a son to be king." They had a wonderful visit. Miriam reminded Shulamit to be sure and tell Nathan or send a message when she was due so she could come and help her deliver again.

Time passed rapidly and as Shulamit's pregnancy was coming to an end she was happy. She would have a large enough home for her expanding personal family. Each wife and her children were considered a family within the larger royal family, but they lived in the palace. Shulamit's new palace quarters were down a long spacious corridor leading outside the palace, though still on the compound. There was also an access hallway under the palace where Solomon could visit her with the privacy she had requested in her Ketubah. Solomon kept his promises, and he impressed her with his extravagance and attention to details.

The walls of her private property surrounded a large inner courtyard full of fruit trees, flower beds, vines growing up the walls, and lots of green grass to run on. There was also a small fountain. Her home was spacious with plenty of room to entertain, with multiple sleeping chambers. All the furnishings in her house were made of cedar and designed with gold inlay from the ceiling to the floor. Large scarlet and purple curtains with gold designs of lions, scepters, and flowers lined the walls and large mirrors. Shulamit was surprised to see a special room designed for a baby with walls painted colorfully of ponds, ducks, flowers, and butterflies. There was even a special baby bed. It was a masterpiece and Shulamit couldn't have imagined its unique beauty. She was overjoyed.

Solomon moved on to build the house of Judgement out of necessity. Ambassadors were coming regularly to Jerusalem to see the Temple, observe his legislation, do business with him, and attend his schools. Solomon liked to greet people with majesty. Six steps with gold lions on the sides of the steps led up to the ivory throne covered in gold. It was set with rubies, sapphires, emeralds, and other precious stones which shone with dazzling colors. Beside his throne were two more large gold lions, and under his throne there was a footstool. Large gold chairs were set on either side of the throne for queens and occasional dignitaries.

Shulamit was privileged to be the first queen to sit on the throne beside Solomon as he entertained his first visitor, the Ambassador from Damascus. The Ambassador brought his tribute payment of gold, silver, and spices to Jerusalem. He then addressed Solomon about increasing trade between the nations. Solomon asked a few questions about how King Rezon was fairing. When Solomon was satisfied with his answers; he then looked over some of the ambassador's products. Shulamit looked at some of the pieces of fine lace, carefully examining silk, linen, and cotton fabrics. Each had intricate designs, and she thought of the beautiful dresses they would make, while keeping an emotionless face. She then handed the fabric back without a word. Solomon also seemed satisfied and invited the ambassador to dine at the palace.

In the large dining hall of the new palace, Solomon invited the ambassador to sit across from him at his table. Shulamit sat at Solomon's right side and his brothers to his left. It was obvious that the ambassador was surprised by Shulamit's extreme beauty, and he had a hard time diverting his eyes from her. Solomon liked this, because displaying a beautiful wife was also a way of boasting of his wealth. Sometimes Solomon brought several of his wives, but he wished to give Shulamit a chance to learn how negotiations were done without other wives being jealous. In exchange for the exports from Syria, the ambassador asked for permission to send students to Solomon's schools.

Shulamit felt an alarm at the idea that this ambassador wished his people to attend Solomon's schools, and she squeezed Solomon's hand to alert him. Solomon was aware of countries sending spies to learn their new skills and answered him wisely.

"I don't allow foreign students in my schools," Solomon said, "unless they are part of my workforce and they were willing to exchange their own skills steel, stonework, and making of lace."

"I will discuss this with King Rezon," the ambassador said. At this, Solomon called for musicians to play music from the instruments that King David had invented. Large trays of desserts were set on the table, and servants poured more wine.

They made small talk and discussed intentions between countries further and Solomon concluded, "I will consider your offer."

Later that evening, Solomon communicated with his bride about how wisely she had behaved in front of one of Israel's most devious potential enemies. "Keep that discerning nose of yours turned toward Damascus, because their King Rezon fled from King Hadadezar of Zobah when David attacked them. Rezon gathered men and became a captain of raiders. Then Rezon went to Damascus and begin to reign over Syria. David took large numbers of their chariots and built a garrison in Damascus for protection. Rezon is not an honorable man. I did not tell you all this before we met the ambassador from Damascus because I wanted to see how well you discerned him. You are such a wise queen; one I can turn to for counsel."

King Solomon took the ambassador to the House of the Forest of Lebanon the next day. It was separated from the Judgement Hall by the hall of pillars made of cedar from Lebanon. This House was formidable. The walls and floor were covered in cedar. Even the vaulted ceiling was constructed with large cedar wood beams. On the walls hung 200 large gold shields and 300 bucklers of alloyed gold. The ambassador was overwhelmed to see the shields and bucklers from the countries King David had conquered, as well as the shields of David's mighty men. But when he saw the shields from defeated Syria his face grew pale.

Solomon's mission was accomplished in showing the military force of Israel was not one they wanted to try and start a war with. Having made his point, Solomon moved the conversation to visiting the gardens.

During this time of building and expansion in his kingdom, Solomon discovered a man named Jeroboam from the Northern Tribe of Ephraim. He was the son of a widow named Zeruah, skillful and hardworking, with a natural leadership talent. Solomon placed him over the labor force of the Tribes of Joseph because he could be depended upon to get jobs done with efficiency.

When Shulamit met Jeroboam at a court event, she had no objection to his talents and leadership. Shulamit never questioned Solomon's choices of leaders. She did note however, that he was not very interested in music or worship. He didn't seem to be spiritually inclined. *Some people are more concerned with worldly values,* Shulamit thought. *Young men whose fathers died had to work hard and bear too much responsibility in their youth* she thought. *It can make them tough and seemingly merciless to those who had it easier than them. But Solomon hired him to get the job done. I pray he is not overbearing on people.* Shulamit was aware that, as Israel became more centralized and market driven, some of the old agricultural culture was changing. While she had enjoyed her privileges, she still loved her roots in the vineyard and her humble shepherding life in the mountains. It was a part of her that would never completely go away.

Just after her youngest daughter Taphath had turned eight, and Shulamit was near to giving birth, another surprise came. Moving about the palace with her full belly, she heard rumors among the servants of the Queen of Sheba. The queen was said to be coming toward Jerusalem. She was making her way from the port of Eilat through the desert with a large caravan of camels laden with gold and spices.

28 THE QUEEN OF SHEBA

Messengers brought news to King Solomon that the Queen of Sheba had arrived on her merchant fleet at Ezion-Geber. She came with a great retinue of horses and laden camels. The richness of her caravan was the talk of the palace. They were now traveling toward Jerusalem. Unaware of the queen's intentions, Solomon felt it best to ride out to meet her. His royal estate included Zabud, his chief advisors, priests, horse masters, and warriors. They were followed by carts loaded with rich foods, wine, and fine clothing. Everyone was excited to meet the famed Queen of the South.

The news spread across Jerusalem like lightning.

"She comes riding on a horse with female guards besides her," said Shulamit's servant, "trailed by a caravan of camels such as we have never seen. They will be here before the full moon."

This should be interesting, Shulamit thought, *I'm glad that I am so large with child that I will not be expected to be there to greet her when she arrives at the palace. I will be able to learn all about her from my hidden vantage point.*

Shulamit did not wish to acknowledge her slight feeling of intimidation. She had welcomed many visiting kings and some of the other queens to the royal court of Israel. Every time, she was at ease, sitting beside Solomon on the throne, sometimes with Bathsheba. But Israel welcoming such a great ruler was without precedent in all of Israel and she was too pregnant to join him.

Shulamit also heard that Solomon had ordered a whole wing of the new palace to be painted and lavishly prepared for the queen and her entourage to stay. It had only just finished construction. Shulamit approved of the move, thinking it a wise one. Only the best hospitality could be given to a queen who had come from the far ends of the earth.

As the queen of the land of spices came through the Eastern gate of the city, the streets crowded with people excited to get a glimpse of her grand procession. Shulamit and her daughters could see a great distance while standing within the high tower on the wall of the palace. Solomon and his soldiers escorted the retinue carrying banners of green, gold, and red. In Jerusalem, people stood on their housetops looking down as the Queen of Sheba entered the city. Shulamit and her daughters walked down to where they could see the queen's entrance more closely.

"Look!" shouted Basemath. "The queen is wearing so much gold!" The queen was indeed draped in a golden cloak with a veil of pearls. "She sparkles in the sunlight. What a majestic white horse too. I love her gold reins and all those colorful stones."

Taphath remarked, "Look at her personal guards." She pointed towards the large spears they carried while riding on decorated red horses. They wore gold bands with feathers hanging down their plaited hair.

"Wow," said Taphath. "Such high leather boots."

"I like the leopard skin skirts."

"Are they sword maids?" Taphath said, staring at the golden girdles holding large swords in their sheaths. Shulamit glanced at Taphath and wondered where she had heard of sword maids.

The trail of camels followed behind, some displaying open boxes of jewels, gold, and baskets of spices. More servants in bright cloaks and matching turbans were adorned with golden girdles and large swords. *This will surely keep people talking until she appears in the throne room of the House of Lebanon to display her gifts before the king,* Shulamit thought.

A few days later, when Shulamit heard the visiting queen would appear in the judgement hall, she joined the other queens behind the lattice where they could observe, but not be seen, to watch this historic event. It was nothing short of spectacle. Bearers, dressed in bright, colorful turbans, bore litters of pearls and incense of bdellium, balsam, myrrh, frankincense, and other rare resins. There were baskets of cinnamon, pepper, cloves, coffee, nutmeg, nuggets of gold, and carts of precious stones.

When the display caravan was finished, the grand entrance of the Queen of Sheba was marked by her two beautiful, darkly colored hand maidens. Dressed in purple gowns and golden shawls, their girdles had long fringes of pure gold to the bottom of the gown. Their faces glittered with paints mixed with gleaming crushed gems that glittered over their coffee-colored mouths, cheeks, eyelids, and eyebrows. After they bowed before the king, they moved to the side and remained on their knees beside the golden lions.

At last, the queen showed herself, emerging from behind the shadows of the cedar columns.

She stepped forward slowly, pacing herself as she met the king's eyes. The Queen of Sheba was tall and commanding, with glowing black skin accented by gold. She continued in a stately manner up the polished cedar steps. Ivory silk flowed over the darkly colored curves of her lovely form. Her black hair was braided with gold beads and held back by two gilded ivory combs.

Her voice carried authority as she announced, "Queen of Sheba greets King Solomon of Israel and Judah."

Solomon stood to welcome her, formally inviting her to sit beside him on a throne fashioned of leopards in golden gilded cedar.

Shulamit stood up, shocked and unsure what to think of this display.

Never has Solomon set a foreign woman beside him on the throne, she thought. *He has rarely even done that with a visiting king. Bathsheba* (who sat on the other side of the king) *is showing no emotions on her face except her trained graciousness. I wish I had her control.*

A sudden onset of contractions signaled to Shulamit that she was approaching her time of birth. All thoughts of a foreign spice queen halted as she turned her attention. Once her contractions came, Shulamit knew the birth would come quickly. She was not one to travail long in labor.

Before the sun went down, Shulamit had delivered another baby girl, who arrived with a loud wailing cry. Instead of Solomon rushing in to greet his new baby, her two daughters sat beside her admiring their new baby sister.

"She is so beautiful, Mama," said Basemath, her finger in the baby's curled hand. "She is strong too."

"I will take care of her," announced Taphath.

"No, I will. I'm the oldest," Basemath demanded.

"You both will," Shulamit voiced before taking a breath. "I'm so proud of you, my daughters. You will make great mothers. I was around your age when my mother had your Aunt Miriam. And I helped raise her. Now, will one of you let your grandmother know the baby is born if she is free?"

Since the baby had her hand grasped around Basemath's pointing finger, Taphath agreed to go and find Bathsheba who was already on her way. When she arrived and saw the infant girl, Bathsheba gave a delighted smile and lifted her up into her arms.

Bathsheba cooed, "How I always wanted to have a girl, but God gave me only sons. Shulamit, my daughter, you have blessed me with the girls I have dreamed of."

Sweet Bathsheba reads my mind although she will never say it. I love my baby, but I have no son. I will never be Queen Mother now. Will Solomon be disappointed? What a time for this, right when a foreign queen is demanding his time. Shulamit turned to her daughters, saying, "Can you girls leave me and your grandmother alone for a little while?" Once her children left, Shulamit looked at Bathsheba and said, "It looks like fore sure I will never be Queen Mother."

"I knew you were thinking that." Bathsheba replied. "Is it really that important anyway? You are still his favored queen. And you will be, as long as Solomon lives. From what I see that it will be for most of your life. You know, I was forced to become Queen Mother, or I would probably have been killed, along with Solomon and all my sons, as there was so much animosity within David's court. The people blamed me for causing his adultery. Without Solomon becoming king, we would have had no protection. I tell you now, I am tiring, and would rather not have been there the entire time today. But I had to be since, you were not there. I will not leave your place to other queens. I'm getting too old for all of this and

Judy Pendell

would rather step down and let you take my place. When your daughters are older you can secure their future by marrying them to good men. I completely approve of Basemath marrying Shira's son. She will make a good Levite governor's wife as she is a born leader. Taphath, I haven't figured out yet. As for this baby she has voice that should carry a tune across Jerusalem. So, my dear, as David said, don't fret about tomorrow, and if you have any real questions, you can always talk to Zadok our priest; he is very favorable toward you and he will always be able to give you wise counsel. You know, I had Nathan the prophet who was also a friend and counselor. Nathan also privately tutored my young princes and raised them up with a fear of God. Zabud, the son of Nathan, and friend of Solomon favor's you and will also give you good counsel. You have much favor in the court."

"Do you think that queen will steal Solomon's heart from me? I saw the way he looked at her."

"My dear girl," Bathsheba empathized, "You have just delivered a baby. You are tired," she smiled as she looked at the newborn baby. "You need rest."

Bathsheba paused and then decided to share another thought to Shulamit. "Solomon has always had this dream that kings and queens will come to Israel and learn about our great God. Perhaps she will become a genuine believer in our God. It is our mission to bless the world, and that does not change his love for you, it enhances it. All you need to do is what you have already been doing. Love our God and continue to worship *Adonai* from the heart. Keep loving Solomon, and you will keep his heart turned toward you and God.

"I hope so," said Shulamit as the baby slept in her arms.

"This queen will pass. Besides she will not stay in Jerusalem, she is a ruling queen in her own country. She cannot give up her responsibility to her people. She comes from a very different culture. There, women rule. I saw my husband, King David, take more brides and have temporary infatuations, but he always came back to me." Shulamit's face darkened at the thought that Solomon could possibly love anyone but her. Bathsheba's words were little comfort. "Just being the loving woman and queen that you are. No one can ever take your place. I am sharing from my life experience. I have seen this play out before."

***

Solomon came to visit his Queen Shulamit and her new princess after some days had passed. He sent vases of flowers ahead of him. When he came, he was joined by servants bearing precious jewels, perfumes, and

299

incense. Solomon never visited any of his queens without bringing presents.

Basemath was holding the baby and smiling. "Isn't our baby sister pretty?" She asked her father.

Taphath stopped playing the harp and said, "She is our baby princess."

"They think she is their baby," Shulamit said, then laughed.

To that Solomon replied, "They are learning to be mothers. What higher call is there for a woman in Israel than to be a good wife and mother?" Placing his hands on the heads of Basemath and Rebecca, he blessed them, "May you be like Sarah, Rebecca, Rachel and Leah."

Without any warning, the baby gave out a loud cry and Basemath handed her to her mother. Shulamit immediately put her to her breast as Solomon looked on with amusement. "She never cries except when she is hungry," Shulamit explained. "And then there is absolutely nothing you can do to comfort her but to feed her."

Solomon looked tenderly toward his baby girl and said, "So, my little princess will have a strong voice to sing with. Shall we name her after your friend Shira?

Basemath added, "Yes, for song. A very powerful song indeed." They all laughed.

After a short visit, Solomon bent down to kiss and embrace his love. He whispered in her ear, "I love to see you nursing our baby, as it always reminds me of the nurturing queen you are in Israel." Then he added that, while Shulamit was in her time of purification, he would be showing the Queen of Sheba around the temple and Jerusalem, and possibly other parts of Israel. He looked at his older daughters and said, "Please take good care of our baby."

Queen Shulamit was happy for his visit and blessings, until she thought of her beloved spending so much time with the Queen of the South. She was so isolated and helpless to do anything. Taking the harp and singing helped to calm her, as in the mountains while tending sheep after her father died. She thought she had forgotten that time in her life, but her situation triggered the old memories. Smiling to herself, Shulamit remembered that an angel had come and comforted her, and she felt more peaceful. She could trust God to get her through this, like David had in the wilderness. "I had fainted unless I had believed to see the goodness of the Lord in the land of the living." *Trust, trust, trust,* Shulamit told herself every time a negative thought hit her mind.

During the next weeks, it seemed that everywhere the Sheban queen went she drew attention. The clothing style of the Jewish women was conservative and stylish. Israelites were not used to a queen with warrior guards dressed in provocative clothing riding horses besides her.

Taphath was fascinated when she heard that her father, the king, had shown the foreign queen his abundant stables and that they were racing with their horses. The warrior women of Sheba were masters on horses. They rode quickly and jumped the horses over fences with considerable skill—skill that competed with Solomon's horse masters.

Stories arrived that the Queen of Sheba sat with Solomon in the Forest of Lebanon's judgment hall. The queen watched how he governed difficult situations. Afterwards, Solomon entertained her in the court's finest fashion with foods and music. Word spread quickly from noble members of the court as they watched their king match wits with an obviously intelligent, foreign woman who was testing him.

King Solomon gave the Queen of the South a royal tour throughout Israel, showing her his expanded roads, military cities, stables, and gardens he had planted. He took her down to the palace he was building by the Sea in Joppa, and up to where he was building a palace in Lebanon. He also showed her the pools he was building outside Bethlehem. He took great pleasure showing the foreign queen all his accomplishments. Solomon expounded to the Queen of Sheba, "I bring the best talents to be found in the world to Jerusalem to build and teach my people their skills."

He took her to the palace where he read from his newest scroll, the Book of Proverbs. To all observers in Israel, the Queen of Sheba was an astute listener, fascinated with this wisdom she had never heard.

But when it was all said and done, this powerful woman was most impressed with the servants. She noticed how happy the servants were, their apparel, and how they waited on them at their table, even Solomon's cup bearer.

"They serve with joy," said the queen, "desiring to please you, and display their talents. The music in your courts is happy and melodious. The way you and your queens sing as you walk up the entryway to the house of the Lord," she smiled broadly, "I have no more spirit in me. It is a true report that I have heard about you, and I didn't believe it until I saw it all for myself."

And so, the people heard of the great queens' pleasure in seeing the glory in Israel. They were not people to go out and proselytize, but they believed in their doing and following *YHWH*, God. People would see their good deeds and glorify their God. They were pleased that their labors brought honor to their country.

Shulamit counted the days of her purification, hoping to soon be out and about and discovering for herself what was going on with the foreign queen. Toward the end of her time, her sister Miriam came to visit again. She walked into Shulamit's bed chamber while she was nursing Shira.

"I tried to come earlier," Miriam said, "but my own baby is just a few months older, and I couldn't bring her out with me yet. She is with my maid in your family chamber." Miriam stopped abruptly as she saw her sister with tears in her eyes looking down at her baby. Closing the door, she said, "I'm your sister, you can talk to me."

Shulamit burst into tears. "I love Shira. Look how pretty she is, and how she smiles at me. But I don't understand how my three children are all girls. I know God loves me, but I don't see how this can be. I'm afraid Solomon is disappointed in me. I have not given him a prince and will never be a Queen Mother."

"So? When did you ever desire to be a Queen Mother?" Miriam asked. "I know that grandiose list of things you wanted in your Ketubah, and never once did you say you wanted to be a queen. You didn't even want to marry a king. You have been living in this palace too long, listening to jealous voices. I know your dream was to worship in the Tabernacle. And that is *all* you ever wanted, besides Solomon. Are you concerned about Solomon and this queen from Sheba? I know there is more bothering you. You can fool a lot of people but not me."

Shulamit looked up from the baby to her sister, aware of her anguish. "I'm so thankful you are here," Shulamit said. "You are one of the few people in this world I can share my heart with and not have to worry about being judged. You are right, I made a covenant of marriage with Solomon, and he has kept all his promises. I also made promises before the Lord in front of the Ark before all Israel. I promised to love Solomon no matter what. Otherwise, what kind of a bride am I?"

Miriam hugged her sister and kissed the baby's forehead. "You are an honorable wife, Shulamit. You will do your husband right all the days of your life. I know Solomon's heart safely trusts in you, and you will never let him down."

Shulamit looked down at Shira, who smiled back at her. She cried a few more tears, then said, "Love is not always easy, is it? But I love God and He will help me love. Call Sheriti to come take the baby. You and I will go worship. I need you to worship with me through this. Shulamit picked up the harp and begin to play while they sang,

> *I will bless the lord at all times*
> *His praise shall continually be in my mouth*
> *My soul shall make its boast in the Lord*
> *The humble shall hear thereof and be glad*
> *Oh, magnify the Lord with me,*
> *And let us exalt His name together*
> *I sought the Lord and He heard me*
> *And delivered me from all my fears…*

"It has been a long time since we worshipped alone together," Shulamite disclosed. "You bring back memories of my childhood worship. I am glad you married Nathan and live nearby. I need you in my life."

"You may have sisters through marriage in the palace, but I am your real sister, and we will always be here for each other."

A few weeks passed and just at the end of Shulamit's time of purification, Solomon arrived to accompany his queen to the temple for the ritual cleansing ceremony. A lamb was sacrificed for a burnt offering and a dove for the sin offering of ritual purity as they honored the sanctity of life. The priest blessed the baby girl according to Hebrew law, and now Shulamit could return to her normal life. But Shulamit felt some hesitance. She requested of Solomon for her servants to carry her baby back to the palace while she stayed a while longer to worship. She had missed her time at the Temple. Solomon acquiesced, as he knew how much worship meant to her.

"Oh, Father in heaven, I have so missed meeting with you face to face and resting in your presence. I miss the music of heaven in your Temple, as I miss the music of Zion in your heavenly courts." Shulamit sat listening to the music and petitioning her heart before the Lord she felt a wonderful cleansing coming over her. She thanked *Adonai* for accepting the sacrifice of the lamb and the dove for her shortcomings and impurities. "Thank you, my father in Heaven. You have made a way for our spirits to be restored to your presence." Shulamit just sat there for a while, soaking in this wonderful time of contemplative worship. Feeling the unction of the Spirit, she lifted her hands to her Lord in praise and gentle worship. The peaceful flow of the Lord rested on her, she finally felt released to go.

She heard someone walking behind her and she turned to see Zadok, the High Priest. What a delightful surprise as they each greeted one another with, "Shalom."

"I heard you had a baby girl that you named after my daughter, Shira."

"Yes, I named her for Shira, my first friend in Jerusalem. My baby's cry pierces the silence with a powerful breath. I hope she shall grow to sing like Shira."

"So how have you been?" Zadok asked.

"I had another easy birth, and my daughters rival one another over who gets to care for her."

"Better, than not caring. You have trained them well."

"Yes, they talk of their dreams of becoming mothers."

"And your dreams?"

"My dreams?" Out of nowhere, Shulamit's two significant dreams, returned to her memory. "High Priest, remember when I first asked you about my dreams? I was sure they were Solomon saying, 'I will never leave you nor forsake you.' And you told me about *The Angel of the Lord.* Do you recall how you said to consider it was not Solomon? I have been thinking about what you said and considering you are right."

"I cannot say for sure, but when I hear words, God spoke to prophets before you, I see a pattern that reminds me of similar experiences and reasons He spoke to them."

He first spoke the words "I will never leave you or forsake you," to Moses as he came out of Egypt and was preparing to lead our people through the wilderness. The next time those same words were spoken were to Joshua as he was preparing to lead our people out of the wilderness into the promised land."

"So, they needed assurance for the tremendous task ahead of them."

"Right."

Shulamit stood in silence as she considered the depth of what the man in the dream said to her.

"My dear queen," Zadok said to comfort her, "no one doubts your call. No one who counts. It is a high call; and being married to a powerful king is not designed to be easy. You did not choose your call, but when you first recognized the voice of God before the Ark saying he had chosen you for his bride, you said 'yes.' I was born into a Levite family, I did not choose to become High Priest, but I recognized the great peace that came upon me when I too, said, 'Yes' to the call.

"Great peace," Shulamit said. "That is what I felt. Perhaps I saw God speaking to me as a man who somewhat looked like Solomon but was not Solomon. I don't understand fully."

"Sweet Shulamit, I have a very hard time with *The Angel of the Lord* being a man. But again, I look back at patterns in the Torah where *YHWH* showed himself to Abraham as a man, and to Hagar, and then to Jacob later at Bethel. He was no ordinary angel. I believe this angel is a pre-incarnate Messiah."

"I don't understand it either my High Priest," said Shulamit. "But I believe what you are saying because I have felt the great peace in saying yes. I have experienced His glory as he spoke to me in the dreams. And it was in the strength of that glory that I led the queens and women in worship at the dedication of the temple when the glory came down. Solomon's interpretation about that glory part was real. It gave me the faith to do what I was called to do."

"It also gave you the strength to be a strong worship warrior at the time Solomon needed you. I know both of you very well, and as a spiritual Father I have seen both of your strengths and weaknesses at important times during your divine calls. I have witnessed That *YHWH* has showed up and answered your prayers and the prayers of the people. The dedication of the temple was one of the biggest events in both of your lives and our nation at this time in our history."

"It is a lot to take in."

The Priest paused for a moment and shared another insight. "Solomon meeting this foreign queen is like a meeting of great minds," Zadok said, "but it does not compare to the meeting of great hearts which you and Solomon have always had. Loves sparks through each of you when you are together and flows to all around you.

I have watched the love between you and Solomon. God is in it. It is a glorious love story in Israel that won't be forgotten after the Queen of Sheba is gone. She is a good woman, and she did come seeking. But she will take back a love and worship for the God of Israel. She can never take your place. Remember too, Queen Shulamit, being a glorious queen and being adored and admired in this world is not what it's all about. We are a peculiar people, yet our true glory is not always seen by all, and even then, only seen by those with spiritual eyes."

Shulamit agreed. "Bathsheba said something like that. Some see, and some don't see."

"Surround yourself with people who have spiritual eyes. Keep your eyes on the Kingdom of Heaven, and the King of the Universe. He is what it is all about. David dreamed of a Zion on earth that would be like the Zion in Heaven."

"Thank you, honorable Zadok. You are a true High Priest. You carry the heart of God and David. I don't totally understand it, but I feel it."

"God has given women a special gift of intuition. Keep it." Then Zadok added, "I heard you are writing a book about your love story with Solomon. Please have a scribe assist you and copy it, so that I may preserve a copy for times to come."

A bright smile lit up on the queen's face. "Thank you for believing in me," she replied. "I am so blessed as a wife of Solomon to be able to have the opportunity to have such a friend as you in my life."

"You are loved by many people, more than you know," Zadok said before he walked away.

Shulamit returned to her palatial home within the palace estate. She asked for a cup of lavender tea and then walked out to her secret place. Hidden behind trees set under a rose covered bower, she sat on a bench and pondered on what the High Priest had shared about the Angel of the Lord. She began to realize that there was a great power in the unseen spiritual realm that directed lives and destinies. She imagined the Angel of the Lord was behind so much of all she did. It was a deep thought to ponder, and she could only imagine the great things of God. It all brought wonder to her heart. As she sat there pondering, she began to sing a song to herself.

It was You, it was You,

It was really You Lord behind it all.
The person who was in my dream will always be You.
I am in your heart, and you are in mine
And nothing can ever separate us.

A deep sense of peace and security came over her. She knew then, no matter what happened in her life the real Lover was the God who sees and watches over her.

She sat there playing her lute and singing, forgetting time, until she heard footsteps. Only if the baby cried would anyone disturb her in her secret place, except for Solomon. As he had done so many times in the past, he tried to tiptoe in and surprise her. But it never worked, just like now. They did what they always did, joined one another in their song. When she heard the echo of a deep male voice she was surprised, but not alarmed. It had been a while since they met in a secret place. They sang together for a time.

Solomon gave her a deep hug and kiss and indications that he wanted to be intimate. When he poured on the charm like that, no matter what was going on in her mind she found him hard to resist. When they arrived in her chamber Solomon led her to the bed and kissed her passionately.

"I have missed you; I have missed you," he confessed.

"And I have missed you, my beloved," Shulamit whispered as in involuntary tear fell from the side of her eye."

"Awe, sweet love, our short time apart makes my heart more aware that without you part of me is missing. My heart has become aware that without you it cannot fully express joy. My song cannot find expression. My inner voice cannot speak, and my sun cannot shine brightly. I have missed you."

"Tell me what you have missed, my love," Shulamit said. She wanted to draw his heart out.

"I have missed the love in my dove's eyes. I have missed the softness of your embrace and the sweetness of your kiss. I have missed that every part of my touch finds response in you. I have missed your beauty, the way your hair flutters when you turn your head. I have missed the sparkle and bounce in your eyes when our hearts and words connect, and our songs began to flow. Your bouncing eyes reflect the rhythms of our hearts. I miss the way my very spirit, soul, and body finds expression with you. The depths of my very being arises within me. When I am with you, you make me more fully myself. And you?"

"You give so much Solomon. You are so full of life and love, and wisdom, that I just want all of you. I want your head of gold, your strong arms and legs are pillars of marble. I miss your scent of frankincense and myrrh and sweet spices. I love the words of fire in your voice. I want it all. When all of you is flowing into me, you make me a fuller me. I miss your presence when you are not here. I've missed your love and intimacy. I've missed you."

"I would not be apart from you for so long were it not for the laws of Purification to keep you and the baby healthy. You have given me a beautiful gift in our sweet baby. But I have missed you."

"Shulamit's heart opened. It found freedom. She became aware that each absence from Solomon only seemed to find that upon reuniting their love grew deeper. They had a shared history in their relationship that had grown and matured over time."

The opening of their hearts, as they expressed their longing for one another, led them into a time of deep intimacy. Later, lying in bed together they spent time catching up on each other's activity. It had been a while since they had really talked. Solomon let his wife know that she could have many baby girls, but she was always his chosen queen, and no woman in the world could ever take her place.

Shulamit needed that assurance of her beloved's love. But she had already won the battle in her heart of loving him no matter what. Her blessed sister, Bathsheba, and the High Priest had stood in the gap between her heart and heaven and helped her overcome perhaps the most difficult trial of her life. God is good. She knew that fully now.

***

A few days later Solomon came to his bride. "I'd like to ask you a favor, my love."

"You know I have never said, 'No' to you," she replied. "What is it?"

"Your fame as a worshipper had gone all over Israel, and beyond."

"Beyond?"

"Yes, those who have come to Israel and observed our Holy Feasts have talked of your worship within the palace and the temple grounds. Now it seems they ask about you as well as me."

"Who are they specifically?" Shulamit was beginning to be curious.

Pacing himself carefully Solomon told his love that the Queen of Sheba had asked that before she left Israel, she hoped she could meet the Shulamit Queen. When travelers had come to her country speaking of the wisdom of Solomon, they had also heard of the glorious worship and music of the temple that went on night and day before the Lord. The travelers talked about the Israelite queens who worshipped with his worshipping bride. Solomon had taken the Queen of Sheba to the temple, his wives leading up the steps to the songs of ascents. She had recognized that, while it was glorious, the real leader was missing.

"How could she know?" Shulamit asked. "I have trained my sister queens who dance with me to lead dances and songs when I am not there. My daughters tell me they do well."

"They *do* well," Solomon replied, "But none are *you*. You carry a joyful, inspirational, living, funny, and spontaneous anointing. No one knows what you will do next. That always keeps anticipation high and alive. No one can do that but you. This queen is very smart, you can't fool her. She has been ruling a country and looks for genuineness in people. She has had to learn to recognize sincerity to survive as a queen. You know how I have always trusted your discernment. Wisdom, discernment, and knowledge are things a ruler must have. There is an element of grooming that must be taught, but not everything can be taught. And you my love, possess these qualities too."

"I do?"

"You forget, when I first saw you singing in the vineyard, I also saw how you inspired your workers to be happy as they harvested. Making hard labor fun is a great art."

"So, what is your favor my king?"

"The Queen of Sheba has asked that she might worship with you."

"She wants to worship with me. Does she understand and believe in our God? You know worship is a heart thing, and as you said yourself, some things can't be taught. Worship comes from the heart."

"You are wise. You will always keep faith pure and not turn it into entertainment for those of impure hearts. But this queen really came seeking for the wisdom of God, and to see if our God is really the real God. She has come to believe. She is a good woman. She is hungry to know everything about our God. I have not seen such hunger since you told me you wanted to learn to read the Holy Scriptures. Wise people seek deeply. They are not content to stand on the shore and wade in the shallow water as the river goes by, they want to dive in and swim in the deep waters. I told her that I have the wisdom, but you are full of heart. Only those who would resist the Spirit of God could resist you. You carry the heart of David in worship and the Father of Israel, and you carry my heart. You know how much I trust you. I think you will find her newly discovered love for our God entirely fresh and inspiring."

"You have asked me a not-so-easy favor."

"Have I ever asked you to do something that I didn't know you could do?"

"No."

"Have I ever failed to assist you, when you felt a task very difficult?"

"No."

"I believe in you. You must know by now that I have only your best interests and heart. Your heart to worship moves Heaven and all the hearts around you. Whatever you need, just ask, as you always have."

29 The Meeting of Queens

Queen Shulamit had long ago learned the effects a mother's emotions had upon their babies. Nursing always forced Shulamit to still her own spirit, so her baby would be calm. For that reason, as she prepared to meet the Queen of Sheba, Shulamit spent time in meditative prayer while she nursed her new baby.

In this imposed calm mood, the queen found herself remembering a promise she had made to God as a girl. She promised *Adonai* that, when foreigners came into the land, she would help them to know the God of Israel. *I guess this is another time to keep my promise,* thought Shulamit.

"Father," she prayed quietly, "I can't do this without your help, strengthen me. Give me wisdom about how to honor you in worship with a queen not of our people." A favorite psalm of David's came to her mind, and she sang it to her daughter. "He who dwells in the secret place of the highest shall abide under the shadow of the almighty." She had not sung that psalm for a while and its peace refreshed her. "I thank you Lord," she prayed again, "for speaking into my spirit and giving me strength."

Filled with holy calmness, Shulamit took an official parchment paper and sent an official invitation to the Queen of Sheba, welcoming her to Shulamit's palace home.

A few days later, with arrangements made for court musicians and her daughters, the Queen of Sheba and her small entourage arrived at Shulamit's entryway. Two female guards preceded the queen. Other servants set down several chests of gifts and then exited. Servants invited the queen and her large group into the main chamber. Queen Shulamit arose. Greeting each other as equals they stood, looking at each other for an awkward moment, until Shulamit extended her hand.

"Welcome," said Shulamit.

"It is an honor to meet you," the Queen of Sheba humbly expressed. "I have heard so much about you."

"I hope that all you heard was good," Shulamit said, gesturing to the chair beside hers.

"I've heard that you can match songs and poetry with that of the king. You are the queen who leads worship in the palace, dancing and spreading joy to all around you. I heard how beautiful you are, and that you are the king's favored wife. Indeed, you are as beautiful as everyone says. I have heard so much that I feel unworthy to come into your presence."

Shulamit, not used to such compliments (except from Solomon), smiled in surprise. "You heard all that of me?"

"I have heard more your Highness," the Queen of the South said. "I heard how you led women dancing on the outer courts of the Temple on the wonderful day of the dedication when glory came down from heaven. I heard that you are full of wonder and spontaneity with lightheartedness and abandoned joy towards your God. I heard you honor tradition, but you are not controlled by it, and how your spirit overflows from the presence of God."

"In the presence of *Adonai*, dear queen, everyone is overcome with joy and gladness," said Shulamit. "At such times, I find no words or feeling to express this joy other than to sing and dance. All Israel danced for joy on that great day of dedication. I just happened to be leading the dances *Adonai* had given me when I worshipped with my sister queens.

"Sister queens," she said thoughtfully. "There is an expression I have never heard."

"I must tell you," Shulamit began, "the first thing I heard about you was from a ship captain from Sidon, named Javan. He said, 'I have to go back to the land of Sheba because the queen there is holding a few of our men captive until we return.'"

"I only held them temporarily," said the queen, abashed. "It was so I could learn the language, for when I came to your country. I had hoped to be able to communicate with you."

"Oh," Shulamit stated. Before she could ask any other questions, the queen explained.

"There was something different about your captain and your countrymen. They were honest in business and would not bow or buy our idols. As queen, I have always learned that where there are good people, there is a good source behind them."

"Javan did say you were beautiful but very tall," said Shulamit. "And indeed, you are. You are the first queen taller than me, and I now know I am not the tallest queen in the world. I was the tallest woman from the mountains where I came from."

"Tall is good," replied the queen. "It makes it easier to be a queen when people have to look up to you."

"Solomon told me I am stately like a palm tree, and it gives me a noble appearance. I never thought of it really. I never expected to be a queen. Solomon and I each laughed about that. Neither of us grew up expecting to be king or queen."

"Yes, but did you not know somewhere deep inside that you were born for more."

"I suppose. Mostly I wanted to worship. But you, you knew when you were born that you would be a queen and rule did you not? I heard about all the gifts you brought in your caravan. I was standing up in the veranda when you entered the palace, but I went into labor and missed the rest." The queen smiled at Shulamit, congratulating her without words. "I heard that you ride a war horse. I also heard you are the sole ruler of your country, a real queen. I have always wondered what kind of woman could rule a country, go to war, and still retain her graciousness as you do. I am astounded that you came here, on such a long journey, to see the wisdom of Solomon and the glory of our *Jehovah* in our Holy Temple on our Holy land. I heard you asked challenging questions of the king to challenge his wisdom. You have found what you came here for, I trust?"

"More than I ever dreamed." Shulamit's face darkened at what she heard, but she sipped her tea and said nothing. The queen continued. "I was groomed to be queen, but I did not expect to become queen so early in life. My mother died when I was fifteen, and suddenly I had a lot of responsibility thrust upon me. I made my share of mistakes. When traders came from your country telling me about your king and your God, I was desperate to learn from a wise ruler. You have no idea how blessed you are to have your great God and King Solomon."

Shulamit's heart began to soften as she realized she could not ever imagine a day her Father in heaven was not looking after her life. The queen made herself vulnerable and Shulamit remembered how vulnerable she felt when her father died at eleven.

"You know," started Shulamit, "I was only eleven years old when my father died. He was the one who taught me to dream, and my dream of worshipping in the Tabernacle nearly died when he did. He was not around to take me to Jerusalem or into the Tabernacle to worship, let alone introduce me to any eligible men as I came of age. What kept my dream alive were the prophecies from the High Priest and my father."

"I have always believed in prophecy and dreams," the Queen of Sheba said. "From one queen to another, that is a truly kind thing for you to say. Solomon said you were a woman of deep perception and insight." Shulamit's face became hot with embarrassment. "I see too that you are a woman of graciousness and deeply sensitive. Do you think that we could ever be friends? If you wish, you can call me by my name, Makeda."

"Makeda, that is nice. You may call me Shulamit."

Tears spilled out of Makeda's eyes. She wiped them, but Shulamit noticed. "You know, I can only cry in front of someone I trust as a friend. A queen can never show her vulnerability. Solomon told me you are his friend, and the one queen he knows he can trust to share his heart with because you will never betray his confidence. You do him good as queen, and that is another reason I wanted to meet you."

Shulamit found herself wiping a small tear in her eye. "Solomon spoke of me to you?"

"Yes, when I asked to meet you."

"Did Solomon say anything else?"

"No, only the expression upon his face when I mentioned your name showed me. No one else could ever take your place. He had an expression of deep tenderness and love, such that I have never seen upon the face of a man when he talked about a queen, he called beloved. Solomon has a kind and tender heart, but I saw in that moment that even if I tried, I would never replace that special place he has in his heart for you."

"That is kind of you to say."

"And besides," added Makeda, "I have a responsibility within my country. I could not stay here even if I wanted to. I must return and rule my country."

"I do sense that you have developed feelings for my king," Shulamit gently inserted into the conversation as she signaled servants to bring in food and drink, anticipating their conversation was about to go much deeper than she intended. "Come," Shulamit said, "let us sit over here on the soft carpet and cushions and share a meal, where we can be more comfortable."

They moved their conversation to the new location, but the queen was undeterred with her subject. Makeda was frank as she took a bite. "Solomon is an easy man to love. I am not used to being treated like a woman. In my country, women rule, and the men are servants. So, I must be strong. Yet, as Solomon taught about the ways of your culture, I realized that something was really missing in me. It was not about ruling, wisdom, and how to make wise judgement. It was the feeling that I missed something from God. A great gift. Something God designed me to be. Solomon made me understand what it meant to really feel like a woman.

"Yes, Solomon, knows how to make a woman feel like a woman," Shulamit agreed. Her tone was neutral, but the queen could hear her awkward feelings as the conversation continued.

"You have men in your country who love their women enough to go to war to defend their families and children," said Makeda. I have people who love me as a queen; but I have no one who loves me as a woman. Your custom of marriage is very protective of women. It allows them an expression of feeling safe and delicately appreciated. Do you know, in many cultures that women are used by men without love or just to have babies, and then they are thrown away when they grow too old to be desirable or give birth to more children?"

Shulamit hid her shock as she sipped tea. "I am aware that other kings bring their daughters here to make treaties with our nation, and the daughters are given no choice about coming here, or who they wish to marry. Some are very frightened when they come, while others are very young. A few are just a bit older than my daughters. Solomon has many queens, but he does not know them."

"He would never force himself upon a woman."

"Correct," said Shulamit. "He has no need." Shulamit smiled sadly. "He gives them time to know our customs and be happy in the palace with other women developing skills and talents they enjoy. He tries to make their lives happy. When they can speak our language fluently, they express that coming here is better than marrying kings in other countries."

"Ah, I see you understand."

Shulamit felt as if she passed a test she did not know she was taking. "So how did you happen to have a country where women rule?"

"I have never been told the exact story," stated the queen, "but it seems that enemy invaders castrated some of the men and took some as slaves back with them. They raped the women and left most of them behind. All that was left in the land were old men and young boys, so the women learned to become warriors to protect themselves and never let that tragedy happen again. Most of the men today do the hard labor. Some are warriors, but the women lead. When we want babies, we go to see the male priests in the temple. When the men of a nation are damaged, it seems something deep inside of them is destroyed, their masculinity as men becomes more effeminate and their desire for women is even destroyed. I have often thought of how this can be reversed in my nation, and now I have hopes that your God can, and your culture can help heal our land. But it will take generations."

Shulamit tried, but could not hide her shock. She offered Makeda more food and drink which she accepted with grace. The women found a bridge to friendship and began walking it slowly. Time had been forgotten as they had talked, and the sound of Shira's loud cry could be heard approaching as her girls brought the baby to her. Quickly putting her baby to her breast quieted the atmosphere. "These are my two daughters, Basemath and Taphath," Shulamit said. "They have desired to meet you."

The girls gave small curtsies and found a place across from Shulamit at the table. Taphath couldn't wait to say, "I saw you riding majestically on a horse. You actually ride your horse into war?"

"Basemath interjected, "Taphath begged our father to let us ride horses, but he would never let us go to war. We are learning how to shoot arrows now. Do you like ruling a country?"

Shulamit could see that her daughters had a lot of thoughts in their hearts that they had been waiting to ask. She thought to quiet them but decided against it. Shulamit was still processing a lot of what Makeda had confided in her."

"Horses are majestic," the queen said, "and they can be ridden for sheer pleasure, not just war." Looking at Taphath's hair the queen said, "You must have a lot of fire in you with your beautiful red hair."

"She has a lot of her father's tribe of Judah within her," Shulamit added.

"If your father allows, I will teach you how to make your horses jump fences and do tricks."

Shulamit looked over at her daughter Taphath, as her face lit up, and wondered where her life was going. "I have ridden a horse with Solomon, but it has never occurred to me to turn it into a show horse. Times are changing. But I will not let her be a warrior. That is where it stops."

Makeda looked over at the baby nursing and asked. "How was your childbirth?"

"Easy," Basemath replied before her mother could, "and I helped her deliver it."

"Basemath is going to become the palace midwife," said a proud Shulamit. My mom was in our village. But my births are easy because I always claim the promises of God. If my heart is right with Him and if I am abiding in the secret place under the shadow of the Almighty, I will have protection."

Makeda looked amazed. "Your promises from your God even make your child birthing easier?"

"Let me sing you a song and you will see the promises," Shulamit said as she handed a full little baby Shira over to Basemath. Taphath brought the harp over. "Solomon and I have written many songs about the secret place, but this was written long ago, probably by Moses. Shulamit began to sing,

> *He who dwells in the secret place of the Most High*
> *Shall abide under the shadow of the Almighty*
> *I will say of the Lord,*
> *He is my refuge and fortress.*
> *My God, in Him I will trust*
>
> *Surely, He shall deliver you from the snare of the fowler*
> *And from the perilous pestilence*
> *He shall cover you with His feathers*
> *And under His wings you shall take refuge*
> *His truth shall be your shield and buckler*

As Shulamit sang, Makeda's eyes lit up with amazement. Shulamit could see in her eyes a real belief in the promises. Rarely had she seen such a response in her own people, let alone a foreign queen. There was an utter joy in this woman. She knew that a great, almighty God held such a deep love and protective nature over His people. Shulamite paused for a moment to let Makeda speak.

"All of my life, I have had to go to war without the knowledge or faith that I truly had a God looking after me. I prayed to a God, but I felt he was distant. I wasn't even sure if He heard my prayers. The burden is immense. Yet I knew someone was protecting me, to bring me to this point of understanding. Sing some more. My heart is being moved within me."

Shulamit invited Makeda to sing with her, and her daughters joined in:

> *You shall not be afraid of the terror by night.*
> *Nor of the arrow that flies by day,*
> *Nor of the pestilence that walks in darkness*
> *Nor of the destruction that lays waste at noonday.*
>
> *A thousand shall fall at your side,*
> *And ten thousand at your right hand.*
> *But it shall not come near you.*
>
> *Only with your eyes shall you look,*
> *And see the reward of the wicked*

Makeda held up her hand to speak and Shulamit paused again. "Your God stops the curses in the arrows coming against you, and demonic spiritual forces," she said. "I see the picture in my eyes alive and real. That is how your God protected your people from Pharaoh and in the wilderness and helped your King David win all his wars. What a powerful God you have."

"Yes," Shulamit replied, "*El Shaddai*. He is our great protector. When we live under his wings, absolutely nothing can harm us. There are even more promises." Shulamit struck the harp another time and continued to sing,

> *Because you have made the Lord, who is my refuge,*
> *Even the Most High, your dwelling place*
> *No evil shall befall you,*
> *Nor shall any plague come near your dwelling*
> *For He shall give His angels charge over you,*
> *Too keep you in all your ways*
> *In their hands they shall bear you up,*
> *Lest you dash your foot against a stone.*
> *You shall tread upon the lion and the cobra,*
> *The young lion and the serpent you shall trample underfoot.*

Again, Makeda made a sign that she had to respond to what she heard. "Your sailors who came to our land, the one who taught me your language, showed me the sign in the stars of strong hero trampling on the head of the scorpion. He said a Messiah will come out of Israel who will break the power of evil. He taught me about the covenant your God made with Abraham. That was part of what made me want to come to your land.

"How wonderful!" squealed Tapheth.

"Later in the year, he showed me the stars where the great lion trampled on the head of the great sea serpent. Sailors must know the stars to guide them in their journeys. But never had I met a sailor who could read a heavenly message in the stars. He told me that out of King David's line would come a messianic king who would trample on the enemy at the end of time. I knew in my heart it was true. You are a very special people with a God who rules over all in the heavenlies. He is the Most High." Makeda continued, "I have always taught my warriors that the battle was more than physical. I knew it was in strength of mind, not to falter under pressure. But I knew there was a spiritual element that the world does not really understand. When the trading sailor told me about how your King David fought wars by praying to His God to help him, it answered all my questions in one moment. You see, I had been seeking for a long time. I entertained many guests in my country and asked about their lands and traditions and what I could learn from them. But I knew there was something unique in what the sailor from Israel told me. It was more than a myth or folk story because something in my spirit rang real to me. I used to stir up my warriors with stories of past battles we won, and myths of God's helping us win battles. But it was to lift their spirits and I did not really believe all of what I was saying. I knew there must be more."

"Since I learned to read, I have searched the scriptures for battle cries," Shulamit added, "there is truth in stirring up minds for battle, but the power of God must be there. That is why I love the psalms of King David for battles. He always prayed and sought the Lord before he did battle."

"Solomon's psalms are great too."

"Yes, about love and peace, which we need for everyday life, but when it comes to war, and stirring yourself, there is nothing like a battle cry. I will show you Deborah's psalm and Miriam leading worship after the Israelites crossed through the Red Sea. Every memorable event needs a psalm to keep the memory alive."

"Even in my far-off country," Makeda admitted, "we heard about Israelites crossing through the Red Sea. I had many questions to ask Solomon, and he answered them in confirmation to the sailor's faith. Now as I sing with you, I know this song is more than just a song; it is real worship of a real God. True recognition of a Father looking after His children, an amazing God you can really love."

Shulamit thought, *Adonai is really speaking into this woman's heart, as she has just proclaimed the next verse of the song. It is amazing how the Lord speaks to us, and we find immediate confirmation.* She went on to sing the final verses of the song.

> *Because he has set his love upon me, therefore I will deliver him*
> *I will set him on high because he has known My name*
> *He shall call upon Me, and I will answer him*
> *I will be with him in trouble; I will deliver him and honor him*
> *With long life I will satisfy him and show him my salvation*

This time Shulamit spoke first. "When Solomon asked me to worship with you, I feared that he was asking the impossible. I have found most of the ruling leaders of the world to be interested in king Solomon's gift for wisdom in ruling, building, animals, medicine, or anything else. Rarely are they interested in the spiritual side behind the anointing. But you are rare, you truly seek the Wisdom of God."

"I appreciate you saying that. You are a queen with the wisdom to perceive the hearts of people. The more I get to know you, the more I can see why you are Solomon's favored bride."

"I have had to entertain many visitors in the royal court, and I have met none like you. You have shown me that a woman can really rule. You have overturned all the lies I have ever heard about women being too weak to rule. But in our history in Israel, we have some strong women in scripture from time to time."

"You should be in the scriptures too, your highness."

"Me? Do you realize that by having only girls, I will never be Queen Mother?"

"But it seems to me you *are* a Queen Mother. Even now. You are the woman Solomon loves, the bride who captured his heart. How many songs have you already written together? I believe your story will be captured in a song that will inspire lovers for generations to come. You are too special to be forgotten."

Shulamit sat there in utter amazement of the words spoken out of the wise queen's mouth. "I will remember the words you just gave me always," Shulamit replied. "I will keep them within my heart." As she thought on this, other thoughts came into her mind that she could not hold back, "You know the court keeps chronicles of all the significant events within the kingdom. I'm sure you will be remembered as a great queen who came from the ends of the earth to learn the wisdom of our king and God."

"I humbly accept your words," Makeda said. Then she added, "I believe that one of your granddaughters is going to sail off to foreign lands, and out of her will come powerful queens who will rule great nations."

"I will remember that, too. But right now, I cannot see how anyone would want to leave our country and go off to foreign lands."

"History is full of amazing turns," Makeda said. "Something about being around you stirs prophecy within me."

"God's presence," Shulamit said. "I feel him here, worship brings *Adonai* and his angels near." Shulamit added to the thought of ruling nations. "You know, Solomon is writing and putting together his book of proverbs and wisdom to teach his princes and governors. The one proverb that speaks to me of the greatness in a nation is, 'Righteousness exalts a nation, but sin is a disgrace to any people.' Moses gave commandments in the end of his writings. 'Now it shall come to pass, if you diligently obey the voice of the Lord your God, to observe carefully all His commandments which I command you today, that the Lord your God will set you high above all nations of the earth.'" Shulamit ushered her daughters out of the rooms, and then continued. "I see in you, Queen Makeda, a woman with spiritual discernment. It has taken me years to even impart to those who worship with me to reach the point where you are today.

"I am honored, your highness."

"The worshipping queens found the dance to be fun and joyful, but I found it more important that they understood the great source behind the songs we danced too. Some were quick to learn. Others will perhaps never really get it. So, I keep an inner circle of worshippers who uphold the spiritual side, and of course the others are caught up in the presence brought on by the true worshippers."

"It is all about heart."

"Yes. There must be heart in real worship. You see, in the last verses of the psalm of David, 'Because he has set his love upon me, therefore will I deliver him, I will set him on high, because he has known My name.' God is talking about those with real heart, who love Him and open their hearts to him. It is like we walk into His heart, and He walks into ours, and we become one."

"Do you mean, like in a marriage?"

"Very much so," Shulamit said, smiling. "But it is a marriage of hearts and spirits. Of course, when having a baby, always claim the 'I will deliver him' part."

"So, we are sisters in heart," Makeda laughed.

"Yes, we are sisters," Shulamit said. "We shall worship as sisters," Servants left to bring more musicians to her quarters. They sensed that Shulamit would move into deep dance and worship and wanted to be ready.

"May we sing the song some more so I can remember it deep within my heart?"

"We shall sing this song as many times as you like. And I will teach you dance steps. My daughters will join in and afterwards I will have a scribe write out a scroll of the song for you." She motioned the servants to retrieve Basemath and Taphath.

They sang the song over and over, dancing until they were lost in the worship. Shulamit knew it was a rare thing when a song touches the spirit so deeply that it can be sung repeatedly until you are completely lost in it while dancing. They were so caught up in their simple whirling circles around each other, when other musicians played, they were unaware. Finally, they stopped to pause for breath. In the pause between the songs Shulamit picked up her harp and played a spontaneous song later named, *Let us Dance Together.*

.

Let us dance together
May the heart of the king go with you
As you return to your land
May you rule as a queen
And not as a man
May you nurture the heart of your people
As only a woman can

Come sister
Let us rejoice together
As queen to queen take my hand
As queen to queen take my hand
May the joy of our shared wisdom
Bless the love in our hearts
For our beloved king
Come sister
Take my hand
Let us sing

Let us praise our King in the Heavens
Who brings hearts into unity
Our Great King of the universe
Whose love sets all nations free
Come my sister and queen
Dance and rejoice with me
That the joy we share together
Will hold our bond together
Till we meet in eternity

Come my sister and queen
Dance and rejoice with me

Dance and rejoice with me
Dance and rejoice with me

The musicians caught the tune and played the song so Shulamit could get up and dance with Makeda freely. Steps came spontaneously for them both. Makeda was the quickest learner Shulamit had ever met. *What a joy* she thought.

"Indeed, you write songs spontaneously," Makeda said. "It is as I have heard."

"I guess the Lord answers your prayers," replied Shulamit. "It has been a while since I have written a song spontaneously. It's nice to know the gift is still there." Shulamit laughed and Makeda joined her.

"I heard you were fun!" They laughed some more.

The two queens spent a few more days together, telling each other stories of their lives. Each was quite different, but Shulamit was beginning to find that the heart of God was a very big heart. It could bring many people together, enlarging people's hearts to love one another.

Makeda finally confessed what Shulamit already suspected when the queen drank the milk instead of the wine offered. Solomon and Makeda had become lovers and she became with child. He wanted to marry, which made Shulamit less sad than she thought she would be. But Makeda refused, as she had her own country to rule. Makeda confided that she was going to take the Hebrew God back to her country. If the queen had Solomon's son, he would be the next ruler in her country.

Meanwhile, Taphath asked her father Solomon, over and over, until he finally broke down and allowed Makeda to teach her how to jump horses. Solomon made sure his master of horses was closely overseeing. Taphath had a natural gift with animals, just as Solomon had. She was even better than many of the princes. *Only God will know where this will lead*, Shulamit wondered in her heart as she watched.

When Makeda finally left Israel, Solomon sent priests, musicians, and a copy of the Torah with her. He gave the queen everything to permit her country to continue to worship the God of Israel. Trade agreements were set indefinitely.

Makeda's last words to Queen Shulamit were to renew her wedding vows with her king. "Take him back to the mountains where you first met. Swim with him in the secret place, as you always wanted to before you married. Enjoy the fruit of the vine and seal your vows within each other's hearts."

30 SET ME AS A SEAL UPON YOUR HEART

While Solomon was escorting the Queen of Sheba out of the country, Shulamit was recording her own adventure with the queen on parchment. When she was done writing, she sighed with a deep feeling of accomplishment. Shulamit had no idea of the destiny her Uncle Jether had spoken when he suggested she be a worship warrior. Nothing her great *YHWH* could do ceased to amaze her.

Life seemed to have come full cycle as she prepared for a journey home. After all this time, she would visit the place she and her shepherd king met. But before that, Shulamit carefully prepared herself for her visit with the king as he returned from his recent travel. She took a multicolored silk scarf and centered it on the back of her neck, crisscrossing it. It rose and fell over her breasts as she tied it behind her back. Next, she took a long fringe belt, also multicolored, and placed it around her lower waist and hips. A softly woven robe of white finished her look as the fringes fell to below her knees underneath.

When Solomon arrived, she welcomed him with a deep kiss and a glass of wine. Shulamit had him sit down in a comfortable chair as she walked in front of him and began to hum. As she did, she slid her robe to the floor, displaying her fringed coverings. She began a new love song as she swayed her hips back and forth and Solomon couldn't help but be entranced by her performance. While moving her ankles up and down to accentuate the sway of her hips and singing,

My king has my heart
His desire is toward me
I am sealed in his heart
Heaven holds the key
And keeps us as one
Your heart within me

And we flow
Together we flow
We move
Like a life-giving river

And we flow

The Worshipper and the King

Together we flow
Full of love
As we flow on forever

I am yours
You are mine
We sway in the flow
Gently dancing
Through the paths
By the way the winds blow

Pride, amazement, and delight played across Solomon's face as he watched. His love for her never ceased to surprise him. She moved and danced, no longer the shy virgin who looked to him for every sign of flowing with him. Now, she was a woman initiating their love making with her kisses. She whispered, almost purring each phrase, as she started to kiss his forehead, cheeks, lips, and neck.

This kiss is for your love for me
This kiss is for my love for you

This kiss is for my deep thankfulness
This kiss is for your loving heart

When she reached his neck, she felt a new song was coming. Still kissing, she let the new song rise from her like water from a fountain:

The king's garden is always in bloom
His desire is always toward me
He's always sending His kisses of love
Forever describing my beauty

I'm lost in the love of my king
His tender love overwhelms me
He's a river flowing within my soul
As he whispers how much he loves me

As a flower in His garden, I bloom
Because of the way He cares for me
He gathers his flower in His hands
And says I'm his treasure and glory

I'm lost in His garden of love

322

He forever tells me I'm lovely
I'm sealed in his heart forever

As so many times in their years together, Solomon reached the point where he could no longer resist his wife. Taking her hand, he rose and led her to the bed. They moved together with sheer joy. Soon, they were loving softly, sweetly, and passionately.

When Solomon finally descended from their mountain top experience, he asked Shulamit, "Where did you learn to dance like that?"

"My ladies care for me," Shulamit said. "They said it is a special dance saved for the wedding night or special occasions."

"Oh," he said as he leaned toward her, "What special occasion is this?"

"My king, my beloved, I long to know you as my shepherd again; the way we knew each other out in the countryside where we first met. I long to go forth to the field, and lodge in the villages, get up early to the vineyards and see if the vine has budded. The mandrakes give off a fragrance at the gates. I seek pleasant fruits, all manner, new and old, which I have yet to experience with you." Shulamit leaned forward as well. She had become excited for her husband once again. "I long to enjoy pleasures we could not experience before we were married. I want to take you to my secret place by the hidden lake."

"Ah," Solomon said. "Your secret place."

"I want to swim with you and dive off the rocks," Shulamit expressed passionately. She kissed her husband. "We can rest under the waterfall and discover all the pleasure of nature."

Thoughts of their first meeting came to the king's mind, just like it was yesterday. He looked at his love and remembered the young girl who danced with him in the hills. She had matured in childbirth, but he saw her youth. She looked like she did when they first met.

"Where did the time go?" Solomon asked. "I see the beautiful mountains where I first saw your face. And I see your lovely face will always be the same in my eyes. Yes, let us go my love. It is time."

"The summer is almost upon us," said Shulamit dreamily. "It will be a great time to go on such an adventure and have a family reunion.

"We shall travel slowly through the countryside and be as you wished—the ordinary shepherd and shepherdess enjoying the local people and scenery as we go."

Shulamit laughed, "And how will Basemath and Taphath jump their horses if they are mere shepherd children?"

Solomon laughed, "Our daughters can come with Nathan and Miriam. We need some alone time to celebrate our betrothal anniversary with your family in the country." Solomon kissed Shulamit, and their plans drifted for a while.

Later, Shulamit packed presents to fill trunks. They would travel with Miriam and Nathan in the wagons. There were so many gifts she wanted to share. Shulamit packed spices from the East, perfume, soft quilts made with feathers, cotton towels, cloth, and linen. She knew her family would never spend money on such things.

Early the next morning, Solomon dropped off some clothing for a common woman for Shulamit to dress in disguise. She smiled at him before he left, then quickly dressed, packing her royal clothing and a picnic for their trip. She met Solomon at the back entrance of the palace courtyard. Their donkey was quickly packed by the servants and soon, they were ready to go. Solomon helped her mount a calm looking donkey and then jumped on his own. He instructed her not to talk until they were out of the gates of Jerusalem and on the road.

Shulamit realized with a smile that she and Solomon had done this, many times.

Getting out unnoticed was not easy.

Riding down the road Solomon looked toward his wife and let her know it was safe to talk. They were protected with soldiers dressed as shepherds on pack mules behind them.

"How do you like your new clothes?" He laughed.

"Comfortable enough," Shulamit answered, "But it has been a while since I rode on a donkey."

"After learning to ride a horse, this is like going back to being the simple country girl again don't you think?" Solomon smiled. "The morning is cool and a good time to keep riding."

"Yes, let's ride until the summer heat comes out."

"Then we can look for a forest of trees to hide and rest in," Solomon said.

"Is that all we are going to do?"

"You tease?" Solomon said, his grin widening.

"Kick in your heals and see if you can make the donkey move a little faster."

With a little pressure from Solomon's thighs, the donkey took off at a speed which startled Shulamit. It made her laugh as they galloped a short while down the road a while. The donkey slowed down again as they started up a hill. From the top of the hill, they looked out over a vast valley. People picking the fruit off the trees that scented the air. Apple trees were in bloom along with citrons and pomegranate. Men shook the olive trees making the olives fall from the trees and land on nets while women were filling their baskets.

It was a busy season.

As Solomon and Shulamit enjoyed the scenery, they discussed how their life had changed from when they first met.

"I'm looking forward to being back in the hills where I first met you," Solomon said, sighing. "I should have known such beautiful hills would create beautiful women, and you were the surprise, and prize of my lifetime."

"I knew God would answer my prayer. But He has answered so much more than I can ever ask or think." Shulamit suddenly burst into Solomon's song about the little hills.

The little hills rejoice on every side
They should for joy they also sing
They shout for joy they also sing
They shout for joy they also sing

They laughed. And then Solomon said, "I will sing you one of the first songs I wrote when I first saw you. He began to sing."

I brought you out of the harvest fields
Where you worked hard for me

I saw your heart in the harvest field
You gave your all for me

And when you discovered my love
You labored as unto me
I saw your heart in the harvest field
You labored in love for me

You knew my words from a distance
You sang my words to me
You put your heart into worship
As you danced before me

I love your soul in worship
I'm coming closer to you
I've been watching your outflow
And I like what you do

Now I am coming to visit you
And draw you closer to me
I'll visit you in your dreams and your song
I want you to dance with me

I've watched you from a distance
And I take pleasure in you
When the time is right, I'll reveal myself
And make a queen out of you

I'm pouring my grace upon you
I am grooming you
My beautiful maiden who works in the field
I'm already in love with you.

While Solomon was singing, the road became blocked by a shepherd leading a large herd of sheep across the road. They were so lost in their own world, neither Solomon nor Shulamit noticed riders on the roadside beside them.

"That song from your heart so reminds me of our Heavenly Father singing through you," Shulamit said.

"After the High Priest told me He was sure Adonai had chosen you, I knew my heart was in touch with His when I wrote that song. To be sure, behind many inspired songs is the spirit of prophecy."

"Even love songs," Shulamit added.

"Especially love songs." Solomon looked over to her with loving eyes and smiled.

They continued enjoying each other's company and soon the roads cleared. Once again, they urged the donkeys to a slightly faster pace. While riding, Shulamit began another song,

My shepherd-king plucked his harp
The mountains begin to sing
Striking my heart like a cymbal
With uncontrolled pulsing
And music carried on wings of wind
Your voice was drawing me in

I ran to the sound of your voice
I was running after a call
Your voice led me to jump and leap
Even over a wall
I was lost in your melody
And my heart wanted it all

I closed my eyes to worship
Desiring to take your song in

Your music, your words, your voice
Within me was transforming
When I opened my eyes at last
I met my shepherd-king

Dressed in rugged clothes
You could not hide from me
Glorious majesty
Opened my eyes to see
The treasure that flowed from you
Only a king could be

At the voice of my shepherd-king,
The little hills danced for joy
A door was opened to heaven
That made the cymbals ring
Let me hear your voice again
Make my mountain sing

Oh, let me hear your voice again
Make my mountain sing
You make my mountain sing!

"You still call me your shepherd king, after all these years. But what is a king but a glorified shepherd."

They laughed and continued singing till they came to the top of a hill where they could see a village marketplace.

"Look," Shulamit said, "There's a marketplace, can we stop and rest and give water to the donkeys?"

"Women love marketplaces," Solomon said, "Even when they have everything they need at home." Shulamit playfully swatted the air in his direction and Solomon laughed. "Of course, it will be fun to talk with the village people."

Shulamit walked through the streets where shopkeepers were displaying their wares. She commented to Solomon that she didn't remember so many pots and pans on display in marketplaces before. Solomon reminded her that the southern Israel and Edom mined the copper and iron. And Ezion Geber provided much of the smelted bronze used in the Temple, but now metals were being used for household items of Israel.

Shulamit remembered meeting merchants coming from the South who were supplying copper, bronze, and other metals. "I need to get out more Solomon. I have been missing things."

327

"The palaces near the sea, and in Lebanon are coming along. Soon enough, you and my wives will be able to stay there during Jerusalem's hot days of summer. I promise you will be out more, but you must be protected everywhere you go."

Shulamit continued walking through the marketplace with Solomon, enjoying herself to the fullest. When Shulamit walked over to a young girl displaying her work from the loom, the girl held out a colorful blanket.

"You have done lovely work," Shulamit complimented, "How much do you ask?" The girl named a price and Solomon took several small coins from his purse. He gave her more than she asked, and when she saw how much she had, the girls face lit up. Shulamit asked the girl about her life and enjoyed hearing about how she had learned so well. Solomon encouraged her to keep developing her skill. Joy erupted from the maiden as she spoke how she liked to dream up pictures to create on looms. Over time it helped her learn how to manipulate the threads better.

"Keep dreaming," Shulamit exhorted. "We are only as great as our dreams." Shulamit realized that she was repeating what she had heard from Solomon several times. *He really has become a part of me. Even my words reflect his love and teaching.*

About this time, a man walked up to Solomon and said, "Excuse me sir, I passed you on the road while you were singing, and I remember your words. You talked about the maiden who worked in the harvest and how you were going to make a queen out of her. Can you tell me how you could accomplish that?

Solomon looked at the man and asked, "Are you married?" The man nodded. "Are you a father?" Once again, the man nodded. "Then," Solomon said, "you are the king of your family, and your wife is your queen. Every day when you wake up, look at your wife and tell her how beautiful she is, and how much she means to you. You watch, she will become what you declare her to be. What you see and say has power.

The man laughed. "That simple? I'll do it."

They continued, buying food from the vendors as they walked. The market was flooded with fresh produce from the season, reminding Shulamit of her childhood. She smiled, remembering how much fun it was when her father took her to the market. Tasting new foods, seeing the items for sale, helping him haggle—all precious memories. Shulamit considered the new spices from the East, now being planted in Israel. It made the food (and air) more flavorful. That too was a sign of prosperous times.

Solomon and Shulamit asked people about the harvest and life in the village. The people were all happy, and their lives were becoming more enriched because of the peace and prosperity in the land. Many were grateful for the safety of the widened roads. It seemed as if they were at the market for such a long time, but it was over quickly, and the heat of the day warned of it's coming.

With the animals well rested and watered, it was time to continue. Shulamit placed the blanket she bought from the young girl atop her own mount. Solomon helped her climb on the donkey again and they continued their journey.

"So," Shulamit said, "your strategy to make me into a queen was to tell me how beautiful I was every day?"

Solomon laughed. "I wondered how long it would take for you to ask about that."

"It was on my mind to ask you as soon as you said it."

Solomon laughed. "It is very important that we are affirmed in our identity before we can walk into our destiny." Shulamit smiled. "My mother was well aware of all the enemies in the court fighting to become the next king. She told me every day that I was born to become king, no matter what the rest of the palace was doing. My mother always built me up, along with my brothers. We were a team.

"Yes, Bathsheba unifies and supports the people she loves," said Shulamit thinking back over her relationship with the Queen Mother.

"Do you remember when we first met? I referred to you as a mare in Pharoah's army leading the other horses into war."

"I do. And I thought about that when I wrote my story about meeting the warrior queen. I remembered my Uncle Jether prophesying to my father that I could not go to war as a man. He said I could be a worship warrior with my music, dancing, and my love for the psalms. And I also remember your vision. Those prophecies set my life of worship into motion step by step, culminating with the Queen of Sheba and I worshipping together."

"Yes," Solomon said. "As she left, the queen said you were the greatest worshipper she ever encountered. She said she did not know it could be possible to fight a battle as strongly in the spirit as in live combat."

"She expressed that to me as well."

"When a great warrior such as the Queen of Sheba meets a great spiritual worship warrior, they realize they have met an equal."

"That makes sense," said Shulamit, humbled. "I felt that."

"That is why, when she asked if she might worship with you, I wanted you to pursue her request. I wanted you to realize your destiny as the worshipping warrior-queen you are." Bringing their pace to a near halt, Solomon looked at Shulamit and said, "I also wanted you to realize why I chose you as both my bride and my own spiritual protector."

Tears came down his beloved's eyes. The sudden insight was overwhelming.

While they were talking, the heat of the day rested on the land like a heavy wool coat. But the heat wasn't so unbearable that they couldn't look for a reprieve. Ahead where the road curved, they saw a small forest of oak, almond, and willow trees. Beyond that a stream glinted. Solomon directed his group toward the water, sending his guards toward a private area by the stream. He helped his beloved bride dismount, grabbing her newly purchased blanket and a few wineskins. They left the donkeys with the guards.

Shulamit and her husband stepped into the stream to cool themselves off, then found a hidden place under a large willow tree. Throwing the blanket down on the ground Solomon said, "I have been waiting for this all day," as he grabbed his love and pulled her down on him. One kiss ignited a burst of passion between them.

Afterwards, they lay beside each other exhausted.

Shulamit lay beside him she and whispered, "Set me as a seal upon your heart, and a seal upon your arm; for love is as strong as death. Jealousy is cruel as the grave; its flames are flames of fire, a most vehement flame. Many waters cannot quench love, nor can the floods drown it. If a man would give for love all the wealth of his house, it would be utterly despised."

Solomon lay there, dazed by her poetry. After a moment, he said, "Those are the most beautiful words you have ever spoken to me. Help me repeat them back to you as vows we make to each other."

They repeated the words,

Set me as a seal upon your heart
As a seal upon your arm
For love is strong as death

Jealousy as cruel as the grave
Its flames are flames of fire
A most vehement flame

Many waters cannot quench love
Nor can the floods drown it
If a man would give for love
All the wealth of his house
It would be utterly despised

Solomon sang the words. And they sang it back and forth to each other until the melody and words stuck; and they fell back to sleep in each other's arms.

After the heat of the day passed, they mounted their donkeys as they continued singing their new vows. They reached a country inn just before dark and had a simple dinner with wine under the stars before they retired early.

They next morning they were up before dawn for the long journey ahead—the final stretch of the way up into the hills.

Solomon said, "If we wish to reach your village by nightfall, we can't stop today, except to rest the donkeys. But yesterday was incredible."

Shulamit couldn't help but smile at her beloved. "Our love is beyond words."

The happy travelers enjoyed the beautiful green scenery before them as they traveled the mountain road.

They saw a few young stags leaping in the hills. "There you are my beloved," Shulamit said as she pointed to them. "Strong, virile, and full of grace and dance."

Solomon laughed. "Only a girl who grew up in the country can appreciate such qualities."

"Only a girl who received inspiration to dance by watching *YHWH's* graceful creatures skip and jump in nature."

"The same country girl," her beloved said, "pleads for me to return quickly like a gazelle and a young stag upon the mountain of spices when I have to go on a long journey."

"Yes, that same lover, longing to dance with her beloved."

They laughed as the smell of lavender and white lilies scattered across the grassy fields created a charming country scent. Shulamit was always fond of crushed leaves on the ground, and the pine trees standing like sentinels opened her heart.

Through teary eyes, she said, "We have been too long away." She was coming home.

"Yes, my Love, we have been long away, but has been an amazing life journey. Many great things have been accomplished for our country, and I could never have done it without you. Call some of your time away from your family a sacrifice but knowing what you left home to accomplish makes going home all that much greater."

Overcome by tears, Shulamit said, "My heart has been truly touched at this moment."

The day of travel seemed to pass quickly, despite the heat, and the sun had gone down as they rounded the last turn of the mountain in the direction of her village. Even with only starlight to guide them, the sound of water splashing down the streams and all the familiar smells of grasses and spicy pine-scented mountain air told her she was home. When the house came into sight, she jumped off her donkey and urged Solomon to walk with her hand in hand to the door.

Her mother and Rebecca ran out and greeted them, full of joy and shouting. "Who is this," cried her mother, "coming out of the wilderness leaning upon her beloved?" They heartily embraced, sobbing joyfully into each other's arms.

"It has been so long Mama; your hair has turned grey," Shulamit said, touching her head. "And Rebecca! How do you still look the same even after all those children you have been having?"

"Mother Miriam, you look lovely," Solomon said.

"Well, come on in," she cried, waving her arms to direct them inside. "You must be tired and hungry after your journey!"

Shulamit watched her mother's expression bend in confusion. She appeared surprised that Shulamit and Solomon were alone. "The children will be coming in the next few days with Miriam and Nathan," Shulamit said, in response to her mother's concerned face. "We just needed a little time alone." She looked lovingly at her husband.

"Your brothers are sleeping in sukkots out at the harvest site. We will see them tomorrow. Come to the table and have a repose. We have a warm meal for you."

Shulamit walked briefly around her country home, noting many changes before she sat down. Many large new rooms had been built along the side of the house, and the floor was now covered in tile. A new stable had been built, able to house more sheep and store grain. The area for cooking had been expanded, and a sizeable table was now placed in the dining area ready to seat a large party. Solomon's quick eye observed everything as well, but he said nothing.

As Shulamit noted the changes, her mother said, "Solomon's wedding gifts, and your help, made much of this possible."

Rebecca came into the room with her two sons. Shulamit and Solomon embraced them all. She told Shulamit, "My three older sons were helping Joshua in the harvest, and Caleb's two younger sons helped with chores at home today."

"Oh Mama," Shulamit said, "You have been blessed. You have worked so hard for many years; keeping it all together after father died. But look at all the Lord has done."

Mama Miriam sang, "The Lord has done great things for us whereof we are glad."

"This," pointing toward her mother, "is where I learned to worship," Shulamit explained to Solomon, who laughed to himself.

***

After eating hot bread and drinking warm goat's milk the next morning, Shulamit explained to Mama that she wanted to take Solomon to her secret place to bathe. Her mother gave a knowing smile and began to prepare a bag with cheese and bread.

Carrying the harp, a wineskin, and the bag from Mother Miriam, Solomon and his wife raced up the hill. At her special spot by the lake, they threw down their belongings. Shulamit pulled Solomon with her, anxious to show him where she dove into the lake.

The water was so refreshing, even in the morning. The king and queen were even more grateful to plunge in the cool water during this, the hottest season of the year. They swam under the small waterfall. Water poured over their heads as they leaned on the rocks, kissing, and embracing each other. This was another of those promises of new and old she made to Solomon.

"I have dreamed of doing this with you since we first met, before we married," Shulamit said, smoothing her hair back.

"You are never without surprises."

"After riding on a donkey for days, it makes this moment even more special. Do you want to see where Rebecca and I dove into the water now?" Shulamit didn't wait for his answer before she started climbing up the rocks by the waterfall. She reached a high bolder and took a great leap into the water.

Solomon followed her without hesitation. When he reached the top, he jumped quickly. He had never jumped from a rock so high, but he would not show himself uncourageous. He was king. He believed himself to be from the same tribe as the Lion of the Tribe of Judah, so he had to be lionhearted. Once he hit the water, he sank deep. Once he came up, he wanted to climb the high rock and jump again. And again. Each time, it became easier. By the third time he jumped, there was no more thought of fear. *Lord, this wife you have given me*, he thought.

After several hours, they climbed out of the river, dried themselves on the rocks, and walked down to the apple tree. Solomon grabbed his harp and played a simple melody he made to go with his love's words.

Set me as a seal upon your heart
As a seal upon your arm
For love is as strong as death
Jealousy as cruel as the grave
Its flames are flames of fire
A most vehement flame

Many waters cannot quench love
Nor can the floods drown it
If a man would give for love
All the wealth of his house
It would be utterly despised

They sang their secret vows to each other, once again sealing them into their hearts.

"Our love is alive," Solomon said, "As long as we are continually writing new songs to one another, I believe God is in our midst. I am going to take our love story and songs and combine them into one long song, a love song, perhaps my greatest song."

He is a true king, Shulamit thought. *They always own what they know will be good. And he is right. He can take my story and make it into a better song than I can. If people believe it came from a king, they will be more willing to listen then if it came from a woman, even a queen. He will put his stamp of authority upon it.*

"That is exciting, Solomon."

"It will be my gift to you, for being my beloved for all these years."

After a moment, Solomon suggested Shulamit go back and help Mother Miriam unpack the gifts that had been taken off the donkeys. "I need to go and check on my soldiers."

Off she went, and off he went, but not just to check on his soldiers. Solomon wanted some time alone to write a song. The melody and the words flowed faster than he could write. Soon there was a song one, song two, song three, and he wrote on the parchment scroll as fast as his fingers could write.

A strong, majestic tune came, and he wrote a wedding song. Then another one came about the bride looking for her husband throughout the city at night. He wrote a ballad about the daughters of Zion asking what was so great about her lover. She described him in great glory, and he saw her glory in a dance of two camps. Nothing could slow the song describing a mature bride as Solomon wrote song six. Solomon came full cycle as he wrote about how he and his bride traveled the wilderness to return to her family for a grand reunion.

At last, Solomon wrote about the bride begging him to return "dancing upon the hills and mountains" like when they first met. As he stopped, he realized the day was over and the sun was about to sink behind the hill. It seemed as if he had only been writing for minutes, and he could not imagine where the time went.

He rolled up his scroll and headed down the hill. The family had just gathered around the table as he arrived. Joining them, he greeted them, announcing that he had written a song and would be happy to sing it after the children were in bed.

The dinner was a very joyful time of catching up with each other's stories.

Joshua said, "My wife, Rebecca, is a very fruitful vine. It seems every year she brings forth another child."

Solomon raised his cup of cheer, "The fruit of the womb is your reward. Let's cheer! Any day now, you will meet my daughters, and we can celebrate some more. We have a quiver full!"

Caleb announced, "The harvests have been full to overflowing, and we have more than enough to fill our family."

Solomon cheered again. "*Adonai* has crowned the years with his goodness. Let's shout for joy and also sing."

The dinner was full of joy and gladness.

Eventually, the ladies put their children to bed while the men talked. Shulamit helped her mother clean up, and soon all the adults returned to the table for fellowship. Joshua, moving Solomon to the head of the table by Shulamit, said, "We would like to hear your song now."

Solomon grabbed his scroll and rolled it out on the table. "Just in case I forget some of the words," he said as he grabbed his harp and began to sing. "Let him kiss me with the kisses of his mouth..." The heart of everyone was moved. They could hardly take a breath as Solomon sang through every verse.

Shulamit sat, spellbound by her husband's song. *Solomon has kept his promise to put music to our story. He seems to have remembered everything of importance. I absolutely love this. It is the most beautiful song I have ever heard.* She praised the Lord as she listened.

Solomon ended his song and there was not a tearless eye in the room. Such overpowering love flowed through the air. God's presence was so strong, no one dared move, or speak. It took several minutes before Joshua broke the silence by clapping his hands together. "Love like this will never be forgotten," he shouted over the clapping.

Shulamit just cried. "This song is so beautiful," she said to Solomon as he beamed. "It is our song. You have not forgotten anything. Everything we spoke of on the way here you put in the song, and more. You have remembered all the important events of our lives, even my prophetic dreams. This song is from God. I will treasure it as long as I live. It is the greatest gift you have ever given me."

"And perhaps to all lovers," Caleb said.

"Sing it again," Mama said. "Only this time, tell the ladies when to sing their part. And let the men join in Solomon's part."

And so, they sang, each one joining in at appropriate parts. Mama Miriam played the flute when needed, and Joshua added some trumpets in the wedding song. Shulamit added tambourine beats."

After they were done, Mama Miriam said, "Your father David brought us many songs to worship to, but he never wrote a love song like this. This song is going to reach hearts that desire love for many generations." The children knew, their mother's words were powerful and prophetic.

They all retired joyfully with love on their hearts that evening. The next morning the men, including Solomon, went out to the vineyards to pick the remaining grape harvest. Shulamit stayed with her mother and sisters, and they baked bread and raisin cakes. Before it got too hot, they milked the goats and made cheese. They also dug vegetables from the garden to prepare for another feast.

Ima Miriam and Shulamit took some private time together while gathering vegetables. "That love song Solomon wrote was beautiful. I was concerned about you when you went to the palace and all you would be taking on. But I knew you were following your heart. Now I can see that God has surely been with you and blessed you. You have grown into a strong woman, beloved wife, and a real queen. I'm proud of you my dear."

"Thank you, Mama. You set the example," Shulamit confessed. "Remember when I said I wanted what you and Papa had. Real love. The Lord gave it to me. Solomon has been so kind and supportive of me every step of the way. His love made everything possible."

"You were made for each other," Mama declared. "I remember as a child you were always fun loving, liking to dance and sing, always dreaming, and always challenging your brothers," she chided. "You were so ready to sing or write a new song. It still amazes me that, as your mother, I know you are still that same person, despite living in a palace and bearing responsibility for supporting your king. You still have your youthful spirit regardless of a very different life."

"I will always be from the mountains. On the way here Solomon said that a king is just a glorified shepherd. I'm still a shepherdess, mom. Only now with a bunch more people who need to be loved and cared for. When I first went to the palace and was around a bunch of women who grew up on royal courts, and I felt out of place. I soon learned that I had an advantage from all I learned growing up in the country. All that I learned from you and Papa prepared me for who I am today. That is why I want my girls to come and see what life is like in the country." Speaking of her girls, Shulamit heard the shouts of Taphath and Basement and ran out to greet them. When Shulamit saw her little Shira toddling in, barely holding her balance, she realized how much she adored her. She ran to Shira and scooped her up. "How was your trip?" she asked her sister Miriam.

"The children were curious, and we had to stop and look at everything, But Nathan is such a patient man, and he is great with children."

Their son Mattathiah, now seven years old, ran up to Shulamit and she hugged him while holding Shira.

"Mattathiah, is so loving. I know he has a special call in the royal line, but I don't know what."

Nathan entered, walking over to Mama Miriam, who was now completely absorbed in her grandchildren, hugging each of them intensely.

She called out to the children, "Your father is out helping your uncles pick grapes if you wish to join him." To her son-in-law she said, "Nathan can you take them?"

"Yes, yes, yes!" they shouted. Grabbing his hands, they began to pull him out of the house and up the hill." The noise did not settle down until the girls were quite a way away.

Shulamit sat down with little Shira, hugging her, and telling her how much she loved her until she was calm and responded to her grandmama reaching out to her. "These lovely moments are ones we want to capture in our minds and never forget," Shulamit said.

That evening, the men returned carrying baskets of grapes. Taphath and Basemath were hanging on their father. The bottom of their skirts stained with grape juice. Before Shulamit could ask what happened; Solomon said, "They insisted on tromping on grapes in the winepress."

Joshua said, "For pampered palace girls from the city, they know how to work."

"Thank you, Uncle Joshua," Basemath said.

Rebecca set out a large copper bath pan, calling out, "Wash up everyone. The food will be ready soon."

The evening meal was a very noisy occasion now that the children had arrived. They were down at one end of the long table except Shira, who sat in Shulamit's lap. Smiling and spilling food all over her, Shira laughed as Shulamit helped her eat. Solomon sat next to her and Joshua at the other end of the table. Shulamit loved to see how much her beloved enjoyed being a part of her family. Here, Solomon was not a king. He was a father, a brother, and a husband, and could speak from his heart without having to constantly weigh his thoughts.

The next few days were full of activity. Shulamit's elder daughters joined their cousins dashing all over the farm. They taught Basemath and Taphath how to milk goats and lead the sheep out into the field. The two princesses caught turtles in the nearby ponds and jumped around on the stacks of hay until their hair was covered with straw.

In the heat of the day, the men took Basemath and Taphath to the large pond and they could swim well. But Solomon did not think they swam well enough to jump off the high rock the way their rough and tumble cousins did.

In the evenings, the family sang and danced. Basemath and Taphath were happy to show off their dancing skills with their aunts and mama. Their cousins enjoyed watching them dance. And later in the night, when the children were in bed, Solomon sang his new love song of all love songs so Miriam and Nathan could hear it. Naturally, they both loved the song, feeling the deep love of Solomon for his Shulamit. But they also felt the love of God singing through him for his bride, and to them individually.

"I feel as though you are singing to me too," Miriam said. It's a love song that will appeal to lovers. Let's sing it again."

They sang it repeatedly, each night at dinner. Hearts opened, overflowing to each other as they sang of setting the seal on each other's hearts.

Mama Miriam sat joyfully watching the happiness in her children's lives.

Eventually, when Solomon announced that they would be returning to Jerusalem before them because of needed business, Basemath and Taphath reminded him of his promise to them. The two were excited to see the place where Solomon and their mother met and fell in love.

"We will have a picnic on the hill by the apple trees, over by your mother's secret place." He laughed, "Which is not so secret as everyone knows where it is."

A few days later, they sat out on the grassy hill. Savory lamb sat roasting on a pit. Sitting on blankets thrown on the ground, the adults drank sweet wine. There was grape juice for the kids. The warm scent of fresh bread, and salads and fruits made the place feel warm and comfortable.

Solomon began to speak, "I was here sitting and hoping to catch a glimpse of the beautiful woman I had seen dancing and singing in the vineyard when I was overcome by the beauty of these mountains. I felt nature speaking to me with a language all its own. It has a language of love that draws lover, so, naturally I began to hear its beautiful song. To hear its own voice. I picked up my harp and began to sing what nature was speaking to me." He then sang the song in his heart,

And the little hills rejoice on every side, lai lai lai
And the little hills rejoice on every side, lai lai lai
They shout for joy they also sing
They shout for joy they also sing
They shout for joy they also sing

Thou crownest the years with thy goodness
And thy paths, they drop fatness
They drop fatness
They drop upon the pastors of the wilderness
And the little hills rejoice, on every side

They shout for joy they also sing, lai lai lai
They shout for joy they also sing, lai lai lai
They shout for joy they also sing, lai lai lai

"And as I sat on this side of the hill there came that same beautiful voice I heard in the vineyard. I thought at first, I was imagining it. But she kept singing. So, I walked to the top of the hill and there she was, singing and dancing with her eyes closed. I kept playing my harp, singing, and dancing around her. Then she opened her eyes. When we caught site of each other sparks flew around. They were flying everywhere. Then we started laughing." Taphath giggled at the thought. "We laughed and laughed and fell to the ground, still laughing.

"When we finally spoke, I remember asking her about herself, and she told me about her brothers trying to push her to marry suitors she didn't want. When she told me she could not marry one because she did not want to kiss him. I asked if she would want to kiss me. She realized what she had accidentally said to a stranger and started backing away. But I knew right then in my heart what her heart felt, and what my heart felt. And that was all I needed to know. I could not let her go."

They all laughed. Then they sang before Joshua and Caleb told their part of the story.

Nathan spoke up. "I was only ten or so when I first saw Miriam. She was cute when she handed my mother flowers, and funny when she curtsied. We became childhood friends." He looked over at his bride, and something passed between them. After a slight pause Nathan said, "What an amazing family you have. We love to visit. I can see why King David loved to worship here. These mountains are full of worship."

"So let us worship," Shulamit called out.

"It is the romance of the mountains, and the beautiful girls born here. Every time I come here; I am filled with song. But I must prepare for tomorrow's departure." Solomon picked up his goblet and said, "Until next time."

With glasses raised, the toast was deep and full of joy, which led to another toast, and another.

It was one of many nights full of stories and song. But it did come to an end and everyone parted to their various places to sleep and prepare for the next day.

In the morning, after a deep kiss, Shulamit whispered her secret goodbye to Solomon. She said it every time he was leaving to go somewhere, "Make haste to return to me my beloved," she said. "Be like a gazelle or a young stag on the mountains of spices."

Epilogue

Upon return to Jerusalem when Solomon's inner circle gathered for dinner in his private chambers, Shulamit and Nathan asked Solomon to sing his love song. Shulamit sang her part with him. Again, there were many tears in the room when he was finished.

The High Priest Zadok was deeply moved in his heart. He looked to Shulamit, who was still teary eyed, and said, "Our king has captured your story exactly as we observed it and you wrote it over the years. We must immediately sing this in the Temple. Your love speaks of the kind of marriage *YHWH* wants with His bride Israel and why He created the joy of marriage—to help us understand and experience His Love and joy in our lives."

Shulamit looked reverently to the now aged High Priest and admitted, "You gave me the courage to write my story as I was learning to read and write, and you gave me the strength to believe in myself as I wrote it over the years. I read my story to Solomon too, as we shared our intimate thoughts. I still read over the wedding blessing you gave when we made our covenant.

"Be to each other a flame protector," you said. "Be to each other a flame igniter, when the world sees how you love one another, they will know you belong to me." I have read your words like a prophecy when I needed encouragement. Your words have always been a fire in my heart. Not as much as Solomon but—"

They all laughed, and Shulamit felt there was no need to continue.

Zadok repeated, "I promised you I would preserve your beautiful love story. Now I promise to make this song of all songs known throughout Israel, and for generations to come. I will create special occasions for it to be sung."

The song became well-loved throughout Israel and was even sung at weddings.

***

The Queen of Sheba returned to her kingdom with the priests Solomon sent with her, a copy of the Torah, and instruments for temple ceremony. She did have a son named *Menelik*, which meant "the son of the wise man." He was raised in the knowledge of *YHWH* and studied the Torah under the

Priests. The Queen of Sheba kept her promise of following the Hebrew culture with a male king, marriage, the rule of law given in the Ten Commandments, solid family structures. Her new ways created a solid foundation to build up their country.

***

Shulamit was able to arrange marriages to her daughters' liking with noble husbands. They were Governor's specially chosen by Solomon in the office of providing food and sustenance for the palace. Basemath married her childhood friend Ahimaaz, son of Ahimaaz and Shira, Shulamit's first worshipping friend in the palace. They lived in the region near Naphtali in the North. They were very happy. Basemath was an outstanding manager of the Governor's mansion and excelled in assisting her husband with his leadership and administrative skills. She brought her understanding of the Jerusalem palace artistry and created a renaissance in the surrounding culture. This included reading and writing being taught to women as well as men. Basemath also pursued winemaking, which she had learned from her mother and enjoyed doing while visiting family in the mountains.

Taphath married Ben Abinadab, who was a governor in Dor on the Mediterranean just south of Jappa. Solomon's Shipmaster, Javan, frequented their mansion with his wife and sons, when he was home from abroad. Like her mother, Shulamit, Taphath was enticed by the stories of his travels and discoveries of new things from other lands. Taphath's sons and daughters also liked hearing about new lands across the sea, especially Tarshish (Spain) which was rich in gold, silver, lead, and copper. Taphath continued her love of jumping horses. Being the adventurous person she was, she also learned about sailing. Later, when civil war and warnings of Assyria invading Israel broke out, members of her family made their way to the Jewish communities on the Southern shore of Tarshish.

***

Shulamit's third daughter had a much more robust impact on her. Shira became a great joy in Shulamit's life. From the time she could talk and walk, she was singing and trying to dance even when her body was not developed enough to make the moves she wanted. Her musical ear for key, pitch, sense of tone, and even rhythm was perfect. If anyone was off in any of those areas, even her young self, noticed it. Shulamit often laughed at the funny faces Shira would make at a wrong note.

Shulamit exposed her to musicians in the palace and took her regularly to the Queen's Court in the temple where she could hear the music. Even from when she was very young, Shira learned the melodies quickly. When her fingers were long enough Shulamit taught her to play the flute and harp, but it took little teaching because Shira practically taught herself. As she approached middle childhood, she recognized harmonies in music and instruments, and knew how the sounds went together to make the best music. She taught herself how to play all the instruments in the temple with little instruction. Shulamit brought her to her worshipping group and at that young age she began to create her own steps to music.

One thing that made Shira so different from her sisters was that she was not interested in all the luxurious lifestyle of the palace. She did not care about dressing up pretty to go to court and meeting kings and dignitaries of other countries. She had a heart totally dedicated to worship. She wrote prayers, songs about nature, and miracles. If she heard a sermon from the High Priest that touched her heart, she wrote a song. She reminded Shulamit so much of her younger self when worshipping was her first love.

But when Shulamit married Solomon, she came to know that her calling also included ministering to and for her king, sitting beside him in court, looking comely for upholding the beauty of the crown. She learned about the life under Solomon's rule: his arrangement of laws into a systemized code, a governing bureaucracy, and increased trade relations that required a high level of social skills. She had also learned that there was heightened schools of knowledge and intelligence, historical chronicles, and poetry flourished under the wisdom of Solomon. Some parts she liked better, such as poetry flourishing, but it was all part of a package that she needed to be a fully developed queen.

However, Shira brought back to Shulamit parts of herself that she had lost. She felt she was doing right in following Solomon, but she really needed to follow God first. Shira awakened her heart to what was most important. Shira continued to love going to the temple and listening to the different courses of priests. After several times of observing the course of Asaph, she heard a singer and musician with a perfect tone in song and musical arrangement. She asked the priest if she could meet him. This son of Asaph, also named Asaph, came to the palace, and played music with her. Their harmonies were perfect, and they knew they were meant for each other. Solomon knew his daughter Shira was not designed for ruling and approved her marriage to a Levite. Hence, the royal line of Judah began to mix with Levites. Out of her union with Asaph came many beautiful songs that went into the temple prayer book of worship.

***

Nathan and Shulamit's sister Miriam had a happy marriage and many children. They were always a blessing to Shulamit and Solomon. Nathan was always a kind humble servant and their son Mattathiah also turned out to be very special. It was through Nathan, the son of David, and his son Mattathiah, that the line of David continued to bring Jesus forth through Mary (Miriam was the ancient name for Mary).

***

Historically, no one knows what happened to Shulamit. At the end of Solomon's life his many foreign women led him astray. To please the foreign wives, he allowed them to build altars to their gods trying to keep the peace with tolerance. Keeping the peace at all costs was another of Solomon's weaknesses which eventually contaminated the Holy Temple. It seems Shulamit was forgotten and not mentioned in the Chronicles of history.

But was she really forgotten?

The High Priest, Zadok (and his Godly descendants), kept his promise to keep her story in the scrolls. It is remembered in the greatest song Solomon ever wrote. He wrote it when he was still young and pure in heart. Shulamit was honored in a greater way than Zadok anticipated—or perhaps ever dreamed.

The Song of Solomon is read every year on Passover at the end of the Seder on the Sabbath during the feast. As the High Priest Zadok referred to, "The Passover is a time of love between *YHWH* and Israel, who entered into a covenant and became betrothed to Him through the Exodus from Egypt."

It is also said, "All the writings in the Bible are holy—the Song of Solomon is the holiest of holiest." Eventually the Song did become more of an allegory.

But we know the real story.

For God is not unjust
To forget your work and labor of love
Which you have shown toward His name,
In that you have ministered to the saints,
And do minister
(Hebrews 6:10).

ACKNOWLEDGMENTS

I have many people to thank. I will start with a prophecy given to me by Jill Austin as an autobiography in her book *Master Potter*, "Passionate lover and friend of the Lord, creative prophetic, dream big dreams, Jeremiah 18:1-6, Psalm 91, storyteller and writer." I believe in prophecy as the most powerful gift. It works its way directly into our hearts, igniting our spirits to give direction to our lives.

Next, I thank all my friends from Jesus People, who believed in me at the conception of my book: Connie Wasson, Chaz Borjas, and Donna Tombuctu. Donna is a midwife who delivered my first two babies. She continued to stick with me as a midwife and helped me deliver this book. I would also like to honor those friends who are now in heaven: Jackie Miller, Michael King, and my daughter Merry. I believe I have many cheerleaders in my great cloud of witnesses.

I thank Judi Bizell who was excited about the name Shulamit because she increased my awareness of being a bride. I thank Jackie Depalmo and all the ladies I danced with on her team. Jackie taught me about being the Bride of Christ. I thank Jackie's sister, Kathy Antonson (in heaven), who expressed her true love of the bridegroom in poetry. We were as iron sharpening iron as we shared poems together.

I thank my many friends who read my poetry book *The Bride is Writing Love Songs* and encouraged me to continue my writing: Sheri Miles, Noreen Smart, Emma White, and Imy Smith. I am grateful to my friends Gail Brown, Rita Stone, Rhonda Cane, Youngin Oh, James Cantos, Claudia Bainqualls, Cindy Jesperson, Piper Lumden, and Kiki Leigh Theilemann; as well as those who read my rough draft and offered corrections and positive encouragement: Justine Wisdom, Linda Schubert, CJ Scott, and Linda Meckler, and my oldest friend from the eighth grade Mary Goetz. I give thanks to Annette Martinez who directed me to KWA, the Kingdom Writers Association, and my friend Amy Todd who patiently listened to me, read my chapters, and continuously said, "You will bless many people."

I thank all the members of KWA (the Kingdom Writers Association), especially the leaders Brae and Jill Wyckoff, who called the scribes together and encouraged all of us to write. I thank Dianne Tylski for leading a writer's group where with that encouragement I wrote over half the chapters in my book. I thank Neil Fraser for his insight that "Lovers are worshippers and worshippers are lovers." I appreciate all his inspiring poetry on intimacy which primed the pump for *The Worshipper and the King*.

There were many books that inspired me, but I will make mention of those that impacted me the most. I mentioned *Captivating* by John and Stasi Eldredge in my introduction. This book changed my whole paradigm for reading the Bible, which I now read from the perspective of the bridegroom pursuing the bride. This framework is apparent from the beginning in Genesis, through the prophetic Song of Solomon, to the final book of Revelation when the bridegroom returns in glory for his glorious bride.

I thank Caz Taylor for his book about the tabernacle of David where the presence of God was there in the Ark for a small window of time. The tabernacle was a precursor to the church where one could go into the presence of God directly. Entering the presence can now happen through prayer because we have the Holy Spirit. Worship goes on 24/7 in Zion's Heavenly Temple, never stopping. That worship is alive today.

Chuck Pierce's book, *Worship Warrior,* informed me heavily, especially the chapter about Leah, who felt unloved after she had given Jacob three sons. When she came to her fourth son, rather than trying to win his love she said, "This time, I will praise the Lord." She named him Judah which means "praise." God chose Judah to be the warrior tribe that kings came from because he was showing Israel that the way to win battles is through worship and praise. "The Lord inhabits the praises of His People." It also means something to me as it is where my name comes from.

I have a special thanks to Dr. Arnold G. Fruchtenbaum and his book *Biblical Lovemaking.* He kept me from giving up on my book. I met him at a Messianic Conference right after I had been bombarded with doubts about how King Solomon had so many wives. At this time, I was concerned that he couldn't love anyone. I asked Dr. Fruchtenbaum if Shulamit was Solomon's sixtieth wife and he said, "She was, but she was the only woman he ever really loved. She was his favorite." I needed that answer. I also loved Fruchtenbaum's literal Jewish perspective on marriage and proper attitudes toward sex, as well as his practical suggestions on enjoying your spouse.

Finally, as I was re-editing (more like re-writing) the last chapter of m book, I discovered Judith Valencia's book *The Emerging Warrior Bride.* My book was already finished, so it didn't affect my writing, but her work confirmed much about what the Lord had been speaking to me about in Song of Solomon as a prophetic book and its connection to Revelation. Her writing also confirmed the Song of Songs was a love song to me personally, as a part of the Bride of Christ. I was thinking, choosing the assignment to write on Song of Solomon, that I was accepting God drawing me to Him as he drew Leah to Him. The Lord draws hurting people to Himself to offer healing through his mighty love.

Many times, in the process of writing this book, I would be awakened in the middle of the night to write down a poem or an idea for my book. If God drawing me to Himself were the only reason to write this book, it would be enough. I received healing through writing this book; but I hope my writing journey blesses my readers.

Above all, I thank my editor, Tiffany Vakilian, for not giving up on me. I appreciate all she did to help me become a better writer. I thank her for her patience, coaching, and editing my writing to improve this story. I would like to acknowledge my son Don, and my daughter Nina, both of whom are better writers than myself. I also thank Nina for my two granddaughters, Zoe and Maya, who have studied hard all their lives and are soon entering college. Zoe wants to keep the world green, and Maya wants to be a doctor. I hope this breakthrough in *my* life leads them to many breakthroughs wherever God leads them.

I am sure there are those I am forgetting to mention. I thank you as well.

Judy Pendell

ABOUT THE AUTHOR

Judy Pendell was born in Jamestown, ND, and brought up in California. There she joined the Jesus Movement and eventually married a worship leader. Together, they ministered across the USA and abroad.

Returning after years of living abroad to a new life and a new marriage, she went through a difficult period of adjustment. Her family scattered over the years, and bringing things back together was particularly challenging. During this time, she had a dream which was more of a visitation from Jesus. In the dream she was first an observer looking down at herself and another person lady standing next to her, of the same height with long wavy black hair near to her knees. They were looking down into the river where a fashion show was going on under the water. Suddenly, out of the river, someone(unseen) came up and gave each of them something green. She was not sure what it was, but it seemed to be an award.

The highlight of her dream was when Jesus appeared, standing on the bridge next to her looking lovingly into her eyes. Judy felt Jesus was going to propose, and she said, "You don't want to marry me, I wrecked a former marriage and the one I have now is troubled." Jesus ignored her words and said, "If I say yes and they say yes, the yes is yes." A group of older men dressed in Biblical clothes appeared on the bridge in a circle next to Jesus on his left and her right. The first one sang, "I say yes," and, around the circle they all sang, "and I say yes," until it came to Judy. She was so caught up in the moment she sang, "And I say yes." Finally, Jesus said, "And I say yes, so yes is yes."

This visitation from Jesus was a dream of her lifetime. Jesus met Judy and was showing her how He loved her, would never leave her, and she was worthy of being his wife. The dream changed her life. Because of it, Judy knows, no matter what happens, she is loved. Shortly after that realization, she began writing this book.

Judy is a retired registered nurse. She also has a bachelor's degree in Liberal Arts and Sciences (Psychology focus). Now, she is returning to her heart's desire in the Prophetic Arts. This is a new day for evangelism. God is bringing together new ways to reach out to people along with time-tested ways of meeting needs in this present harvest of souls. She has attended Fire Academy at Tsidkenu Church and studied with Bethel's School of

Supernatural off campus at Lamplighter Revival Center, San Diego.

Judy has volunteered in San Diego Healing Rooms and Lifeline Ministries in nursing homes. She is presently engaging in outreach street evangelism ministries, which include healings, salvations, deliverance, and breaking off traumas. Judy also traveled with an Art that Speaks ministry team to Zambia this past year. Prophetic art is part of a growing renaissance with Christians across the globe, being used to speak into people's hearts and open them to receive more from the Lord.

Prophetic Art also includes writing, poetry, worship dance, videos, movies, etc. Judy is a member of the Kingdom Writers Association and hopes to be a participant in helping spread the gospel through the arts. She has written a poetry book called *The Bride is Writing Love Songs*. One can find poems from this book there.

My Dream and Visitation from Jesus
The Dream that inspired *The Worshipper and the King*

I was standing in the center of a theme park where children played around a clear blue lake. There was a two-dimensional unicorn running through the park, near a gazebo where my (now ex) husband sat talking to a Duke and Duchess we knew. In the dream, I was still his wife. The Duke and Duchess were offering him a job working with their children and my joining him was part of the job. When I heard that, I said something inappropriate. This ruined the interview for him.

My ex-husband became angry and said, "You destroy every opportunity we get."

Before I could even react, the scene changed.

I stood on a bridge between a medieval castle and a grandstand full of sitting people. A colorful fashion show was going on under the castle's surrounding water. To my delight, people were diving into the water from the grandstand. As I looked into the water, I somehow rose, transported above the scene. From my new perspective, I observed myself from the outside. Rather than be surprised, I was at peace. Beside me to the right, a woman with long dark wavy hair (almost down to her knees) stood, looking regal.

I sensed that we were going to be honored in some way. I saw the color green. It could have been an award, or clothing given to someone of a certain distinction. Green represents prosperity, freshness, and new beginnings, so I became excited to receive.

From nowhere, Jesus appeared on the bridge to stand with me, and the woman was no longer there. He looked at me very lovingly, and I knew within my soul that he would propose to me.

I said, "You don't want to marry me. I mess up every relationship I have ever had."

He just looked at me with love, as if not wishing to respond to my negativity. Then he said, "If I say, 'Yes—'" and as he spoke, 12 elderly men dressed in long biblical-looking robes instantly appeared and stood beside him. He continued, unphased. "—then yes is yes. And I say, 'Yes.'" Jesus began to sing, "I say, 'Yes,'" and though I could not really hear it, I knew his tune. The group of people formed in a circle with me to the right of Jesus.

The man to his left began to sing, "And I say, 'Yes.'"

One by one, each person took their turn around the circle, singing, "And I say, 'Yes.'"

When it came to me, I was so excited I too sang out, "And I say, 'Yes!'"

Jesus closed the loop and ended the song, "And I say, 'Yes.' So yes is *YES*." Then he took my hand and led me away from the group, back outside of the medieval castle to a clearing. Behind him stood a majestic mountain covered with a vineyard just beginning to ripen. There was also a mansion (or perhaps it was a castle, but it was out of focus). Jesus continued looking at me with his loving, compassion, but it took me a moment to be brave enough to meet his eyes.

Eventually, I looked up.

When I met his gaze, love surrounded me, making me brave and bold. I said, "I haven't been a very good wife, but I will be the best wife I can."

Then I woke up.